MAGNETIC

CARISSA MILLER

For Easton, Emmy, and Cohen.

Thank you for believing in me so much,
that I had no choice but to believe in myself.

To Michael,

For loving me, all of me,
even the brokenness and scars.

"We are all broken,
that's how the light gets in"

-Ernest Hemingway

PROLOGUE

She knows what waits for her in the darkness. Fear grips her throat—making it difficult to breathe—as she turns in desperation to look at the woman beside her bed.

The same thin, gold frame, adorned with tiny pearls and delicate, red roses, has been on the girl's bedside table for six years, a gift from her father on her eleventh birthday. Longingly, she stares at the dark-haired beauty smiling back at her from the black-and-white photograph, and pleads—*don't leave me.*

Her eyes grow heavy with the passing hours. The weight of paralyzing fear and years of sleepless nights pull at them without cease. In one last desperate attempt to stay awake, the girl studies every feature of the woman—the way the soft, black curls fall perfectly around her face; her flawless skin; the dark eyes that flicker with happiness; and above all else, her captivating smile.

But as always, the girl's efforts are in vain.

She falls asleep. Then she dreams.

She is standing in the quaint kitchen of her childhood home wearing her favorite outfit—a white lace dress that highlights her dark sun-kissed skin and gold sandals that tie around her delicate ankles—and placed on the table in front of her, as always, is a birthday cake. The glow of the ten purple (her favorite color) candles blind her. Intuitively she knows who holds the cake. She knows the angelic face, and the melodic rise and fall of the woman's trademark, soprano voice as she sings out the same familiar song she sings every night— Happy Birthday to You.

The girl leans forward and blows out the candles. As the light fades away and smoke rises, sadness overcomes her. She looks up. The familiar face that filled her with love and comfort is gone. It's replaced with the face of someone else—someone unknown; someone that fills her with fear.

Desperate to leave, the girl pushes back from the table and lunges for an exit. But there are no windows. No doors. Reality hits. An all-consuming sadness attacks her, leaving her cold, emotionless, perhaps even dead inside.

She knows it's the last birthday she will ever celebrate. She knows part of her is doomed to stay in that room of darkness, forever a ten-year-old little girl—never aging—and always afraid of the dark.

CHAPTER 1

As we pulled out of town, I refused to turn around. My heart ached as our van lurched onto the paved two-lane road that led to the highway. I knew I was foregoing my last opportunity to see our little house—white siding chipping away in spots here and there, black painted shutters, and the massive oak tree on the front lawn with a tire swing endlessly swaying back and forth in the Ohio breeze. I could picture the whole scene and though I longed to steal one last glance, I refused.

We continued down the road to the highway and I thought of our porch swing, the one all three of us would swing on every night, weather permitting, as we watched the sun disappear behind the horizon in a sea of oranges and pinks and pastels so beautiful, they took my breath away. When I heard Mr. Solomon's mangy dogs nipping at our tires, I knew we were almost to the highway. A sudden urge to look at the pesky mutts nagged at me, because I knew they were the last piece of home I would encounter before we turned onto I-70 and I was forced to say goodbye forever. But still, I stared forward.

My dad's worried glances in my direction increased the closer we got to the end of town. When I could take it no more, I put my earbuds in, pulled my Ohio State lightweight hoodie over my head, then yanked it angrily over my eyes. Over the past five years, I had perfected the art of shutting my father out. Today would be no different.

I leaned my head against the headrest and peered out the window. It was rolled down—of course—to combat our nonexistent air-conditioning system. I caught a glimpse of myself in the rear-view mirror, hypnotized as I watched the long black tendrils peeking out of my hoodie whip wildly in the Ohio wind. Through the waves of darkness clawing at my face, I saw eyes the color of dark emeralds staring back at me in the reflection. They were my dad's eyes, the only physical attribute I inherited from him, but just as I saw a stranger when I looked at my dad, I also saw a stranger staring back at me in the rear-view mirror.

I glanced away, needing a distraction from my tangled thoughts, and turned my mind to my two best friends, Grace and Charlie: summers lying in the field behind Grace's house, looking up at the sky and dreaming about the day we would leave our small town; winters bundled up in our snow gear sledding down the hill in front of Charlie's house; singing in the church choir and listening to my dad's deep voice thundering down from the pulpit on Sunday mornings. Sunday-afternoon church potlucks and riding our bikes to the Shop and Save for dollar treat bags; basketball games with the neighborhood boys and forbidden parties in the fields outside of town; dragging main, aimlessly wandering up and down the thoroughfare of our small town in Kyle Murphy's Mustang convertible, and making out in the back seat of his car behind the bowling alley. With my eyes still closed and my hands stuffed in the pocket of my hoodie—the one Grace gave me when we started our senior year only two months before—I remembered laughter and love and all that was wholesome and good about growing up in Brookville, Ohio, population 5,589.

As we continued our exodus, my peaceful reverie was interrupted by a familiar pull from somewhere deep within. A neglected place deep inside of me awakened and when it did, I heard a soft, eerie whisper on the wind, calling to me from the darkness. The voice beckoned me to open my eyes and remember, but I wouldn't obey without a fight. I snatched my phone out of my lap and turned the volume up—angry lyrics streaming into my earbuds—one last, desperate attempt to force the unwanted voice out of my mind, even though I knew my attempts were futile.

Please don't make me remember that road.

I tried bargaining and when that didn't work, distraction. I pushed my thoughts toward Grace and Charlie—forcing myself to hear Grace's thunderous laugh ripping through the cold Ohio air when we went sledding down Old Man Thompson's hill—anything to forget the darkness calling to me, but my attempts to distract myself were all in vain. Finally, I quit bargaining and accepted my reality.

This is the only way out of town. I can't avoid it forever.

I took a deep breath, peeked out from under my hoodie, and faced that which called to me—a menacing one-lane dirt road stretching off into the distance. Darkness clawed its way up to the surface, but I was stubborn and headstrong and just as I had perfected the art of shutting my father out, I had also perfected the art of pushing those unwanted memories to the back of my mind. Over the years, I learned to suppress the memories of fear, the memories of tears, the memories of pain, the memories of sadness, and most of all—the memories of her. I quickly closed my eyes, pulled my hoodie back down, and pushed back at the darkness, refusing to let it emerge. As we passed the road, the memories threatening to surface acquiesced, finally, and settled back down to that place I learned to store them over the years—a little black box in the deepest part of my soul where they stayed locked and hidden away. Forever.

I glanced over at my dad. He turned to meet my gaze then smiled his silly, lopsided grin at me. I immediately averted my eyes. I hated the guilt that permeated my soul when he smiled at me like that. I deserved his hatred after everything I'd done to him but instead he always forgave me and turned the other cheek, just like he always preached from the pulpit.

I knew my dad would never tell me the real reason we were leaving Brookville—always protecting me even though I didn't deserve it—and I would never tell him I already knew it was all my fault. Staring out the window into the darkness, watching the mile markers pass, the silence loomed between us as I contemplated how badly I wanted to apologize to him for all the stress and anxiety he was forced to endure because of me; but the mile markers continued to pass, one by one, and I said nothing. Just like always.

My dad and I had an unspoken pledge of silence. I don't remember exactly when it happened. I just know that one day I realized there was a great divide between us, an endless chasm formed by words that had never been spoken, hurt that had never been expressed, and most of all, questions that would never be asked. We didn't even know what to say to each other anymore, so we said nothing at all. Yes—silence was how we learned to operate, ever since "we" became just the two of us. So, I would never tell my dad I knew why we were really leaving Brookville and in turn, he would never tell me I was the one to blame for him losing his job. Instead we would file it away with all the things left unspoken between us over the years and leave them somewhere in the middle of nowhere in Ohio, along with all the other darkness.

Sometime in the early afternoon, my dad pulled into a McDonald's in Illinois after we had been driving in complete silence for somewhere close to seven hours. I quit counting eventually, knowing our trip would take much longer than it should thanks to our antiquated and unreliable means of transportation. Every possession we owned was packed to the brim in the back of a decrepit fifteen-passenger church van the congregation so kindly bestowed upon us as our tainted parting gift. I rolled my eyes as I hopped out of the van and saw the fiery orange letters emblazoned on the side of the faded black paint job—Brookville Church of God. I hated that stupid van, an ever-present reminder not only of my preacher's-daughter upbringing, but also of the church that fired my dad for my transgressions.

We made our way inside then placed our orders, and as I took slow sips of my Diet Coke, the spirit of a truce slowly began to wash over me. I decided to stop punishing my father. We both knew it was *me* who deserved to be punished anyway.

"Dad, tell me about this new job," I said as I took another bite of my McDonald's hamburger. I'd refused to hear anything about it before we left.

He peeked up from his grilled chicken sandwich and answered cautiously. "Well, I'm going to be teaching at a school there." My jaw dropped and he quickly answered as if a little bit wounded. "I do have a master's degree, you know, and I guess with my experience teaching night classes at the community college as well as a recommendation from your Aunt Cordelia's employer, they thought I was suited for the job."

"Oh yes, Aunt Cordelia." I said her name with equal parts sarcasm and animosity. I still hadn't come to terms with the fact that my dad had received a letter from a long-lost aunt, my mother's sister apparently, and had been communicating regularly with her for almost a month now. "So where exactly is this teaching job Aunt Cordelia helped you get?" I asked.

"It's at a very prestigious school in Tulsa. It has a strong academic focus but also a religious affiliate. I'll be teaching a senior-level religious-studies class."

Silence resumed and the tension between us mounted as I noticed he was trying to build up the courage to tell me some crucial bit of information he'd neglected to mention.

"What is it? Just tell me already."

He answered with reservation. "Elyse, the school I'll be working at is called Heritage Hall Preparatory Academy, and…" He took a deep breath. "You're going to school there. You get free tuition since I'm a teacher."

A fire ignited inside of me. Not only did he use my full name—he knew I preferred Elle—but he was also telling me, not asking, that this was my fate. So much for the promise he made me years ago. I squeezed my paper soda cup, staring at him. The fire threatened to rage out of control. It slowly consumed me, burning tangibly within, licking my fingers and my toes then moving upward at a steady pace. From the time I was a little girl, the same fire burned, always pushing me toward anger, toward rebellion, toward disobedience and most of all—toward defiance. I knew, before long, that I would be incapable of containing my rage. His words echoed in my mind—Heritage Hall Preparatory Academy. I hated the name and I hated what it represented—another broken promise; more rules and regulations; more opportunity for failure; more expectations I wouldn't be able to live up to; more people looking at me like I was broken when they realized I wasn't the same as the other snobby prep-school kids.

I was forced back to reality when the McDonald's worker walked up and broke the awkward silence.

"Um, excuse me ma'am, may I take your trash?"

Neither of us moved or even acknowledged she'd spoken. We merely resumed our stare down of each other until eventually she realized she was infringing on some tense, unspoken father-daughter moment. She tucked her tail and walked away.

"Heritage Hall Preparatory Academy?" I asked quietly but incredulously.

He promised I would never have to be homeschooled again; I could go to public school. He promised me I could decide. So much for that.

I repeated the words again, loudly. My tone acidic. "Heritage Hall Preparatory Academy, Dad?"

"Elyse Rose Christiansen." He answered my tone with warning of his own—use of my full name. "You *will* go to Heritage Hall Preparatory Academy. The decision is already made."

In that moment, I lost all control of the fire. I stood, yanking my chair back, enjoying the terrible screech it made.

Dad jumped out of his seat. "Elyse—Outside. *Now.*" He whispered with unmistakable authority but his words held no bearing over me.

"How could you do this to me? You promised I would never have to go back to being homeschooled again. You promised I could go to public school."

"Elle, you're not being rational. It's not like when I was homeschooling you. It won't be like that, I promise." He held his hands up and spoke calmly, soothingly, but it was too late. The fire raged past the point of control per the norm, and in the middle of a McDonald's in Illinois, I threw my empty Diet Coke at the window.

"I don't believe your promises! I refuse to go to some snobby prep school!" My throat started to close off and I found it difficult to breathe, recalling the isolation I felt as a child, sitting in my little green desk in our small church parsonage, longing to go to real school with Grace and Charlie. I was a prisoner then and now he wanted to imprison me again, this time at a prep school with millions of rules and regulations, where I was destined to fail.

When I awakened from my fit of anger, my dad was dragging me by my arm and throwing me into the fifteen-passenger Brookville Church of God van. Everyone in the entire fast-food restaurant was staring at us, but I was accustomed to it by now. Their shocked and judgmental glances didn't faze me.

My dad slammed the door, hopped in the van, and screeched out of the parking lot. We drove in silence for what seemed like eternity. I stuck my earbuds in and looked out the window, refusing to talk to him as mile after mile passed us by. Slowly my dad's frustration began to subside and I saw a look on his face I tried to decipher—was it sympathy, sadness, or regret? It was always so hard for me to read him and since most emotions went unspoken between us, I could only guess. He never had to guess with me though. It was always anger, perhaps with an occasional side of resentment or hostility.

He gave me the space I needed for a long time—I think it was hours—then he reached over and gently pulled the tiny speaker out of my ear.

"Elle, this is going to be good. For both of us," he said with that unnamed look I had now identified as sympathy.

I gave him a slight nod and a half smile. Shame raked my body. *I'm sorry Dad. For everything.* But our pledge of silence kept me from speaking the words out loud, so I closed my eyes, then drifted off to sleep.

When I closed my eyes, I was still in Ohio. I was with Grace and Charlie and it was a sunny day in early fall. I knew it was fall because I could feel it in the air, that familiar smell of leaves beginning to change and that unnamed but ever recognizable scent on the wind signaling a new season was coming. The wind was blowing and the first leaves were just beginning to fall, swirling through the air in beautiful arcs as they fell from their branches and rode the wind before finally finding their new home on the ground beneath the trees.

Fall was my favorite time of year. We were laughing as we rode our bikes down Main Street, our dollar bags from the Shop and Save tucked in our back pockets. I was in the lead followed by Grace and then Charlie. We passed Main Street and pulled onto the two-lane road that led to my house and I quickened my pace in excitement. Not long after I turned onto the road, something began to feel very wrong. I turned to look over my shoulder for reassurance from my friends but when I did, they were no longer there. The laughter dissipated and I realized there was only me, all alone with a vaguely familiar road stretching out in front of me.

Something told me not to venture further down the road. I knew I should turn around and run back to Grace and Charlie, toward the light and the laughter, and run away from the road in front of me—the road that led to darkness. But my mind was already set. I glanced over my shoulder one more time but only to say my goodbye.

Determined, I pushed off and stood up on my bike pedals to hasten my trip down the dark deserted road. An unknown force beckoned to me, telling me to press forward even though the darkness threatened to envelope me. Storm clouds were rolling in on the horizon ahead of me and a foreboding washed over me; still I continued.

The light was gone now. I could no longer see where I was going. The clouds rumbled and a bolt of lightning struck in front of me, illuminating a path I hadn't seen before. It was a dirt road. Fear ripped through my entire body, handicapping me, yet inexplicably my body began moving of its own accord. I was being pulled down the path—part of my soul was calling to me from the end of the road—and I had no choice but to travel forward to be reconnected with the missing party of myself. I dropped my bike and started walking down the road into the pitch black of night. I slowly fumbled my way; one foot in front of the other. Another bolt of lightning illuminated my path and when it did, I saw something I recognized—an old blue Volvo station wagon.

I was in darkness again, confused, frightened. I had to find my way to that Volvo. I wanted to run as fast as I could but the darkness made it impossible. There was another flash of lightning followed instantly by a loud rumble, then I saw the blue Volvo yet again. This time I thought I saw the outline of a shape standing beside the station wagon but I was covered in darkness again before I could be certain. Something seemed so familiar about the vehicle, about the road, and most of all, about the shadow of a person.

In the pitch black, I broke out into a run. I was compelled, desperate to get to the end of that road. Someone I loved was in danger. They needed me. I tripped and fell, scraping my knee on a rock. Blood trickled down my leg but I pushed myself back up and continued to run blindly. I heard a scream tear through the silence of the night and a chill shot up my spine. *I know that voice.*

The lightning flashed again and there she was, standing at the end of the road. I was almost there. I could make it to her. I could save her. Then the lightning was gone and so was she. I was in total darkness, unable to move. Why won't my legs answer me? Why won't they run to her? A thunderous roar broke the silence, lightning bolts striking down from the sky all around me, allowing me to see into the darkness. There she was again!

My chest tightened with a force that took all the air from my body. Her beautiful light blue sundress was ripped, shredded into strings and tears that hung in odd places. Her hair was matted and tangled. Blood poured down her body, forming a deep-crimson pool that stained the ground. She looked at me with love and tenderness. My heart shattered into a million unsalvageable pieces, seeing her disheveled and broken. Then her voice called to me as she reached her blood-soaked hand out.

"Elyse...."

She was gone again with the blackness. I still couldn't move. I struggled with all my might but no matter how hard I tried, my legs refused to do as I told them. I had to get to her. She was dying and only I could rescue her. Only I knew where she was—at the end of that wretched one-lane dirt road.

One more flash of lightning was followed by a thunderous clap, but this time I couldn't see her or the blue Volvo. Rain poured around me and my feet were still stuck in the ground. I called out to her. I opened my mouth and screamed as loud as I could but my screams were drowned out by the torrential downpour. I looked down; my legs were trapped in thick mud and though I struggled against it with all my strength, they refused to budge. The rain poured down in a tumultuous assault and I noticed the water was rising all around me. Soon I would be under water. I panicked as I realized the water would cover me and I would drown—unable to move, unable to get to her, unable to save her. I closed my eyes, and with one last breath my cry ripped through the silent, dark night.

"I'm coming, Mom!"

When I awoke, my dad was grabbing my arm, eyes wide with concern. I was disoriented. My eyes darted around, trying desperately to get my bearings and confirm I wasn't in that nightmare, that I wasn't on the one-lane dirt road again. It was still dark outside but I saw light creeping up the horizon in a beautiful display of intermixing oranges and yellows. My dad had been driving all night apparently, no doubt fueled by the adrenaline rush provided by the fight with his sullen teenage daughter. I glanced to the right. Outside of the van window, a sign read, "Tulsa, 30 miles." I took several deep, calming breaths.

I'm in Oklahoma. I'm not on that dirt road again. I'm in Oklahoma with my dad and I'm safe.

But deep within I heard a familiar voice chastising me, telling me I was never safe and never would be. I shoved the unwanted thought back down into that little black box and began the process I was so accustomed to—my coping mechanism—denial, avoidance, and most of all, running away. I was always running away from that dirt road until my next nightmare unavoidably brought me back.

My pulse slowed and the fear started to subside. I glanced over at my dad and saw the worry in his eyes, that little crease in his forehead showing as he pulled his brows together in deep thought. We never talked about my nightmares, yet another silent agreement the two of us had. He was always there when I woke up screaming though, holding me in his arms, comforting me.

"It's just a dream. Just a dream, Elle," he would say over and over until I calmed down.

There was nothing else to say. Yes, it was just a dream, but it was also my reality. Every time I closed my eyes, I risked finding myself on that bloodstained dirt road, screaming her name but never able to get to her. I was never able to save her.

My dad broke the silence by turning on some music on the archaic radio player. He kept pushing a button until he finally found one with no static. I heard a raspy man's voice and a bass guitar playing one slow beat. I recognized the song instantly, having been brought up with a steady flow of 60's and 70's rock thanks to my dad's music preferences. It was a classic by Three Dog Night. My dad laughed out loud and started beating his hands on the wheel of the fifteen-passenger van as though he was playing the drums for the Rolling Stones. I couldn't help but smile. Even I had to admit how apropos the song was considering our current set of circumstances. When the song hit the refrain, my dad turned to me with an infectious grin plastered on his face, asking me to join him in his mood and forget the torture of my dreams. Music. It was something we had in common. Music always helped us bridge the Great Divide that stretched between us and sometimes threatened to separate us forever, it seemed. Music made us feel like a normal, loving, father and daughter. Music made us forget the darkness, even if only temporarily.

My dad winked at me as he continued to croon the lyrics in my direction, and a smile slowly crept across my lips in response. I was finding it impossible to hold onto my sullen mood. Before I knew it, I was playing the air guitar to his drums as he belted out the lyrics.

"Well I've never been to heaven but I've been to—" he turned to point at me.

On cue, I sang out. "OKLAHOMA!"

Then we joined in together; I took the harmony a major third above the melody he was singing, breaking out in my air-guitar solo as my dad's rich laughter filled the whole van.

I looked over at him and my heart was filled with love. Sure, he was moving me to a state that I had absolutely no desire to live in, ever, and making me go to a school that sounded like something straight out of a horror movie in my opinion, but I loved him. He was all I had, especially now that I had to leave Grace and Charlie. By the time we finished our duet, I forgot about my nightmare entirely. I even had a slight smile on my face.

"See those lights up there?" my dad said. "That's Tulsa."

When my dad told me we were moving, I allowed myself to get temporarily excited. That was, until he revealed our destination—Oklahoma. Of course we were leaving Ohio for perhaps the only other place in the continental United Sates that was more inconsequential than my own home state. When I envisioned leaving Brookville, I dreamed of skyscrapers and culture and oceans; trendy universities where I could lose myself and forget my small-town preacher's-daughter upbringing—New York, Los Angeles, Chicago, even Dallas. I wasn't that discriminatory. Instead, Oklahoma. But then again, I guess that is what I deserved after all I'd put my dad through over the past several years.

I knew absolutely nothing about Oklahoma. My preconceived idea of the small, Midwestern state primarily involved cowboys and farms, horses and cows. So as we pulled into Tulsa, I was pleasantly surprised to see a booming city. It wasn't as big as Cleveland, which was the only city I'd ever been to before, but I found myself thinking it looked mildly promising as we continued our journey into town.

Tulsa was nothing compared to the skylines of New York I'd seen in pictures and books, but there were some tall buildings that peppered the horizon. Without a doubt, Tulsa was much bigger than Brookville. There were bright lights, tall buildings, highways intercrossing each other, and a huge silver arena that said BOK on the side of it. I saw a flashing billboard advertising an upcoming concert at the silver building—One Republic—one of my favorite bands. *Bands never came to Brookville.* My eyes darted with intrigue from shiny building to building, realization dawning that perhaps, Tulsa, Oklahoma, was proving to be—unexpected.

We were on a large highway and passing exit signs every mile—Memorial Avenue, Yale Avenue, Lewis Avenue. I heard my dad put his blinker on and sat up slowly, trying to look like I lacked any interest whatsoever in where we were going but simultaneously trying to peer over the dash to see where we were. We were exiting on a street called Utica Avenue—a strange name for a street. In Brookville, we only had a few streets and they were all your typical names—Main Street and First, Second, and Third Avenues. After that it was mainly county roads that were just numbers.

We exited on Utica Ave and pulled up to a stoplight. I couldn't help it. My curiosity was fully piqued. We both sat there in silence, playing our usual games, while the left-turn signal clicked at us for what seemed like an eternity. Finally, dad turned onto Utica Ave and I could no longer maintain my cold act of indifference as we drove by a shopping center unlike anything I had ever seen. It was full of aged brick and stone buildings; gorgeous, mature trees beginning to show the first sign of fall colors; quaint little restaurants with outdoor seating areas; fountains and brick-paved paths; and a massive stone sign that read "Utica Square". We continued our drive past the picturesque area as I turned around to read the signs of the fancy stores—Saks Fifth Avenue, Anthropologie, Miss Jackson's.

We're definitely not in Brookville anymore.

This was not at all what I was picturing when my dad said he was moving us to Oklahoma. Suddenly we were on a road with massive trees stretching up to the sky on either side, their branches so heavy with leaves that they dipped down to kiss the top of our church van as we drove. The whole scene reminded me of a different era—as if I'd been transported to *Gone With the Wind* where Scarlett O'Hara rode in her horse-drawn carriage up a mile-long path lined with oak trees rooted there for centuries—to find a beautiful white mansion waiting at the end of the road. But there was no white mansion at the end of this street. Instead, I saw a large red-brick gate with a stone sign encased in the brick. Engraved upon the sign were the words "Heritage Hall Preparatory Academy" and then in smaller letters, "established 1905". I quickly turned my head and looked away in disgust.

Dad tried to keep things light. "I just have to run inside to drop off my license and pick up my new-teacher information packet. Do you want to come in with me and check out the school?"

I didn't even acknowledge him. We pulled into a parking spot and I slumped down even further into my seat. He paused, giving me an opportunity to change my mind, then let out an exasperated sigh before hopping out of the van, leaving me alone to sulk. A few minutes passed, and I grew bored of my bad mood so I pushed myself forward and rolled down the window slowly—the hand crank got stuck on a few turns—so that I could look around. The buildings were the picture of uniformity—red brick intermittently peppered with aged stones and thick mortar bleeding from between the bricks. Paired with the black windows, massive turrets, and cast-stone entrances around the doors, it reminded me of a mausoleum I once saw in one of Charlie's murder-mystery shows he was always forcing Grace and I to watch. I had no doubt some would find the look aesthetically pleasing—almost castle-like with its rooflines stretching toward the sky and immaculate landscaping spreading across the grounds—but all I could see was more rules, more trouble, and more failure.

I was burdened by the weight of my current circumstances, overwhelmed by sadness and even hopelessness. My dad still wasn't back so I pulled out my dollar-store sunglasses and put them on, then laid my head back and closed my eyes, trying to forget. A few minutes later I heard him turn the key to the church van once, twice, then three times. Finally, it roared to life after a long groan of resistance but then quickly died again. Apparently, I wasn't the only one exhausted by our cross-country exodus.

I knew the protocol, so I jumped out of the passenger-side door and went over to the driver's side while my dad made his way to the front of the van and popped the hood. He gave me the signal and I turned the key in the ignition while I slowly pumped the gas pedal. The van sputtered then slowly rolled to life while my dad continued to mess with some wires under the hood. He slammed the hood down and winked at me, giving me a big grin and a thumb's up. I waved at him and signaled to the seat across from me. He nodded then jumped into the passenger side, allowing me to give him a break from being behind the wheel for a few minutes.

We pulled onto the long drive that would lead us back to Utica Avenue and as we approached the gated entrance to the school, a gust of wind blew, carrying with it a slight, faint beat. At first, it was just a slow beat in the distance that I turned my head toward, curious to find the source. Then I saw a flash of light as a black truck pulled out onto the road in front of us, the beat continuing to grow louder as the monstrosity of a vehicle approached us.

The truck was unlike anything I'd ever seen in Brookville. Everything about it seemed to shine from the metallic black color of the paint, to the jet-black rims on the wheels. Kyle Murphy from back home had a subscription to *Truck Trend* magazine and every month I would watch him flip through the latest edition as he drooled over the shiny, expensive trucks displayed on each page. As the truck approached me from the distance, I couldn't help but think to myself, *That thing looks like it just drove off the front cover of one of Kyle Murphy's magazines.*

Expensive cars never impressed me, or any material possessions for that matter, but even I couldn't help but notice the amazing means of transportation before me. An inexplicable force was drawing me to look in the direction of the truck even though I wanted so badly to act disinterested. As I waited to turn left, the truck continued to approach the school and I saw the blinker begin to flash, signaling that the driver intended to turn right into the school.

The truck was close enough now to see a tag on the front. It had a modern logo with two H's intertwined—Heritage Hall—then, beneath the two letters I saw the word "baseball". The driver of the truck was a Heritage Hall baseball player. I looked away, disgusted.

My dad pointed toward the left, indicating that was the way we needed to turn. *Ugh.* I slammed my blinker down—signaling left. The truck approached, the engine rumbling loudly as he neared our church van. My heart began to beat rapidly as the truck neared. I rolled my eyes beneath my sunglasses but only for my own benefit; I was confused by my visceral response to the proximity of the truck and annoyed at my inability to control my reaction. I looked away, waiting for the truck to pass. A few seconds later, I heard the roar of the engine right in front of me and knew the driver was pulling into the school. My eyes were forced in the direction of the truck against my will. My head turned, just as he pulled into the narrow drive. Merely an arm's length separated our two vehicles. His window was rolled down, as was mine; and our eyes met.

The driver of the truck wore dark fancy sunglasses with prism lenses that seemed to reflect an aura of colors. I'd never seen anything like them before in my life. But even more intriguing was that I could see past his sunglasses and I knew he had crystal-clear blue eyes.

How in the world did I know his eye color?

Even though his sunglasses were on, I knew the boy's eyes were that of a calm sea—clear, tranquil, and above all else, soothing. His eyes—I suddenly knew I had seen them before though I had no idea where—spoke to me, whispering words I longed to hear in a long-forgotten place that no one was ever allowed, calming the storm that raged within me. I was completely and utterly lost, stripped bare. I couldn't maintain a clear thought so I stared, unabashedly, attempting to memorize every detail of the boy before it was too late, and he was gone.

He wore a black-and-grey flat-billed baseball hat turned backward and a white Under Armour shirt that clung to his broad shoulders tightly, perfectly showcasing his broad chest and taut muscles.

Later my mind would tell me that only seconds passed when we drove by one another, but in that very moment time stood still—the ostentatious black truck and our worn-out church van, frozen in the middle of the Heritage Hall drive. We were suspended in time, staring indefinitely into one another's eyes and somehow seeing past that, into each other's souls. A deep, hidden part of myself awakened.

I struggled to orient myself, looking around frantically to find myself driving away from Heritage Hall Preparatory Academy. I don't know how long my dad had been saying my name. I was in my dream world where all I could see was a black truck and a pair of blue eyes that called to me, piercing straight through the wall long erected in the dark depths of my soul and making their way to a hidden black box where I allowed no one. Those eyes. They were all I could see.

CHAPTER 2

My dad touched my arm and slowly, unwillingly, I emerged from my daydream. I was unable to focus. The only thing I seemed to remember was a pair of enigmatic eyes seared forever into my memory. I longed to see the blue-eyed boy again, craving the calm I experienced when he somehow whispered to the storm in my soul.

"Did you hear me?" His voice was laced with concern. "I said to turn at the next stoplight."

The sound of the turn signal brought me back to reality. I tried to push the boy in the black truck to the back of my mind. My dad told me to roll down the window and he gave me a gate code to enter. I entered the numbers and then slowly, the gates creaked to life. Before they inched open, I took note of an iron filigree circle at the center of the gate with a large "M" inside of it. I wondered what the "M" stood for.

I pushed on the gas pedal as the gates swung open to let us pass. Our church van groaned its disapproval, sputtered twice in protest, then began to inch forward. We made our way up the driveway, if the long road that led to the house could even be called such, and I couldn't help but think how out of place we must look driving the Brookville Church of God van on this immaculate property. The lawns were perfectly manicured; green stretched for what seemed liked miles on both sides of the road. Large oak trees peppered the lawn in perfect increments and the morning sun shone perfectly through their branches to enlighten flower beds planted amongst the grounds. I was so engrossed in the perfection I barely heard my dad tell me to stop.

The Thompsons from my hometown in Ohio had the biggest house in all of Brookville. Their house was two stories tall, one of the only homes that was more than a single story in our entire town. It sat on two acres and had a wraparound porch, two living rooms, five bedrooms, and a study with a fireplace. They invited us over for dinner one time when I was a little girl and as I wandered around their home, I pretended I was a princess, living in a castle. In my youthful naivety, I thought the Thompsons' spacious white house was a mansion.

The house that we were in front of at this very moment made the Thompsons' house look like a shack. None of the words I possessed in my vocabulary could define what I saw stretching out in front of me. It was more than a mansion. I would have called it a castle but it was far too majestic and modern. The house was made of white stone and had graceful shutters painted in an elegant bluish-green color. There were at least four—or did I count five?—towering fireplace chimneys stretching out from the roof. Off in the distance I saw a large body of water—much bigger than the pond behind Charlie's house back home—with a beautiful fountain in the center. There was a tiny wooden structure at the far shore—it looked like a picturesque little cabin—and a long deck with a dock at the end that stretched out onto the water. The estate—yes, that was what a monstrosity like this was called—sprawled on for days. It was massive and commanding, yet somehow managed to emanate the feeling of a home. On the way up the drive, we passed a fort that had been carefully built into one of the old oak trees that had a rope swing and a ladder hanging down from its branches.

My dad told me to pull around to the back of the house. He seemed to be looking for something. Finally, he found what he was searching for—a smaller, less grandiose driveway, then at the end of that road, a quaint little cottage. He signaled for me to drive in that direction.

Once we reached the small cottage—which was still probably bigger than our house back in Brookville but compared to the "M" mansion, it suddenly seemed like a cottage—I pulled over. My dad jumped out of the car, then grabbed our overnight bags and made his way up to the front door. I followed him. He reached up to grab a door knocker that was nestled somewhere amidst a beautiful fall wreath made of fresh flowers, pinecones, and berries, then he tapped lightly, three times. I heard footsteps coming toward the door then slowly it cracked open to reveal a familiar face.

The person I saw standing before me in the doorway of the little cottage was a total stranger, yet I felt I knew her. Maybe it was her smile, warm and inviting with two huge dimples. It could have been her thick dark hair pulled back from her face and pinned with two long knitting needles. Perhaps it was her dark-brown eyes that seemed so recognizable. Though I had never met her before, I somehow felt that I knew this woman well.

My dad looked at me and said, "Elle, this is your Aunt Cordelia."

I don't know how long I stared at her, standing there saying nothing at all with my arms crossed in a subtle—or perhaps not so subtle—stance of defiance. How rude of me. But I had never been one to care much about niceties anyway. She broke the silence as she stepped toward me, wrapping her arms around me, and embracing me in a hug that whispered love and tenderness.

I didn't like to be hugged. I didn't like to be touched at all for that matter, and everyone who knew me accepted my boundaries without refute. So, I nearly stumbled backward, my body stiffening in surprise when this woman I had never even met reached out without hesitation and pulled me into the grasp of her arms, violating my preferences. Even more surprising, was the fact that I let her.

Aunt Cordelia finally released me then scooped my bag up and scurried inside. She led us into a small but inviting living room where a fresh batch of zucchini bread was sliced on a serving plate. Beside it sat three tall glasses of lemonade. We sat and ate while making awkward small talk about the Oklahoma fall weather and our trip—careful to leave out the part about the temper tantrum I threw at the McDonald's in Illinois, of course.

After we had eaten, my dad raised his arms and yawned. He had driven through the night with no sleep. The next thing I knew, my dad was being shown to one of the three small bedrooms in the cottage and I was left alone with my Aunt Cordelia.

The way she looked at me made me uncomfortable for some reason, so I made my way out of the living room and into the hallway, attempting to find shelter from her prying eyes. I discovered a hallway so covered with pictures, I could barely see the walls beneath—black-and-white photographs of smiling strangers staring back at me. There was a young Cordelia with a handsome, chiseled man in uniform, his arms wrapped around her small frame protectively as he stared down at her with a loving smile. There were more pictures of the adoring couple— on their wedding day, under a large oak tree on the property, and on a boat in the middle of a pond. I took several more steps down the hallway—watching the couple age—noticing several pictures of them with a dark-haired boy and a dimple-faced baby girl with Shirley Temple curls tickling at her face. *That must be Cordelia's husband and children?* Then I took one last step, reaching the end of the gallery of memories, my eyes resting on a picture that took my breath away. I gasped out loud, nearly dropping my lemonade.

The picture was of two young girls. They were breathtakingly beautiful with their dark, thick hair that fell down their backs in cascading waves. They were laughing and had their arms wrapped around one another in an embrace so candid and full of love and laughter that it was evident they weren't posed. I stared at the black-and-white picture, leaning over to get closer and yet closer still, until my nose almost touched the frame. It was the girl on the right, the one with the longest hair and the smile that was so charismatic and full of life, I couldn't stop staring at her. She left me captivated. Her smile touched her eyes and made you want to laugh right along with her and she had the biggest dimples I had ever before seen, other than when I looked in the mirror at my own. I was so mesmerized that I didn't even hear my aunt walk up behind me.

"Isn't she the most beautiful thing you have ever seen?" I heard the whisper of pain and longing in her voice as she continued. "That was your mother, when she was your age. She was seventeen years old when we took that picture." She looked lovingly at the photo then brushed her finger over it as if wishing to be back in that moment. "You remind me of her," she said, and before I could ask her anything about the picture or my mom, she turned and walked away. I glanced her way, frustrated, as she walked out of the room, leaving me with a million unanswered questions.

That's all she's going to say? You've got to be kidding me.

But she was gone, the pain she felt evident on her face as she left the room, and I knew that my questions about my mother would go unanswered; just like they always did.

I had to get out of the cottage. I walked back to find my dad unpacking some of his clothes in the small bedroom at the back of the house.

Why is he unpacking? My questions about how long we planned to stay with Cordelia would wait. The need to get fresh air and clear my head was my new priority.

"I'm going to go on a walk, Dad."

His eyes shot me a warning. "OK, but don't go far."

I nodded my head in agreement then turned and left the small cottage, the one with the picture of my mother when she was my age hanging on its wall. I walked up the brick pathway, my mind consumed with tangled thoughts—trucks, photographs of a young smiling beauty with dark hair and dimples, Heritage Hall Prep with its tall stone buildings and iron gates, arguments with my dad, nightmares about a dirt road, and most of all, those blue eyes that kept materializing in my mind.

I needed a distraction from the chaos that was my life so I went searching for one. I continued walking around the property until I heard a rhythmic pounding. I knew it was coming from the basketball courts so I made my way over to the gate and pushed it open. There, standing before me, was my distraction. Distractions were my best friends. Grace and Charlie were fairly good at coming up with distractions for me when I needed them, but more often than not, I found I had to discover them on my own. And this six-foot tall boy before me, who looked to be my age, was the perfect discovery. His shaggy light-brown hair blew in the wind as he dribbled up and down the court. He was athletic and clearly knew what he was doing with the basketball. He jumped into the air, draining a shot from the three-point line; then he turned and looked at me. Yep, he was exactly what I needed to forget the absurdity of my life.

I walked up to him and smiled but purposefully didn't talk first. He smiled back.

"Hey. I'm Caleb," he said.

"Give me the ball, Caleb," I said with a smirk. Let the flirting commence.

"Oh, you like to play basketball?" There was a playful taunting in his eyes.

I knew this song and dance well. Big macho guy thinks little girl can't shoot the basketball. Big macho guy thinks little girl can't beat him at basketball. This was going to be fun. I batted my eyelashes and peeked up at him coquettishly.

"I used to play a bit when I was little."

He took the bait. "Let's play a game then."

"What type of game?"

"Knockout. Do you know how to play that?" A confident grin was plastered on his face.

"I do think I remember how to play that one," I said with naivety in my tone. "But what is a game without a bet of some sort?"

"What do you want to play for?" he asked, dribbling the ball nervously and looking up at me with reservation.

I paused, placing a finger to my lips in concentration, pretending to think. It was all an act since I already knew exactly what I was going to say. "Oh, I don't know. Is there anything in particular that *you* want?" I turned around and stared at him, putting emphasis on the last two words as I said them. His mouth dropped. He was easy to read so I knew what he would say before the words came out of his mouth.

"If I win, we go out."

I widened my eyes feigning surprise. "And if I win?"

"I don't know. What do *you* want?" A hopeful smile replaced his earlier confident grin.

I looked around. Distractions… My eyes landed on a red sports car parked beyond the fence.

"Is that your car?"

He nodded.

"Cool."

He beamed with pride at my praise. Thankfully he didn't detect the slight sarcasm in my tone.

"If I win…I take your car for a drive."

His jaw dropped. "You want to take my car for a drive? It's a stick shift."

"That's OK. I've driven one a few times before."

He seemed cautious, nervous.

I bet his parents don't allow anyone to drive his fancy car. I rolled my eyes at the thought. It made me want to win the bet even more.

We stared at one another for a while. Finally, he broke the silence with a confident, "OK, let's do this."

I reached out my hand. "Let's shake on the terms. If you win, we go out tomorrow night. If I win, I get to take your car for a drive." As our hands touched when we shook hands, I could feel that familiar attraction igniting between us. I always had fun at this game.

"Deal," we both said in unison as we shook hands.

I took the ball from him. I dribbled it once, twice, three times, then I pulled up to drain a jump shot. I thought I was going to have to pick his jaw up off the floor when he saw me shoot. I turned around, shrugged my shoulders, and gave him an ornery smile.

"What? I told you I played a little." I threw the basketball at him hard and as it hit him in the chest I said, "Why don't you go first."

Still unable to speak, he grabbed the basketball while I ran over and picked up a spare. He shot his first shot and made it then I shot and made mine as well. He shot again and made another free throw. I shot and made mine. This game was getting boring.

"Why don't we make this interesting and scoot back to the three-point line?" I challenged him.

He arrogantly took two steps back. "Are you sure you can handle it?"

I took two steps toward him so that I was only inches away from his face then said in a sultry, soft voice, "Are you sure that *you* can handle it?" Then I stepped up and shot a three pointer and made it.

My diversion worked. He shot and missed. I ran for my ball and sprinted back to the three-point line while he made a mad dash for his rebound after the miss. Before he could get the ball and do a layup, I made it back to the line and drained another three pointer.

His jaw practically touched the floor. I walked up to him confidently, holding out my open palm. He failed to budge.

I took my tone up an octave, making my voice sugary. "Would you pretty please give me the keys to your fancy red sports car since I just kicked your ass in knockout and won the bet?"

He pulled his keys from his pocket and reluctantly dropped them into my hand. "Are you sure you know how to drive a stick?" His concern wasn't cute.

I walked around and took my position in the driver's seat as he huffed his way around to the passenger side. "Well I'm not letting you drive without me there."

"So get in." I waved toward the passenger seat.

"Are you *sure* you know how to drive a standard?" His hands shook slightly as he buckled his seatbelt.

I pressed on the clutch and ripped it into reverse, winking at him playfully. His discomfort fueled me. "Positive, basketball boy."

We backed over some small tree limbs that had fallen from a large oak tree with ease then I stopped, pushed the clutch up into first gear aggressively and peeled out as we took off. The wind blew through my hair. I threw my head back and laughed. It was the first time I had laughed since I found out that we were moving. It was my typical laugh—loud and energetic. I glanced over and basketball boy was staring at me in wonder. I knew in that moment that he was falling and I decided I would let him. After all, I needed a new distraction in this town where I knew no one and coincidentally, he was a pretty cute distraction.

We sped through the streets and even though I had no idea where I was, neither of us seemed to care. He changed the radio station and each time a new song came on we laughed and started belting out the words. He reached over and grabbed my hand and I let him.

Eventually we made our way back to the "M" mansion.

"So do you live here?" I asked as I pulled over by the basketball courts.

"No, I live down the street and come over and use the basketball court sometimes."

We hopped out of the car and he walked around to my side, snaking his arm around my waist and pulling me to his side.

Again, I let him. We walked over to a tree and I knew what was about to happen. He pulled me into his body and I rested my hands on his chest; then I looked up at him with anticipation. As expected, he bent down and kissed me. What was unexpected is what happened as he pressed his lips to mine—a pair of blue eyes floated to the surface of my mind. I may have kissed the boy I just met at the basketball courts, but those blue eyes were all I could see, again.

CHAPTER 3

I was still in a trance—thinking about the mysterious boy from the parking lot, although someone else's lips were on mine—when I heard my dad's voice.

"Elle, I think it's time for you to come inside. *Now.*"

I slowly pulled away from the boy I was kissing and peeled his arms from around my waist. He stared at me with longing as if my dad was not standing only ten feet away from us, nonverbally threatening him with his eyes.

"I'll pick you up at eleven tonight. For a party," I heard basketball boy say in my ear.

"Ok," I whispered back as I pulled away.

I needed to forget still. I needed to forget the last twenty-four hours. I needed to forget fights with my dad; saying goodbye to Grace and Charlie; the picture of my mom at my age; nightmares; but most of all, I needed to forget those blue eyes that haunted me.

"Pick me up at the courts," I said, then I turned and walked away from the boy I had just met, glancing over my shoulder one last time to mouth to him, "no lights," as I pointed toward his car. He nodded at me and although I wasn't looking at him, I could feel his eyes on me. I knew he watched my every step as I walked toward the cottage with my dad.

I had plenty of experience sneaking out. I was fourteen the first time I did it. My dad told me I couldn't go to Grace's house to stay the night. Perhaps because he knew my real plan was to go to Kyle Murphy's house for a party instead.

Kyle Murphy was sixteen years old when I first met him. My dad finally lifted my imprisonment, otherwise known as being homeschooled, and allowed me to go to Brookville High my freshman year. I saw him in the parking lot on the first day of school, all his jock friends gathered around him and his yellow Mustang convertible. I—of course—was being dropped off in my dad's beat-up minivan, much to my dismay. I quickly learned that Kyle played basketball, football, and baseball—a trifecta that made him a god amongst the Brookville student population. Kyle's parents allowed him to have parties at his house because they didn't care in the least what he did, which also helped solidify his popularity vote amongst the students of Brookville High. Needless to say, when he invited me to his party the first weekend of school and my dad thwarted my plans by telling me I couldn't stay the night with Grace, I had to find a backup plan.

That was the first night I snuck out. Then I did it again, and again, and then again. Eventually I was sneaking out five nights out of the week to go to a party, go to the field, go over to Kyle's house, or just to get out and prove to myself and my dad, even though he didn't know I was gone, that nobody was going to tell me what I could and could not do. I was a born risk taker even as a child but after that night on the dirt road, something changed. It was almost as if I chased death; or at least I wasn't scared of it. I loved the adrenaline rush I felt when my feet hit the ground and I tasted the freedom of no curfew and no rules. So when I thought about sneaking out of my aunt's house that night, all I felt was the thrill of a challenge.

At ten o'clock that evening, I decided to start my mock bedtime routine. I stood up and yawned, for dramatic effect of course, then told both my aunt and my dad good night. Slowly— to give the impression that I was oh so tired—I sauntered down the hallway then turned toward the bathroom. I didn't want to raise any suspicions so I knew it was necessary to pretend to wash my face and brush my teeth. I went in the bathroom and turned on the water, letting it run for a minute or two while I checked myself out in the mirror.

Being that I had no female figure around during my teenage years to teach me how to apply makeup or wear my hair or pick out clothes, I had to teach myself pretty much everything. This meant that the extent of my make-up application was usually a little powder, sometimes mascara, and a quick dab of lip gloss. Fortunately, I had my mom's olive-toned skin that stayed tan year-round. I also had been gifted with her thick nearly-black hair that had a constant slight easy wave to it, and her long black eyelashes that made my green eyes stand out even more against my dark skin; I was a bit of a tomboy, whether by choice or forced by circumstance I was not certain, but nonetheless it was who I was. I finished finger brushing my hair and quickly applied a dab of powder on my cheeks and nose then looked in the mirror.

I guess that will do. I wish Grace was here to help me do my make-up. My heart ached. I was so alone, and I knew it was all my fault. I pushed the pain away, stuffing it down to my little black box.

After my mock bathroom routine, I went back into the bedroom and changed out of my pajamas into my favorite ripped-up skinny jeans and a black fitted crop top. I completed the look by tying my favorite flannel around my waist then I hopped into bed fully clothed and waited for my dad to walk in and peek at me, a nightly ritual I had come to always expect. Finally, I heard the door crack and I breathed in and out heavily to give the impression that I was asleep—once, twice, three times. I heard the door quietly shut and I waited for another minute or two before I jumped out of bed and tiptoed across the room to find two pillows in the closet which I strategically placed under the covers in the shape of a sleeping body. I pulled on my black ankle boots, pushed open the window and hoisted myself up, then slowly climbed out into the dark Oklahoma night, my heart beating rapidly as I escaped my aunt's home. For some reason I pictured her face as I pushed the window shut and a twinge of guilt washed over me at the thought of disappointing her. Surprised, I pushed the feeling away. I made my way up the brick path, forcing the unwanted thoughts of my aunt out of my mind. Basketball boy was waiting there, lights off just like I told him. His obedience sent waves of annoyance through me. I forced a smile and waved at him then jumped into the convertible. He kept his lights off and slowly pulled onto the drive. Before I knew it, we were heading out of the massive gates and away from the "M" mansion property. We wound through neighborhoods slowly, music playing and my hair blowing in the wind, until we came to another one of the gated entrances. He pushed a button inside of his car and the gate opened.

"This is my house," he said, pointing to the large brick and stone structure at the end of the driveway. "My parents are out of town and I'm having a party. Thought you might like to meet some people from school." He gave an endearing, genuine smile.

That's so nice of him to leave his party and come pick me up.

But of course I couldn't bring myself to acknowledge his kindness. I wouldn't allow myself to be vulnerable in that way. As we continued up the drive to basketball boy's house, my thoughts transported me to my sophomore year.

Grace was a mess, unable to snap out of an ongoing depression after her boyfriend of two years broke up with her. I was fiercely protective of Grace and hated to see her in pain. I wanted to bear the burden for her, because I was strong, because I knew I could handle the pain; but I couldn't take it from her and that killed me.

"Charlie what are we going to do? We have to help Grace snap out of this. I'm really worried about her."

He didn't answer; his body tensed. I could read him like a book.

I rolled my eyes. "What Charlie? Just say it. I know you're thinking something."

He paused, contemplating his next words carefully. "You don't get it, Elle." He was gentle, as always, and there was a wisdom about Charlie that was atypical for a sixteen-year-old boy.

"What's that supposed to mean?" I was defensive.

He looked at me with kindness. I knew his next words would sting from the truth. Charlie was always painfully right. I braced myself.

"You don't open your heart to anyone Elle, so you can't understand how it feels to love someone then lose them."

I looked away in pain. "Actually, Charlie, I think I know perfectly well what it feels like to love someone then lose them." I turned his words against him, uncomfortable with the truth of his implication.

"You know that's not what I mean," he argued, sympathy ringing in his words as he reached out to comfort me.

I refused his peace offering, slamming his bedroom door in his face and stomping away. The pain of his words stung the entire walk home—mostly, because I knew he was right. I never opened my heart to anyone after that night on the one-lane dirt road.

"Elle?" I heard basketball boy call my name, returning me to the present.

"Oh yes. Thanks for the invite. I can't wait to meet some of the fine students of Heritage Hall," I said with mock excitement.

Apparently he hadn't been schooled in the art of sarcasm because he just grinned. I turned my head and rolled my eyes again, even bigger than the first time. I was bored with basketball boy. He hopped out of the car without even opening the door then walked around and grabbed my hand to help me out. He kept a tight lock on my hand as he led me inside his house and up a flight of stairs to his bedroom. I tried to subtly shake free. No luck.

"First I want you to meet my best friend. I've told him all about you," he said with excitement.

Thank goodness he was in front of me on the stairs or he would have seen me roll my eyes at him for the third time in less than a span of five minutes. Not only did he not understand my sarcasm, but he was already telling his best friend about me as if I was his girlfriend. I just wanted to have fun. His seriousness was stifling.

We were at the top of the stairs and at the end of a hallway a bedroom door was cracked. I felt myself pulled in the direction of the stream of light peeking through the crack of the door. Basketball boy pushed open the door and lying on the bed, arms crossed behind his head, was a beautiful boy with a baseball hat on backward. I scanned his body because I really liked what I saw and it was utterly impossible not to stare at something so perfect. Finally my eyes made their way up to his face and it was then that I saw them—the exact same crystal-clear blue eyes that had been haunting my every thought since the Heritage Hall parking lot.

We learned about magnets in sophomore-year science class. I hated science but when we were told about an invisible magnetic field between two objects that relentlessly tries to bring the two objects together, I was mystified. When I walked into basketball boy's bedroom, something similar seemed to be happening—something magnetic. My legs were shaky and I couldn't control my body. I grabbed the handle of the door to steady myself, desperate to make my body respond to my commands instead of obeying the silent, magnetic force that was calling me toward the boy on the bed in front of me. It was overwhelming; I had to fight with determination to keep myself from being yanked directly to his side and I was sure my struggle was evident on my face.

Pull it together, Elle. This is ridiculous. It's just a boy. A complete stranger for that matter.

I searched his face for a sign he was feeling the same undeniable force, but I only found indifference; it was unnerving. *How could he not be feeling this?*

I heard basketball boy's voice but wasn't registering his words until my name was spoken. I came to and realized he must have been introducing me to the blue-eyed boy.

"This is Elle," I heard him say.

Basketball boy stood there and looked back and forth between the two of us, waiting for someone to break the silence. Neither of us did. My heart was pounding. I was paralyzed, unable to respond, unable to even move.

The doorbell broke the silence.

"I better go get that," Caleb said as he ran past the door and down the stairs.

It was just the two of us. The second Caleb left, the invisible force I had been feeling doubled in intensity—so strong now that I was sure my feet would literally be pulled off the ground against my will. Did he feel it? He must. I stayed rooted where I was and still nothing was said as we continued to stare at one another indefinitely. Finally, I heard the blue-eyed boy speak as he continued to lie casually on the bed in a position of complete indifference—which was totally pissing me off yet somehow simultaneously intriguing me.

"Elle?" he said with a tone of sarcasm and disinterest in his voice. "What? Like the letter or something?"

Fire burned inside of me at his words and I let go of the door to cross my hands over my chest in one of my trademark moves. Then I slowly raised an eyebrow and gave him my signature "who the hell do you think you are?" look.

"I'm sorry, I must have missed *your* name?" I said to him, answering with sarcasm of my own.

He paused, a slight smile playing on his lips as if he was trying to figure me out. "It's Maverick," he replied with cool confidence.

"Maverick? What? Like Tom Cruise in *Top Gun* or something?" I spat his sarcasm right back at him.

He pushed his perfect, muscular frame off the bed and stood to his full height. My eyes followed his every move.

Oh. My. God. My thoughts were incoherent.

He towered above my five-feet seven inches; he had to be at least six-foot four—perhaps taller—and his broad, athletic shoulders made him look even more commanding. His jawline was defined, the picture of masculinity, and underneath his hat, dark hair peeked out in a perfect disheveled mess, framing his face. The contrast made his blue eyes seem even more crystal clear. As he walked toward me, I couldn't help but think he looked like he walked off one of those huge Abercrombie and Fitch posters—the ones I saw at the mall each year when I went to Cleveland with Grace and Charlie for our annual back-to-school shopping trip.

He is perfection. I was gaping. I chastised myself and looked away from him, briefly, in a feigned attempt to regain my composure; but my eyes were quickly drawn back by the force calling me toward him. He was intimidating—a feeling I was completely unaccustomed to—as he walked straight up to me until our bodies were merely inches apart. He leaned down and as he got closer, I found it difficult to breathe. I stood there waiting in anticipation, glancing up at his towering body. My eyes traveled upward until they found what they were searching for—those captivating blue eyes. The second I saw them, I was completely and utterly lost yet again.

My thoughts jumbled. All I knew is that he was so close, but not close enough. I desired above all else—perhaps more than anything I had ever wanted in my entire life—for him to touch me. I wanted him to kiss me so badly that my body ached for it; but he wouldn't. The longing was driving me insane. Finally, he leaned in.

He's going to kiss me. So he does *feel it too.* I was triumphant as I closed my eyes in anticipation for what I longed for—his lips on mine. But the kiss never came. I opened my eyes, confused. He was inches away from my face, a look of amusement on his face that infuriated me.

"You wish, Baby Girl," he whispered into my ear. Then he walked out of the room, leaving me longing for his touch and begging for that invisible magnetism to force us back together.

The fire worked its way through my body. I wanted revenge for the rejection the blue-eyed boy had dealt me. Without thinking—because I always acted without thinking when the fire burned—I stomped down the stairs and walked right past the crowd of teenagers gathered in the entryway and living room dancing to rap music. I scanned the room and found basketball boy. I confidently walked up to him, wrapped my arms around his waist and pushed my body up against his, grinding to the beat of the music and twisting my hands through his wavy brown hair. I used his hair to pull his face toward mine and as we got so close that it looked as if we would kiss, I let go and turned around to where my back was facing him. I threw my arms around his neck then moved my body up and down his while swaying seductively to the music.

As we danced, the fire burned stronger. I searched the room, desperate to see those blue eyes. I finally found Maverick—he was leaning against the wall with that smug look of indifference on his face—but his eyes, they seemed to smolder with an emotion I could not quite identify as he watched me put on my racy public display of affection with his best friend. I heard cat calls and people whistling but it didn't stop me. All I could do was stare at Maverick. I was spellbound by him.

My trance was interrupted abruptly as he walked up to a girl across the room and grabbed her by the hand. She had long blonde hair that fell to her waist and was wearing the shortest cheerleading skirt I had ever seen; of course her body was nearly perfect too. I stared in horror, disgusted by how basic she was, as Maverick dragged the blonde cheerleader onto the dance floor and pulled her against his taut body. They danced while I watched in shock, the fire burning inside of me blazing to an intensity I had never before experienced. He moved her tiny frame effortlessly to the beat of the music as undeniable jealousy poured through my body. I wanted that to be me in Maverick's arms.

I walked out of the room, afraid of what I might do if I had to continue watching. I walked through the kitchen and out onto a sun deck, lost in my own thoughts—frustration, annoyance, and most of all, anger toward myself. As I sat on the sun deck and tried to make the world make sense again, my thoughts were interrupted when I heard a girl's voice behind me.

"Hey new girl. Way to make an impression."

I turned and saw a girl with curly shoulder-length brown hair and an endearing smirk on her face. I liked her instantly. She was witty, which was a non-negotiable for me when it came to friends. Her hair was cut into a mismatched tapered bob and she wore cutoffs with black combat boots that laced above her knees. A tattered shirt hung off her right shoulder and read, "Be Yourself."

Please be my friend. Embarrassment washed over me. How desperate could I be?

I hung my head. No way she'll want to be my friend after what I did in there. *Why can't you ever just chill out and think before you act?* I had asked myself that question a million times and of course I already knew the answer. When the fire burned, it was all consuming. I couldn't stop it. I wasn't capable. The fire controlled me, not vice versa. I was still chastising myself when I finally heard the witty brunette speak again.

"I guess you already met Caleb?"

It took me a moment to register who she was talking about. "Oh, you mean basketball boy?"

She broke into a fit of laughter. I smiled. It was a wonderful sound. It sent me back to days with Charlie and Grace. I wanted that friendship, or at least something similar, here.

"I guess you could call him basketball boy, but his *actual* name is Caleb," she said, eyeing me with slight disapproval.

I hung my head again as I realized the weight of my actions. I was so desperate for a distraction, I hadn't even considered Caleb's feelings. He deserved better.

"I take it you guys are together by the PDA I saw going on in the living room earlier?" She interrupted my thoughts with her question.

"No, we definitely are not together," I clarified.

She looked relieved, but confused. "Oh because I walk up to random strangers and dance with them like that, then almost make out with them at parties all the time."

"I met him earlier today," I admitted. "He was playing basketball by my aunt's house and we hung out." I left off the part about our kiss.

"I see. So you *met* him today at some basketball courts." She raised her eyebrows suggestively. "And by tonight you are almost making out with him in the middle of a party full of people you have never even met?" She paused for dramatic effect and looked at me expectantly. I shrugged my shoulders. She laughed. "Well, congrats. Definitely not a bad catch for being the new girl. Caleb is awesome…."

I recognized the emotional incantation she put on the syllables of Caleb's name. Grace used to do it when she had fallen for a guy. She didn't offer any information but she didn't have to. I knew that this girl I was talking to—hopefully my first friend in this new town—had a hopeless crush on the guy I made out with earlier that day.

Could this day get any worse?

Remorse washed over me as I realized the predicament I found myself in. Suddenly the exhaustion of the last twenty-four hours hit me and I could barely hold my head up. I needed a bed and quickly. Tomorrow I would make all this right, I vowed to myself.

"Well, I think the new girl has made enough of an impression for one evening." I stood up and dusted off my jeans then looked her in the eyes and smiled my biggest, most genuine smile—the one that showed off my dimples. I hoped she didn't sense my insecurity as I offered her my hand. "My name is Elle by the way."

Please give me another chance.

She smiled back warmly and took my hand for a firm handshake. "Mine is Carly."

Carly. That was a perfect name for her. I was flooded with gratitude toward the cute witty girl with the tapered bob as she walked me toward the front door. Every single person looked at me disapprovingly on my way out, but thanks to her, I wasn't alone.

Tell her how much you appreciate her.

"It was really nice to meet you Carly," I said. I couldn't bring myself to say more and I hated myself momentarily. *Why is it so hard for you to open up to people?*

"You too," she said with a friendly smile. "I'll see you at school on Monday?"

"Sounds good. It will be nice to know someone on the first day. Thank you for being so nice to me." I looked away, embarrassed. It was all I could bring myself to say.

"No problem," she replied. "I'll look for you. You're going to need some support after tonight." She laughed.

I had no response. I would be facing my first day at a new school on Monday and after tonight, it would undoubtedly be full of sideways glances and whispers.

Oh well. It's not like you're not used to that already. I hoped that things would be different in Tulsa, a fresh start so to speak. But the fire inside had already ruined my chances at that. I wanted to go home, go to bed, and forget.

"Bye Carly. See you Monday."

I was walking down the driveway and toward the gate when I heard the door slam behind me then felt someone grab my arm from behind. I didn't have to turn around to know who was touching me—Maverick.

I was surprised—confused even—when I turned toward him and in his eyes, I thought I saw anger. He seemed upset with me though I couldn't fathom why. I ripped my hand away from him.

"What's your problem?"

"Where do you think you're going?" Answering my question with a question of his own only further infuriated me.

It was so confusing, the rush of unfamiliar emotions I was experiencing when I was in the presence of this cryptic boy. I found myself vacillating between wanting to throw myself into his arms—giving into the magnetism that was at work between the two of us—and wanting to shove him as hard as I could and tell him to get the hell away from me.

"I'm walking home," I said decisively.

He laughed mockingly. "No you're not." His tone was so authoritative. It was maddening and intoxicating at the same time.

No one tells me what to do.

I stepped toward him, using my index finger to point up toward his massive, muscular chest to drive my point home.

"*Yes*. I am," I said defiantly though I was not at all sure why I was arguing about this.

"Maybe you didn't hear me." He grabbed my hand that I had used to point at him with and pulled me into his chest. "I said, *no, you're not.*"

We were so close that I could feel him breathing on me; that ever present, invisible force field pulled me toward him, always calling us even closer together still, like two magnets never satisfied until they find their rest in connection. He stared at me, his blue eyes penetrating past the surface of my emerald eyes and piercing their way into my soul—pressing uncomfortably on that little black box that I allowed no one to touch. That little black box in the depths of my soul shifted again. It was tangible, uncomfortably foreign yet calming. The fire that burned inside of me began to subside—ever so slowly—as I lost myself in his eyes. For the first time in my life I realized I wanted to do exactly what I was told to do. I didn't want to fight. I didn't want to push him away. I didn't want to let the fire burn rampant, telling me to defy; to break the rules; to shut him out; to run away. For the first time in my life, I wanted to submit to someone else's will.

My heartbeat quickened, nearly beating out of my chest. Emotions began to rise inside of me; emotions I had spent years trying to quell. The lid on that little black box that I kept so perfectly hidden in the depths of my soul began to peek open. It was terrifying. I couldn't breathe. My heartbeat increased yet again, to the point that I thought it was going to pound right out of my chest. My throat was closing off. The world started to swim. The lights outside of the house started to go black. Everything was spinning out of control.

The last thing I remembered was his blue eyes as I was falling away from them but this time he didn't look angry; he looked concerned. He looked like he cared.

CHAPTER 4

When I woke up, it was to a pair of blue eyes; but they weren't his. I struggled to find my bearings, glancing around the room in a daze of confusion. My memories started coming back and slowly. *I'm in Oklahoma.*

I felt him before I saw him, that invisible force between us alerting me to his presence. I pushed myself up to a sitting position and looked around, desperate to find him, but it was my new friend Carly that I saw first, sitting in a chair next to the bed. I gave her a little smile when I saw her, grateful that she was there by my side.

A strange sensation pulled my thoughts away from Carly. *What's that feeling? Who's touching my arm?*

I turned to look toward the opposite side of the bed, realizing that Caleb was sitting beside me, gently stroking my arm with concern. I immediately turned away, my eyes scanning the room. They were satisfied when they reached the corner. He was sitting in a chair—arms folded behind his head; hat on backward with dark wavy hair peeking out from underneath; toothpick hanging out of his mouth; and, of course, he had a smug disinterested look plastered on his beautiful face.

When I saw him, our exchange in the driveway flashed through my mind. *Can anyone tell how red my face is?* I remembered being in his strong arms. I remembered him being so close that I could smell his spearmint gum. I remembered my heartbeat increasing and my chest wanting to explode right out of my chest. I remembered my throat starting to close off, my breathing becoming labored, and finally, the feeling that I was fighting for air; then—nothing.

"What happened?" I asked.

It was Caleb who answered. "Mav said he found you in the driveway and you had passed out. Are you OK?" He moved to stroke my face with concern.

I grabbed his hand and moved it away, hoping he would get the hint and stop touching me, then I glanced over at Maverick. I watched, enamored, as he flipped the toothpick in his mouth back and forth, back and forth. I couldn't stop staring. It was so distracting. I envied that toothpick. I thought I saw him wink at me—ever so slight—but it was such a quick movement that I couldn't be sure. I laid my head back on the pillow in exasperation, glancing around to take in the strange surroundings of a bedroom I'd never before seen—I assumed in Caleb's house.

"Can someone please take me home?" I asked. "I just want to go to bed."

Caleb jumped up, much to my disappointment. It was silly of me to hope that it would be Maverick, since Caleb was the one who brought me to the party, but I couldn't help but dream. I longed to be alone in his presence.

Out of the corner of my eye, I saw Maverick rise out of his chair. I was in a trance—as usual—as I watched him command the room with his very presence. I saw his mouth begin to move but I was so captivated by how handsome he was that I didn't hear a word he said. His mouth stopped moving and it was then that I noticed everyone in the room was staring at me expectantly, though I didn't understand why.

"Would that be OK?" I heard Caleb ask as he began stroking my arm again. I pushed it away instantly. "Mav said he'd take you home since he's going there anyway and he's right, I do have a lot of cleaning up to do here. I'm happy to take you myself though," Caleb explained. He started to stand up and make a motion toward me. "I'm just going to take you myself so I know that you are home safe," he said decisively.

"No!" I said to Caleb—perhaps with a bit too much desperation in my voice.

Everyone's curious eyes shot toward me at my sudden outburst.

"It's just that I know you have so much cleaning up to do after the party and now I've just made your night more difficult," I backpedaled. Caleb took my hand as I spoke. I resisted the urge to pull away again, appalled at how terribly awry my plan for a fun distraction had backfired now that I had met Caleb's best friend. "Please, just stay here and I'll catch a ride with Maverick, uh Mav, umm Maverick." I was so confused about what to call him but most of all, I was petrified that someone would recognize the tone of reverence with which I spoke his name.

Caleb was indecisive. "Well…I guess I do have to get this placed picked up before my parents come home tomorrow or I'm going to be in so much trouble," he finally said. "Can I have your phone please?" He reached his hand out to me.

I reached into my back pocket and pulled out my archaic cell phone—the one that I had been told repeatedly by my father was only to be used for emergencies. Carly, Caleb, and Maverick all stared at it in disbelief, but it was Carly who spoke up first.

"Are you freaking kidding me? That's your phone? Um, two-thousand and five called and they want their Motorola flip phone back," she said as she laughed loudly. I loved her already.

"Oh I'm so sorry everyone. Let me just run out to my shiny red Porsche that my *daddy* bought me and get my brand new iPhone." I twirled my hair around my finger and gave my best spoiled-brat impression.

Caleb was undaunted.

"Can you text on this phone?" He really was the epitome of a gentleman. That twinge of guilt hit me again.

"Yes," I said with indignation, "a little."

"OK," he said as he programmed his number into my phone. "Text me when you get home so I know that you made it back safely."

I nodded, knowing I would do no such thing. I stood up. My legs were shaky but I wasn't about to show anyone my weakness. I braced myself on the headboard then pushed off into a determined walk. Caleb followed me and insisted on helping me down the stairs. He nearly carried me the entire way to the car, helped me in, and had I allowed him, I think he would have buckled my seat belt for me.

I have to straighten all this out tomorrow. I'll just tell Caleb I'm not interested in dating and put in a good word for Carly. Everything will be fine.

Caleb said goodbye to me and reminded me for the fifth time to text him when I got home. Then he shut the door and it was just the two of us—just Maverick and me—finally. The second the door closed the invisible force drawing me toward him magnified to a point that was almost unbearable. The tension was palpable. I glanced over at him, hopeful that I would see something in his eyes that might tell me he was feeling the same undeniable force that I was, but he gave nothing away. I glanced aside, anxious to hide my flushing face.

Maverick started his truck and began to pull out of the driveway and as he did, his fancy radio flashed "XM radio - Hits 1". I heard a lone piano chord strike through the silence of the night followed by a male's voice.

I couldn't stand it: the haunting melody on the piano; the hypnotic voice ringing through the speakers; the words that seemed so apropos—*you've got my head spinning, can't get you out of my mind, you're my end and my beginning;* the magnetic force pulling me to the mysterious boy who sat beside me; all the confusing emotions bombarding me all at once. I was unhinged.

We sat there in total silence and listened to the melody ring out—each note and each word intensifying the invisible connection—as the music called us toward one another and the man's voice repeated one line over and over. *I give you all of me and you give me all of you.*

We pulled up to a red light. Every nerve in my body was humming, begging me to turn in his direction. The strange sensation was impossible to resist. At the exact same moment, we both gave into the magnetic force and turned toward one another. The intensity of the emotions passing between us nearly took my breath away. The only time I had ever experienced an emotion that strong was when I lost my mother. Looking into Maverick's eyes, I felt the same depth of emotions as that night, but instead of sadness and pain, I felt something completely new—a feeling I had never before encountered; it was an all-consuming fire that burned inside of me, leaving me exhilarated and confused and afraid and euphoric all at the same time.

I was consumed with trying to decipher the complicated feelings I was experiencing when our moment was abruptly shattered. Maverick reached for the knob on the stereo. He covered his emotions with the indifference he always wore across his beautiful face.

"I hate that song." He changed the radio station then continued driving down the road as if that indescribable and beautiful moment we shared hadn't even occurred.

Demoralized, I shrunk down in my seat and looked out the window. With a new rap song playing on Maverick's ridiculous stereo system, the tension that loomed between us lessened significantly, and I hated the silence. I wanted to ask him a million questions. I wanted to know everything there was to know about the mysterious and unreadable boy sitting across the truck from me—yet another thing I could now add to my list of firsts that I seemed to be experiencing since meeting Maverick. Normally I didn't care to know anything about any of the guys I dated. The less I knew, the less attached I'd be. With Maverick, everything was different.

I broke the silence. The words felt strange rolling off my lips but what was stranger still was that I found myself wanting to tell him about her, about someone that I never talked about to anyone—ever.

"It's Elyse," I said stoically, refusing to look at him. He was silent and strangely, in his silence, I found myself wanting to divulge more. "Elle...like the letter?" I said, mocking him from earlier. "My name is actually Elyse and I was named after my—" I took a long pause as I tried to force myself to speak the word that I never spoke— "my...mother." I finally spit the word out with a sharp exhale, my shoulders slumping in relief.

He didn't respond at first and I noticed I wasn't breathing, anxiously anticipating his response to my confession.

"Beautiful."

That was it. All he said was that one little word; and as he said it, a little place in my heart that had long been forgotten slowly cracked open. When it did, I heard more than that one little word. I heard something unspoken.

I looked away, closing my eyes and forcing myself to take deep breaths. *Pull it together Elle.*

We pulled up to the massive iron gate with the "M" insignia and it automatically opened. I vaguely remembered Caleb saying something about Maverick taking me home since he was going there anyway.

"Wait a minute, *you live here?*" I said in horror.

"No, I just have a magic gate opener in my truck that opens all the gates in the city of Tulsa," he deadpanned.

I don't know why it made me so mad when I realized he lived at the "M" mansion, but it did. Perhaps because I had already made my mind up that the people who lived in the mansion were pretentious jerks that I would hate, and although I was confused about my conflicting emotions toward the mysterious boy that sat beside me, I was certain that it wasn't hate that I was feeling toward him—not in the least.

A familiar fire started to burn inside of me again. I didn't understand how he could make me feel such a vast array of emotions in such a short period of time. It was completely exhausting. I was on a roller-coaster ride against my will— never knowing which way was up or down, and never knowing when I was going to be catapulted upside down or in a different direction—and just like a roller-coaster ride, I found the emotional onslaught I was experiencing in Maverick's presence both exhilarating and utterly frightening.

"The 'M' on the gate stands for Mason," he said softly, almost apologetically for some reason. When he said his last name I noticed that he glanced over at me—almost expectantly—but I had no idea why.

"Maverick Mason huh?" I didn't hide the criticism in my voice. "Sounds like some terrible soap-opera-star name to me." I crossed my arms and looked out the window, satisfied. *I'm sure everyone who meets you worships the ground you walk on pretty boy. Well, not me.*

Slowly a smile spread across his face; then he laughed. It nearly took my breath away. Warmth spread throughout my body and that invisible force began tugging endlessly at my soul. I wanted to hear it again. *I want to be the one that makes him laugh like that.*

"No is the answer," he said, interrupting my private thoughts.

"No is the answer to what?" I asked, confused.

"No I was most definitely not named after Maverick in *Top Gun,*" he admitted with a chuckle. "And you are the first person who has ever asked me that by the way. Maverick is a family name. It's my mother's maiden name. So, I guess we are both named after our mothers."

He looked at me tenderly when he said that we were both named after our mothers and it made me uncomfortable.

"Well I would get used to that if I were you." I wanted to backpedal as soon as I said it, but it was too late.

"Get used to what?" he asked as he pulled to the top of the hill that led to the cottage and pushed his truck into park. He looked at me, eyebrow raised, awaiting a response.

I took a deep breath, resolving to finish what I had started, then locked eyes with him. "Me being the first," I said with confidence.

We stared at each other, searching one another as so many unspoken feelings passed between us, each of us trying to read the emotions on the other's face. The tension escalated; I felt that familiar tug—that magnetic force intensifying. His blue eyes burned into mine, and I was positive that he felt it as well. Then with a deep breath, he shook his head and covered his features with determination and decisiveness. In a split second, smug and indifferent Maverick had returned, much to my disappointment. I decided to change the subject.

"So how long have you lived here anyway?"

"Always. I grew up in Tulsa," he answered. "What about you? What's *your* story?"

His eyes searched me with scrutiny. I looked out the window in a desperate attempt to avoid his prying gaze. *It's like he knows.* I rubbed my sweaty palms on my jeans and took a deep breath, feigning triviality.

"Well as you heard at the party, I'm the 'new girl' so obviously I just moved here."

He stared at me with disapproval. My palms began to sweat again and I glanced away. *Does he know I'm avoiding his questions?*

"That's it? That's all you're going to tell me?"

"Yep, it sure is."

He leaned in. My breath hitched.

"You're sure about that?" He was shamelessly aware of how good looking he was, and wasn't afraid to use it to get his way. I had to look away not to give into his charms.

"Totally sure, Top Gun."

There was a pause. I glanced over, pleased to see he seemed amused by me, perhaps even intrigued.

"OK. You can just tell me when you're ready." He sounded so cocky.

The fire burned inside. "Oh really? I can just tell you when I'm ready? Are you serious right now?"

This guy is absolutely infuriating.

"That's what I said. You can just wait and tell me when you're ready." He carried so much certainty in his voice, as if he were my puppet master, giving me permission to wait and tell him later, but absolutely positive I would do what he wanted—eventually. I hated it, and I loved it all at the same time. It was exhausting and exhilarating.

I huffed, crossing my arms with force.

"Well, I wouldn't hold my breath if I were you."

He smirked.

"You're something else, Baby Girl, you know that?"

He was driving me crazy—our constant banter, the onslaught of emotions I was feeling that I didn't understand, his annoying pet name for me that I simultaneously loved and hated.

"You better stop calling me that," I said with all the strength I could muster. I reached for the door handle, jerked it up, then hopped out of the truck and slammed the door. I didn't bother turning around.

"I'll stop calling you Baby Girl when you stop calling me Top Gun, *Baby Girl.*" He said it again, just to irritate me further.

I whipped my head around, gave him my hardest eye roll, then continued to stomp my way down the hill to my aunt's house.

"Aren't you going to say thanks for the ride?" he called after me. His antagonism was never ending.

I stopped in my tracks, then turned on my heel and walked toward him purposefully. He held my gaze as I continued toward him and with each step, I felt the force between us intensify, always pulling us toward one another. I approached him but I had to push onto my toes to reach him because of the monstrous tires he had on his truck. I crossed my arms and rested them on his truck window, leaning in so that we were only inches apart. The magnetism between us was undeniable.

"You're welcome…" I said, pausing for dramatic effect before continuing in an even lower voice, "for allowing *you* to give *me* a ride home."

I tried to read the emotion I saw gleaming in his eyes right before I turned to saunter away. Either he was angry, or he secretly loved my defiance. I couldn't tell which—maybe it was both. We seemed to have the same erratic effect on one another.

I heard Maverick call after me.

"You better go text Caleb. He'll be worried." There was bitterness in his tone. I refused to acknowledge his comment.

"Hey Elle, one more thing—tell Miss Cordelia I said hi."

With those final instructions, I heard his truck roar to life then his engine throttled as he slowly pressed the gas and drove away, stretching the magnetic field between us further and further apart. As his truck disappeared over the hill, I still felt that endless pull fighting to bring us back together.

CHAPTER 5

I was a prisoner to my own thoughts—my mind racing—as I replayed every word that passed between Maverick and me. I remembered his touch, the way my body responded innately when he placed his hand on my hand; and I longed to feel him again.

I was so caught up in reminiscing about my time with Maverick that I didn't even notice there was someone else in the room when I crawled back through the window of my little cottage bedroom. I flipped on the bedside lamp and started to undress before I recognized the uncanny feeling of someone else's presence. When I peeked over my shoulder, I started at the sight of my Aunt Cordelia in a wooden rocking chair, knitting away with her knitting needles, her face showing no recognition of the fact that her seventeen-year-old niece had just climbed through her window at three o'clock in the morning.

"Good evening Elle." I was surprised not to hear a hint of anger in her voice. "Did you have a nice time with Maverick?"

How does she know I've been with Maverick?

I was so confused by the entire interaction—her calm demeanor, the fact that she wasn't yelling at me or threatening to ground me, and even more so that she knew it was Maverick who brought me home that evening.

"Um, no not really," I finally responded with bitterness, thinking about our interaction both outside Caleb's house and in his truck. We sat there for several moments, her teetering back and forth softly in her rocking chair and me standing awkwardly at the edge of my bed awaiting my judgment. She broke the silence first.

"I shared a room with your mother when we were growing up," she said with a hint of nostalgia. "She was quite the escape artist as well, did you know?" She peeked up over her spectacles and temporarily ceased the movement of her knitting needles. "I see you seem to take after her."

I was too shocked to speak, unable to comprehend that I was speaking to an aunt I had never even met until today, and she was openly talking about my mother. My wall began to falter—the one I worked five arduous years to build—as I stared at my aunt, but saw my mother instead. I fought the urge to run to her and wrap my arms around her, finding solace in the arms of the woman who reminded me so much of my own mother. I wanted to smell her hair and see if it smelled like my mom's. I wondered if she used the same lavender-scented shampoo and if her hair would feel like silk when I brushed it, just like my mother's. I wanted to stay up all night long and ask her a million questions. Momentarily, I wanted to let down my walls for her; but I couldn't. I had operated for far too long under my current set of rules. So out of fear, I refused to let them go. I turned and looked away, and I shoved the unwanted emotions I was feeling toward my aunt back into my little black box, and I slammed the lid shut.

Where was she all those years? Where was she when I needed her...

With my wall back intact, I lashed out at my aunt. "If you knew her so well, then why have I never even heard of you before?"

64

Her body stiffened in defense, her eyes narrowing as she stared at me with a challenge building. "You never knew me because your mom left when she was your age. She ran away and I never saw her again." A deep and painful sadness resonated in her words.

She held my gaze and in her eyes, I saw heartbreak. I wanted to walk over and comfort her, which was unexpected. We shared the same pain, Cordelia and I, and whether I wanted it to or not, the shared connection was forging a bond between the two of us. We both knew the excruciating pain of loving someone more than life itself, then losing them. As much as I wanted to deny what I was feeling for this stranger I had just met, I could deny it no longer.

My body moved of its own volition, walking across the room toward my aunt. I stopped in front of her rocking chair, then silently reached out my hand to her. She dropped her knitting needle and grasped onto it with an obvious desperation. We didn't look at one another. Perhaps we both knew it would be too much for the other to take. Instead, we stayed there in silence—two women who had suffered the same unbearable loss. We were unified in a similar grief that only we could truly understand. In complete silence, we comforted one another, telling each other in our own unspoken language of pain—*you're not alone.*

It was my aunt who broke the silence first. She reached her hand up and stroked my face with affection and I let her.

"You look just like her." Then she stood and walked out of the room, turning to me before she shut the door behind her. "Go to sleep now, Elle."

Those were her only words but I heard what was implied— no more questions, Elle, not tonight. She couldn't handle questions about the sister she had lost; the sister she was never able to say goodbye to; the sister who crawled out of their bedroom window when she was seventeen years old, and never returned home. Although I had thousands of questions I needed to ask, I respected her request and remained silent as she walked out the door.

Our eyes met one last time as she shut the door and in that moment, I saw my mother. I allowed myself to remember instead of pushing the memories away like I usually did. I saw her in the kitchen, her red-and-white checkered apron on, Christmas music blaring and the smell of sugar cookies wafting through the air. I jumped up onto the countertop as she smiled that smile of hers—the one that reached out and touched the depths of your soul and made you feel so happy and full of life; then she took a huge scoop of cookie dough and held it out for me to enjoy as she placed her index finger over her mouth as if to say, "Shhhh…this is our little secret," as she glanced knowingly at my father in the next room.

The memory ended abruptly and I was back in my aunt's cottage in Oklahoma. I took a deep breath and remembered one last thing before I stuffed everything back into my little black box—that was the last Christmas I ever saw my mother. I crawled into my bed and exhaustion overtook me; I quickly drifted off to sleep.

I found myself on a familiar dirt road. I walked slowly down the road. The clouds began to move in. A storm was coming. I turned around and saw the light behind me but it was only a quick glance. I didn't even bother to listen for the laughter of Grace and Charlie. I knew I would walk into the darkness. I always did.

I heard a low rumble and saw the first strike of lightning. There in the distance was the blue Volvo station wagon at the end of the road as it always was. I started running into the darkness, desperate to get to the blue Volvo. The lightning struck again and I saw her at the end of the road, long black hair flowing wildly in the twirling winds created by the storms. Her blue sundress was ripped and torn to shreds, hanging off her body in disarray. She was as white as a ghost and her normally beautiful features were disfigured by pain and fear.

I have to save her.

I started running faster. The lightning struck again and this time I saw a figure behind her—a shadow of a man with no face. My mother stood in front of him, blocking me protectively and not allowing me to see but an outline of grey shoulders behind her. My body cowered instinctively as I felt the evil emanating from his dark presence.

It was black again and I was consumed with handicapping fear. If I didn't get there in time, I knew that he would kill her. I tried to run into the dark night, compelled to save her, but my feet were stuck. No matter how hard I tried, I couldn't move them. Another strike of lightning tore through the dark night and I looked down to see that I was in quicksand. I thrashed and pulled at my legs desperately but the harder I tried, the more I sank into the sand. The lightning struck again and somehow I was only feet away from her. I saw her standing there, blood running down her face, covering her dress, then finally pooling in a deep, scarlet puddle on the ground beneath her. She held something out in her hands, an object I had seen her offer me so many times over the years, though I didn't know what it was. As the lightning flashed one last time, I saw her brown eyes staring at me with sympathy and love before the night became pitch black yet again.

I thrashed desperately, screaming into the night but as I struggled, I only sank deeper and deeper into the quicksand. It crept up my torso then covered my shoulders. I pushed my chin up to the sky and sucked in what would be my last breath as I waited hopelessly for it to claim my entire body. Lightning struck and I opened my eyes one last time. It was then that I realized I wasn't alone. I saw a pair of piercing-blue eyes and suddenly I was lifted out of the pit of despair by a set of strong arms. As he sat me down, I realized that light was creeping its way up the horizon in a display of oranges and yellows and pinks. It was no longer dark and I was no longer alone. The boy with the blue eyes found me, and he saved me.

He took my hand and I didn't question him. I let him lead me and together we started running down the dirt road except as the sun rose, I saw that we were on a different road altogether. We were on a long dirt road but it wasn't the dirt road I was accustomed to seeing in my nightmares. In every direction that I looked, I saw green grass and the horizon; then I saw a large black structure in the distance moving up and down, up and down without cease. I scanned the horizon and saw several more of the large structures. Oil wells.

We continued to run and when my legs tired to the point of exhaustion, he picked me up and carried me with ease in his strong and steady arms. He carried me into the horizon with confidence and although I had no idea where he was taking me, he had my complete trust. Finally, I saw a set of shapes in the distance, a row of small structures that created a dark silhouette on the morning horizon. They were small wooden houses that appeared to be identical in every way except for the occasional different coat of paint on the exterior. As we approached the houses the boy with the blue eyes set me down, letting me take the lead for the first time since he rescued me. Surprisingly my feet moved with certainty toward a house at the end of the street.

It was painted yellow—the only house on the street painted that bright color—and something inside of it called to me. I moved toward it slowly and as I neared, I saw a beautiful circular shape hanging from the door. I noticed the round object was adorned with colorful beads and feathers and it moved melodically with the wind. It was a dreamcatcher; I recognized it from a book I had to read about Native American culture—a requirement for my freshman history class. I was mesmerized by it. I stared at the feathers swinging back and forth in the wind for a few seconds before I finally took the steps that led to the front door.

I reached up to knock on the door but before I could, I heard a noise and the door slowly creaked open. I was calm, at peace even, though I had no idea what was behind the door. As the door creaked open, I saw a silhouette of a woman. She wore a white dress made of leather that touched the floor. The dress was adorned with beads and feathers, just like the dreamcatcher, and her hair was done in two long braids of dark hair intermixed with strands of silver that indicated her age. Her beautiful smile lit up when she saw me; it touched her wrinkled eyes. Without a word, she lifted her hands and offered me a dark, wooden box. I recognized the box instantly; I recognized it because it was the same ornately carved wooden box that I had seen my mother hold out to me in her bloody hands hundreds of times before in my dreams.

CHAPTER 6

I woke up disoriented. I looked around, confused. The little yellow house and the woman in the white dress were nowhere to be found. I rolled over to look at the old-fashioned alarm clock on the bedside table and saw that it read 5:35 a.m.—way too early to be up for the day—but after tossing and turning for several minutes I accepted that I wouldn't be falling back asleep.

I pushed myself slowly out of the bed then walked on my tiptoes over to my suitcase, cringing each time I took a step as I heard the old wooden floors groan their resistance. I made it across the room, finally, then opened my suitcase and unzipped the top pocket. There I found my old sketchbook as well as my pencils, paints, and pastels—the ones I had found in the back of my closet when we were packing to leave Ohio. I tried to throw them away, attempting—unsuccessfully—to convince myself that I didn't want them and would never use them again; but something stopped me as I walked toward the trash can. I couldn't find the will to part with them. My mother had given them to me and perhaps, because my artistic abilities were yet another trait I had inherited from her, I wasn't ready to turn my back on them forever.

I walked over to my bed with the sketchbook; then I took a deep breath as I opened it for the first time in over six years. As I flipped through trying to find a blank page, I saw a beautiful display of colorful pictures. I wanted to look through each picture I had drawn, and happily reminisce. *The little girl who drew those pictures is gone forever.*

I flipped past images that spoke of another time and found a blank page. Then I started drawing with my pastels.

I drew a beautiful Oklahoma horizon with oranges, yellows, and purples spanning the sky. Then I pushed the corner of my white pastel across the horizon in little strokes, dotting it with thin wisps of clouds. Next I drew a long, straight road with green grass lining either side of it. I drew movement in the grass—just like I remembered it from my dream—blowing gently in the Oklahoma wind. At the end of the road, a row of colorful wooden houses, little squares of uniformity differentiated only by their shade. I accentuated one house above all others—a yellow house in the center of my picture— and on its front porch a beautiful dreamcatcher that blew melodically in the Oklahoma breeze. I drew everything just as I had seen it.

I sat my pastels down and felt exhausted yet satisfied. It required me to open a part of my soul that I had not used in six years and I was oddly at peace as I admired my art work.

I threw the sketchbook on the bed and saw my alarm clock said it was a more acceptable hour for waking. I thought I heard some movement in the kitchen so I threw on my robe and decided to face my punishment from the night before.

I walked down the little hallway and into the kitchen to find my aunt making coffee. There were massive cinnamon rolls sitting on the table, oozing with butter and white icing. My mouth watered. My dad was sitting at the table, his reading glasses on and his face buried in the newspaper. My heart pounded in my chest, wondering which of his possible punishments he would dole out this time—months of being grounded, no cell phone, loss of privileges with friends, or my least favorite of all: writing Bible verses that corresponded with my particular offense.

"Elyse," my dad said, then took a long pause as he slowly refolded the paper and laid it on the table.

I cringed. Use of my full name was not a good sign. I held my breath, waiting for my verdict.

"We need to do some shopping today."

I stared at him in disbelief. My heart sputtered out a few confused beats.

My eyes shot to my aunt. Her back was toward me, but I could tell she was listening. Why didn't she tell my dad?

I grabbed a cinnamon roll from the plate in front of me. "Thank you, Aunt Cordelia," I said as she grabbed her mug of coffee and joined us at the table. I made sure to lock eyes with her. I hoped she knew I was thanking her for so much more than breakfast.

The next thing I knew, my dad and I were walking outside and loading up in the Brookville Church of God van to commence on our discount-uniform shopping trip, which I was wholeheartedly dreading. As we pulled off the little road that led to the cottage and onto the main road that would take us past the Mason mansion, I was suddenly acutely aware of the invisible force field that connected me to Maverick. I slouched down in my chair, knowing that he was close and terrified that if my dad saw me look at him, he would recognize the connection that resonated between Maverick and me. We drove past the basketball courts. When I could take it no longer I finally glanced toward Maverick. I found him instantly, running up and down the courts in a pickup game of basketball with Caleb and four other friends. Our eyes connected and even from a distance, his gaze burned into my soul.

My dad and I drove off the property and made our way to the discount-uniform shop in town. When we arrived, the saleswoman was expecting us—thanks to a call from my aunt—and she directed us to an area that was full of Heritage Hall's used uniforms. She started going over the dress code for the Academy and I immediately tuned her out. I hated listening to rules. Finally, she walked away and left my dad and I staring awkwardly at the Heritage Hall clothing section. I had never even been shopping with my dad before and it was obvious that our little outing could not be over fast enough—for the both of us.

"Uh, umm…" He muttered awkwardly as he gestured toward the clothing section.

I interrupted to help put him out of his misery. "How about you just go sit over there…" I chuckled as I waved to a seating area on the opposite side of the store, "and I will let you know which ones work."

I grabbed an assortment of plaid skirts and white-and-navy collared shirts then disappeared into the dressing room. I tried on each skirt and although I thought they were all hideous, they did fit. I looked at the price tags and realized that two of them were significantly less than the others, so I decided on those. If I was going to wear an ugly plaid skirt, it might as well be the cheapest ugly plaid skirt I could find to help my dad out. I came out of the dressing room holding the two skirts and a few shirts with the same HH logo I had seen on Maverick's truck. Seeing the logo made me think of the first time I saw him. Suddenly I was bombarded with thoughts of his piercing-blue eyes, the feeling of his touch on my skin, and his quiet confidence that left me beguiled. I could never seem to escape him.

"Elle." My dad's words awakened me from my daydream and, flustered, I walked toward the counter and handed over my second-hand clothes. I felt a rush of guilt as I watched my dad count out $72.39 to pay for my uniform.

"Um, thanks dad," I said awkwardly. "I really appreciate it."

"You're welcome Ells," he replied, giving me a playful wink. I smiled back, enjoying his use of the nickname he called me when I was a little girl. As we walked out of the discount-uniform store, I tried to recall the last time he called me Ells. It had been too long to remember. I liked it, though I refused to tell him. I playfully nudged him with my shoulder and he looked at me with surprise then nudged me back. As we walked to the car, I couldn't help but notice that the tension between us—since arriving in Tulsa—seemed to have lessened, even if just slightly.

We jumped in the Brookville Church of God van and I glanced over at my dad as we drove away. I had so many questions but I knew I had to ask them carefully if I wanted answers. Over the years, the topic of my mother had become completely obsolete between the two of us. She was never spoken of, in fact we made an unbelievable effort to never even use her name. Neither of us knew how to function with her gone. Neither of us knew how to talk about our feelings. Neither of us knew how to escape the immeasurable pain when we thought of her.

"Dad?" I asked with reservation, testing the waters.

He quit humming and turned to me. "Yes Elle?"

"Why did I never even know about Aunt Cordelia until now?"

His shoulders stiffened. He waited awhile, breathing deeply. "Because I didn't know about her myself until a few weeks before we moved here."

I stared at him, dumfounded. "You're trying to tell me you didn't know your own wife had a sister?" I said, my intonation rising with each word.

He paused, then tried to change the subject. "How are you feeling about school starting on Monday?"

I wanted to laugh at what a terrible choice that subject change was, but I had tunnel vision. "Dad, please. I need to know," I begged.

He pulled up to a stoplight, then took a deep breath and let it out before he spoke. "Elle, when I met your mother she was seventeen years old. She told me her parents had passed away and that she had no family. We never spoke of it again after that because..." He trailed off and dropped his head. My heart hurt for him.

I reached my hand out to him in a gesture of comfort. I knew the agony caused by talking about her because I had felt it myself; so normally I honored our unspoken agreement, but today I had to break our rules.

"Because what, dad?" I pressed.

His brow drew together in concentration and I knew he was trying to find the strength to speak his next words. "Because I loved her too much to ever ask her about it again. I could tell it caused her so much pain. I just wanted to take her pain away and make her happy."

I sat there in silence, dropping my hand from his. The fire started to burn and I wanted to stop it. But I couldn't.

"You're telling me that Mom was only seventeen when you met her and that she told you her family was all dead and you never spoke of it again, but it turns out they aren't all dead?" I could hardly make sense of the words as I spoke them.

"Yes," he said. "That's what I'm telling you." I could hear the finality in his voice and I knew he was done speaking on the matter. I, however, was just getting started.

"So we moved to Okla-freaking-homa, to the middle of *nowhere* to live with Mom's dead sister—who isn't actually dead—that we had never even heard of until a few weeks ago? Is that what you are telling me right now?" I didn't even try to hide the anger and sarcasm in my voice. The fire burned fast, growing inside of me. My heartbeat quickened and my breath became short and labored. We both knew what was about to happen. I was not in control. The fire was taking over.

"Elle?" I heard him but it was as if he was calling to me from miles away, not from just a seat away in our church van. I sensed his concern. I could barely hear him. I was slipping away.

"Elyse Rose…breathe!"

They were the last words I remembered hearing before everything turned to black.

CHAPTER 7

I awakened to find us sitting on the side of the road in a neighborhood I had never seen before. My dad sat there watching me, a look on his face that was a mixture of concern, fear, and sadness. I hated when he looked at me like that.

"Let's go." I waved toward the road dismissively and looked away, anxious to avoid his concerned, prying eyes. Finally, he started to pull onto the road and I let out a relieved sigh. I didn't want to talk about it and he knew that.

My dad and I didn't discuss my "episodes", which is what I called them. The doctors said they were severe anxiety attacks brought on by Post Traumatic Stress Disorder. Whatever they were, I had been a prisoner to them ever since the night I watched my mother die.

My dad peered over at me, concerned, and I knew he wanted to break the silence but wouldn't. It was another unspoken rule between us. Don't ask if everything is OK because we already knew what the answer was to that question; the answer was no. It was always no for both of us. Everything wasn't OK. Nothing had been OK since we lost her.

We pulled up to the cottage and I hopped out quickly, anxious to shut myself away in my room. My father's voice stopped me.

"Elle, I thought I would get my guitar out?" He said it with a question in his voice then stood there awkwardly, waiting for my response. I knew what he was really asking. He wanted us to speak to one another in the only language that we were able to communicate in—music. My heart softened when his eyes searched mine, begging me to meet him in the middle for once. After all that I had put him through, how could I say no?

"Let me run these clothes inside and I'll meet you back out here."

I ran to my bedroom, threw my clothes on the bed, then grabbed my guitar. When I walked back outside, I found my dad already strumming away so I sat down and listened to him play. I breathed in and out, over and over again, as I let the troubles and frustrations from the past two days fade away with each melodic note. I looked around and marveled at the beauty of the Oklahoma leaves beginning to change in early fall, then finally, I let my eyes close and I began to play. I joined my dad in a familiar rhythm and beat, finding our connection through the notes of the music. His voice rang out and I followed, singing the harmony to a song I knew every word to by heart.

We sang all three verses of my dad's favorite hymn—It Is Well With My Soul. I knew why he always wanted to sing that song; because my dad earnestly hoped and prayed that the words would come true and that one day it would be well with our souls again, that peace like a river would flood our souls. I loved him for that. I loved that he could hope. My hope, on the other hand, died when I was a ten-year-old little girl, when I held my mother's hand as I watched her bleed to death.

I was finishing the last chorus when my pulse began to race and that dark spot in the depths of my soul began to call to me, pulling me back to reality, commanding me to open my eyes. I fought to stay where I was, afraid—for some reason—of who I knew would be standing there when I returned to the present. Eventually the song was over and the deafening silence slowly forced me to open my eyes. Standing in front of me was Maverick, holding two bags of groceries in his strong arms.

Oh. My. God. He just heard me singing.

My aunt walked out of the front door. Finally, she broke the awkward silence. "Maverick this is Mr. Christiansen, your new religious-studies teacher."

Maverick was staring at me, stripping me bare with those blue eyes of his and I desperately wanted to look away, to run from the intensity of his gaze; but I couldn't. Eventually, he tore his eyes away from mine and sat the groceries down, then grabbed my father's hand and gave him a firm, proper handshake.

"Nice to meet you Mr. Christiansen."

"Nice to meet you as well, son."

My mouth was dry as my dad and the blue-eyed boy exchanged pleasantries.

Is this seriously happening right now? My dad and Maverick are meeting? I wasn't sure why I was so horrified, but I was.

"Elle, this is Maverick Mason. He's a senior at Heritage Hall too." My aunt turned to me and completed her introductions even though she knew they were only for show. She knew we had already met. "Maverick this is my niece that I told you would be coming to stay with us. Her name is Elle."

Maverick walked toward me and the force between us surged, becoming more difficult to fight with each of his approaching steps. He was directly in front of me and I was holding my breath in anticipation as he reached out his hand to me. My hand instinctively went up to meet his without me telling it to do so.

We're touching again.

I was bombarded with an onslaught of emotions. I was lost, completely undone. The second our hands met, I was suddenly wandering in a desert, dying of thirst but only being given a drop of water to sustain me. Maverick merely touching my hand was not enough to quench my undying thirst. It only made me long for more.

I was interrupted by my dad's judgmental glare. I worried that he could somehow sense the undeniable force that connected us. Maverick winked at me before he turned around and I was irritated by his playful behavior in front of my dad; but I also loved it. I rolled my eyes at him but simultaneously tried to suppress a smile.

I was always so unhinged in his presence. He was both infuriating and intoxicating, a mixture that left me completely enraptured. I could not escape him—not in my dreams and not in my reality. Maverick Mason—he was everywhere.

He walked straight past me with no acknowledgment—which made the fire simmer inside of me—and put the groceries on my aunt's kitchen counter. I watched as he walked around her kitchen with obvious comfort and ease, unloading her groceries for her. Meanwhile, I sat there with my arms crossed and stared at him, scowling. Eventually I felt my dad nudge me and I looked up to see his questioning eyes on me, wondering why I was being so rude to the young man he thought I had just met. I softened my glare and let my arms fall to my side as I heard my dad begin to make polite small talk with Maverick about Heritage Hall, what his interests were, and how he liked living in Tulsa. I acted disinterested but secretly hung onto every word that came out of his perfect mouth.

My dad and Maverick were still making small talk when I heard my aunt's phone ring in the next room.

"Yes, she's here. May I ask who's calling?" I heard her say, then she walked into the room holding the phone out to me.

"Hello?" I said sheepishly as my dad, Maverick, and my aunt all stared at me in unison. I turned my back to them as I put the phone to my ear.

"Hey there," I recognized the voice instantly. It was Caleb.

"How did you get my aunt's phone number?" I accused. I glanced into the next room to see my dad eyeing me suspiciously, probably because he knew all too well that when boys started calling, trouble usually followed.

"I'm sorry what?" I was so engrossed in staring at Maverick that I hadn't even heard Caleb's words.

"I said I wanted to ask you about something," he said.

"How did you get my aunt's phone number?" I didn't even try to hide my annoyance.

"I had to ask Maverick for it," he admitted. "You haven't answered my texts." I looked at Maverick in the next room and glared at him with disdain. He matched my stare.

"What do you need to ask me?" I said, still in a trance as I glanced at Maverick from across the room.

He seemed almost angry at me, his penetrating blue eyes making me uncomfortable as he glared at me from the next room. For some reason, I found myself fighting the urge to go to him and say that I was sorry, even though I didn't know what my transgressions were. I hated his disapproval—I wanted to right it, and that was a feeling I was completely unaccustomed to.

Maverick brushed by me as he put some eggs and milk into the refrigerator and I was certain it was on purpose, so that he could see my reaction to his touch. As if on cue, I inhaled sharply when his skin touched mine and my heart began beating rapidly, my breath coming in short, accelerated bursts when it did return to me, betraying me. He turned to me as he leaned into the fridge and he stared into my eyes, obviously noticing my reaction, then he pulled away and shut the door. I thought I saw that little trademark wink, as he turned and walked away.

He was so puzzling, seemingly angry at me for unknown reasons one minute, then playful and flirtatious the next. Even more confusing was my reaction to him. Whether he was being playful or mysterious or controlling, I undoubtedly was being drawn to him. I wanted more and more of him even though I found him so difficult to understand. I was being drawn to every single part of him by a force that I found impossible to comprehend and even more impossible to resist. I wanted to be nowhere but in his presence.

I stood there reflecting on the epiphany I had just experienced regarding my feelings about the enigmatic boy who I knew nothing about except that he lived in the mansion up the hill; drove a truck that cost more than my house back in Ohio; was best friends with the boy I had nearly made out with in front of half the members of my soon-to-be school; possessed eyes that haunted my soul in a way that I found both frightening and enchanting at the same time; and he played baseball. I also knew that staying with my aunt, in her cottage on the back of the Mason estate, provided an increased opportunity for seeing Maverick; and because of that—and perhaps other reasons as well—I found myself dreading the day we would have to leave.

"Elle?" The words were almost a shout as they came through the receiver. I had been caught daydreaming again. I glanced up, startled, and thought I saw a smirk spreading across Maverick's face.

"I said do you want to go to Maverick's party with me tonight?" I heard Caleb ask.

"Um, I need to ask my dad," I responded awkwardly, thinking to myself that no, I didn't want to go to the party with Caleb because I wanted to go with Maverick himself.

"OK well ask your dad if you can go," Caleb said.

"I'm kind of busy right now," I retorted.

He was persistent and I could tell that there was no way I was getting off the phone with him until I asked. I decided to just get it over with as quickly as possible.

"Um, Dad, can I go to a party tonight?" I said.

"What kind of party?" my dad asked with scrutiny.

It was as if Caleb could hear what was going on in my aunt's house. "It's just a fall party that Maverick's parents throw every year!" he answered. His enthusiasm was exhausting but I knew he was my ticket to the party and more importantly, to being in Maverick's presence again; so I continued.

"It's a fall party at…um, um," I paused, somehow finding it difficult to speak Maverick's name out loud in his presence, "Maverick's house," I finally spat out with embarrassment.

My dad looked at Maverick and when he did, his expression softened. Apparently he wasn't immune to the powers that the boy with the blue eyes possessed either. I listened as my dad and Maverick talked and I heard some details that Maverick was giving about the party—something about a swim-in movie night in their heated pool and games afterward. I didn't really hear much of what he said after the swim-in movie in the heated pool part because I was stuck there. I had never even heard of a heated pool before much less some type of a movie theatre in one. I found myself wondering what in the world his dad did for a living. I had so many questions for the mysterious Maverick Mason.

My dad's laughter brought me back to reality and I realized that he and Maverick were done talking and Maverick was leaving, which inexplicably left me feeling panicked. I hurried to get off the phone with Caleb.

"Um, my dad said OK so I will just meet you there." Maverick glanced at me as I said those words.

"No. I will pick you up at seven," Caleb disagreed. I sighed audibly, annoyed with him but running out of time to argue.

"OK, whatever."

"Awesome! It's a date!" His response was much too enthusiastic in contrast to my clipped and annoyed tone and I found myself thinking that it most definitely was not a date—a fact I planned to clarify for Caleb that night.

I hit the end-call button and rushed to the front door to try to see, or better yet, talk to Maverick before he left. By the time I got outside, my dad and my aunt had already said their goodbyes and Maverick was walking toward his truck. I carefully observed his every move as he walked away. His canvas belt didn't seem to be doing its job. The top of his boxer shorts peeked out—ever so slightly—from his low-slung fitted jeans that somehow hung loosely from his hips just perfectly, yet simultaneously hugged him in all the right places. My face flushed at the thoughts that rushed through my head. I looked away, but only temporarily. The draw was too strong and it brought my gaze back to Maverick within seconds. This time I kept my eyes focused above his waist, noticing his black V-neck T-shirt, the front tucked in on one side but hanging out loosely on the other side and at the back. His arms peeked out from the edges of his T-shirt, just enough to show the defining lines of his lean muscles. Dark hair peeked out from the edges of his baseball hat, which he was wearing backward, just like the first day I ever laid eyes on him in the Heritage Hall parking lot. He was magnificent—in every single way—from head to toe.

Maverick was almost to the truck. I was so entranced by studying him, I didn't even realize he'd turned back around and his beautiful blue eyes were locked on mine. *Oh crap he caught me staring at him.*

"Nice to meet you, Elle. Sounds like you have a date with Caleb so I guess I'll see you tonight at the party." He acted so cavalier.

I was livid and I couldn't decipher if that was because Maverick had gotten the last word in again, or because he had referenced me having a date with Caleb. As I replayed his words over and over again as he drove away, I realized it wasn't what he said but the way he said it that infuriated me. He said the words with complete indifference, as if he couldn't care less whether or not I went on a date with Caleb. That made the fire inside of me burn in a way that it never had before. As I watched Maverick drive away—his truck engine rumbling loudly and the beat of his bass music reverberating through the air—I let myself accept that I knew exactly what it was that I was feeling toward the enigmatic boy with the blue eyes. It was desire.

CHAPTER 8

I lingered outside of my aunt's cottage long after everyone went inside, staring at the road that just carried Maverick away.

I have to know if he's feeling this strange connection.

Standing in my aunt's driveway, I made a decision—that evening at the party I would find a way to talk to Maverick about us.

I walked back into the house and made my way down the tiny hallway to my bedroom, eager to be alone with my thoughts. When I walked into my room, I noticed that the bed was made, my clothes were picked up, and my sketchbook had been moved; it was placed on the little desk by the window, which was not where I left it. Neatly stacked beside my sketchbook was a package of new colored pencils, pastels, and paints.

No, she did not come in here and look through my sketchbook.

Anger coursed through my veins. My aunt had looked through my drawings without asking—a clear invasion of my privacy.

It's actually really sweet of her to go to the trouble of buying you those art supplies.

I wanted to be thankful. I wanted to let go of my anger and I tried to suppress the fire that was beginning to burn, but the fire was always too strong.

That's so wrong of her to go through your personal belongings without asking first. You have to say something.

Of course, the fire won, and I found myself walking down the hallway in a determined stride, to confront my aunt.

"Aunt Cordelia?"

She was knitting away in her rocking chair, and glanced up at me sweetly over her tortoise-shell reading glasses.

"Is there something I can help you with sweetheart?"

Ugh. She's so darn nice. It makes it impossible to stay mad at her.

"Did you go through my room?" I finally asked.

"Well dear, this is my house the last time I checked and I didn't know picking up a room in my own house was a crime," she answered kindly.

"It...uh, it's just...I don't like people to look at my sketch-book." I stammered, dropping my head in embarrassment, completely unable to meet her gaze.

Seriously, Elle? She's letting you live with her and has been nothing but kind and you can't let her look at your drawings? What is wrong with you?

Guilt flooded my body and I fought the urge to tell her she could look at my sketchbook anytime she wanted. I envisioned myself pulling up a chair beside her and flipping through my drawings with her, allowing her to shower me with praise and tell me how I was just like my mother; but I pushed the urge away, entirely uncomfortable with being that vulnerable.

"They're such lovely drawings, Elle. You're so talented, like your mother."

I cringed and looked away. I envied the way she mentioned my mother so freely; but she didn't let my reaction stop her from continuing.

"I have the picture of the yellow house and with your permission I would like to frame it."

Normally in such circumstances, the fire would have burned so much that I would have whipped around in protest to tell her there was no way in hell she could have my painting; no one was ever allowed to see my art.

"Sure...that's fine," I conceded, surprising even myself. Then I turned and walked away. *What just happened? I'm totally losing my mind.*

I threw myself on my bed, taking deep, calming breaths, and trying to push all the unwanted emotions back to their designated place in my little black box. My phone beeped twice—interrupting me—and I realized I hadn't touched it for almost twenty-four hours. I picked the little black device up and saw several missed text messages and phone calls from Grace and Charlie, as well as some texts and calls from an unknown number. My heart skipped a beat. *Maybe it's Maverick.*

But I knew it was wishful thinking. I unlocked my phone and opened the texts from the unknown number, to find several worried text messages from Caleb. I sighed and threw the phone down on my bed without responding to any of them.

I needed Grace and Charlie, but I was too confused to call them. Grace would pepper me with questions about Tulsa and boys and where we were staying and of course, boys—again. Boys were always Grace's favorite topic, ever since we turned ten years old. I was exhausted just thinking about her interrogation. Her bubbly personality and incessant positive outlook on life was always in stark contrast to my dark and brooding moods. We were opposites attract, Grace and I, and it was just one of the many reasons I loved her so much. Charlie was somewhere in the middle, grounded and mature beyond his years, always the voice of reason. He was the cord that tied us all together—me at one end and Grace at the total opposite, then sweet and steady Charlie in the middle, connecting us all.

That was our perfectly imperfect little triangle. Sadness gripped my heart as I thought of my two best friends back home in Ohio, but no matter how much I wanted to call them, I wouldn't. I couldn't, not until I figured out the mess I had already gotten myself into in Tulsa. I couldn't disappoint them, not again.

My mind was racing, trying to sort everything out. Caleb was unbelievably sweet and handsome, protective and gentlemanly, kind and thoughtful, and any girl would be lucky to have him as a boyfriend. The truth was, he deserved to date someone who could give him more than just a broken heart, which was all I would ever give him. I had to find a way to tell him that there was only one person I had any interest in and unfortunately, that person happened to be his best friend.

As I lay on my bed evaluating my predicament, I finally decided on a solution—that night at the party I would tell Caleb the truth; then I would talk to Maverick and tell him how I felt about him. Butterflies danced in my stomach. I hoped by the end of the night I would be right where I wanted to be— with Maverick Mason.

I ran to my backpack with a renewed sense of nervous excitement for the evening. I had a plan and I was going to execute it but first, I had to get dressed. I fished through my backpack and found the two little red pieces of fabric that I was looking for—Grace's red bikini. I borrowed it the night before we left Brookville when we snuck out to go to Kyle Murphy's for one last swim party. Thankfully I never returned it. My modest black one-piece from the old lady section at JC Penney—the preacher's-daughter special—was not going to do the trick tonight.

I glanced at the clock and realized it was 6:45 p.m. I rushed around the room in a frenzy, quickly putting on Grace's bikini then pulling my black old-lady swimsuit over it. I knew the drill; my dad would check to see what I was wearing before I left the house since it was a swim party. He couldn't know that I planned to wear Grace's little red two-piece, so I would wear the black swimsuit over it and take it off when I got to the party. I threw my frayed cut offs on and found my favorite blue flannel shirt, then slipped on my black flip flops. I checked the clock again and realized I was running out of time so I grabbed my bag and ran for the front door in a hurry.

"I'm going to the party. See you guys later..." I called my goodbye to my aunt and dad. I was almost out the door and could nearly taste my freedom when I heard my dad's booming voice.

"Elyse Rose Christiansen, get back in here." I didn't have time to defy him and get in an argument so I complied.

"Yes Dad?" I said, perhaps a bit too sweetly.

"What are you wearing to this swim party?" he asked.

Ugh. Get over it Dad. I'm seventeen years old for God's sake.

With a huge roll of my eyes, I slowly pulled my flannel shirt up to reveal the black, ugly, one-piece grandma swimsuit that covered my midriff. He nodded his approval but looked at me suspiciously. I knew what was coming.

"Hand it over, please." We both knew the "please" was just a formality. He reached out and took the bag out of my hands.

"Dad, I really have to go now!" I said desperately as he searched my bag. It was 6:53 p.m. and I was running out of time.

"You have to be home at ten o'clock Elle. Not one minute later or you're grounded," he said as he continued to fish through my bag.

"OK! See you at ten o'clock dad." I grabbed my bag from him and ran out the door.

I had to leave the cottage before Caleb arrived. It was all part of my plan. He would come to pick me up and realize that I had left without him. Without a doubt my plan was hurtful and rude but I hoped it would give him just a small indication of what I was capable of, hopefully dissuading him from further involvement with a girl who could be so thoughtless. I told myself that I was just saving him from the agony of falling for me.

It's too late for that. I pushed away that snide little voice in my head—the one I hated because she was annoyingly right most of the time, or all of the time.

I ran out the front door and made my way up the path to the Mason Mansion, my anxious anticipation becoming greater with each step. As I climbed the steps to the enormous mansion, my heart beat in rapid succession and my stomach did flip flops. For the first time in my life, I was going to tell someone how I felt about them; and I wanted more than anything for him to feel the same way that I did.

I rang the doorbell and waited. The massive wooden front door started to crack open just as I heard footsteps coming up the stone stairs behind me.

"Hey there you," I heard a familiar voice call from behind me as I felt a pair of arms wrap tightly around my waist. It was Caleb. At that exact same moment, the front door swung open, allowing me to stare into a pair of blue eyes that burned into my soul. I stood there in shock, completely mortified at how my plan had backfired. I closed my eyes, willing the horror of the moment to go away.

This is not happening. Please tell me this is not happening right now. I am not standing on Maverick's front steps with Caleb's arms wrapped around me. NO.

Finally, I inched my eyes open to accept my reality. My plan to get to Maverick's house early and talk to him alone was over before it began.

My eyes never left Maverick's; he walked beside me—the air thick with his disapproval—and Caleb walked two steps ahead of us, dragging me into the house with excitement, across black-and-white checkerboard marble floors and past a double-sided, two-story staircase. The opulence of Maverick's magnificent home surrounded me, but did not interest me in the least. I could only look at one thing—Maverick's haunting blue eyes.

I have to get him alone and talk to him.

He was angry with me—really angry—and I wanted more than anything to make his disapproval go away. My body tensed when he looked at me; my stomach was in knots that made it difficult to breathe; and for some reason, I couldn't stand the thought of him being upset with me.

I followed the boys to the backyard—willing Caleb to let go of my waist with every step—but he wouldn't. We came to a row of lounge chairs beside the pool and I sat down. Caleb immediately sat right beside me. I watched Maverick's eyes simmer with displeasure as his best friend pulled me closer to his side.

I have to get out of here.

I stood up. "Can you guys tell me where the restroom is?"

I needed to be alone to regroup, to clear my head, to think; but mostly I had to escape the intensity of those blue eyes, speaking directly to that neglected place in the depths of my soul with merely a look.

Maverick and Caleb pointed me in the right direction and I made my way to the bathroom. I splashed some cold water on my face then looked into the mirror, disgusted with myself.

Seriously Elle. How do you get yourself into these impossible situations?

I took a few deep breaths to regain my composure, then slipped out of my clothes and took off my black grandma suit to reveal the red bikini. I put my cut offs back on and tied up my flannel shirt to reveal a tiny patch of my copper skin, then unbuttoned one of the buttons on the top of my flannel shirt. I reapplied some lip gloss, then looked at myself in the mirror and gave myself an internal pep talk.

You've got this, Elle. Pull it together.

I walked out of the bathroom, determined to change my fate and redirect the course of the evening.

When I walked out of the bathroom I nearly ran right into the blonde cheerleader from the night before and my stomach dropped.

Great. This evening seems to be getting worse by the second. "Well hello there." She spoke first and although her words were nice, I heard everything but a friendly greeting. "Your name is Elle, right?" she asked in a sickeningly sweet, fake voice.

Oh please. Don't act like you don't know my name, girl.

I rolled my eyes and didn't even try to hide it. "Yeah, it's Elle," I deadpanned while looking around to plan my escape route.

"I heard you're dating Caleb Bradshaw already. Way to go girl. Caleb's a great catch." I knew her words were insincere.

"Nope. Not dating Caleb," I retorted, giving her no more information.

She looked me up and down, then crossed her arms and gave a little huff.

"Well it sure looked like you guys were dating by how you were dancing with him."

"Oh that? That was nothing." I laughed dismissively, even waving my hand for added dramatic flair, then reveled as her jaw dropped at how lightly I was taking my dance performance from the night before. "We're totally just friends."

"Just friends huh?" she challenged, raising an eyebrow in judgmental scrutiny.

"Yeah, like I said, *just friends.*"

We stood and stared at each other, and the longer she looked at me with her condemnation, the brighter the fire inside of me burned.

"I have my eye on someone else anyway," I added, knowing my confession would drive her absolutely crazy; then I turned and walked out of the room, satisfied, and knowing I never wanted to be friends with the blonde beauty that probably ran Heritage Hall Preparatory Academy.

I made my way through the Mason Mansion, passing stranger after stranger, before I finally saw someone familiar.

"Hey Carly!" I was so relieved to see her smiling face.

"Oh hey new girl," she teased. "You dance all over any boys you've barely even met before at this party yet?" She rolled a sucker around her mouth lackadaisically, awaiting my response.

I instantly remembered why I liked her so much. "Not yet, but the night's still young girlfriend so I'm sure I'll manage to do something shocking before it's over."

Carly let out a deep belly laugh at my comment and wrapped her arm around my shoulder to walk through the house with me. I was flooded with gratitude.

Thank you, Carly. I don't know what I'd do without you.

Carly ushered me into a large game room with more video games than I had ever seen in my life, plus arcade games, ping-pong tables, a pool table, and even a skee-ball machine like the little Fun House back in Brookville had.

Seriously though. What in the world do these people do for a living? I wanted to ask Carly, but before I could, she was grabbing me and pushing me down on the huge white sectional that was in the back of the game room.

"I have someone you have to meet!" Carly introduced me to one of her best friends, a short soccer player named Madison who had a genuine smile and dressed like a fashion goddess. I instantly liked her.

The three of us talked for several minutes before a tall dark-haired beauty walked over to us with a shy smile on her face. She wore all black and I could instantly tell that she had an artist's soul.

"It's Macey!"

The girls introduced me to their other best friend, Macey, and I quickly realized that she was quieter than the other two girls but she perfectly rounded out their trio.

I spent the next hour or so laughing and talking with my new friends and feeling genuinely happy for the first time since I had arrived in Tulsa. I was so happy, in fact, that I temporarily forgot about the messed-up triangle I had created with Caleb, Maverick, and myself.

My peaceful time with my new girlfriends abruptly ended when Madison—the ringleader—decided that we all needed a change of scenery. As I walked outside to the pool area with the girls, I was acutely aware of Maverick's presence. The magnetic force beckoned me toward him and as usual, it refused to be ignored. I glanced around frantically then finally found him in the pool. He was floating in an oversized raft that looked like a chair, and plastered to his side looking adoringly into his eyes instead of at the movie she was supposed to be watching, was the blonde cheerleader. The fire inside me raged and I envisioned myself jumping into the pool and ripping her off him, grabbing a handful of her bleached blonde hair and using it to pull her away from his body.

I couldn't tear my eyes away from him—his flawless taut body on display as he floated in the pool. I admired his smooth tan skin and counted the indentations of the lean cut muscles on his abdomen. O.M.G., *That's way more than a six pack.* I moved up his body, slowly, taking time to appreciate everything I saw until finally, my eyes landed on his beautiful face. Maverick was watching me, flipping a toothpick back and forth in his mouth and staring at me with his signature look of apathy. It infuriated me that I couldn't read him.

"Elle, c'mon, a group of us are going to play truth or dare," I heard Caleb's voice from behind me and realized he must have finished his game of pool in the game room. His arms encircled me.

"I actually better go home," I said to Caleb. "It's getting late." I pushed his hands off my waist and stepped backward. Truth or dare was a disaster waiting to happen for a girl who had more secrets than the entire school combined. My pulse began to race and my body was being pulled backward, alerting me to Maverick's presence. I knew he was standing right behind me even though he hadn't spoken a word.

"C'mon on, Brookville. You scared?" he chided.

I turned to stare into his piercing-blue eyes, a look of challenge spreading across my face. "You wish Top Gun," I spat without thinking. No way was I going home now.

I thought I saw him laugh. He brushed by me and walked into the pool house. The blonde cheerleader was attached to his chiseled arm as if some unwanted parasite, but it didn't stop him from turning around to look at me, or giving me that trademark wink of his.

The fire burned inside, and of course, I followed him.

CHAPTER 9

Do not go inside that pool house. You can't play truth or dare and you know that. That voice of reason was screaming inside my head, begging me to turn around and run home; but my mind was made up the second Maverick accused me of being scared.

"Elle, you're staying, right?" Caleb was always such a gentleman, even though I didn't deserve his niceties. I let him guide me into this pool house.

"Of course I'm staying," I said decisively, and the reason why was staring at me from across the room. Maverick was standing on the opposite side of the living room, one of his legs pushed up against the wall causing his swimsuit to ride up just enough so that I could see his chiseled thigh beneath. That smug know-it-all look was covering his beautiful features as he flipped that toothpick back and forth effortlessly between his lips. I shot him my most cutting look then rolled my eyes, just for good measure. I thought I saw him wink at me, and the fire burned in that new way only he could elicit.

I found a place in the back of the room, hoping I could avoid being asked any questions during the game, and observed the Heritage Hall students playing truth or dare with amusement. *These prep-school kids are so tame. This is very different than playing in Brookville.*

My mind wandered to the last time I had played truth or dare and an unwanted vision of me jumping from the roof into

Kyle Murphy's pool, sans clothes, flashed through my head. I never backed down from a dare. Unfortunately.

"Elle, truth or dare?" Madison interrupted my thoughts with her question.

I paused, weighing my options.

"Truth." I liked my chances with truth since no one in the room knew anything about that one-lane road in Ohio.

"OK," Madison said sweetly. "How many boys have you kissed?"

Twenty pairs of prying eyes stared at me. None of them knew anything about me, and I didn't want this to be the first thing they learned. I struggled to formulate a plan to avoid the truth, my heart racing, as I glanced around, inquisitive eyes awaiting my response. Then, I had a stroke of genius.

"Zero," I answered sweetly, feigning innocence.

The whole room erupted.

"No way!" I heard skeptical voices argue. "That's not the truth. That has to be a lie!"

Whispers circulated throughout the room about my dance performance at the party the night before. I glanced over to catch Caleb staring at me, arms crossed, with a triumphant look on his face as everyone relived my public display of indecency from the previous night. I immediately looked away, embarrassed, unable to hold his gaze. I knew that dance didn't mean to me what it did to him, just like I knew I wasn't fooling anyone with my innocent act. I didn't care what everyone else thought though. There was only one person in the room I was concerned with and he was staring at me from across the room, his blue eyes searching me as always. Maverick gave away nothing, flipping his toothpick back and forth in his mouth, driving me crazy. Slowly he pushed himself off the wall and walked toward me with a quiet confidence that made my heart skip. My breath was shallow, becoming more labored with each of his approaching steps, the force between us magnifying as he neared. Finally, he stopped right in front of me and I craned my neck to look up at his massive frame that would dwarf most grown men. He intimidated me, yes, but I refused to allow him or anyone else to see that. I matched his confidence, standing up straight and squaring my shoulders. The room was silent, waiting for the master of the room to speak. He took his toothpick out of his mouth lackadaisically, my eyes lingering on his lips a bit too long as he did.

"You lose. You lied." There was finality in his voice.

"I didn't lie," I argued, "and I definitely didn't lose either." I raised my chin in defiance and tried to make myself stand taller. "I said zero because I have never kissed a boy—" I heard some more rumbles throughout the room so I crossed my arms and finished my point, "—*first*." I added with sarcasm.

We stood there in a standoff for what seemed like an eternity as the room around me erupted into laughter and cat calls and arguments about whether I answered honestly based on the semantics of the question.

"How many boys have *you* kissed is what was asked." I restated Madison's question with extra attention on the word "you" in the statement. Maverick's eyes stayed glued to mine. The way he looked at me was both frightening and thrilling; and I both loved it and hated it simultaneously. "I answered the question a hundred percent truthfully," I said with mock innocence. "I—" I drew the simple vowel sound out for much longer than it needed to be held for dramatic emphasis, "have never kissed a boy *first*."

The whole room was laughing, seemingly amused by my play on words, except for Maverick. He leaned in a little closer and I couldn't breathe, which seemed to be my body's constant visceral response to his proximity, then I heard him whisper something meant only for my ears.

"You'll kiss me first." He spoke with absolute assurance. Then he started to walk away, but as he brushed past me he turned around to say two more words, "One day." He cocked his head up as he said it, an expression of smug self-assurance covering his handsome features, and I had to fight with every power I possessed to keep my body from running toward him and crushing my lips to his right then and there, in a room full of people. I grabbed onto the wall, attempting to steady myself, but mostly because I didn't trust myself; it was physically painful to fight the force that was drawing me toward him.

I followed Maverick's every step as he walked to the opposite side of the room, longing to see his eyes again and hear him speak to me, telling me that he felt the force between us too; but when he turned around, Maverick wore his mask again—his signature look of indifference. My heart sank.

"Elle loses. She didn't answer the question truthfully." Maverick spoke with authority.

I heard the room erupt, half of them stating their disapproval and agreeing with my side of the argument, the other side stating that Maverick's assessment of the situation was fair. An overwhelming mixture of rage mixed with desire flooded my body as I watched the cryptic boy who commanded the room with his very presence. He was intoxicating.

My body moved of its own volition across the room, toward Maverick. The undeniable force between us was too powerful to fight any longer. The room was full of laughter—the party in full swing—but to me, there was no one else in the room but him. I pushed my way through the crowd, determined, and our eyes burned into one another's souls as I approached him.

"Meet me outside?" I waited in nervous anticipation to see if he would comply.

He nodded his agreement.

We walked past the throngs of dancing teenagers and made our way out the front door, then outside and to the side of the pool house. We were alone. Every nerve in my body was alive, humming an electrifying song that only he could elicit with his presence.

I turned to face him, determined to confront him about our unspoken connection, but I lost myself the second I saw him. His eyes—they leveled me. They searched my soul without permission, leaving me exposed and vulnerable. I wanted to look away, to find reprieve from his steely gaze and the way it ripped through my soul to that neglected place I allowed no one; but I couldn't. I couldn't look away because I needed more of him. I always needed more of him.

"Maverick, I know." As soon as I spoke the words, I wanted to take them back.

"You know what? Say it," he commanded. He was going to make me say the words out loud, and I wanted to, once and for all. He put his arm on the wooden post behind me and leaned in toward me, hypnotizing me. We were merely inches apart, and I could barely breathe. I willed myself to focus.

"I know about this." I motioned back and forth between the two of us.

"Oh do you now?" His tone was cocky, yet playful. He pushed his body closer to mine and as he did, the force between us raged uncontrollably, begging us to connect.

"Yes, I do." I swallowed hard and closed my eyes, resolving to finish what I needed to say to him. I opened my eyes and met his gaze with determination. "And I know you feel it too."

I couldn't breathe as I waited with anticipation to see how Maverick would respond to my bold declaration. He didn't speak, but out of the corner of my eye, I saw his hand move toward mine. Upon his slightest touch, my entire body ignited. I was overwhelmed, panicked even, but I didn't run. Instead, I turned to him and allowed him to see the fear in my eyes.

Maverick opened his mouth to say something but the words never came. Instead he squeezed my hand with purpose—once, twice, then finally, three times. The third time he squeezed my hand, he peered into my eyes with unparalleled passion. He was communicating something unspoken to me, begging me to understand what he couldn't—or wouldn't—say out loud. I was puzzled, not quite certain what he was trying to convey. My eyes burned into his, trying desperately to read what he was trying to say to me in our unspoken language, but before I could figure it out, Maverick shattered the moment by dropping my hand. He turned to leave, glancing at me one last time before he walked inside the pool house. When our eyes met, I saw his mask of indifference again; and my heart shattered into a million tiny pieces.

"You better go say goodbye to Caleb. He'll be worried if you just leave again." Then he turned and walked away.

He was gone. I fought to regain my composure, frightened, as I realized my little black box—the place where I stored away every unwanted emotion and memory and feeling—was compromised. I unknowingly let the lid fly open in that moment with Maverick, so distracted by him and those hypnotic blue eyes, that I didn't even know I was opening that forsaken part of my soul. I was exposed and vulnerable, and that was terrifying to me. Panicked, I frantically worked to slam the lid shut on my little black box. Eventually, I was successful; but as my heart slowly closed itself off yet again, I was overcome with a sadness I had never before experienced.

In that moment, standing on the front porch of Maverick's pool house—alone—I allowed myself to accept a sobering reality: something prolific had happened inside of me when Maverick touched my hand and squeezed it three times. His blue eyes tore their way into the depths of my soul and blew the lid off my coping mechanism. I didn't want to run away anymore. I didn't want to shut him out. I didn't want to build a wall that would keep him out. Although I didn't know if I was capable of it, I realized and accepted that I would try to open my heart up for him; and only him.

Beautiful acceptance washed through my body and I was at peace momentarily. Then worry and anxiety crept in as I looked through the door and realized that Maverick Mason, the one person who made me want to open my heart again, was walking away from me out of respect for his best friend. He refused to hurt his best friend, regardless of what he felt for me; I knew that. Defeated and alone, I stared at the door of the pool house for several minutes then finally, I left, making my way over the hill at the back of the Masons' property, toward our cottage. I heard my phone beep and pulled it out of my back pocket to see a text from Caleb.

"Where did you go and why do you keep disappearing on me?"

My heart dropped when I read his text. I knew he cared about me and I also knew that I had led him on, purposefully, so none of the mess in which we found ourselves was his fault. However, frustration ran through me. He was the reason I couldn't be with Maverick, and I resented him for that, no matter how unfair it was.

I continued down the path back to the cottage—my mind spinning—trying to formulate a solution to my predicament with Caleb and Maverick.

I'll text Caleb and tell him how sorry I am for leading him on. I'll tell him I just want to be friends and that I don't want to hurt him.

If you don't want to hurt him then why did you lead him on in the first place? There was that unwanted voice of reason, but I didn't push her away this time. I knew she was right. Regret washed over me and a memory floated to the surface of my mind.

We were standing in the kitchen and I was holding a puppy that I took from Mr Thompson without permission.

"Elle, I specifically told you we could not have the puppy, and you disobeyed me. You took one anyway."

"But Mom, I love him."

"Elle, you directly disobeyed me and there will be a consequence. You have to return the puppy. We can't keep him."

Tears cascaded down my cheeks.

"Mom, I love him so much. Please, please, please let me keep him. It will break my heart if you make me take him back."

She brushed my tears away. I could see the pain in her eyes, but I could also see her strength and decisiveness.

"Elle, I need you to know something, sweetheart. If you would have come to me and talked to me, we could have figured out a solution together. Maybe your dad and I would have even let you get a puppy if you would have been willing to take care of all the responsibilities. But instead, you lied to Mr Thompson and did things your own way, and now you have to pay the consequences of your choices. You will return the puppy."

Her words echoed through my mind. "You will pay the consequences for your choices." All these years later and I was still the same. I acted without thinking. I did things my way, then I had to pay the consequence. I sighed.

This is my fault.

Disgusted with myself, I continued my walk of shame back to the cottage.

Out of the corner of my eye, I sensed a movement in the distance and I strained my eyes out into the darkness. I swore my eyes saw the shape of a person—a woman—dressed in white. I blinked in disbelief and rubbed my eyes, struggling to see into the pitch black of night again; but the woman was no longer there, and I questioned if I had even seen her in the first place. Fear crept through my body and I couldn't shake the uncanny feeling that I was being watched, so I turned around and hurried into the safety of the little cottage. My dad was waiting up for me just as I expected.

"How was your evening?" he asked.

"Fine," I said unconvincingly.

"Elle, that was very rude for you to leave before that boy Caleb got here to pick you up," he scolded.

"I know, dad." I dropped my head in shame.

"Well, you should treat other people the way you want to be treated, Elle."

The fire burned even though I knew he was right. I hated it when he used the Bible to guilt trip me. "I said I know dad. The Golden Rule. I got it."

"You owe him an apology." I could tell he wasn't going to budge so I took out my phone and drafted a text.

"Sorry about leaving before you got here tonight." I flashed the screen toward my dad. Then I hit send.

"There. You happy? I apologized."

His gaze held disappointment. Inwardly, I flinched. Did I want to be this person? Who disappoints her father, her aunt, herself?

Finally, he returned to reading his book. I walked to my room and didn't bother to wash my face or take off my clothes. I just plopped down on my bed and closed my eyes. As I drifted off to sleep, I saw Maverick outside on the porch. I let my mind linger on the memory of his hand on mine, squeezing it firmly—once, twice, then a third time. I replayed the same memory over and over, desperate to stay in that moment, eagerly trying to decipher what it meant.

I faded off as I felt him squeeze my hand—three times— and as I let go and gave into sleep, I had a vision of my mom sitting on the steps of our parsonage. Her black hair was blowing in a light summer breeze and her cheeks were bronzed from the sun, making her teeth look so white that they glowed when she smiled at me.

"I love you," she said.

One, two, three little words.

That night I slept in a peaceful slumber that had eluded me for years, not waking once to find myself in a nightmare that ended on a dead-end one-lane dirt road. Instead, I dreamed of summers at the farmer's market with my mom; riding my bike through the town with Grace and Charlie; singing "I'll Fly Away" with my mom and getting a standing ovation at church; and finally, I dreamed most of all about lying in the back of a truck under fall leaves that had changed to orange and yellow and burgundy with a boy who had the bluest eyes I had ever seen. We lay there peacefully, laughing and talking and finding solace in each other's arms. Then he leaned over and kissed me on the forehead—once, twice, and then three times—and I felt the same peace wash over me that I did when I remembered my mom telling me those same three little words.

"I love you."

CHAPTER 10

My dad let me sleep in the morning after the party. When I woke up, I looked at the clock and realized it was Sunday, and it was after 1:00 p.m. I took a deep breath and lay my head back down on the pillow, reveling in the fact that I wasn't at church on a Sunday for perhaps the first time in my entire life.

I smelled my aunt cooking in the kitchen but I wasn't ready to leave the solace of my bedroom. I wanted to lounge in my bed and think about Maverick—remembering every interaction between us the night before—especially the part outside the pool house where he grabbed my hand and squeezed it three times. I was thinking about his searing blue eyes and how my entire body ignited when he touched my hand, when a knock at the door interrupted my daydream.

"Elle? Are you up?" My dad's concerned voice floated under the door.

"Yeah, come on in, Dad," I answered.

I yawned and stretched out from underneath the covers as he walked in with a breakfast tray. He placed the homemade waffles on the bed in front of me. For some reason, I got the impression that the waffles were a peace offering.

"Well I guess your aunt wants to have a family meeting today." There was awkward tension in his voice. He said "family" and "meeting" as if they were foreign words that he did not understand and it made me giggle. He looked up at me in surprise. With a mouthful of waffles and the Oklahoma afternoon sunshine peering through my window, my dad and I sat on a bed and laughed together for the first time since I could remember.

I finished my waffles then my dad took my tray away and left the room, giving me privacy to get ready for the day. I fished around in my bag for some clothes, briefly wondering what our plan was for unpacking and questioning whether we were going to live permanently with my aunt or get a place of our own. My heart fell when I thought of not staying in the little cottage on the back of the Mason property.

I finally found the pair of jeans I wanted and threw them on with a white graphic tee and a pair of Converse, then left my bedroom to join my aunt in the living room. My aunt started our "family meeting" as soon as I sat down.

"I just want you both to know how happy I am to have you here and that you're welcome to stay here as long as you want. I want you to see this as your home as well."

"Thank you so much for your generosity, Cordelia," my dad almost interrupted her, "but we plan to find a place of our own very soon. I've already been looking."

She waved at him dismissively. "Well that's fine John but I want you to know you are welcome here and I would love for you to stay." My dad and Aunt Cordelia made eye contact and a slight, unspoken tension hung in the air. It made me uncomfortable.

My aunt went over some small house rules, then proceeded to tell us some different information about the property, the estate, where we could and could not go, about the gate code and that it changed at the beginning of every month, and finally, she told us about the Masons, the owners of the estate. I was on the edge of my seat, hanging on her every word.

"I'm employed by Mr. and Mrs. Mason. They know you're staying here with me and have asked me to tell you that they're so happy to have you here as well. They plan to invite us all up to the main house soon for dinner so they can meet you."

My face flushed red with embarrassment at the thought of my dad and Maverick and Maverick's parents all being in the same room. I fought the urge to ask my aunt a million questions about the Mason's and most of all, about Maverick and her relationship with him; those questions would have to wait until I was alone with my aunt, so I asked something else instead.

"Do you mind me asking what your job is? What you do for the Masons?"

"I'm their nanny," she answered. "Well, I was their nanny." She looked away, longing evident in her eyes, but I thought I saw something else as well—pain. "Now I watch over Maverick and the estate when they travel for business, which is frequently." She paused and looked at me with scrutiny. "I helped raise the Mason kids," she finally added, a stern look in her eye that made me want to look away. She seemed worried.

She loves Maverick. She's warning me. But there seemed to be something more in her eyes—fear.

As I processed the information, she continued to watch me and I knew how intuitive she was. My father was completely clueless about what was going on between the Masons' son and me; my aunt on the other hand, was most definitely not.

"I want you both to know this cottage belongs to you as much as it does to me," she continued. "My parents lived here before me, and Elle—" she looked at me as she used her hand to motion around to the small but cozy cottage— "your mother and I grew up here."

I was speechless. A million questions circled through my mind, but I couldn't formulate words. *My mother lived here? My mother grew up in this very cottage.* I looked around the little room and imagined a dark-haired, copper-skinned girl running around with a laugh that filled the house and dimples permanently etched into her cheeks as she smiled. Pain ripped through me.

"Elle, I know there's so much you want to know," my aunt said with sympathy. "I have so many questions myself." She looked up at me with tears in her eyes. "I want to get to know the niece that I never knew I had and I know you want to learn about your mother and the family you never knew you had." I watched a lone tear stream down her face as she continued with caution. "I want you here and I want to tell you everything that you want to know, but we have to take it slow."

My dad broke into the conversation, and I shot him a glare, which he didn't notice, of course. "Cordelia, we're so thankful for your kindness. We'll only stay here temporarily until we can find a place of our own but we appreciate your hospitality so much. I was planning to go look at some housing this afternoon actually but we might need to stay here for at least a few weeks until I can find the right place."

I rolled my eyes. He hated anything emotional.

Cordelia shook her head dismissively and our emotionally charged moment was over. "Of course. Feel free to look at other housing but please know this house is as much yours as it is mine." She paused as if making a calculation in her head. "Your grandfather helped build this cottage Elle," she finally added.

My jaw dropped. I had a grandfather—my mother's father—and I wanted to know more about him. I sat up in my seat.

"Your grandparents' names were Henry and Margaret Smith and your grandfather oversaw the grounds on the Mason estate years ago. He worked for the people who owned the estate before the Mason's and when we moved here, they said we could live in the little cottage on the back of the property if my dad would help fix it up. It was just a run-down shack back then, but your grandfather was so talented. He did all the work with his own two hands." She spoke of him with so much pride and I loved the twinkle I saw in her eye when she mentioned her father. It made me smile. I felt a connection to him though I never even met him.

"After the Masons bought the property, they allowed me and Paul to continue living here and even deeded the house to me." It was the first time I heard her mention the man in the military uniform, her husband I assumed. I wondered what happened to him, and I wondered why they never had any children, but didn't dare ask. I hated the pain I saw on her face when she was forced to remember. "They were so sweet and understanding after I lost Paul..." She trailed off, her eyes darting out the window with longing and sadness.

So she lost her husband. I wanted to go to her and wrap my arms around her. This gentle woman of strength and beauty before me, she had endured far too much pain yet wore her scars with grace and dignity. She had every reason to be bitter and angry, but instead she was kind and patient. Something shifted inside of me, was it that little black box again? *I want to be more like Aunt Cordelia.* I pushed the thought away as quickly as it had come to me, slamming the lid shut on my unwanted emotions.

"The Masons let me have the house and employed me as their children's nanny."

We stood there peering into one another's eyes—my aunt and I—a silent communication passing between us that only we could understand; and I knew that our exodus to Oklahoma was in no way a coincidence. My dad, on the other hand, was only taking in the facts.

"Thank you again, Cordelia," he said almost robotically.

My aunt and I continued to lock eyes as my dad's words went nearly unnoticed.

"I'm going to go work on my lesson plans for tomorrow now unless you have anything else we need to talk about?" he asked.

"Yes, absolutely," she answered cordially, her eyes still locked on mine. "That's all I wanted to talk to you about."

"Thank you so much again, Cordelia," he said as he walked out of the room.

We were finally alone, my aunt and I, with so many questions looming between us.

"Aunt Cordelia?" I asked, waiting to see if she was open to one more question or if she had given me all the information she planned to share for one family meeting. She gave me a slight tilt of her head and I took that as an invitation.

"How did you find us after all these years?"

She paused, for a long enough period of time that I was uncertain whether she would answer my question or not.

"Your mom wrote me…"

I couldn't comprehend her words. My mom was dead. I watched her die nearly six years ago. I held her in my arms while she bled to death. Aunt Cordelia must have seen the confusion and pain written on my face so she gently stood up and came to sit by me on the couch, placing her hand lightly on my leg. I didn't push her away.

"Elle, she wrote to me before she died. Your dad told me that she died six years ago on November seventeenth. Is that correct?" she asked.

I nodded my head yes, unable to speak.

"A few months ago, I found an unaddressed letter in my mailbox with my name written on it in her handwriting."

My heart beat furiously. I struggled to breathe as she continued.

"But when I opened it, the letter was dated November seventeenth, two-thousand and nine. Your mother somehow wrote to me on the day she was murdered, but I didn't receive the letter until six years later."

What is she talking about? This is making no sense. My mom wrote to her sister on the day she was murdered?

It was too much information for me to process. My head swam and my stomach felt nauseous. I couldn't stay in that living room one second longer.

Go before you have another episode.

"I have to go," I mumbled as I stood.

My aunt allowed me to walk out of the room, understanding I needed space. I put on my shorts and a fitted tank top then tied up my running shoes. As I hit the front door, no one even bothered to ask me where I was going. They just let me run away.

I pressed play on my iPod and took off in a run, pounding the ground angrily with each step, taking out my frustration and anger on the pavement. I pushed harder and harder, sweat dripping and with each step tension released from my body.

I rounded the back of the property when a path appeared that I had never seen. Curious, I turned to run up the path and as I did, I recognized that familiar pull, like a magnet being drawn to its counterpart. The pull directed me to a green fence, and I knew without a doubt who I would find there.

A boy my age crouched in a catching position as a hard POP rang out. He slammed his hand in his glove, then pulled out a baseball, shaking out his catching hand.

Another boy, who filled out a white dry-fit perfectly and wore black athletic shorts and a backwards baseball hat, stood on the pitcher's mound, laughing at his friend. My entire body ignited with uncontrollable desire. He pulled another ball from his pocket, drew his leg up, and in one swift movement he plunged forward and hurled the ball into the catcher's glove, so hard I thought surely the catcher's hand would fall off at this point. When the ball popped, he glanced up at me. His confident stance seemed to falter; he knew something was wrong with me. He started to walk toward me but I stuck my headphones in, gave him one last dismissive look, then ran away.

Running away was something I had perfected. It was all I knew. I had been running for years and had no plans to stop. I ran back to the cottage so swiftly that by the time I walked through the front door I was panting and barely able to stand.

My aunt was sitting on the couch waiting for me. She patted the couch next to her. My mind told me not to move forward and to turn and walk down the hall toward my bedroom; but my body betrayed me and walked toward her of its own accord. I craved the comfort she provided, and I was losing the will to fight it.

I sat down beside my aunt and she protectively put her arm around my shoulder and pulled me in for a hug. I lay my head on her shoulder, melting in her embrace. We sat there in knowing silence for as long as we both needed.

CHAPTER 11

After my run, I went with my dad to several appointments he had made to look at various condos and apartments. There were several small, two-bedroom places that were nice enough, but I recognized the tension in the air each time the realtor told my dad the asking price. We didn't have the money needed for the down payment. Surprisingly, that was just fine with me. I wasn't ready to leave my aunt's cottage anyway.

I moved through the rest of the afternoon and evening in a daze, still struggling to process the information my aunt had provided during our family meeting. That night at the dinner table, I pushed my food around on my plate while my aunt and dad discussed the next day—our first day at Heritage Hall.

I helped clean up after dinner then went straight to bed; that night I awakened to my own terrified screams but this time I wasn't in my dad's arms. My aunt was sitting beside me on the bed and I allowed myself to scream into the night freely as she held me and rocked me in her arms. I fell back asleep, finally, with her sitting next to my bed in a rocking chair. She held my hand until I could find sleep again and I welcomed her soothing presence.

The alarm went off at 6:00 a.m., and I moaned my resistance. After a night full of nightmares, it felt like I hadn't slept at all. I turned the alarm clock off and saw my aunt still beside my bed. Neither of us mentioned what had happened the night before as she stood up out of the rocking chair then grabbed a piece of my thick, dark hair and twirled it around her finger lovingly.

"I'll make you some breakfast before school," she said as she walked out of my room.

I ate my breakfast then my dad ushered me into the Brookville Church of God van in a hurry, anxious to get there on time for his first day as a teacher at Heritage Hall Preparatory School. It was the beginning of October so it was an odd time to start a new job at a school but my dad explained to me that the woman who had the position before him quit suddenly. He said it was divine intervention that he got a phone call from an old buddy from seminary about the position the same week that he lost his job. I felt that little voice inside telling me it was more than just divine intervention, but I kept those thoughts to myself.

We pulled into the school parking lot. It was empty, which was a relief. I would rather not be seen on my first day at a new school in a fifteen passenger van with "Brookville Church of God" emblazoned on the side in fiery orange letters. We drove around to the back of the building and parked under an oak tree far in the back then walked in together, both of us weighed down with as many religious studies books as our arms could carry.

I helped my dad set up his classroom and prepare for his first lesson plan. He talked about his plan for teaching the class and I was pleasantly surprised to see that he seemed truly excited about his new job venture.

"You're going to be great at this, Dad. I can tell."

My words shocked both of us.

"Thanks Ells," he said with an awkward smile. "Do you want me to go with you to get your schedule and find your classes?"

"Um, no. I don't think I want my dad to walk me around to find my classes on my first day at a new school. Talk about social suicide," I teased.

We both laughed. Something was different between us. I felt it yesterday morning, sitting in my bedroom when he brought me the waffles, and then again in his classroom as we laughed together. I wasn't sure exactly what was different, but whatever it was, I liked it.

My palms were sweaty and my heartbeat erratic as I walked toward the principal's office. The anticipation of my first day at school wasn't what was making me nervous though, it was the uncertainty of seeing Maverick. I was unsure of how he would act toward me. Would he be cold, calculated and controlled, or passionate, caring, and kind? His moods were so confusing and even more baffling was that regardless of who showed up today, I longed to see him; to be in his presence; to feel his blue eyes piercing all the way down to the depths of my soul; and above all else, to experience his touch.

"Hey, new girl." Carly's familiar voice interrupted my anxious thoughts. "You ready for your first day at Heritage Hall or what?" She grabbed the schedule out of my hand. "Let me see that!"

We looked over my classes, comparing my schedule to hers then she told me what classes I would have with her, Madison, and Macey. So far the day was shaping up to be pretty good and there were only two classes that I didn't have with at least one of my new friends. I found myself wondering if I had any classes with Maverick and at that very moment, the magnetic pull engaged. I glanced up as the front doors of the school opened and although the light shined brightly behind him, I saw the outline of his broad shoulders and I knew it was him. It could be no one else.

The halls had filled with students while I was in the principal's office and they were bustling with activity; but when Maverick walked down the hall, everyone stopped what they were doing and turned to watch him—everyone including me. He walked by and as he did, he glanced over at me momentarily. Our eyes connected and that new fire began to burn—the one I recognized as desire. Carly looked at me, then at Maverick, then back at me again. She was perceptive, I could tell. I grabbed her arm and turned to walk away.

"What's the deal with that Maverick Mason guy?" I asked her as we made our way to first hour, trying to sound nonchalant.

She laughed out loud and said his name as if it were holy. "Maverick Mason..." She sighed. "Well for starters, he is insanely rich, obvi. His grandparents started some oil company that makes more money than God and he will inherit the Mason empire someday," Carly said with a tone of awe in her voice. I wanted to tell her that I couldn't care less about the Mason empire and his inheritance. I wanted to know about *him*, but before I clarified she continued.

"He is smart and is an amazing athlete and every girl in school wants to date him but he won't give anyone the time of day." I tried to remain calm and not show how interested I truly was when I responded.

"You're telling me he doesn't date?" I asked.

"That's what I'm saying. He has never asked a single girl out. Ever. Margot Weston has been after him since middle school and he won't even pay her any attention."

"Margot Weston?"

She pointed as she rolled her eyes and I followed her finger across the hallway to see the blonde cheerleader standing around talking animatedly to a group of girls who were dressed exactly like her.

"Oh," I said with disgust in my voice. "Yeah I had the distinct misfortune of meeting her the other night at the party."

Carly laughed loudly. I smiled at the sound. Her boisterous laugh was one of the many things I loved about her.

"I know right. Isn't she awful? Everyone worships the ground she walks on but it's nice to see that someone else can finally see through the pretty exterior to the monster inside."

"Oh trust me, I see the monster."

Carly lowered her voice, placing an arm around my shoulder and leaning in to deliver the gossip she was about to impart. "So Margot and Maverick's parents own this massive oil company together. Rumor is they *have* to get married. Like their parents are going to make them or something."

My eyes widened. "Yeah right Carly, this is the twenty-first century and I'm pretty sure arranged marriages aren't a thing." I spoke with certainty but my insides were churning. *Surely not.*

"I'm just telling you what I've heard," she argued. "That's why Margot is always hanging all over him and trust me, she has acted like Maverick belongs to her ever since we were kids."

The fire burned inside at the mention of Margot thinking Maverick was hers.

"Well I'm pretty sure he's not a possession and he doesn't belong to her *and* no one can make him get married to someone he doesn't want to marry." I didn't hide my disgust at the thought.

Carly looked at me and raised an eyebrow, then crossed her arms. "Why are you asking all these questions about Maverick anyway?"

I met her gaze, a knowing glance passing between us, trying to decide whether to confide in her or not. "I'm just curious because apparently my aunt was his nanny." I decided on a half-truth, hoping she would buy it.

Carly shifted back and forth uncomfortably at the mention of my aunt being his nanny, but just as I was about to ask her why, the bell rang.

"C'mon we gotta go or we are getting sent to detention."

Carly grabbed my arm to drag me into class but not before I turned to glance over my shoulder. I needed to see Maverick one last time. Our eyes met instantly—a triumphant smirk forming on my lips upon learning he was most definitely watching my every move—but the second I saw his expression, my almost-smile vanished. His steely regard sent tremors of uncertainty through my body. *Did he know we were talking about him? Why does he look pissed?* Our eyes stayed locked until Carly gave me one last tug into the classroom and pushed me into my seat.

"Hurry up, Elle, you don't want to get in trouble on your first day."

Preoccupied, I sat through an English class on Shakespeare's *Othello*. I thought I heard Mr. Jacobs mention jealousy as a theme throughout the play when he began his lecture, but everything else was lost. My mind was reeling—about Margot and Maverick, their supposed family connection, and more importantly, Carly's reaction when I mentioned my aunt being Maverick's nanny.

I went through the entire day hoping that Maverick would be in one of my classes and I dreamed that in a stroke of luck, I would be seated next to him; but that never happened. The only time I saw him was at lunch and unfortunately as I walked by with Madison and Carly, Caleb jumped up and scooped me into a huge hug right in front of him.

"There you are girl!" Caleb shouted excitedly. I remained stoic as he lifted me off the ground in a giant embrace. "How has your first day been? What classes do you have left? Let me see your schedule so I can see if we have any classes together."

I heard the questions he was asking but all I could do was look at Maverick and wonder what he was thinking. He looked away as Caleb talked to me and my whole body ached with the sting of his disapproval. Caleb asked me to come sit by him and motioned to the table he sat at with Maverick and their other jock friends, but I assured him that I couldn't because I promised Carly, Madison, and Macey that I was going to sit with them. He was disappointed but that didn't deter him from leaning in to kiss me on the cheek before he walked away.

"I'll see you after school, OK Elle?" he called to me, loud enough for half the lunchroom to hear.

I gave him a half-hearted smile then sat down at the lunch table with my friends, only to realize that I had no appetite yet again. I pushed my food around on my plate and tried to find the will to ignore the force that kept pulling me to the boy sitting two tables away; a feat I found completely impossible, not to mention miserable.

I went through the rest of the day meeting new friends and, overall, liking the new school that I had such a negative preconceived notion about. When the final bell rang, I went to my dad's classroom to tell him I was going to hang out in the parking lot with some friends, then I walked outside. Immediately, I saw Maverick standing by his truck with Caleb and some of their other friends. Caleb waved me over and since Madison, Carly, and Macey were nowhere to be seen yet, I decided I had no other choice but to walk to Caleb, who was waving frantically at me. As I approached, the same aching I experienced at lunch overcame me yet again as Maverick looked at me, then away with disinterest. He nodded at his friends.

"Later guys," I heard him say as I walked up. He glanced at me once but only for a split second as he brushed past me to walk toward his truck; then he started his engine and backed out in a hurry, screeching his tires on the pavement as he drove away.

My heart sank, burdened by the overwhelming sadness of my reality. Maverick was going to ignore me and act like the moments we shared were nothing. The fire burned, but it was out of anger toward myself.

You should have never allowed yourself to feel anything for him. These feelings were the exact reason I built my wall of indifference in the first place—for my protection.

I forced myself to mask my hurt and made small talk with Caleb until my girlfriends finally came out of the school.

"Hey Caleb, I'll talk to you later," I said when I saw the girls walking toward me, relieved to finally see them.

"OK. I'll call you tonight after practice," he promised.

He did call me that evening but I didn't answer. Then he called my house and when I heard the phone ring I jumped up to go take a shower, telling my aunt I couldn't talk. Avoidance. I didn't know what else to do.

The next morning I woke up and went to school and it was the same routine as the day before—Caleb finding me in the halls and giving me a big hug and sometimes even a kiss on the cheek; finding me at lunch and asking me to sit by him and me refusing, saying I had to sit by my girlfriends; then him happily telling me he would wait for me in the parking lot after school. I was beginning to feel like I was in a bad dream by the end of the week, going through the same monotonous motions every day.

With each passing day Maverick seemed to shut me out more; his coldness toward me made me question whether the moments we shared together were but a figment of my imagination. But then I would remember him squeezing my hand three times, while his blue eyes touched my soul. No matter how cold he was to me or how much he ignored me, I knew that we shared at least that one beautiful moment, and no one could ever take that memory from me.

That afternoon after school my dad had to stay late and work on lesson plans for the next day so I decided I would pass the time by going to the computer lab and doing some research. I typed "Mason Oil Tulsa Oklahoma" into the Google search engine and hit enter.

I searched through and quickly realized that the actual name of the company was WestCo Petroleum. When I entered the company name into the search engine, I had over a million hits so I decided to hit on the "About" tab on the company's actual web page.

As I read, I learned that WestCo was an oil and gas exploration and production company that originated in the early 1930s by a man named George Mason—Maverick's great grandfather. However, it was Maverick's grandfather, George Mason's eldest son—William Mason—who was responsible for bringing the company to its current state of prominence in the oil and gas industry. William's discovery of oil in Oklahoma, the Osage county region to be more specific, provided the foundation, which ultimately grew the company as the third largest oil producer in the world as well as being in the top twenty-five companies for gas production. I scrolled down and saw pictures of Maverick's great grandfather, George, his grandfather, William, and then his father, Miles.

Another notable mention in the historical account of the company was the addition of a partner, James Weston, who bought into the company and became an equal partner in 1959. The article ended by stating, "the Mason & Weston families will continue as pioneers for the oil and gas industries into the twenty-first century."

At the bottom of the page was a beautiful portrait of a picture-perfect family dressed in all black and white, a crisp white background highlighting their perfect features. On the left side of the picture, standing next to his father, was a younger version of Maverick. He somehow seemed different in the picture—lighter, perhaps, the smile at his lips a bit more carefree, less controlled. I stared at the picture and memorized his every feature. If he wouldn't speak to me or acknowledge my existence anymore, at least I could admire him in the picture on the computer screen. I noticed he had the same strong and masculine jawline as his father, as well as his dark hair and broad shoulders; but his crystal blue eyes—those he got from his mother.

I studied the little girl standing to the right of Maverick in the picture—her smile was a crooked, endearing grin and light-brown ringlets played at her face. She was significantly younger than Maverick and his arm was on her shoulder protectively. *I think that's the little girl in the pictures in my aunt's hallway. It must be Maverick's little sister.* I wondered why he never mentioned his little sister and felt a bit indignant, but the snide voice in my head quickly laughed at me, reminding me I barely knew him at all. I dismissed the unwanted voice and scrolled down the computer screen—leaving the Masons behind—to land on a picture of the Weston family, immediately noticing the blonde cheerleader who was constantly hanging onto Maverick. She was sitting on the edge of a leather chair, with pristine posture of course, in a black pencil skirt and an immaculately starched white button-up blouse. Her mother sat beside her—hair dyed platinum just like her daughter's—and they smiled the same smile; a cold and insincere smile that would be considered beautiful by the world's standard, but not mine. Behind them stood a man with dark hair slicked back, with streaks of grey that showed his age. One of his arms was on his daughter and the other was on the back of the dark-leather chair. Beside him stood a young man that looked exactly like him, thin and wiry, pointed nose and sharp features that some would consider handsome. As I looked at the picture of the family that many would consider picture-perfect, showing a family exuding power and wealth, a cold shiver ran down my spine.

I was engrossed in my research when I heard the door creak open. I quickly hit the x on the top of the screen.

"C'mon Elle, time to go home," I heard my dad say.

I turned off the computer and walked out of the room with my dad, heading back to our temporary home—the little cottage on the back of the Mason estate. For the rest of the evening, the picture of the Weston family materialized in my mind. Each time it did, an ominous feeling overwhelmed me. It was the same feeling I experienced when I rode my bike down a one-lane dirt road in Ohio, the night I lost my mother.

CHAPTER 12

That weekend, my dad and I were busy going to appointments with a realtor again. We looked at several small houses as well as numerous apartments and condos, even though I knew we wouldn't be moving anytime soon. My dad would need more time to save enough money for a down payment, thank goodness. I needed more time with my aunt before we moved. *And with Maverick.* I didn't even bother ignoring my little voice in my head. I knew she was right.

I ignored Caleb's texts throughout the weekend asking me to go on a date with him, to meet him at a party, and one final desperate plea asking me to meet him at the basketball courts on Sunday night. He was relentless and so was I—at ignoring him. Guilt overwhelmed me each time I saw one of his texts or phone calls. I wanted to fix what I had done but I didn't know how to. So, I did what I knew best. I ran away, and I built a wall.

When school started on Monday it was the same routine as the week before. I tried, unsuccessfully, to get Maverick out of my mind as I walked the halls and sat through my classes. He was cold and indifferent toward me and I was starting to succumb to the sadness of acceptance that perhaps the moments we shared were a figment of my imagination and I was just like every other girl in the school—apparently not good enough for Maverick Mason.

When I got back to the cottage after school, I immediately went to my bedroom and changed into my running clothes. I needed to forget my frustrations. I ran hard—my angry music blaring through my headphones—pounding my feet into the ground and ridding myself of confusion and anger with each step.

As I came over the hill that would lead me back toward my aunt's house, a familiar pull ignited. I made my way through the front gate and saw Maverick standing at the front door of our cottage. The fire burned uncontrollably—my emotions running rampant—vacillating between anger and desire.

Get a grip, Elle. I hated how out of control I felt when I was in his presence.

"Where's Cordelia?" He didn't even bother to say hello, his words clipped and abrasive.

"Well hello to you too." I crossed my arms and scowled at him.

"Just tell me where she is," he said in his normal bossy, controlling tone.

I gritted my teeth. "Yes, your majesty. Your wish is my command," I said as I dipped into a mock bow.

He let out a long, frustrated sigh. "Can you please just tell me where Cordelia is, Elyse?"

I knew he said my full name to irritate me.

"Don't call me that," I said, stepping closer to him and pushing up on my tiptoes in an attempt to look more intimidating next to his massive frame.

He laughed out loud. Instinctively my hand lashed out to hit him in the chest. He grabbed it with a smirk on his face.

"I. Hate. You," I spat at him vehemently as I struggled to rid my hand from his grasp. I regretted the words the second I spoke them.

Anger lit his eyes; it frightened me, but I refused to apologize.

He leaned in, and his closeness took my breath away. "No, you don't."

We stood there—inches apart—searching one another while the magnetic connection between us intensified with each passing second, begging us to connect.

"Mav, is that you?" He dropped my hand quickly as my aunt interrupted our emotionally charged moment. "Now why in the world have you stayed away for so long? I haven't seen you in weeks!" I saw him glance in my direction before he turned his large frame toward her, scooping down to give her a big yet gentle hug.

"I know, I know," he said apologetically as he shot another accusatory glance in my direction. "Listen I can't stay long but I just wanted to run down and give you a birthday hug and tell you that my mom wants you to come to dinner tonight if you can."

It was Aunt Cordelia's birthday? My face flushed. *Pay better attention, Elle.*

I wanted to get her a gift...maybe I would draw her another picture since she seemed to like that.

"You get inside this house right now Maverick William Mason, or so help me—"

"OK, OK, you win." He threw his arms up, indicating a truce, then held the door open for her. Maverick followed her into the kitchen and sat at the table while she poured him some lemonade and brought him a plate of cookies. I left them alone, sitting in the next room with a book and unsuccessfully trying to distract myself from the undeniable force calling me into the next room. The minutes ticked by, each one an eternity, as I fought the urge to join them.

"Elle, could you help Maverick carry these to the car please?" I heard my aunt call to me as she walked into the living room carrying a pan of her delectable homemade cinnamon rolls. His arms were already full with a plate of her chocolate-chip cookies. I hopped up to comply with her request.

"Sure."

As I took the cinnamon rolls from her hands, she caught my eye and a knowing glance passed between us. I looked away, embarrassed by how much she seemed to understand, and started walking toward the door. We came to the entryway and Maverick reached up to open the front door then stopped, something catching his eye. I followed his gaze and saw that he was looking at the picture I had drawn of the yellow house. I didn't realize that my aunt had framed it and hung it in the entryway of the cottage.

"Where did that come from?" He pointed toward my picture.

I remained silent. I didn't want him to know I was the artist.

"Who drew that?" he asked again, more forcefully than the time before.

"I did," I finally answered.

His eyes burned into mine and I no longer saw indifference.

"Beautiful," he said as he looked at me, not the picture. I couldn't be certain, but I wanted to believe that the picture wasn't the only thing he was calling beautiful.

"Thanks." I glanced away, my face heating up.

"When have you been there?"

"Been where?" I was confused.

He pointed to the picture hanging on the wall. "To the reservation? When have you been there?"

My eyebrows furrowed. "Are you saying you recognize this place?"

"Yes," he said with certainty.

How could Maverick possibly know of a place that I thought only existed in a dream?

"It's the old abandoned Osage Indian Reservation, right?" He was obviously confused as to why I was questioning him about something that *I had* drawn.

"Um, yeah," I lied. "I saw it in a book about Oklahoma that my aunt had and I just thought it was pretty so I sketched it. How do you know about the reservation?" I asked, trying to be nonchalant.

"I grew up going there with my dad. His company has tons of oil wells out there. I used to love going out there with him when I was a kid."

"Cool. Is it close to here?" I pressed.

I swore he could read my every thought. "Why do you want to know where it is so bad?"

"I don't want to know where it is so bad. I was just making small talk," I lied, desperate to get him off my back.

"You're lying. I can tell."

"Whatever Maverick, no I'm not. Just leave me alone." It was infuriating how well he could read me.

"Elle, I'm going to ask you one more time. Why do you want to know where the reservation is?"

You can't tell him. He will think you are completely insane.

"I don't know. I was just curious after I saw the picture in the book, OK?" I sighed in exasperation, my eyes landing everywhere but on him. I had always been a terrible liar.

He nodded as if privy to my innermost thoughts, and I thought I saw disappointment in his eyes, or was it hurt?

Suddenly my heart ached with loneliness. I saw myself on a one-lane dirt road, drowning in quicksand, a strong arm reaching toward me, saving me, pulling me out of the pit of death right before I went under. A pair of blue eyes were my beacon in the dark, bringing with them safety and most of all, protection.

My breathing was erratic as I glanced around nervously, trying to regain composure. *It's not too late. Tell him the truth. Ask him to come with you.* I faltered. I struggled to find the words, opening my mouth and trying to force them out; but they wouldn't come. So instead, I took a deep breath then turned and walked away, keeping my wall intact—as high and as strong and as impenetrable as ever.

CHAPTER 13

Before Maverick's truck drove over the hill, my mind was already devising a plan to get to the reservation. I had no car. I also had absolutely no idea where I was going or how to get there. Minor problems, right? I decided to start with the latter—determining where the reservation was and how long it would take me to get there—then I would deal with how.

I walked into the living room, annoyed to see my father sitting there. The only computer in the cottage sat on a small desk in the corner of the living room, making privacy nearly impossible.

I sat down at the computer and typed "Osage Indian Reservation" into the search engine then clicked on one of the maps that Google provided me with. The reservation was in Osage County; it looked to be about forty-five minutes northwest of Tulsa. I found a piece of paper and a pencil on the computer desk then scribbled directions from my aunt's house to Osage County and then, to the reservation. When I was done I carefully glanced over my shoulder to find my dad consumed in his chosen reading material for the night. I sighed in relief and quickly closed out the results from my search.

Patience was never one of my better virtues so of course I decided to leave for the reservation that night. My aunt had dinner plans with the Masons for her birthday so my dad and I sat alone in the house that evening as I watched every minute tick slowly by on the clock above the fireplace mantle. I tried to consume myself in the latest book I was reading but was too distracted. My eyes scanned the page but instead of the words I saw a tiny yellow clapboard house, an old woman in a long white dress with two long braids, and as always, those blue eyes burning into my soul. Finally, I looked up and saw that it was 9:00 p.m., and although it was early for me to go to bed, I didn't think I would raise suspicion if I said the right words.

"I have to get up early tomorrow to study for my biology exam before class so I'm going to bed." I stretched as I faked a big yawn. My dad looked up from his book, his eyes showing his fatigue.

"Yeah I think I better call it a night too." He sat down his book and stood up to walk to his bedroom, pausing to ruffle my hair and give me one of his big goofy grins. "G'night, Elle," he said.

"Good night, Dad." I stood to walk into the kitchen, acting as though I was getting a drink of water while I carefully eyed him walking down the hall toward his bedroom.

Once I heard his door close, I started quietly but frantically opening the drawers in the kitchen, looking for a flashlight. I found one just as I heard my aunt open the front door. I quickly stuffed the large flashlight in the back of my jeans, hoping that my flannel shirt covered it in the back, then grabbed a glass and filled it with water.

"How was your birthday dinner, Aunt Cordelia?" I smiled at her.

"It was so lovely. Thanks for asking, sweetie."

She proceeded to tell me about how Mrs. Mason had served her favorite meal and even had the chef make her favorite dessert, some fancy French-sounding dessert I had never heard of called crème brûlée. I listened, nodding my head and smiling appropriately, but I was distracted. All I could think about was getting back to my bedroom to be alone and finish planning my departure.

"I'm so glad you had a nice evening," I said. "Happy birthday, Aunt Cordelia."

With that I walked out of the room, and an unwanted memory floated to the surface of my mind after I spoke the words "happy birthday" to my aunt. It was the morning of my tenth birthday and my mother woke me up with my favorite breakfast—her homemade blueberry pancakes. The pancakes were stacked high and protruding from the stack were ten purple candles, my favorite color. She smiled that smile of hers—the one that showed her beautiful dimples—as I heard her angelic voice sing out, "Happy birthday to you, happy birthday to you, happy birthday Elyse Rose, HAPPY BIRTHDAY TO YOU." Then I blew out my candles.

The memory ended there as my aunt's touch brought me back to the present. I looked up to see sadness in her eyes and realized I had been standing there thinking of my mother for an undisclosed period of time—pain and longing etched on my face, no doubt. I hated when my aunt looked at me that way; it made me feel damaged, broken. I quickly forced a smile.

"Well goodnight!" I said, with perhaps too much fake enthusiasm. Then I turned and walked out of the room, thinking about how I hadn't celebrated a single birthday since that day. My eleventh birthday was spent burying my mother. My birthday had become—in my mind—the second worst day of my life. I wanted to remember the last birthday I had with her, and no other.

My aunt's eyes watched me as I walked away and I hoped that she couldn't see the flashlight. As soon as I closed the door, I ripped the flashlight out of my back pocket and went to work. I took my books out of my backpack and replaced them with the flashlight, then I added my notebook with the directions I had written down, my cell phone, and a black hoodie. I arranged the pillows on my bed and flipped off the light in my room, sitting in the corner and waiting, just waiting. I sat there, watching the seconds on the clock tick by slowly, as I heard everyone in the tiny house go through their nighttime routines.

When the house was completely silent, I waited for another twenty minutes, hearing nothing but my own anxious breaths, then I pushed myself to my feet; it was time. I glanced at the clock and noticed it was only eighteen minutes after ten o'clock, earlier than I would normally sneak out when circumstances warranted extreme measures.

I quietly opened the window and pushed myself through the small opening, hopping down to the ground and landing in a crouch. My foot landed on a twig and it snapped, loudly. I cringed. I stayed in my crouched position, frozen, my heart beating rapidly as I listened to make sure I was still unnoticed. When I felt confident no one had heard me, I carefully reached up and closed the window, then stepped away from the house, choosing each step with caution and precision. I closed the gate to the house quietly and made my way to my dad's church van, silently praying to myself that it would miraculously start the first time.

I hopped in the van and slowly pulled the door shut then inhaled and exhaled deeply—two times—before I turned the key. The engine rolled over instantly and a smile fueled by relief spread over my face. I put the van in gear and rolled down the road with no lights on until I got to the main gate. As I approached the massive iron gates they slowly lurched open.

Once I had cleared them, I turned my lights on and pulled out onto the main road.

Within ten minutes the Tulsa city limits were behind me and I saw the sign for highway OK 11W. I drove into the darkness, away from the lights of the city. The stars in the sky burned brighter out here and I was all alone, except for a pair of headlights far off in the distance that I occasionally saw flashing behind me.

I began to pass old two-story houses that obviously had been beautiful once upon a time but now sat ravaged by time—paint chipping off the wood, sagging porches, and broken windows. Without looking at my directions, I pushed the turn signal and pulled onto a county road. The radio was on but oddly there was an eerie silence that deepened as I traveled further into darkness. I didn't need to look up or check my directions; somehow I knew exactly where I was going. Something was drawing me into the darkness and at the end of the road, I knew I would find a yellow clapboard house.

The road narrowed then suddenly turned sharply to the right. I made the sharp turn, then found myself on a narrow gravel road. I drove on into the night, and although I had never been on the road before, I recognized it as the exact same path I had drawn from my dream. There was not a single street light. Only my headlights shined into the black of night. I could see nothing beyond a few feet in front of the van, but I knew that on either side of the road, flat Oklahoma prairies stretched on endlessly for miles. I knew that where the grass met the sky, oil wells dotted the horizon and pumped up and down without cease.

Finally, I came to a fence with a gate that was open, but not large enough for a car. I pulled over to the side of the road and parked the van. I should have been scared—a teenage girl, alone on a gravel road in the middle of nowhere—but I was at complete peace.

I pulled my backpack out, put on my black hoodie, then without hesitation, I shut the van door and turned my flashlight on. I saw the outline of a row of houses before me and I knew what would be waiting for me in the middle of them. I put one foot in front of the other and passed one house, two houses, then another. The houses were lined up perfectly on either side of the street, just as I remembered them from my dream. I passed three more houses then my flashlight met the form of a house in the distance. It was separated slightly from the others and though the darkness was all consuming and my flashlight lacked the power to show me the color of the house, I knew that it was yellow.

My legs moved forward, stepping purposefully, and as I climbed onto the threshold, I noticed a dreamcatcher blowing in the wind. Just as it did in my dream, the door cracked open as if welcoming me inside and a light orange hue emanated from a tiny, flickering candle. As the door continued to open of its own accord, the soft light from the candle illuminated the shape of a woman standing inside the tiny house—just as I knew she would be.

Unafraid and feeling an inexplicable calm despite the unknown, I walked through the door and stepped into the house that called me to it. The room was dim; a small fire burned in the fireplace. The modest kitchen could barely be seen off the living area and in between the kitchen and living room was a small corner for a table. Around the table sat four tiny wooden chairs.

I stepped further into the house and approached the woman. Our eyes met. They were black—the color of the charcoal that I used to help my mom pour into our grill on our back porch in Ohio—and as I stared into the blackness I knew that she had experienced immeasurable pain and loss, grief and suffering; but I could also see that she was strong and courageous. I saw her spirit, and I knew she was a fighter.

I longed to know her. I yearned to sit down and lose myself in her story. I ripped my eyes away from hers and took in her slight but sturdy frame; her long dark braids laced with silver-grey hair that shone in the candlelight like a halo; her white leather dress hanging to her knees where it split into tiny strands of leather that fell to the floor and ended with small blue and silver beads. I turned my eyes back toward hers but neither one of us broke the silence. Eventually she reached behind her and grabbed something off the table, never taking her dark eyes away from mine.

She slowly pulled a dark wooden box from behind her back, then she moved her weathered hands toward my chest in a gesture of offering. She still didn't speak and I realized with sadness that perhaps she was not capable. As I looked at the object in her hands more closely—the dark, aged mahogany wood carved with intricate details—I knew that it was meant for me. In my hands, it felt at home.

As I took it from her, her eyes spoke of happiness, relief even. We stood there, both of our hands on the wooden object, our dark eyes peering into one another's souls. A hundred questions passed through my mind, but as I found the courage to ask, I heard a noise outside. I turned quickly to look behind me. Headlights glazed through the open door.

The peace was gone, replaced instantly with fear. When I turned back to the woman, she had vanished. It was as if she had never been there but I looked down and saw in my hands a reminder that she had been—the dark wooden box she had given me.

I shoved the box in my backpack as I heard more noises outside, then boots walking up the steps toward the threshold. I glanced around frantically, finally seeing a small window cracked open on the opposite side of the living room. I ran toward it, pushed it open, then pulled my body through the window and jumped, landing softly on the ground below. I sat there quietly, my heart beating so fast I thought it would come out of my chest. A heavy pair of boots—or perhaps it was two pairs—stomped around the house. Trepidation washed over me as I looked up to see that I left the window wide open. I heard the footsteps walking toward the window and acted without thinking, standing up and slowly, quietly pushing my body away and around the edge of the house. I turned the corner and hide my body on the opposite side of the house, just as I heard someone crank the window open even further.

I didn't dare use my flashlight but once I cleared the side of the house I took off into a sprint toward the church van. I passed several of the clapboard houses before I heard a door slam, followed by tires screeching. I ran harder, not daring to look behind me and finally made it to the van.

The engine rolled over on the first try—thank God—and I put the van in gear and stomped on the gas pedal, peeling out of the dirt just in time to pull out in front of a pair of headlights I saw glaring behind me. I was being followed.

The decrepit old church van was giving me all it had to give—which wasn't going to be enough. I could see headlights behind me inching closer and closer to my bumper until I felt a hard nudge from behind. My head lurched forward and hit the steering wheel upon impact and my body reacted by slamming on the brakes. The vehicle behind me swerved to dodge the church van and when it did, it came into view of my left side-view mirror. The vehicle was jet-black—the windows tinted the color of midnight—and although I was never one who had paid any attention to the make or brand of cars, I knew this was some type of a Suburban or large SUV. The Suburban went off into the ditch but something told me the detour was only temporary so I punched the gas pedal and made my way down the road, desperately trying to outrun it. I saw the turn to the highway appear in front of me and felt a renewed sense of hope as I pulled onto the smooth paved road; but my hope died almost instantly when I glanced in my rearview mirror and saw a pair of headlights pull onto the highway not long after me.

I pushed the gas pedal to the floor again but I knew it was useless. There were no other lights on the highway, no one to save me, and the black vehicle was gaining from behind.

I'm going to die on a road in the middle of nowhere, Oklahoma, just like my mom died on a road in the middle of nowhere, Ohio.

Anger rushed through my blood at the thought of my mother's death, and the fire ignited, leaving no room for fear. *I'm not going down without a fight.*

The black SUV pulled up beside me and I jerked the wheel to the right then back to the left, slamming the church van into the body of the vehicle. The van pushed the SUV off the road but only for a second. As we both pulled back onto the road, I saw a pair of headlights in the distance moving toward us quickly and my heart skipped a beat, daring to hope; then the black SUV slammed into me with such force that the church van veered off the road, into the ditch, and I lost control. I was surprisingly at peace as I let go of the wheel and accepted that I had no control over what happened to the vehicle or to me. The side of the van scraped a fence, then broke free and plowed through a field. Trees appeared; I was heading straight for them. I braced myself for impact. Then everything went black.

The salty taste of blood in my mouth awakened me. My head rested on the steering wheel heavily, and bright lights shined in my face. Searing pain shot through my head and my vision blurred. I strained to make my eyes cooperate and when they did, they saw the shape of a vehicle.

The person in the black SUV. They're here for me.

But then an invisible force awakened inside of me, pulling at the dark depths of my soul. I closed my eyes and succumbed to the pain but before I did, I saw a pair of beautiful blue eyes clouded with fear and concern. It was Maverick; he was my beacon in the dark. His eyes—they were begging me to be OK; to hang on; to stay—for him. He was commanding me not to let go, and I knew that I would do whatever he asked.

My body was lifted out of the truck by a pair of strong arms, the movement causing excruciating pain to shoot throughout my body.

The wooden box. I couldn't leave without it.

"My backpack," I pleaded. Maverick reached back toward the van with one hand.

As we drove I was in and out of consciousness and although I was in immeasurable pain, I was also euphoric, because I was in his arms. I opened my eyes and heard him whisper my name softly then my eyelids grew heavy and started to close again. I heard him yell my name in desperation.

"Elle! Elle, stay with me. Don't you close your eyes, Elle! Stay here."

I tried—for him—but it was impossible to hold on any longer. I let go and fell away from him, finally giving into the unconsciousness that called to me.

The last thing I remembered was a strong hand squeezing mine—once, twice, then three times. I drifted off thinking about my mom standing on the front porch of our house in Ohio, looking at me and saying three little words.

"I love you."

CHAPTER 14

I awoke in a haze—an incessant beeping interrupting my slumber—and I scanned the room slowly. My aunt sat in a chair by the window, covered by one of her hand-knitted blankets. My dad sat beside me in a chair, his head lying on my bed as he slept.

I kept looking, desperately searching for Maverick, but when I tried to move, pain radiated throughout my head. *He's not here.* My heart sank.

Suddenly memories came flooding back to me in no particular order—a black SUV running me off the road; a woman in a white dress; my head on Maverick's lap as he called out to me to keep my eyes open; a yellow house; and an intricately carved wooden box.

The wooden box. I pushed myself up to a sitting position—panicked—the machines in the room sounding off with my sudden change of position, alerting everyone in the room that I was awake. My dad's eyes shot open.

"Elle?" he said tenderly. He was already at my bedside.

"When can I leave?" All I could think about was finding my backpack and the wooden box.

He looked at me like I was crazy.

"Elle you've been asleep for days. You have concussion, a broken wrist, and some broken ribs."

So I'm not leaving anytime soon. My head was swimming as I took in my surroundings. I tried to move my arm toward my head to stop the pounding, but when I did, a shooting pain ripped through my arm. I had to stifle a scream. My ribs were sore, so sore I didn't want to breathe. The pain was excruciating. I lay my head back down on the pillow, exhaustion consuming me.

"Honey, Maverick told us everything." My dad said the words with disappointment in his voice. I took a deep breath, trying to discern what "Maverick told us everything" meant.

"He did?" I asked, praying that Maverick hadn't told my dad the truth about the reservation and the black SUV.

He changed his look to one of reproach but I still saw tenderness in his eyes. "We know you were sneaking out to go the fair with some friends, Elle."

Relief flooded me.

"I'm so sorry Dad." The cover story Maverick told my dad was a lie, but my apology was heartfelt.

"We're just so thankful Maverick saw the van leaving and decided to follow you."

I looked up as he held water to my mouth and I sipped. *So that's how Maverick knew where I was.*

"Mmmm-hmmm," I said, waiting to see where else the cover story went.

"He said your tire exploded on the highway...I'm so sorry, Ells. I knew the van needed new tires but I didn't know it was that bad." His voice cracked on the last few words. I hated to see him in pain but even more so, I hated that I always seemed to be the one causing it. *Say it Elle. Say you're sorry.*

"Dad, I'm so sorry. I'm fine. Everything is going to be OK." I reached my good hand toward his—the one that wasn't screaming out in pain at the slightest movement—bridging the

Great Divide between us. He squeezed my hand lightly, looking up at me with brokenness in his eyes. Guilt permeated my soul, making it difficult to breathe. *You're so selfish. You never think before you act and your dad always has to pay the price.* I looked away, fighting back the tears that threatened to spill forth. I couldn't hold his gaze as I repeated my heartfelt apology one more time, a whisper really, but I knew he heard me.

"I really am sorry Dad." Somehow, we both knew I was apologizing for so much more than just sneaking out.

"I know, Ells." And my dad was forgiving me for so much more too.

My aunt was now awake and at my bedside as well. "Thank God he was there. Thank God he found you."

Tears fell down her cheeks freely. I looked at her in astonishment, unable to grasp how she was so at peace with allowing others to see her emotions.

I felt Maverick's presence nearby; there was an awakening inside me—beckoning me toward him—and as if on cue he walked through the door. I couldn't help but smile when I saw him and he smiled back at me; then he gave me that trademark wink, making the butterflies fly wildly inside my stomach. We didn't even attempt to take our eyes off each other as my dad spoke to us. Something had shifted between us.

"Well speak of the devil—" my father chuckled at the irony of his statement—"or I guess I should say you are our angel, saving Elle the way you did." His eyes rested on Maverick, so full of gratitude I thought he might cry.

Maverick didn't acknowledge my father's words. He did nothing but stare at me with his piercing blue eyes, speaking into my soul without uttering a sound. He leaned into the door frame, that crooked cocky smile playing at his lips and the force between us surged uncomfortably. I wanted to tell everyone to leave so I could be alone with Maverick.

"I was just telling Elle how you followed her when you saw the van leaving the property—thank God—because if you wouldn't have been there when that tire exploded and seen her accident..." he refused to finish his thought. We all knew what he was thinking anyway so there was no need.

"Yes sir," Maverick answered without looking in my father's direction. He couldn't—wouldn't—tear his eyes from mine. "Thank God I was there." He looked at me with disapproval and I met his gaze with defiance. Then he winked at me again and within a second my emotions went from defiance to uncontrollable desire.

My dad walked over to Maverick and shook his hand, a look of eternal debt evident on his face. "Thank you, son. For saving my daughter's life. I owe you everything."

"Mr. Christiansen there's no need to thank me, really. I'm the one who's thankful I was there and could help."

My dad let go of Maverick's hand.

"I'm going to go check at the desk to see when the doctor will be by to see you today."

My aunt stood and started to follow my dad through the door but on her way out of my hospital room, she stopped to give Maverick a gentle hug. When she pulled away from him, I noticed she didn't let go of his hand. Instead she pulled Maverick by the hand—leading him—to the side of my bed. She stood there, looking back and forth between the two of us, then placed his hand on top of mine and held it there firmly. With a maternal look of approval in her eyes, she patted our hands twice; then she walked out of the room without a word.

We were alone. The invisible force between us intensified and I found it nearly impossible to speak, all my efforts focused on resisting the desire to pull my body off the hospital bed toward his. He broke the silence first.

"Well hey there, Baby Girl," he said with an affectionate smirk on his face as he came to sit on the side of my bed. I was exhausted, but not too tired to partake in our endearing banter.

"You know I hate when you call me that."

"You love it," he challenged. "And I would argue I've earned the right to call you whatever I want."

I knew what he was implying. He had saved my life after all.

"What in the hell were you thinking, Elle? Stealing a church van to drive to an abandoned reservation in the middle of the night? Are you kidding me?"

I looked away, desperate to avoid his scolding glare and even more desperate to avoid his question. *He will think you're crazy if you answer that. Change the subject.*

"How did you find me out there, Maverick?" I noticed my words came out slower than expected, and were slurred. The entire room seemed hazy and the incessant beeping of the hospital machines were lulling me to sleep. *It must be the pain meds. Focus, Elle.* I still needed answers to some lingering questions about the night of my accident.

"I was outside in the garage working out when I saw your dad's van pull off the property."

"And?"

I could tell he would share no more unless I pulled it out of him. I stared at him expectantly, refusing to break eye contact with him until he gave me more details. Finally, he caved.

"And I remembered how strange you were acting when I saw you at the house and asked about the reservation so I decided to follow the van. I was—" He paused, his beautiful blue eyes staring into the depths of my soul. Our unspoken connection allowed me to read his thoughts, but I still wanted to hear him speak the words. My heart was pounding as I waited for the confession I longed to hear.

"—I was worried about you. I couldn't stand the thought of you leaving and not knowing where you were going and if you were safe or not."

Maverick was worried about me. My heart leapt. I was totally flattered at his revelation of concern, but of course, I refused to show him. I answered with a snarky response instead.

"Stalking is illegal in all fifty states by the way."

"Why don't you press charges then, Brookville? You might want to mention I saved your life while you're at it though," he countered.

I loved his irritating little nicknames for me—Brookville and Baby Girl. Only Maverick Mason could somehow make those two terms endearing.

"I guess I'll let you get away with it *this time*, since you did save my life and all."

"Yeah, that's what I thought."

His cocky tone only pushed me to antagonize him further.

"I do have a few suggestions for you before you consider pursuing a career in this whole Mr Knight in Shining Armor thing…"

He cocked an eyebrow and I noticed a playful gleam in his eye. I knew he loved when I challenged him, even though he would never admit it.

"I'm all ears, Baby Girl."

"You might want to work on your timing."

"Oh really?"

"Yeah, really, since you pretty much got there too late and I almost died." I pointed at the white dressing wrapped around my head which I was quite certain made me look like the

Mummy. The mood suddenly turned serious and I regretted my words. He was hurting.

"You think I don't know I was almost too late…" The torment I saw on his face ripped through my soul. His pain was almost too much to take. *This has to do with more than just my accident.* That little voice in my head spoke to me and I knew she was right. There was something Maverick wasn't telling me. I reached across my body with my good arm to comfort him. I couldn't stand to see him in agony.

"Maverick, I was totally just kidding. I'm sorry. It's not your fault at all. All of this is my fault." He stared off into the distance and I hated the look of torture on his face. It was as though he was reliving a nightmare, but for some reason I wasn't sure if it was the night of my accident or something else altogether.

"I was trying to keep my distance, but I ended up losing you at a turn then it took me awhile to find where you had gone. I know I was almost too late and I will never forgive myself…"

"Maverick, look at me." Slowly, he brought his face back to mine. "Seriously, I'm fine. Everything is fine. You saved my life and I wouldn't be here if it wasn't for you."

He reached out and touched my face with tenderness. "What were you doing out there, Elle?"

I shook my head. "It won't make sense even if I tell you."

"Try me." He held my gaze.

I was scared, terrified to open up after years of closing myself off and running away, but when I looked into Maverick's blue eyes, I wanted to do what I had never done before—tell someone the truth. Plus, the pain meds seemed to be hindering my inhibitions. I wanted to tell Maverick Mason all my secrets.

"I have dreams." I had still been undecided on what I was going to do when suddenly the words spilled forth. He had a power over me that I couldn't comprehend, and I had no choice but to open myself up to him. "I guess I should call them nightmares or visions. Honestly, I don't really know what they are." I shook my head back and forth. How could I explain what I didn't even understand myself? My throat started to close off and my heartbeat increased. I closed my eyes and breathed deeply and as I did, he stroked my arm gently, soothing me. "I've had these dreams or nightmares ever since the night my mom died."

I never dared to speak of that night, not to anyone, and as I sat in a hospital bed staring into the enigmatic eyes of a boy I hardly knew, I realized I was going to do what I had never done before, for him. I lacked the strength to fight, to build a wall high enough and strong enough to keep him out. Maverick Mason—he was everywhere. I had no choice but to let him in. The lid of that little black box in the depths of my soul slowly cracked open; and for the first time ever, I welcomed it.

"She died when I was ten. Days before my eleventh birthday, actually." The words were freeing as they slipped from my tongue. "I was sitting on the couch watching TV, waiting for her to get home from the women's retreat she had gone to, when I had my first dream. It was more like a vision, really. It was like I was actually there. Everything went dark and all of a sudden I was on that one-lane road where she died." I paused, feeling vulnerable.

He probably thinks I'm certifiably insane.

He sensed my insecurities. "Elle, it's OK. You can do this," he coaxed.

"I don't know how but I was there. I saw my mom and she was terrified. She was running away from something, and she was covered in blood." I shook my head, desperate to rid myself of the vision of my mother trembling with fear. "When I woke up, I got on my bike and went looking for her. I found her less than a mile from our house on the exact same dirt road I had seen in my vision. I heard her scream." I looked away and fixed my eyes to look out the window of the hospital room, no longer able to speak as the sound of her blood-curdling scream resonated in my ears. Still all these years later, it chilled me to the core. I took several deep breaths, regaining my composure. "I turned down the road and ran toward her but when I got there it was too late. She bled to death in my arms, Maverick. I couldn't save her."

I dropped my head, exhausted yet relieved. By allowing my wall to come down, I realized how all-consuming it had been to hold it in place for all those years. My entire body sagged out of emotional and physical exhaustion; then he was there, enveloping me in his strong arms. He rocked me back and forth as cleansing tears fell silently down my cheeks. He brushed my hair gently away from my face and consoled me by repeating the same words, over and over. "I'm here, Elle. I'm here." For the first time since that night she left me, I didn't feel utterly alone.

I don't know how long I cried, but when I was done with my cathartic release, I knew I needed to tell him the rest.

"Maverick?" I pushed myself out of his arms and looked at him with uncertainty.

"What is it, Elle?" He knew there was more to the story.

"I had a dream the night I moved here and when I woke up I drew what I saw in that dream."

Confusion was evident in his eyes.

"It was the picture you saw hanging in my aunt's house. That's what I drew," I clarified.

"The old reservation?"

I nodded my head. "When you recognized the place I had drawn from my dream, I knew I had to go there. I knew something was there for me."

He looked at me in disbelief and I gave him time to process as we sat in silence. "So, you're telling me you have dreams about the future too?" he asked with disbelief. I was embarrassed, afraid he wasn't going to understand, as well as defensive at the doubt I heard in his tone.

"I don't really know," I said with frustration. "All I know is that the night my mom was murdered I was sitting on my couch and then all of a sudden everything went dark and I was on that very road where she was murdered. I saw it happen. Then I went to the road and I found her there, exactly where I had seen her. Was that the future that I saw or the present? Was it a vision or a dream? I don't know what it is. I don't have the answers."

"Elle," he said soothingly, "I believe you. I believe every word you're saying. I'm just trying to take it all in and understand." He stroked my arm, soothing me with his touch, and I opened myself up to him yet again.

"I guess after the night my mom died, I just had night-mares. They aren't typical nightmares though, because it feels like I'm there. It's terrible. It's like I'm reliving the same horrific night over and over again—me ending up on the same dead-end road with my mom bleeding to death in my arms. Sometimes a man with no face is there and I know he's who murdered my mom but I can never see him. And I can never save her. Those two things never change." He nodded, coaxing me to continue. "The night I moved here—the night after I met you—I had a different kind of dream. It was more like that one I had the night my mom was murdered. I was on the dirt road and I was drowning in quicksand, and then I saw your eyes. You were there and you lifted me out of the quicksand, then suddenly we were on a completely different road. It wasn't dark anymore and we ran together down the road until we ended up in front of a yellow house—the yellow house on the reservation. I went inside and a woman was waiting there for me, and she gave me a wooden box."

At the mention of the wooden box, I panicked, realizing that I had no idea where my backpack was. As usual, he read my mind.

"Don't worry I have it."

"My backpack?" I questioned.

"Yes, you told me to grab it when I pulled you out of the van."

"Where is it?"

"It's out in my truck. Do you want me to go grab it?"

"Yes please, if you don't mind." I was desperate to see if the box was there, or if the woman in white was all a figment of my imagination.

"I'll run out and get it and be right back."

Maverick was gone in an instant and as he walked out of the room my mind filled with frenzied thoughts. My head hurt and I was exhausted. I closed my eyes—desperate for reprieve from the pain—but was interrupted only moments later by the sound of my father's voice.

"Elle, the nurse says your doctors won't be around to check on you until later this evening. Since Maverick is here—" He looked around the room.

"He'll be back any second," I assured him with a weak voice. My head was throbbing and the pain was growing steadily. "He just had to run out to his truck to get something."

"Oh, OK," my dad said. "Well if he's fine staying with you for a little bit, your aunt and I were going to run to the cafeteria and get a bite to eat."

"Of course I don't mind staying with her," I heard Maverick's voice as he walked back into my hospital room. He was holding my backpack.

A nurse followed Maverick into the room. She was young—probably early twenties—with long strawberry blonde hair, and although I was hyped up on pain meds and my head was throbbing, it was impossible to miss how her eyes appreciated Maverick. I glared at her as she came to my bedside.

"Are you in pain?" she asked.

"I'm fine." I spit the words at her, perhaps with a bit too much venom.

I glanced across to see Maverick cross his arms and smirk. He knew I was pissed she was checking him out. I gave him a hard eye roll.

"You need more pain meds." She pushed a button beside my bed then walked out of the room. "I'll be back to check on you in a bit."

Don't Bother. I didn't want her anywhere near me. Actually who was I kidding. It was Maverick I didn't want the pretty little nurse to be around. The pain meds started kicking in instantly. My eyelids felt heavy and the world was in a haze. I glanced up through heavy lids to see my dad staring at me as if I were a china doll that might break.

"Dad, I'm fine, I promise. Go get some food," I encouraged him with a weak voice. I knew I only had a few more minutes and I wanted them to be alone, with Maverick.

"Are you sure?" He didn't want to leave me.

"I'm sure, Dad. I'm just going to rest." My words were slow and labored and I closed my eyes, lingering a bit too long.

When I opened them, my dad was patting Maverick as he walked out the door.

"Take good care of my girl."

"Always, sir."

We were alone again. Maverick sauntered toward me, his hands stuffed in his pockets, making his low-slung jeans ride even lower on his hips. His eyes raked over me as he approached my bedside and his lip curled up into that sexy half smile of his. The way he looked at me, it made that new fire burn uncontrollably—a burn I thoroughly enjoyed. The sensation gave me a second wind, and I opened my eyes, forcing myself to make the most of the last few moments I had with Maverick before the pain meds forced me to sleep. As he stood by my bed, I noticed what he held in his hand. *The backpack.* I reached out for it.

"Elle, why don't we do this later? You need to rest."

I ignored his concerned look and signaled for the backpack. He handed it over, reluctantly. I couldn't unzip it with only one hand. "Can you help me please?"

He looked at me tenderly then unzipped the bag for me. My heart beat erratically as I reached in and searched. *Is it really there? Or did I imagine it all?* My hands hit a solid object. My heartbeat increased in response. I grasped my fingers around it tightly. Then finally, I pulled out a dark wooden box I had seen so many times in my dreams, and now in reality.

"What is it?" Maverick asked.

"I don't know. When I had my dream—or vision, or whatever the heck it was—I saw an old woman dressed in white in the yellow house on the reservation." I paused, worried to continue because I knew how crazy it would sound, but eventually, I found the will to speak, fueled by my desire to be free—once and for all—of the burden of secrecy I had carried for so long. "Maverick, when I went to the reservation the woman I saw in my dream was waiting there for me, and she handed me this."

I held up the box for him to see and we both stared at it with uncertainty. Finally, I grabbed the box and tried to open it, with no success. Then Maverick tried with the same results. Nothing we did would make it budge. It was almost as if it was one solid piece of impenetrable, beautifully carved wood. Eventually, we both gave up. Frustrated and confused, but most of all— utterly exhausted and in pain—I put the wooden box back into my backpack for safekeeping.

We were engulfed in complete silence, Maverick processing all the information I had just given him and me trying to grasp what I had done.

I can't believe I just told him everything.

I took deep breaths and with each breath, I struggled to keep my eyes open. The pain meds were in full effect. My thoughts were jumbled and the world seemed like a dream world. My eyelids were so heavy. I could fight no longer. Maverick leaned forward, touching his forehead to mine, and at his touch, my heart relaxed into a steady rhythm.

I thought I heard him talking to me as I closed my eyes and gave into the sleep that called to me, but I wasn't sure if it was real or it was a dream.

"I'm here, Elle. Always."

Before I drifted away, I felt three gentle kisses pressed to my forehead and in the depths of my soul I heard him speak three little words. *I love you.*

CHAPTER 15

Days passed—each the same as the one before—as I counted down the minutes until I could leave the hospital. My body was almost healed. The only reminder of my accident was the gash on my forehead that was still healing—I wondered if it would leave a scar—and the sling my arm was in to protect my wrist. The doctors said I would soon be able to move to a soft cast. My ribs were still sore but seemed to improve each day. I tried to sleep as much as possible—that was what the doctors said I needed more than anything to heal—but every time I closed my eyes one of three things was waiting for me: the black SUV; the woman in the white dress; or my least favorite, the man with no face. The highlight of my day was when six o'clock rolled around; that was when Maverick came to visit me after baseball practice each day. I lived for the moment he walked through the door of my hospital room and I could forget my nightmares, even if it was only temporary.

Maverick refused to speak about the night of the wreck. Anytime I tried to bring up the events that happened at the reservation, he would just shake his head.

"Shhhh…" he would whisper quietly into my ear. "We don't need to talk about that right now."

I knew he was only trying to protect me. He wanted to give me time to heal before we were forced to face reality; but I was frustrated. I needed to start working through the mystery of the woman in white, the carved wooden box she gave me, and more importantly, who tried to murder me and why.

"You know we have to talk about it at some point?" I asked Maverick on the third day he came to visit me when he still refused to address the subject.

"Yeah but not today," he responded with gentle authority.

I let Maverick continue his charade because in all honesty, it was so therapeutic to finally be in his arms, that nothing else even mattered to me. Somewhere inside darkness called to me though, and I knew my nightmares were beginning to return. I would inevitably have to face all the dark roads in my past— both the one-lane dirt road in Ohio and the road to the reservation. I couldn't run from them forever.

On the start of my second week in the hospital, Maverick walked into my room with a black backpack thrown over his shoulder.

"Hey Baby Girl," he said, winking at me as he walked in.

"Well hey there, Top Gun." I loved our banter.

My aunt had fallen asleep by my bed wrapped cozily in one of her quilts but slowly awakened when she heard Maverick talking to me. A smile of happiness spread across her face when she saw us together. She stood to leave, knowing intuitively that we wanted to be left alone with the enormity of the emotions we experienced in each other's presence. The room was crowded when anyone was there but just the two of us.

"I'm going to head on home." She walked toward the bed and kissed me on the forehead.

"Okay, Aunt Cordelia, thanks for coming." I squeezed her hand.

"Maverick are you OK to stay with Elle until her dad gets here? He has a meeting at the school tonight so he won't be getting here until later."

"Absolutely. Go get some rest." He gave my Aunt Cordelia a big hug then walked her to the door.

As soon as she stepped out of the room, the atmosphere changed. The force between Maverick and me magnified significantly. I patted the bed. *Please let this visit be different than all the others. I can't wait for this much longer.*

Patience had never been one of my better virtues; or one I possessed at all for that matter. Maverick had been coming to see me every night for over a week and during that time he would lie in my bed beside me; hold me in his arms as I fell asleep; kiss my forehead; and even fall asleep next to me; but there was one thing he refused to do—kiss me.

He knew what I craved and I knew he wanted the same—I could see the way he looked at me with hunger in his eyes—but for some reason, he refused to give in. I was growing more impatient by the day. Never before had I wanted someone to kiss me so badly. I was perplexed and frustrated by his gentlemanly behavior.

As he sat on the bed, our eyes burned into each other's with desire. I pushed myself onto my elbow in anticipation, longing desperately for him to give into our connection. Maverick made a movement, leaning in toward me, and my heart started beating rapidly; then abruptly, the moment between us ended as I watched Maverick throw himself back onto the pillow of my hospital bed, and laugh.

"What?" I almost yelled with indignation as I forced myself up to a seated position and backhanded him across the chest. "What in the world are you laughing at?" I asked again when he didn't answer immediately. He kept laughing.

"Don't you remember that night we played truth or dare?" he finally said when he regained his composure.

A memory flooded back to me from Maverick's party. *You'll kiss me first. One day.*

"*That* is why you haven't kissed me?!"

"Yep!" He casually folded his muscular arms and placed them behind his head on the pillow, amusement playing on his beautiful blue eyes. I was momentarily distracted by how amazing he looked with his muscles bulging beneath his athletic T-shirt and the laughter touching his face.

I had to look away to regain my composure.

"You've got to be kidding me, Maverick." I rolled my eyes and crossed my arms, staring at him with disdain.

"Pretty sure I'm serious," he said matter-of-factly. "I decided that night that I wouldn't kiss you first."

I let out an exasperated sigh. "It was just a joke, Maverick, a loophole so I wouldn't lose at truth or dare."

"Still, you made such a big deal out of it and it made me want to be the first." He leaned in closer to me, placing emphasis on his next words, "*I'd get used to it if I were you.*"

"Get used to what?" I was confused, watching humor play at his eyes, and knew that I was missing something.

"Get used to me being *the first.*"

The corner of my mouth twisted up in a half smile as I remembered that first night I was alone with Maverick in the truck, and I spoke those very words. I remembered how I felt, embarrassed at my candor, but unable to regret speaking the words. Because I knew they were true—I wanted to be Maverick Mason's first everything; and now he was telling me the same.

I glanced over at the clock and it read 9:00 p.m. I was suddenly so fatigued I couldn't even partake in our endearing banter one second longer. I could barely keep my eyes open. Although my headaches were getting better, I still hadn't fully recovered from the wreck. Maverick knew what I needed before I even asked. He stood and turned off the light then crawled into the bed next to me, pulling me toward his chest gently. I rolled toward him and he kissed my forehead tenderly—three times. I breathed him in and a feeling of complete and utter peace enveloped me. When I was with him, everything in the world was right. He made me forget all my pain; all my loss; all my fear; and all my nightmares. I closed my eyes and gave into the serenity of being exactly where I belonged, even if it was for but a moment.

I was with Maverick and we were walking down an idyllic pathway on the back of the Mason property. It was fall; I knew because the trees were shaded in deep colors of burgundy and magenta and fallen leaves were peppering the ground that we walked on. Maverick stopped and put a gorgeous heart-shaped necklace around my neck then kissed me on my lips, three times. My heart was content as we walked hand in hand down the pathway lined with massive, colorful oak trees.

As time went by and we continued our walk, I noticed the trees were no longer colorful. My feelings of peace began to dissipate and with each step we took, there were fewer leaves on the trees. I looked up; dark storm clouds were slowly obscuring the sky. We finally reached the end of the path and I glanced around in horror, realizing that I no longer even knew where I was.

I ripped my hand from Maverick's, no longer feeling safe, and I turned to see that he wasn't there. Standing next to me was a faceless man. He was much smaller than Maverick—only a few inches taller than me—and he wore a grey, tailored suit.

Fear gripped my body, making it impossible to move. I screamed as he reached out for me—his long skinny fingers clawing at the necklace I wore around my neck—then I thrust myself away from his grasp and ran in the opposite direction. I ran down a long, menacing, familiar dirt road. It was pitch black but I sensed the man was chasing me, only a few steps behind as always. I stumbled and fell. His hands wrapped around my neck. They clawed at me, desperately searching for something, until he grasped what it was he was looking for— the heart-shaped necklace. I fought him. I struggled and kicked and tried to push his hands away from my neck as I screamed out into the night, the name of the one person who could save me.

"Maverick!"

"Elle?" I heard him calling my name but it seemed distant as if in a dream. My head throbbed and the pain forced me to sit up. I looked around, confused, then I saw that the clock said midnight.

I'm in my hospital bed. I'm not in that nightmare.

Maverick was in my bed, holding me. My face flushed, burning with heat, at the realization he experienced one of my nightmares. I looked up at him—vulnerability in my eyes— terrified that he would want to run away when he saw my brokenness.

Please don't leave me alone.

He grabbed me and wrapped me up in his strong arms, relieving my anxiety instantly with his touch.

"I'm here Elle. I'm here," he consoled. "I'll always be here." His words of assurance were exactly what I needed to hear. We sat like that for several minutes—me in his arms as he comforted me with his presence and his words—until I finally pulled away.

"What did you hear?" I asked him.

"I just woke up when you started screaming my name. What happened?" His eyes pleaded with me to divulge the details of my nightmare but I struggled to find the words.

"Elle, please tell me," he begged with his blue eyes for me to confide in him.

"I had a nightmare," I said with reservation.

"What was it about?"

I hesitated. *He'll think you're crazy.*

"Elle, you can tell me."

As usual, our connection allowed him to hear my unspoken thoughts and fears. He looked at me with tenderness, begging me to continue. I took a deep breath and closed my eyes, resolved to do the unthinkable.

"We were walking on a pathway on your property. It was a gorgeous fall day and you gave me a heart-shaped necklace. You put it around my neck." My eyes darted away from his face as I divulged that detail of the dream. "We were walking down the path and it started getting dark. I turned around and you weren't with me. I was with a different man but I couldn't see his face; it was the man with no face who is always there in my nightmares, the man who killed my mom. I ran away but he chased me and when he caught me, he attacked me and tried to rip the necklace you had given me off my neck."

He paused, taking in all the information. "What does it mean?" he finally asked.

"I don't know," I said with exhaustion. "I never know what they mean."

"What was with the necklace?" He seemed agitated.

"I told you I have no idea." I matched his tone, frustrated with his continued questions that I didn't have the answers to.

"Well, who was that guy chasing you?"

"Maverick. *I don't know.* I've been having these nightmares since I was eleven years old and I've never made any sense of them. There's a man in my dreams sometimes but I can't ever see his face. I have no idea who he is."

Maverick pushed me aside gently as he stood up from the hospital bed.

Great. He's leaving because you're crazy and screwed up.

My heart hurt as I watched him walk away. He moved toward the bag he carried into my hospital room. He pulled out a black folder, then he made his way back to the bed and sat down beside me.

"Before I show you this, I need you to promise me something." The urgency in his voice frightened me. I nodded. "I need you to promise me that no matter what happens—no matter what we find out or where it leads us—that you will never put yourself in harm's way again." He grabbed me with a force that startled me. He repositioned my body easily with his strong arms, as if I were a little rag doll, and pulled me so closely to him that I was almost sitting on his lap. "I need your word that you will always tell me everything, so that I can protect you. I need you to promise me that you will let me help you and you won't try to do things on your own." I could hear the desperation in his words and I realized we shared the same greatest fear—losing each other—but there seemed to be something more behind the terror in his eyes. "Promise me," he pleaded.

"I promise."

Liar.

I silenced the unwanted voice in my head and focused on Maverick's blue eyes. "I promise Maverick." I reached up to caress his beautiful face to assure him.

He was apprehensive, as if he heard that voice whispering too. I couldn't look him in the eyes, so I scooted closer to him and repeated my promise again.

"Maverick, I promise. I'll tell you everything and let you help me."

Finally, he accepted my words, then he reached over, grabbed the mysterious black folder, and opened it. Tucked neatly inside was page after page of newspaper articles, pictures, pieces of paper with hand-scribbled notes, and magazine clippings. As I flipped through the information in the black folder, I landed on a small square picture that held my attention. It was an old black-and-white photograph, so worn that the edges of the picture were frayed. I saw something I recognized.

The wooden box.

A dark wooden square sat in the hands of a beautiful young woman with thick hair hanging to her waist in a sheet of long ebony silk. She had eyes the color of black coal and beautiful dimples etched into her cheeks. Beside her stood a handsome man who looked to be somewhat older than her. He had on a suit jacket, a vest, and a tie, and he wore his dark hair slicked back from his face. He didn't smile though she did.

I was drawn to the captivating young beauty in the picture. Her smile seemed familiar. Though I'd never seen her before in my life, somehow I knew her. I leaned into the picture and examined it more closely; it was then that I realized the young beauty wore something around her neck—a beautiful heart-shaped necklace. It was undoubtedly the same necklace I had just worn in my nightmare.

CHAPTER 16

I continued to stare at the information in the black folder—and as I did, the fire within began to burn.

"What is all this?" I pushed the folder angrily toward Maverick.

He looked at me—obviously confused by my anger.

"I mean how do I even know I can trust you? Where did you get all this crazy information from? Now that I think of it, why were you even there at the reservation that night?"

I was completely out of control and a familiar and unwanted constriction pulled at my throat. I gasped for breath but no matter how hard I tried, I seemed incapable of forcing air into my lungs. I looked at him in desperation, grasping my throat and struggling for each breath.

He moved toward me slowly and scooped me up easily with one arm, then he held me firmly but gently, until I quit struggling to breathe and my gasps turned into soft sobs. I didn't need him to speak; we didn't need words. I knew what he was telling me with his presence—that he was there and he always would be; that I could show him my nightmares and my panic attacks and my anger and my scars and my fears and he wouldn't run away—he would still be there for me. As he held me in his arms, he communicated one word to me, without ever speaking it: unconditional.

I fell asleep in his arms and when I woke up the black folder was missing from the bed as well as any sign of my temper tantrum and subsequent anxiety attack. I knew Maverick was there; I could feel him. I looked around to find him asleep in the chair next to the bed as I noticed the first signs of the sun beginning to peek through the window of my hospital room.

He stayed the night? My dad is going to kill me.

"Maverick wake up. You have to leave!"

He sat up, seemingly unaffected by the urgency in my voice.

"Elle, your dad knows I stayed the night," he said calmly, with sleep still in his voice.

My jaw must have hit the floor. "What?" I was so shocked that I was incapable of forming any other words.

"Your dad called late last night after you—"

I looked away, knowing what he was going to say.

"After you *fell asleep.*" He changed his words and didn't mention my anxiety attack, causing me to look up and give him a sweet smile of gratitude.

"I can't believe he was OK with you staying with me." I was still in shock.

"Well he didn't have much of a choice. He insisted on trying to fix the church van even though they said it was totaled after your wreck. It broke down when he tried to drive it home and he he had to get it towed back to Cordelia's place."

"Total shocker the Brookville Church of God broke down."

We both broke into laughter at my caustic comment.

"I mean seriously, this is going down in the history books for me—the day my overbearing, rule-obsessed overprotective father allowed a boy to stay the night with me. I never thought

I'd see the day when he would let me be alone in the presence of a boy, much less stay the night with one."

"Well, I'm not just *any boy*," Maverick said with that confident, pushing-the-limits-of-cockiness shine in his eye.

"No, you are definitely not just *any boy*, Maverick Mason."

I gave myself a moment to appreciate him, sitting in the recliner by the window, with the soft morning light streaming through the window to highlight his beauty in an almost angelic way. He was gorgeous in that ruggedly handsome meets all-American boy type of way. He was strong yet gentle. He was quiet but confident. He was self-assured yet humble. He was controlling but caring. He was everything, and he was mine. He saw me staring at him and that lopsided half grin spread across his face. He winked at me and the fire inside of me burned, but in that new foreign way that only he seemed able to evoke.

"Well *good morning to you too*, Baby Girl. See something you like?" Apparently, desire was evident in my gaze. I couldn't help but smile.

"You know most girls would take offense to their boyfriend calling them *Baby Girl*."

He paused and uncertainty washed over me as I realized what I had said. *Idiot.*

"Well you are most definitely *not* just any girl, Elle Christiansen," Maverick teased. I let out a sigh of relief when thankfully, he seemed unfazed by the mention of the word "boyfriend".

In our unspoken form of communication, I could read what was beneath his words. I had shown him every side of me—the uncontrollable fire that burned inside, the temper, the panic and anxiety, the fear, the scars, the nightmares, the defiance and lack of reason—and yet, he was still there right beside me. Not only was he still there, but he seemed to be telling me with those piercing blue eyes of his, that he loved what he saw.

I looked away, uncomfortable from the intensity of his gaze and the next thing I knew Maverick was on top of me in one swift moment, pinning me to the bed and smiling at me with a grin that made me laugh uncontrollably.

"Maverick, what are you doing? I'm injured."

"You look just fine to me. *More* than just fine actually." He brushed one of my dark locks away from my face, his eyes burning into mine with desire. Then, he lowered his body slowly toward mine and as he did, the mood shifted. The laughter stopped and the magnitude of my need for him took my breath away. He moved until the muscles of his abs brushed against my body, then he hovered over me as we stared at each other, each of us begging the other with our eyes and our bodies to give in, to stop fighting that magnetic force that was calling us to connect. I couldn't resist the urge to touch him. I moved my hand and touched his chest, then let it travel down his abs—feeling each indentation from the muscles hiding beneath his shirt. I rested my hand on his belt buckle. Our breathing was labored. We were so close, all it would take was one of us moving an inch.

Kiss me.

But he didn't. His willpower remained intact as he pushed himself forward and kissed my injured forehead, then moved down—ever so slowly—and kissed the tip of my nose, then another purposeful movement and he was positioned right over my lips. I held my breath and waited anxiously, anticipating the feeling of his beautiful lips on mine. But again, it never came.

"No, Elle Christiansen, you are most definitely *not* like other girls," Maverick said as he nudged my face to the side so he could kiss my cheek. "But you're *my* girl." He whispered the words into my ear, speaking them emphatically—almost possessively—and my heart erupted with happiness, a triumphant smile spreading across my face.

I was speechless. I just looked up at him, holding his gaze, and let sweet surrender wash over me. *I'm your girl, Maverick Mason. Forever.*

Maverick's phone beeped several minutes later and interrupted our peaceful embrace. He pulled his phone out of his back pocket and looked at the screen.

"It's your dad. He's on his way here, and I have to get to school. We don't have much time." He pushed himself to a sitting position and looked at me with concern. "Elle, we have to talk about that night on the reservation and I need you to stay calm."

I nodded my head decisively. "I'm ready."

He moved toward his bag and grabbed the folder and a fancy laptop that I realized was his personal computer.

"We only have a little bit of time before your dad gets here so we have to be quick." He handed me the black folder again. I felt like we were in a business meeting and he was my boss which annoyed me, but I played along. "You need to read all of this information from front to back and we can talk about it later today when I come back to see you." He paused to look at me, making sure I was comprehending his request. "Elle?" I nodded my head yes. "It's the history of the abandoned Osage reservation. Read it carefully and I want you to take notes and write down anything that stands out to you with this—" He reached into the bag and handed me a shiny gold rectangle and a keyboard that apparently went with it. I stared at the electronic device he had just given me, dumbfounded.

"What's this?"

He stared me down with his authoritative glare. "Looks like an iPad with a keyboard to me." His tone was sarcastic, but I also detected a warning. "You have your own email account set up and all the newest software and apps. I also downloaded some music and books for you," he added.

"Are you serious right now Maverick? You can't just go around buying me iPads."

"Yes, I can," he said definitively, "and you'll take it and say thank you, because its *rude* not to accept a gift." He paused—staring me down—daring me to challenge him.

The fire started to burn within. I crossed my arms defiantly, but he didn't seem to heed my non-verbal cues.

"I want you to have this too." He reached into his bag and pulled out another electronic device that I knew well but had never owned, an obnoxiously large iPhone with a gold finish that matched the iPad he had already given me. I started to open my mouth in protest but he shot me a warning glance, silencing me again. He seemed pained, and the look in his eyes took my breath away, rendering me speechless.

"Please Elle, just take these, for me." He was no longer controlling and commanding, but vulnerable. He was begging me with his eyes, pleading me to understand his request, and I knew that I would do anything he asked when he looked at me like that. "I need to know you are safe after what I saw that night on the reservation." He shook his head as if trying to rid himself of some terrible nightmare. "Holding your head in my lap while you were bleeding and unconscious, not knowing if you would make it—" His eyes were so full of agony. I wanted to grab him and comfort him. I scooted my body closer to his and took his hand. "If something ever happened to you…" he trailed off and didn't finish his words; but there was no need. My heart was already softened by his confession. I reached up

176

and touched his face, cradling his chiseled jawline gently in my hand.

"Maverick, this is all overwhelming to me. I've never been given gifts like this before and it makes me uncomfortable. I don't know how to accept them. I mean, it's just awkward…"

"What's awkward about it?" He looked perplexed.

Ugh. We are from such different worlds. How do I explain this to him?

"You know—" I couldn't find the words to describe how I was feeling.

"What?" He pushed me for an explanation.

"You know, just us barely knowing each other, and you buying me these expensive gifts and…" I trailed off, not wanting to say the last part of what I was thinking for some reason.

"And what, Elle?" I could tell he wasn't going to drop it.

"And it's just awkward, using your dad's money to buy me expensive gifts, Maverick." I put my hands on my hips to really drive my point home. "I don't care how rich your dad is. That's not normal to buy a girl you just met iPad's and iPhones."

"So I guess that's what you think of me? That I use my daddy's credit card for everything?" Clearly he was wounded by my words. I immediately regretted what I'd said to him.

"I'm sorry. I just assumed that—"

He interrupted me. "Well don't assume Elle."

"I'm sorry Maverick, I didn't mean to offend you. There's just so much we don't know about each other I guess."

He softened, reaching up to caress my cheek. "Well how about we get to know each other better, and we ask questions and learn and don't make assumptions about each other? I know we're from different worlds but that's what I love about us.

Opposites attract right?" He winked and I melted. *He just said that's what I love about us.* My insides were doing somersaults.

"This is all just new and I'm scared. I don't understand any of this—" I trailed off, unable to speak the words that I was feeling. Instead, I motioned back and forth between the two of us and looked into his eyes, hoping that he would understand what was unspoken—that it wasn't the black SUV or the nightmares or even the man with no face that I feared the most. What was most terrifying of all, to me, was the depth of the emotions I was feeling for him. Craving his touch and affirmation, I pushed my body into his and lay my head on his massive shoulder.

"So how about I go first—Elle, I have my own money that has nothing to do with my dad, OK?" I was relieved to hear him address me with gentleness in his tone again. "Please don't insult me again by not accepting something that I give you or insinuating that my dad bought it." His words were soft, but demanding. I nodded my head. I could tell he meant business and didn't want to fight.

What does he mean he has his own money? I pushed my curiosity away, knowing it wasn't the time to press the matter.

"Like I said, I'm sorry I offended you, Maverick. I mean, trust me when I say I've never been in this situation before. Buying brand new iPads and iPhones for girlfriends really isn't the norm in Brookville. We don't even have an Apple store for God's sake." I tried to force the conversation to a more lighthearted mood, but it didn't seem to be working.

"It's not the norm in Tulsa either, Elle. We are kind of dealing with some extenuating circumstances here."

"Exactly. So we'll figure this out together right?" His sullen mood was stifling.

When he didn't answer, I picked up the iPad and iPhone to illustrate that I was ready to meet him in the middle. "Thank you *so much* for my shiny, pretty, new, gold electronic devices, Maverick." I was being sarcastic, yes, but we also knew I was being truthful. "Your wish is my command, sir, so will you please tell me exactly what you would like me to do with these?" I held the two devices out to him, confessing my surrender. My knowledge of technology was limited—I had no clue how to operate an iPad or an iPhone.

Maverick showed me how the iPad worked with the keyboard then he demonstrated how I could create my own account in Google and login. I stared at him in awe. He was a technological wizard; I was technologically challenged—*opposites attract*. I chuckled at the thought.

"What?" His tutorial was interrupted by my laughter.

"Oh nothing, I guess I'm just sitting here wondering, is there anything you're not good at Maverick Mason?"

"Stick around Baby Girl, I've got a lot of things I can teach you."

He winked at me, then continued his crash course on my new fancy devices, though I really didn't hear a word he said. He was far too distracting. He went through the apps on my iPad and showed me a library full of music he'd downloaded for me.

Well that was really sweet of him.

I reached out and squeezed his hand.

"Thank you, Maverick, I really do appreciate this."

He nodded his head and continued. *He's so serious about all this.*

"Give me that," I grabbed the iPad from him playfully. I was tired of being so serious.

"Elle, we only have a few minutes. I have some stuff I have to show you." He was perturbed but it didn't stop me.

"I want to see what songs you downloaded for me."

"Just look at them when I leave."

Is he embarrassed? That's so un-Maverick Mason like. It made me want to continue pressing the issue.

"Nope I want to look at them now. Let's see..."

The first song I saw nearly took my breath away: "All of Me" by John Legend. I flashed back to that night in the truck, the first time Maverick and I were alone, when those melodic chords struck through the night. It was literally painful not to give into the magnetism drawing us toward one another in that moment. I looked at him, desire burning.

"I like that one."

He matched my gaze. "Me too."

"Let's see, what else is on here." I flipped through the music, shocked at how well he seemed to know my music preferences. "One Republic?! I love One Republic. How did you know?"

"Just a lucky guess. They're one of my favorite bands too. Did you know the lead singer is from Tulsa? I saw him perform at Cain's one time and it was so awesome."

"What's Cain's?"

"It's a famous ballroom in downtown Tulsa. Just a cool small venue that musicians play at. And I got to meet Ryan Tedder backstage. It was so cool."

"Of course you did." I deadpanned. "Just curious, do you ever think to yourself, *My life should be an episode of Lifestyles of the Rich and Famous?*"

He reached across and tickled me for mocking him. I slapped his hands away, wincing in slight pain.

"Watch the ribs, Top Gun. Remember? Near death experience, like, last week." I pointed to the wound on my head and cradled my ribs. He glanced away, pain etched on his face. I hated how he seemed to take personal responsibility for my accident. I needed to change the subject before I lost him.

"Okay so tell me more about meeting Ryan Tedder. I would die to see One Republic in concert."

"You really are into music aren't you?" He seemed truly interested.

I looked away, reminiscing sadly. "I guess when everything seemed out of control, I could always lose myself when I would play. It made me forget. At least for a little bit."

He looked at me with pity. It made me uncomfortable. I hated when people looked at me like I was broken. I changed the subject again.

"So if you're lucky I'll play a One Republic song for you some day. I have several favorites from their new album. But only if you're lucky." I nudged him with my shoulder.

"I don't know. I've been feeling pretty lucky lately." His eyes smoldered, and I knew what he was implying. He stole another glance before he turned back to the iPad, all business yet again. Maverick opened a Google document for me and showed me where to type notes as I read through the information in the black folder.

"So, the last chief before the reservation was abandoned was this guy—" His tone was serious. I forced myself to pay attention.

He pointed to a picture of a tall, statuesque man standing beside a fire in the middle of the reservation. He wore a magnificent feather headdress that highlighted his dark skin and high cheekbones, giving the overall impression of regality. I couldn't tear my eyes from the chief.

"His name was Chief Joseph Blackwater," I heard Maverick say.

I knew he was still speaking—highlighting the areas he deemed important in the black folder he had provided me with—but I was not giving him my full attention. I was enthralled by the pictures of the reservation before it had been abandoned. Beautiful dark-skinned children with shiny black hair stood in front of a school house. Energetic young women in long camel-colored dresses danced in front of the largest fire I had ever seen in my life. I also saw several more pictures of Chief Joseph Blackwater, always in the same headdress and always commanding the undivided attention and respect of his people.

I continued to flip through the pictures until a specific black-and-white polaroid caught my eye. I stopped on it. The chief was in the center of the picture and he had his arms lovingly around two people—a strikingly handsome man in a suit on the left, and on the right, a breathtaking young woman. Her hair was jet black as the darkest starless night and her eyes were the color of coal; but what gripped me more than anything was her captivating smile. She had two dimples that stretched across her face and there was something about her that left me spellbound.

Chief Blackwater, the intriguing young beauty, and the man in the suit, all stood on the threshold of a small, wooden small house and although the pictures were in black and white, I intuitively knew the color of the house they stood in front of—it was yellow. I was finding it difficult to breathe as I looked at the pictures and an ominous premonition overcame me.

"Elle, you have to breathe. You have to stay with me." Maverick's touch brought me back to the present. I turned my head from the pictures and took three deep breaths then blew the air out slowly, willing myself not to panic again.

"Why are you showing me all of this?" I was so confused.

"Elle, I think your mom was murdered for a reason."

What did he just say?

"Elle, are you listening to me? We have to find out what happened to your mom or I'm afraid that you'll be next."

I couldn't speak. My mind reeled, repeating the same words over in my head, trying to process them unsuccessfully—*your mom was murdered for a reason.*

With those final words, he buried his head on my lap. Fear permeated my soul as I realized that I wanted to be with Maverick Mason forever, but the magnetic force that bound us together—as strong as it was—would perhaps not be enough against the darkness that chased me.

CHAPTER 17

Maverick took the black folder from me and stashed it on the table beside my hospital bed when he heard my dad talking to the nurses outside my room. I reached for the cell phone and iPad and tried to hide them in the drawer as well.

Maverick looked at me suspiciously.

"I don't want my dad to see these," I admitted.

"Let me handle this, Elle."

"Maverick, please don't. You don't know what my dad's like. He will *not* be OK with this."

"Elle, I got this. Trust me." He disappeared into the hall for several minutes which seemed like an eternity to me. When I could take it no longer, I hopped out of my bed and tiptoed to the door where I could eavesdrop.

"Yes sir, I understand," I heard Maverick say. "It must have been so hard for you too that night and I know her safety is the most important thing to both of us."

There was a long pause then I heard my dad's voice, broken with emotion.

"I almost lost her Maverick, just like I lost her mother." I couldn't believe what I was hearing. My dad never mentioned my mother to anyone, and now he was opening up to my boyfriend? I found myself wondering what power Maverick possessed that he was able to get not only me, but my father as well, to open up after years of closing ourselves off to the world.

"Mr. Christiansen, Elle told me about her mother—"

"She did?" my dad interrupted Maverick, shock evident in his voice.

"Yes sir, she told me everything."

There was another long pause then I heard my dad's voice, again marked with emotion.

"I'm so glad she told you. She hasn't talked to anyone about losing her mom, not since she was a little girl."

I'm sorry, Dad. I didn't know how to talk to you after she was gone. I'm sorry I shut you out.

"Well I think she's ready now sir. Maybe the two of you could talk?" Maverick posed it as a question but I knew him better than that. He wasn't asking, he was telling my father it was time for him to talk to me about what happened to my mom.

"Yes, I think we should."

I heard movement outside my door so I ran back to my bed before I was caught eavesdropping on their conversation. My dad and Maverick walked through the door just as I made my way back into my hospital bed.

"So, good news," my dad proclaimed with a smile on his face. "The doctors said today is the day."

"Thank God," I said. "I'm so ready to get out of here."

"I have to head to school," Maverick told us. "If you guys need anything just let me know." He glanced at me with his most authoritative glare. "Text me as soon as you leave the hospital and when you get home, Elle." He didn't even bother to say please. *He's infuriatingly bossy.* My response to his demand was nothing but a glare.

He leaned over and gave me three sweet kisses on my forehead and as he pulled away I heard him whisper in my ear, "Don't forget your homework." I nodded my head then watched Maverick shake my dad's hand and walk out the door. I hated watching him go.

When I looked up my dad was watching me with curiosity. He could tell that I was different; that something inside of me had shifted; and that the change in me had everything to do with the mysterious Maverick Mason. My dad wanted to ask me about him—it was obvious—so I changed the subject before he had the chance.

"Dad, would you tell me about how you and Mom met?" He stopped dead in his tracks then turned slowly, a look of pain plastered on his face.

"Sure Elle. Anything you want to know." Apparently the conversation with Maverick had been influential after all.

I sat in silence for a minute, pondering how in a matter of weeks my world had been turned upside down; and although it was chaotic and frightening and utterly disorienting, somehow everything that was happening felt right—especially this conversation that was finally taking place between my dad and me. He leaned backwards in his chair and pushed back on one leg, then crossed his arms behind his head and assumed his storytelling position. I listened, enthralled, as he purged himself of decades full of memories that I never even knew existed.

"I met your mom my first week of seminary. I went to the library to meet my study group and when I walked in, my eyes caught the new girl that was working behind the desk. She was captivating, and I couldn't take my eyes off her the entire night." The look in his eyes made me slightly uncomfortable, like I was infringing on a deeply personal moment; but I wanted him to continue so I said nothing. "I watched her for nearly three hours then finally got the courage to go ask her out. She told me no." He chuckled to himself at the memory. "I was relentless though. I came back to the library every single night and every night, I asked her to go to dinner with me. She still said no; but one night when I asked her if I could walk her home after work, she finally said yes."

I was captivated as my dad described how he walked my mother across campus—enchanted by her smile and her laugh and every word that she spoke—until finally they stopped at a tiny efficiency apartment one street over from the campus.

"Elle, when she opened the door I saw that she had nothing." He said it as if he were still appalled at the thought. "She had a sleeping bag on the floor and no other furniture".

My dad was lost in a sea of emotions. A mixture of happiness and love, but also extreme sadness and pain, coexisted on his face as he continued to tell his love story—the one I knew ended in tragedy.

"Your mother was only seventeen years old when I met her and I asked her to marry me after only three weeks of dating." He revised his statement. "Well I guess I should say that I begged her to marry me. It was too fast and we were way too young...and I knew she didn't even love me yet."

What? Mom didn't even love him when he asked her to marry him? I was caught off guard by his statement, disturbed by the honesty of it.

"But I knew I loved her enough for the both of us and the rest would come in time," he said as a smile spread across his face. "I knew she would fall in love with me once she let that wall of hers down. I knew I could protect her and keep her safe and never let her get hurt again and I knew she would love me one day, if for no other reason than loving me for how much I loved her..."

"What do you mean you would never let her get hurt again dad?"

He looked disoriented as I awakened him from his private walk down memory lane with my question.

"I'm talking about your mom's accident."

I was thoroughly confused. "You mean the night she died?"

"No, Elle."

"Dad, what you are talking about?" He could sense my agitation.

"Well she never wanted you to know. She didn't want it to upset you." He seemed indecisive, like he didn't know if it was OK to tell me or not.

"Dad, I understand you didn't want to tell me when I was little but I'm not a kid anymore," I pushed back.

"I don't know. She never wanted me to tell you."

I reached out my hand to him. "Dad, look at me." He looked up, uncertainty and pain evident in his eyes. *"She isn't here.* It's just us, just you and me. And I'm asking you to tell me everything. I need to know." I tried not to sound too desperate but in actuality, I was. I needed more details of my mom's story— all the details—in hopes that somewhere in her story I would find the clues that I needed to unlock the secrets to not only her past, but mine as well.

My dad finally submitted. "A few weeks before I met her, your mother was found on the side of a road a few miles outside of town. Some students who were hiking found her badly injured and unconscious and took her to the hospital. She had severe amnesia and couldn't even remember her name. One of the nurses finally realized her name was Eleanor—she found it written on the back of a picture in the necklace she wore around her neck."

The necklace I always saw her wearing? I made a mental note to ask my dad more about that necklace. A stirring in my spirit told me I needed to know more…

"After your mother left the hospital, one of the local pastors helped her get into an efficiency and found her a job at the library. I met her the day she started her new job and we were married exactly one month after her accident." He shook his head in disbelief. "I look back and realize how rash everything seems—us getting married so quickly—so soon after an accident and without her knowing who she was, but I loved her so much, Elle."

He looked up at me, pleading with me to understand and although I was angry that so much had been hidden from me, the sadness and pain reflected in his eyes made it impossible for me to stay mad at him.

"I asked her over and over to marry me and finally one day she said yes. She said who she was in the past didn't matter because her future was with me. We went to the courthouse that day. She took my last name, and we never spoke about the past again." When he raised his head I saw a lone tear slide down his cheek and I wanted to reach out to comfort him, but after years of us both shutting the other out emotionally, the action felt foreign and uncomfortable so instead I kept my hands placed stoically on my lap, waiting anxiously for his next words.

"I know it was selfish. Please forgive me, Elle. I wanted her so badly for myself that I allowed her to not even address her past. I allowed her to let me be her only family instead of searching for hers. I wanted her all to myself and then I lost her." He put his head in his hands and rocked back and forth, attempting to console himself unsuccessfully.

My heart hurt watching my father—so broken, so vulnerable, so lost having to live without the love of his life. I stood and walked toward him and sat my hand on his back lovingly. I said nothing. I just sat there until he was done, my hand firmly on his back, until he wiped his face and stood up from his place of mourning.

"Please forgive me, Elle. I shouldn't have kept the truth from you for so long." With that final admission, we both looked at each other and nodded our heads in silent understanding, an unspoken agreement to leave our conversation in that hospital room and never speak of it again. I would never make him bear the pain of telling that story again. But before we walked out I asked him one last question.

"Dad, I remember Mom always wearing a heart-shaped necklace. Was that the same necklace she was wearing when they found her?"

"Yes," he answered. "She never took that necklace off. I think, in a way, it was her only connection to her past."

"Where's the necklace now?"

"When she died, we buried her with it." With those final words, he walked out of the room. I knew he could handle no more talk of his wife, the woman he had loved and lost—forever.

My mom was buried in the heart-shaped necklace that I saw in my dream. I wasn't sure what it meant, but I knew it was important—somehow.

I pulled out my shiny new gold iPad. I quickly opened a Google Docs like Maverick had shown me and typed down the highlights of my dad's revelations.

- Mom's body found washed up by river in Ohio;
  she was wearing a necklace when they found her

with a picture that had her name written on the back—the heart-shaped necklace from my dream. She was buried with it on.

- Hospitalized. Had severe amnesia when she woke up.
- Mom and Dad married quickly.
- Mom said she didn't want to look into her past.

I closed my iPad, exhausted, and needing a distraction. I immediately perked up when I glanced down and saw my new iPhone. *I can FaceTime with Grace and Charlie now that I have an iPhone!* My heart ached with longing for my childhood best friends. We had talked a few times since I moved but our schedules always seemed to be off, and we had been playing phone tag for what seemed like eternity. I missed them so much it hurt.

I picked up the phone and dialed Grace's phone number—I knew it by heart. She picked up on the second ring. When I saw her face, I was overcome with happiness and also, crushing loneliness at the same time.

"Elle, is that you? OMG did you get an *iPhone*?" I saw the shock on her face and couldn't hold back my laughter.

"Hi Grace! Yes, I have an iPhone now."

"What?! Johnny C bought you an iPhone?" I laughed at her use of my dad's nickname—Johnny C. She and Charlie had called him that since we were kids. She leaned into the phone, her face so close to the screen I couldn't even make out her features anymore. "Wait, is that the *new* iPhone? What in the heck did you guys win the lottery or something?"

"Yes, Grace, it's the new iPhone and no, Johnny C definitely didn't buy it for me. I mean c'mon, you know him better than that."

"Well, then who did because I know you didn't buy it."

I acted offended. "Why would you say that?"

"Oh I don't know. Maybe because never in a million years if you had that kind of money would you choose to spend it on an electronic device."

It was scary how well she knew me.

"True." I laughed. "So how have things been in Brookvville? What's the latest gossip?"

She wasn't letting me off that easy.

"Where'd you get the cell phone, Elle?"

I paused. Even though I couldn't see her body I knew her hand was on her hip. She wasn't letting me change the subject.

"My boyfriend bought it for me, OK?" I held my breath, waiting for the onslaught I knew was coming.

She shrieked so loud it hurt my ears. I rolled my eyes in response and listened as she rapid-fired questions in my direction about Maverick. I couldn't help but smile at her excitement. She had always been boy crazy.

"Well you just asked me seventy-two questions and there is no way I can remember them all but his name is Maverick. He's a senior too at the school I go to—Heritage Hall Preparatory Academy, and actually, he lives in the house up the hill from my aunt and I guess she—um—was his nanny when he was growing up."

Her eyes were so wide I thought they would pop out of her head. For once, I rendered Grace speechless, which was not an easy task.

"I know, when I say it all in one sentence like that, it sounds absolutely crazy." *Because it is crazy.* I pushed the unwelcome voice in my head away.

"Wait a minute, where are you by the way?" Grace suddenly realized the surroundings in the background.

"I'm in a hospital."

"What?" She looked terrified.

"I just got in a little accident. Everything is OK."

"Just got in a little accident? Elle, you are really freaking me out."

"Listen, everything is OK Grace, I promise."

Liar. I silenced the voice inside my head. I had always been protective of Grace. It was my job to make sure no one ever hurt her, even if that meant protecting her from the demons in my own life.

"I don't believe you, Elle!" She was starting to panic. I went into full-scale recovery mode. I knew just how to distract her.

"Grace, I promise. Everything is great here and it was just a minor accident. I got to miss some school and you know how I love that. But seriously, I'm just totally bored here and need you to distract me. Tell me about who you are crushing on these days."

She looked skeptical but I knew she wanted to give in. If there was one thing Grace couldn't resist, it was being asked about who her latest crush was. I watched her start to relent, and I was relieved. Grace couldn't know about all the darkness in my life. I had to protect her from it all, just like I always did.

I listened to Grace tell me about her latest crush—Dawson Williams—and we caught up on Charlie and all the latest Brookville gossip, until a knock on the door interrupted us.

"Someone's here. I gotta run."

"Wait! Is it Maverick? Let me talk to him. I want to meet him!"

"Grace I gotta go. I miss you so much and I'll call you soon. Tell Charlie hi for me!"

"Elle!"

The desperation in her voice stopped me from hanging up.

"I'm worried about Charlie. He hasn't been himself since you left."

My heart sank.

"Really? OK I will give him a call and check on him."

She looked relieved.

"That'd be great. I'm really worried and just don't know how to cheer him up."

I heard another knock at the door.

"Gotta go Grace! I'll talk to you soon and I'll give Charlie a call ASAP."

Just as I hung up, the door cracked open and I saw a dark curly mop of hair that I recognized well.

"Well there she is, Miss Midnight Escapee. Hey if you're going to sneak out and go on a cross-country excursion in the Brookville Church of God van, can we get a phone call next time so we can get in on all the excitement?"

Carly bounced through the door first, trailed by Madison, then Macey. But my breath caught—not in the good way—when I saw another face walk in behind them. It was Caleb. He glanced at me with uncertainty as he walked into the room, and I looked away, guilt overtaking me.

"Sorry to disappoint you but I have no more excursions planned as of now, especially since I totaled the Brookville Church of God van and will probably never be allowed behind the wheel of another vehicle again."

Madison walked up and sat beside me on the bed, concerned etched on her sweet face. "God, we've been so worried about you, Elle. Maverick's been keeping us updated but he told us we weren't allowed to come up here until you were strong enough for visitors."

Another twinge of guilt gripped me at the mention of Maverick's name. I resisted the urge to glance over at Caleb.

"Ugh he's so bossy. How do you handle it?" Carly interjected dramatically, twisting a lock of her curly hair around her finger.

I was mortified and shooting them all looks of death as they continued to talk about Maverick in Caleb's presence. They didn't get the hint.

"Oh, I can think of about a million reasons she can handle it, starting with those washboard abs of his," Madison said dreamily, staring off into the distance as if she was envisioning Maverick standing in the room. I cut my eyes toward her with warning, annoyed at her daydreaming about my boyfriend.

"So what's been going on at school you guys?" I changed the subject quickly.

"Really you're the main topic of convo these days. Heritage Hall has definitely never had a student sneak out in the middle of the night, wreck a church van, then land in the hospital for a week." Caleb finally entered the conversation and I was relieved, his comment seeming to break the unspoken tension between us. I tilted my head toward him and let a sweet smile play at my lips. I was trying to bridge the gap between us.

"Well that's definitely something I'm kind of used to unfortunately." Everyone laughed.

"Yeah you sure do know how to make an impression that's for sure." I heard what was unspoken in Caleb's words as the memory of us on the basketball courts together flooded into my mind, against my will. I pushed the thought away but not before I heard that nagging voice again. *You owe him an apology.*

We chatted and Carly, Madison, Macey, and Caleb caught me up on what I had missed at Heritage Hall during my hospital stay. I laughed and made small talk but guilt was consuming me. I had to make things right.

"Hey girls, would you mind going to check on my dad and ask if he's heard anything from the doctors yet?" I stared at them with purpose, willing them to read what was unspoken. *I need to be alone with Caleb.*

Of course, it was Macey who finally picked up on my cues; Carly and Madison were completely oblivious.

"Oh, sure we can do that." She stood up to walk out but Madison and Carly didn't follow. She grabbed Carly by the arm, "C'mon girls. *Let's go.*" Carly stood up with a huff and looked at her with confusion but fell in line when she saw the way Macey was looking at her. Madison got up and followed suit as well. Then finally, it was Caleb and me in the room together—alone.

He stood sheepishly by the door, his chestnut hair playing around his cautious eyes.

"So how've you been Elle?"

I preferred to skip the small talk.

"Hey Caleb, I've been wanting to talk to you."

"You have?" The hope in his eyes made my heart hurt.

"Yeah, I owe you an apology."

He didn't disagree.

"Look, you've been nothing but nice to me and I've been nothing but rude and insensitive to you. I just want to say I'm so sorry for that and if you can forgive me, I would love to be friends."

He looked up, sadness in his eyes and I wanted to hug him, but I knew that wouldn't help. He tried to cover his melancholy with a smile, but it didn't touch his eyes.

"Sure I can forgive you, and I appreciate the apology."

I dropped my head in shame. I was undeserving of his forgiveness and I knew it.

"If you can give me another chance I promise I can be a great friend."

Again, I saw him wince at the use of that word but I had to communicate that's all we were. The silence loomed between us as we both avoided the inevitable. It was him who finally spoke first.

"Look, Elle, Maverick talked to me about you guys."

My eyes widened in shock. *Maverick never told me he talked to Caleb about us.*

"He did?"

"Maverick's my best friend. He's been my best friend since we were little kids. We've been through *a lot* together." He stared off into the distance as he spoke and I saw pain in his eyes, something unspoken. "We're not going to let a girl come between us." He said it matter-of-factly, like the decision had already been made.

I let out an audible sigh. "Thank God, because I was feeling so terrible thinking I caused problems between the two of you. I would never forgive myself if I messed up your friendship somehow."

"He told me how he feels about you, Elle, and sure, I was pissed at him at first but when he explained…"

I interrupted him, desperate to learn more about Maverick's clandestine confession to Caleb.

"Explained what?"

He eyed me with caution, not falling for my line of questioning, much to my disappointment.

"Look, Maverick told me how he feels about you and I can see how you feel about him. What else is there for me to do but accept it and move on? So…" he walked toward me, hand held out in a peace offering. "Friends?"

I reached my hand toward him with a smile, resisting the urge to beg him to tell me what Maverick said about his feelings toward me. It was physically painful. I wanted to know so badly but I knew asking would only hurt Caleb further, so I didn't.

"Friends." We shook hands firmly.

"Well that's done then."

I nodded in agreement. "You're a good guy Caleb, and you deserve a great girl."

As if on cue Carly walked back into the room, shattering the moment between Caleb and me, for which I was thankful.

"We have good news, Elle!"

"We found your dad and the doctor is giving you clearance right now to go home," Madison interjected.

I sighed in relief. "Thank God. I'm so ready to get out of here."

Caleb said his goodbyes and the girls helped me pack up my belongings then left as well. I waited impatiently for my dad to come back with the wheelchair that I had to ride in to the car. I heard my new phone ding at me.

What's going on? I told you to text me.

I typed out my response. *Aren't you supposed to be at baseball practice? PS, you're being bossy and controlling again.*

The screen made a little signal at the bottom that I decided must indicate he was texting me back, then I saw the words pop up.

You love it when I boss you, Baby Girl. Admit it.

I was smiling from ear to ear, uncontrollable desire coursing through my body. I loved our endless banter, even when he was being annoying.

No, I don't. By the way, I think I'm going to get to leave the hospital tonight. I'm waiting on my dad to get back.

Awesome. Don't forget to text me when you leave OK? And when you get home too.

I sighed. He was so overprotective—yes, it was over the top and something told me even a bit unhealthy perhaps. I pushed that unwanted thought away though, unwilling to deal with it in that moment.

I sent him an OK emoticon.

That's my girl. See you soon.

I put my phone down on the bed and took a deep breath, falling back into my pillow. I was euphoric, and sometimes it was still difficult to grasp that *the* Maverick Mason wanted *me*. Finally, my dad came walking into the room pushing a wheelchair, interrupting my thoughts about Maverick.

"Your chariot awaits my dear." He gestured toward the wheelchair.

I laughed. "Remember that time Mom broke her leg and she refused to let you push her out of the Brookville hospital in the wheelchair?" The words spilled out before I could stop them and I realized my mistake—breeching our unspoken agreement. I was on pins and needles, waiting for my dad's response, begging him to meet me in the middle. Finally, he laughed and I sighed in relief. I had been holding my breath and didn't even realize it.

"Boy do I ever. She liked to kill me when I told her she had to ride in the wheelchair. That's just like her to refuse. She walked down two flights of stairs on those crutches just to prove to me she could do it without the wheelchair."

The nostalgia hung in the air between us, heavy with the pain of missing her. My dad reached down and lifted me into the wheelchair, lingering a bit too long when he sat me down. We both knew I could walk myself into the chair, but we welcomed the comfort from the contact. I smiled at him as he let go and deposited me in the chair. He leaned down and kissed the top of my head, mussing my hair as he pulled away.

"Love you, Ells." I saw the longing in his eyes and I wanted to return his sentiment. *Say it, Elle.* But I pushed the voice away, uncomfortable from years of shutting my father out, and unable to handle any more change in that moment.

My dad loaded me into my aunt's small car and we headed home. We had only been on the road for five minutes when I heard my new phone beep. I reached into my bag and saw a text from Maverick.

I told you to text me when you left the hospital.

I rolled my eyes as I typed a response. *I forgot. I was just hospitalized for concussion you know?* I typed an emoticon to make the text seem lighthearted but in actuality, his text concerned me. I could ignore the pit in my stomach no longer. I picked my phone up to shoot an accusatory text.

How did you know I left anyway???

He didn't respond so I shot out another text.

Stalker. Please tell me you aren't tracking my new cell phone somehow because that's totally creepy.

Finally, he responded.

Elle, I just need to know you're safe. I told you, I can't lose you.

I paused, not sure how to respond. Then I finally typed out two words.

Not OK.

I threw my phone down, vowing to talk to him about his control issues the next time I saw him. I knew he was concerned, overprotective even, but I had an unwelcome premonition that something far more was fueling Maverick's control issues, and it scared me for some reason.

CHAPTER 18

When we pulled onto the property of the Mason mansion that ever-present force was drawing me toward Maverick but I attempted to push it away; I knew I would have to wait to see him, though I didn't want to. My aunt prepared a homecoming meal for me and I needed to put in some face time with the family. Not to mention, I needed to talk to my aunt about my mom. She was the only person who could provide me with more insight into my mother's early years.

My aunt came rushing out when she heard the car pull up and I let her wrap her arms around me. She hurried me inside to sit down at the dinner table and enjoy the feast she made for me. We made small talk at the dinner table, but no one dared to speak of the events that happened the week before, for which I was grateful. I ate my meal and helped my aunt clean off the dinner table before stretching and telling everyone I needed to go back to my bedroom for a rest.

My aunt clearly didn't want to let me out of her sight. She ushered me back to my bedroom as if I were a glass china doll that could shatter into a million pieces at any moment, tucking me in and sitting down beside me on the bed; I recognized her concern as the opportunity I needed to ask my questions.

"Aunt Cordelia?"

"Yes sweetie?" she answered gently.

"Can you tell me about my mom?" I said the words softly, unsure of the answer I would receive but desperately hoping for a yes. Silence passed between us as she peered into my eyes, searching.

"You've been through a lot, Elle. We can talk about this later when you aren't so tired." I could tell she was avoiding the subject so I reached out and grabbed her hand, preventing her from walking out of the room.

"Please."

I wasn't afraid to beg. She continued to stare at me indecisively as I pushed myself forward to a seated position and stared into her eyes with hope.

"What do you want to know?" she asked.

Everything. But I knew I needed to start small.

"What was she like when she was younger?"

A slow smile spread across my aunt's face as she answered. "She was charismatic. She was fearless, strong, brave, and her smile lit up a room. I was so proud every day of my life, to be Eleanor's little sister."

I smiled at the description. It was exactly how I remembered her.

"Tell me more please, Aunt Cordelia."

She sighed and let out a deep breath—I held my breath as I sensed her reluctance—but thankfully, she eventually began her account of their childhood.

"Our mother was a proud full-blood Osage Indian. Her name was Margaret Smith and she grew up on the Osage Reservation in Oklahoma."

My grandmother grew up on the Osage Reservation that I went to? That cannot be a coincidence.

"Your Grandma Maggie lived there until she met your grandfather. His name was Henry Smith and she moved to

Virginia with him where they were married. That's where they raised us—your mother and I."

I wanted to ask my aunt so many questions about my grandmother, and the Reservation, but I knew I shouldn't interrupt her walk down memory lane.

"Our mother taught us well despite what others said about us being *uneducated half breeds*," she spat the words out vehemently and I knew her anger was directed at someone in specific, though I didn't know who. "She taught us reading, math, English, and history but she also taught us about our ancestors. She taught us the way of our people—how to find beauty in what surrounds us and how to heal from what nature gives us. She taught us what couldn't be taught by sitting in a desk in a classroom. She taught us the way of the Osage People."

I hung on her every word as my aunt gave a full account of a childhood with my mother, a childhood I never even knew my mother had. Eventually her tone changed and she began to speak about times of sadness—of their mother's untimely death and her dad's struggle to teach them and provide for them once she was gone.

"Not long after Mom died, our dad got a job offer to be head groundskeeper on an estate in Oklahoma—"

"—The Mason estate," I interrupted. She nodded without pause and something stirred inside of me again, a churning of moving pieces I did not fully understand.

"But back then the estate didn't belong to Mr. Mason," my aunt explained. "The owner offered my dad free housing—a small cottage we were able to live in if my dad would fix it up and do the work. And the job also offered tuition to a new private school that would be opening."

"Let me guess, Heritage Hall Academy?"

My aunt nodded her head indicating my suspicions were again correct, and the stirring inside continued, one more piece of the puzzle sliding into place, allowing me to recognize yet another connection between my mother's past and my present.

My mother went to Heritage Hall Academy too? This is getting so weird.

My aunt continued, interrupting my private thoughts. "To our dad, the offer was an answer to prayer in a time of sadness and loss. Me and your mom were reluctant to leave our home in Virginia but he assured us that moving back to Oklahoma was the answer to all our troubles." She looked off into the distance, a forlorn look in her eyes as she remembered the pain of a past I was making her relive. "We didn't even put up a fight really. We knew how sad he was with Momma gone. Our little house was so small, we could hear him cryin' himself to sleep every night." I saw her wipe a tear from her cheek. "The pain of losing his wife and the stress and worry of how he was going to provide for us was just too much for him. We knew he had no option but to take the job offer in Oklahoma."

I reached over and consoled her while I selfishly prayed that she wouldn't stop talking. After a small break, she continued.

"We finally made it to the cottage after a long two-day drive. The owner of the property—James Weston—sent his two sons to come welcome us because *he was too busy to come himself.*" I thought I detected a hint of hatred in her voice when she spoke of James Weston. "His sons were named Nathan and Philip. They stayed to help my dad move a few of our belongings out of our truck and into the cottage and I think they were both already madly in love with your mom by the time they left our cottage that night." She paused, looking out the window to collect herself before she continued. "It was

James Weston's youngest son, Nathan, that your mother began spending more and more time with though. They couldn't stay away from each other even though I begged her to stop seeing him. It was like they were connected by some unexplainable force. You could feel it when you were in a room with them. When they were together, it was like no one else existed but the two of them. They *couldn't* stay away from each other."

She paused and looked up at me, a mixture of fear and sadness in her eyes, and I knew she was trying to communicate so much more than she was saying.

Is she comparing what is going on with me and Maverick to what my mom felt for Nathan Weston?

I was uncomfortable at my aunt's unspoken insinuation. But as I searched my feelings, I realized what was upsetting me more than anything—that I knew how my mom's story ended and she didn't end up with the boy she had such an undeniable connection to—Nathan Weston. I shuddered at the thought as that snide little voice in my head began chirping in my ear again, telling me I wouldn't end up with Maverick either; that what we had was too all consuming and eventually it would self-destruct; that I was like Icarus flying too close to the sun, and eventually I would burn.

Your story with Maverick will end the same as your mother's did with Nathan. I shook my head then buried it in my hands.

"What happened to them Aunt Cordelia? What happened with my mom and Nathan?" I had to know, even though I didn't want to know at the same time.

"They secretly dated for two years. So madly in love they couldn't stay away from each other even though it was forbidden for them to be together. They'd meet in their secret spot—a massive old oak tree that sat on the back boundary of the Weston estate. Nathan would read Eleanor poems he wrote to her and your mother would sing to him. I followed her one time…" She looked into the distance, trailing off, and I knew she was transported to a different time, a time when her big sister was still living.

My aunt continued to paint a picture of forbidden love between a young, spirited daughter of a poor groundskeeper and a quiet, disciplined son of an affluent oil baron who was next in line to inherit a company that he didn't want to own.

"Nathan's dad —James Weston—refused to accept their relationship. In fact, he forbade them to be together. I could never understand it but he seemed to hate your mother the second he saw her." She shook her head as if she still couldn't understand it all these years later. "Everyone always loved your mom, Elle. Everyone. But for some reason when Nathan introduced Eleanor to his father, he was horrified. You should have seen the look on his face—like he had seen a ghost or something. It was so strange."

"Why in the world would he hate my mom?" I asked in complete shock.

"I don't know. We could never make sense of it. We were invited to the main house for dinner one night but James Weston just walked out of the room when Nathan introduced him to your mother, then our family was asked to leave before dinner even started. Nathan sent a note to our house later that night saying he was no longer allowed to see Eleanor. His father even had our scholarship removed from the school so that your mother couldn't go to Heritage Hall. It broke Nathan's heart—and your mother's. But they found a way to be together anyway. No one could keep them apart. Not even James Weston."

I was certain I heard hatred in her voice when she said his name this time. My aunt quit talking and looked out the window. She was in pain and my heart hurt for her, but I needed her to finish.

"Aunt Cordelia? Please tell me what happened to my mother and Nathan."

She took a deep breath and pressed on. "One day Eleanor and I came home and we heard our dad and Mr. Weston arguing so we snuck into the kitchen to listen. Mr. Weston was yelling at our dad—'Keep your *trashy daughter* away from my son or else I swear I'll kick you out of this damn house, Henry!' But I'll never forget what daddy said back—" She half-smiled, a slight glimmer in her eye as she recounted her dad's response— "'*I think you've got a few things backward here Mr. Weston. Your son would be the luckiest man alive if he had the honor of being with my Eleanor.*'"

My aunt continued recounting the details of that night as if in a dream. "I'll never forget what he said to my dad: 'My son is going to run WestCo Oil one day, Henry. He can't be with an uneducated, half breed. I would rather see him dead.'" I watched as a tear ran down her cheek. I reached out to comfort her.

"What happened, Aunt Cordelia?"

"My dad punched Mr. Weston in the face for calling us uneducated half breeds is what happened. Then Mr. Weston told my dad to be off his property in three days, or else he would have him thrown into jail. Eleanor and I snuck back to our bedroom and went to bed that night and when I woke up, your mom was gone. I never saw her again." The tears flowed freely down her face in a steady stream.

"I'm so sorry Aunt Cordelia."

"I should have known," she whimpered with agony. "I knew her better than anyone. I should have known she would do something drastic." I decided I needed to push my aunt for more information before she shut down from all the pain she was having to relive.

"What do you mean she ran away and you never saw her again?"

She lifted her hands from her head and wiped her tears away. "That next morning when I woke up I found a note she had slipped under my bed and I knew she was gone."

"What did the note say?" I asked.

She answered slowly, looking off into the distance as if she could see the actual letter in her mind. "Take care of Dad. Love you always, Eleanor.'"

"Aunt Cordelia, where do you think she went?" I was desperate for more information.

"I don't know. All I know is who she went with."

"Who?" I pressed.

"Nathan Weston of course."

"She ran away with Nathan?" I asked, almost in shock.

"Yes," she replied as if I should have expected that response. "They were so in love, Elle. They planned to be together forever, and since they knew his father would never allow that, they ran away together."

I couldn't assimilate the words. The person I grew up with—the mother I had always known—was a complete stranger. I was finding it difficult to reconcile the strong but demure preacher's wife who raised me with the fiery, passionate girl who would run away to be with a forbidden love. I pushed away the unwanted feelings I was experiencing and forced myself to continue asking my questions. I still needed answers.

"What happened to Nathan and my mom?"

"I don't know, Elle."

"What do you mean you don't know?" My words came out with an edge of unintended anger.

"Nathan's truck was found the next day in a river twenty minutes outside of town—" She paused, calculating her words, then looked me in my eyes before she spoke them. "He was dead."

I allowed the weight of her words to sink in as I processed that my mom had been in love with someone else before she met my dad—so in love that she ran away to be with him—and he died tragically, drowned at far too young an age at the bottom of a river. I had to know more.

"Well if Nathan died and my mom ran away with him then how did she end up in Ohio married to my dad?" I tried to remain calm as I asked for more information but I knew my aunt could tell I was disconcerted. She sat her hand on top of my leg, attempting to calm me.

"Elle, I don't have any answers. We were told that she wasn't with him that night, that she wasn't in his truck and he was found alone, already dead. But I know it was a lie." She shook her head adamantly. "I know she ran away with Nathan. She wouldn't have left without him." My aunt looked at me with desperation in her eyes, willing me to believe the words she spoke. I could tell it was a story that others did not believe.

I believe you even if no one else does.

I reached out my hand to her and nodded my head in acceptance. She was encouraged by my response to her story so she continued.

"James Weston was never the same. They said he lost his mind after Nathan died. He put his house up for sale and moved to a secluded mansion thirty minutes outside of town. He basically became a hermit. Your Grandfather Henry and I drove ourselves crazy trying to get to him. We went to his house every single day for months, but his security turned us away." She looked at me with unparalleled pain. "We only wanted answers. We knew that Eleanor and Nathan ran away together but they refused to acknowledge her or their relationship. We tried to get the police to listen. We begged them to get involved in our search and told them our theory of James Weston being involved but they just laughed at us." She was on the verge of sobbing as she continued. "We hounded the press, the police, anyone who would listen, and they treated us like we were crazy. They said she was obviously a runaway and there was nothing more they could do. No one would help us." She buried her head in her hands and cried.

"I'm so sorry, Aunt Cordelia." I knew my words could not touch her pain, but I said them anyway in hope of bringing her some sort of comfort.

"My dad lost his mind searching for her. He was arrested a little over a year after your mother ran away, caught breaking into Mr. Weston's residence, and he went to prison for breaking and entering." She hung her head in defeat and she spoke her next words. "He died in prison within the year."

My heart ached, realizing that the kind and patient woman sitting before me had lost her mother, her sister, and then her father, all in a short period of time. Without stopping to think, I wrapped my arms around her and hugged her while she cried. I was done asking questions. My aunt had told me all that I needed to know to start unraveling the mystery of my mother's death. All I wanted to do was make her pain go away.

I will fix all of this. I will make you happy again.

We held each other indefinitely, both comforting one another in the stillness of the night as gut-wrenching pain ripped through our souls. Finally, she released me quietly and placed a gentle kiss on the top of my head before she walked out of my room. As she grabbed the handle of my door she paused and turned around to look at me. I saw a faint tired smile on her lips.

"You're so much like her, Elle. I don't understand it all, but I thank God for bringing you to me after all these years."

I watched as a lone tear made its way slowly down her face, then she walked out of my room and shut the door, leaving me to reflect on the memories of a hidden past that had come to light—a past that somehow held the keys to unlocking the mystery of my mother's murder which was perhaps my only hope at having a future.

CHAPTER 19

I was walking down a long hallway at my dad's old church in Ohio. Light permeated through a small crack in a wooden door at the end of the hallway and somehow, I knew I was meant to walk toward it.

I continued forward, the hundred-year-old wooden floors moaning their resistance with each step I took. I paused at the threshold of the door, momentarily listening to the voice inside my head that screamed in protest, telling me not to lift my hand toward the door; but as always, I silenced the voice of warning and raised my hand to push the door open.

As I stepped inside, I saw large windows that permitted light to pour in, illuminating the bright white walls of the room. The room was completely bare save for two items—a solitary figure in a black suit standing with his back facing me, and an antique gold mirror that stood on an easel in front of him. I was drawn to the figure in front of me and a familiar pull forced me toward him. He was magnetic.

I stepped toward him and as I approached I could see the broad masculine set of his shoulders; I knew without a doubt that he *was* the force drawing me into the room. I continued walking toward him with ease, longing to touch him and anxiously awaiting his strong muscular arms around my body. As I drew near to him, he still didn't turn around so I placed my hand on his back and pulled myself up to peer over his shoulder and into the mirror. I saw my reflection. I was glowing, standing there in a white dress I had seen only once before in a picture—when my mother wore it on her wedding day.

As I stared into the mirror, I lost myself in his blue eyes. He was the epitome of masculinity in his black suit that perfectly encased his wide-set shoulders, and the dark color of his suit somehow made his blue eyes even more bewitching; I almost didn't recognize myself in the radiant white dress that hugged my curves tightly and highlighted my dark copper skin and long ebony hair. Together, we were picturesque, and I was at complete peace standing there beside Maverick. I wanted to remain in that moment forever.

Slowly, however, the feeling of peace began to dissipate and the room grew darker. Panicked, I glanced to the left and then to the right; the walls were slowly changing from white to gray. Soon it would be pitch black in the room.

I grabbed Maverick's arm and looked to him for solace but instead saw a face I didn't recognize. He was also tall but his head was covered with sandy blonde waves and his eyes were dark brown. The sadness I saw reflected in his eyes took my breath away. I knew he was Nathan Weston, my mom's long-lost love from her previous life—the life she kept hidden from me and my father. I tore my eyes away because I couldn't stand to see his pain and as I did I saw my reflection in the mirror yet again; I was not myself. I was my mother. The sight of her made me forget my fear and confusion. All I cared about was feeling the comfort of her touch, so I stepped toward the mirror with my hand outreached.

All the light was being sucked out of the room, replaced by a suffocating darkness. I knew I should run but I couldn't find the will to leave her. I saw the reflection in the mirror move her hand toward her throat, grasping at something. My eyes struggled to adapt, finally making out a heart-shaped necklace around my mother's neck.

I knew immediately that it was the same necklace I'd seen my mother wear when I was growing up—the rose-gold heart that found its home right beneath her collarbone. The reflection began to fade, but not before I saw my mom make one last movement. She moved her other hand toward her chest and in it I saw she grasped tightly to a small, leather-bound book. Then she was gone.

I was standing in utter darkness, feeling more alone than ever upon the realization that both Maverick and my mother were gone. Suddenly a bolt of lightning struck the ground right outside the window and as it did I saw myself in the mirror again. My hand was wrapped around the necklace now hanging from my neck and as I grasped it tightly, blood began to seep through my fingers. The thick red liquid began to trickle down my white dress, covering the beautiful silk slowly, inch by inch, leaving it stained deep scarlet. Lightning flashed again and in the mirror stood a dark figure in a grey suit directly behind me; he watched with evil satisfaction as I slowly bled.

I sat up in my bed, gasping for air; I reached for my phone and shot out a text. I had to get out of that room. I needed Maverick.

Can you meet me?

The response was immediate.

Yes, boathouse in 5 minutes?

I found the "okay" emoticon and hit send. Then I pushed myself out of bed and pulled on my black running tights and tennis shoes, and quietly made my way down the hall, through the living room and kitchen, and out the garage.

It was a five-minute walk to the boathouse, and the entire time I was replaying every detail of my nightmare. An eerie presence in the darkness pressed in on me with each step I took. I quickened my pace. Finally, I saw him, the outline of his broad shoulders standing in the darkness as he peered out into the water. His back was turned toward me—hoodie pulled over his head, shoulders slumped, and hands pushed into the pockets of his black jogger pants. I could sense his pain even from a distance. *He's hurting.* All my troubles melted away when our invisible connection allowed me to experience Maverick's heartache.

What's wrong with him?

I walked up behind him and placed my hand on his shoulder, tenderly. He turned around slowly and smiled a half smile. It didn't touch his eyes. Pain ripped through my soul at his obvious sadness.

"Hey, Baby Girl."

"Hey, Top Gun."

I dropped my hand and intertwined my fingers through his, then lay my head on his shoulder. We fit together like puzzle pieces, and he felt like home.

"Are you OK?" I already knew the answer.

"Fine." He glanced at me and gave me that signature wink. It didn't hold the same swagger it usually did.

He's lying.

"You know you can talk to me, Maverick?" I pleaded with my eyes. He looked away, shifting back and forth uncomfortably.

"I know, Elle. You don't need to worry about me." He covered his face with his mask and my heart sunk, sad at the realization he wouldn't open up to me. But somehow our connection told me to be silent—that he wasn't ready. I knew if

I pushed, I would only push him away. So I didn't press the issue further.

I took a deep breath and exhaled, allowing the comfort of his presence to wash over me. We stood there for several minutes, neither of us needing to talk to communicate what the other was feeling. Then he stirred, taking me by the hand and pulling me toward a bench underneath a massive oak tree that sat overlooking the water. The moon was full, illuminating the water in a breathtaking reflective display, and the night was still in an ominous way that whispered foreboding; but I didn't care, because I was with him. Maverick sat down and pulled me onto the bench beside him, putting his muscular arm around me in an embrace so comforting and protective, it made all my worries and fears—even the visions of my bloody nightmare— fall away. I was overcome by my need for him.

I leaned in slightly and turned my lips toward him. The force between us surged, drawing us even closer still. I leaned in further to obey its calling, inviting him to meet me. But he pulled himself backward suddenly, placing both of his solid arms around the back of the park bench and refusing to touch me.

"Just so we are clear, *you* are going to have to kiss me first." He smirked.

The fire inside raged at his rejection but quelled immediately, overcome by the powerful new burning I experienced in his presence alone. I was consumed by desire for him.

He crossed his arms behind his head, again refusing to make contact with me, leaning back even further into the park bench with an attitude of total indifference. I no longer cared about our little game. All I could think about was finally feeling his lips on mine.

You want me to kiss you first? You got it.

With one swift movement, I pushed myself up and swung my right leg over his lap, straddling him. The magnetism between us awakened further, begging us to connect in a new, uncontrollable way I found almost painful. I knew his desire was just as unbearable as mine. His blue eyes were burning with passion, making him more irresistible than ever. But he still refused to remove his arms or sit up from his relaxed, lounging position.

I cannot believe this guy's self-control.

I pushed myself forward and placed my hands on either side of his arms on the back of the bench, pausing only to appreciate the bulging muscles my fingers grasped onto beneath his hoodie. I leaned in slowly, until every inch of our bodies was pressing against each other—except for our lips. I let go of his biceps, placing my hands on his face with purpose, caressing his strong jawline, running my fingers slowly across his beautiful lips, and smiling to myself as I reminisced about that first night I saw him, when he flipped a toothpick back and forth in his mouth and I dreamed of the moment that I would be the one touching his lips. Finally, my dream was coming true.

As our lips moved together in unison—softly and smoothly in perfect rhythm—a sweet release encompassed my entire body and soul. I surrendered to the force drawing me toward Maverick since the moment I first saw him. We moved as one and I was complete in that moment with him, fully experiencing the beauty of our transcendent connection at last.

He let go of his arms, uncrossing them from behind his head, and placed them in my hair, gripping me with just enough force to remind me that he was in control—always in control—and I succumbed as he quickened the pace. I allowed him to pick me up, wrapping my legs around him, as he walked us toward the boathouse. Our lips never left each other's as he pushed the door open with a kick to reveal a small room with a cot in the corner of the tiny room. He lay me gently on the cot, then positioned himself on top of me and held himself suspended above me, looking into my eyes with so much passion I almost couldn't hold his gaze. He placed three gentle kisses on my forehead—no need to speak what they meant, because I already knew—then he lay down beside me on the cot and pulled me into his strong arms. My body melded into the shape of his perfectly—as though we were created to fit together as one piece—and as I lay beside him, I was whole.

We spent the entire evening in the boathouse, enjoying our newfound unity, and feeling home at last in the comfort of one another's arms. Maverick asked me about my past, about my life in Ohio and about my friends, and finally, he asked about my mother. I talked openly with him, sharing information I had never told anyone before and with each secret told, I experienced the beauty of freedom in my confession to him.

I let my tears flow as I cleansed myself from years of not allowing myself to feel. He just sat there in silence—knowing what I needed as always—caressing my hair, wiping my tears away, and giving me the comfort of his presence and the peace of his unconditional love.

I shared my burden with Maverick and as I realized he would help me carry it on his strong shoulders, beautiful serenity washed over me, calming me and quieting the fire within. There wasn't room in my soul to love Maverick with the passion that consumed me, and hold onto the darkness and the hatred and the fear that had also consumed me for years. So without a second thought, I let go of that little box in the depths of my soul once and for all. I let the lid fly off and years of hatred and resentment spilled forth in a therapeutic release.

Then, when it was empty, I replaced the darkness that had lived in my soul for six years, with the light of him.

When we saw the sun beginning to peek above the horizon, we were forced to face the reality that we would have to leave the comfort of each other's arms. Maverick's face grew serious as he pushed up to a seated position, carrying me with him.

"We have to talk. We don't have much time," he said.

"I know," I said with disappointment, realizing that we had to re-enter the real world—the world in which someone tried to murder me and someone had already successfully murdered my mother. "I need to tell you what I found out from my dad and my aunt," I told him.

I shared my dad's revelations with Maverick—about his relationship with my mother, her accident, the amnesia, and the quick wedding, then I went even further back and told him about my mom's forbidden love affair with a rich young boy named Nathan Weston, who died tragically.

"Elle, did your aunt tell you the name of Nathan's dad?" The tone in his voice frightened me.

"Yes. His name was James Weston." I answered him with certainty.

The shock on his face was evident. "I know who James Weston is," he admitted.

I stared at him, struggling to process the words he had just spoken. "How?" I finally asked.

"I've only met him one time, when I was a little boy. He's old and is kind of crazy. Mostly what I know about him my dad told me. Long story short is that James Weston is my dad's business partner and he was my grandfather's business partner before that. He bought into the company as an equal partner in nineteen fifty-nine. From what my dad has told me, Mr. Weston was a very affluent man who was well respected in Tulsa and throughout the country. He was apparently indispensable with business relations when he and my grandfather started the company. He was sort of a legend." Maverick paused momentarily then turned to me. "You told me that your mom was in love with a boy named Nathan?" I nodded my head in agreement then he continued. "That has to be James Weston's youngest son, Nathan Weston. He died in a tragic car accident when he was only eighteen years old and my father said it changed Mr. Weston forever. He sold his house—to my grandfather actually—and moved to a compound outside of town where he spent his life locking himself away from the outside world. He's still very much involved though and has fifty-one percent ownership, but he runs the company through his oldest son, Philip Weston. My father never sees James and all his business dealings are with Philip now. By the way, Philip Weston is Margot Weston's dad in case you hadn't realized that yet by the last name."

We sat there in silence as we watched the sun break the horizon in the distance, knowing—with sadness—that our time was coming to a close. I grabbed his hand and lay my head on his shoulder.

"I think we both know our next step." I looked up at him and as our eyes connected, I knew we were in complete agreement. "We need to find out anything and everything there is to know about James Weston."

CHAPTER 20

As Maverick made his way back up the hill that would lead to my aunt's house, I knew I should be nervous about getting caught; I had—after all—left in the middle of the night and spent the whole evening with my boyfriend; but I didn't care. After everything I learned about my mom, her past, Mr. Weston, Nathan Weston, forbidden loves, and tragic deaths, I didn't have room to feel anything but confusion.

We pulled up to the house and Maverick leaned in to give me a kiss before we were forced to separate.

"I'm glad you texted me."

"I'm glad I texted you too."

Maverick dropped his eyes and I noticed a pained expression.

"Hey, are you OK?"

He paused, measuring his words. "I just worry about you when I'm not with you," he said as he intertwined our fingers and squeezed three times. He grasped onto me tightly, refusing to let go. He looked insecure, panicked even; an unwanted memory triggered. I had seen that look before—when I was in the hospital. Suddenly I remembered a lingering question I needed answered.

"Hey Maverick? When you texted me after I left the hospital…"

His eyes shot toward me and tension filled the air. He knew what I was going to ask before I spoke the words.

"How did you know I left the hospital at that very moment? You texted me the second we were driving away."

He refused to make eye contact, staring out the window instead. His silence spoke volumes.

"So you *are* you tracking my cell phone somehow." I didn't really pose it as a question. I already knew the answer. I crossed my arms, staring him down and waiting for a response.

"Elle, someone tried to murder you for God's sake. I'm just trying to protect you."

"You know what Maverick? I get that you're worried but that doesn't give you a right to track my cell phone without permission." I uncrossed my arms and pointed a finger at him, really attempting to drive my point home. "That's level-ten crazy and I won't put up with it."

Pain covered his beautiful features, contorting his face into a mask of fear. We stared at one another and somehow our connection allowed me to see into his soul. He was helpless—terrified even—and I couldn't reconcile the brokenness I saw in the boy before me with the strong, confident Maverick Mason I knew. I could see his vulnerability and didn't want him to hurt any more so I scooted over toward him, grabbed his strong jaw, and kissed him gently on the cheek.

"Maverick, thank you for worrying about me. But it's not normal to track my every move. You know that."

He dropped his eyes, recognition of the truth of my words evident on his face. I handed him my phone gently, and he took it, knowing what I wanted him to do.

"Turn it off."

He went to the settings section of my phone, then to the privacy and swiped a green button to the left.

"There. It's off."

He seemed thrown, anxious even. I knew there was something he wasn't telling me but it wasn't the time to push him. My heart hurt, seeing him in pain, and I wanted it to stop.

"Hey Maverick?"

He cocked his head toward me, waiting to hear what I had to say.

"Thank you," but somehow I realized that wasn't enough so I said two more words, "for everything." He knew what I was saying, our connection allowed him to hear what was unspoken—thank you for saving me; for protecting me; for worrying about me; for loving me; for seeing my brokenness, my hurt, my pain, and all my scars, and still choosing to see me as beautiful, even with all my imperfections. He softened, and the pain in his eyes lessened finally, much to my relief.

"You're welcome." Then he added two little words as he leaned in and gave me a peck on the cheek—"For everything."

We were running out of time as the darkness was beginning to turn to dawn and with each passing moment our chances of getting caught increased exponentially. I forced myself out of his truck and the second I did, the force that connected us pulled me back toward him. It was physically and emotionally painful as I took each step away from him on my way down the path to my aunt's house. I wondered to myself if it would ever get easier being away from him or if I would always feel this pain in his absence, an undeniable primal need to be reconnected to him.

I sneaked around the back of my house and climbed in through my window then quickly crawled beneath the covers. I was beginning to give into sleep when I heard the door crack open then slowly close again, followed by my dad and aunt's voices.

"Is she still asleep?"

"Yes. She needs it though. Let's just let her sleep in and maybe she can go to school at lunchtime."

With that, I closed my eyes and gave into peaceful sleep.

When I woke, it was after 11:00 a.m. I immediately picked up the phone and saw some missed texts from Maverick. I texted him back.

I slept in. See you at lunch.

I got ready in record time, knowing I needed time to make a phone call before we left. It was lunchtime back home and if I called at just the right time, I could catch Charlie before he went to fifth hour. He picked up on the second ring.

"Hey, Ells. I heard you got a new iPhone."

I sensed his judgment immediately, and it stung.

"Grace has been running her mouth all about it, I'm sure."

He laughed, but it seemed off.

"You know how she loves a good story."

"So what's new with you?"

He stared at me through the phone, not answering my question.

"Grace told you she's worried about me, didn't she?"

Charlie and I, we didn't know how to pretend. He wanted to cut to the chase.

"Yeah, she did."

"Well, I'll be fine. Don't worry about me."

"How about you don't tell me what to do."

I saw a hint of joy in his brown eyes at my comment.

"There's the hot-headed Elle Christiansen I know and love." The way he said my name made something stir inside of me. He seemed different somehow.

"Why don't you stop being so freaking stubborn and tell me what's got Grace so worked up. She's saying you aren't yourself and she's worried about you. And we both know that she has a new boyfriend so if she's noticing anything other than that, you must be acting *really* off."

He laughed, rubbing his chin as if reflecting on my words. "True...true."

"So quit making me ask, Charlie. You know I'm worried about you."

He reached up and grabbed the bill of his Cincinnati Reds hat, bending it over and over, reshaping the bill. I noticed his nervous habit and I waited. I knew he was about to talk.

"It's just not the same without you, Ells. I miss you."

"I miss you too, Charlie. It's not the same here without you either."

We stared at each other, the sadness looming, a million unspoken emotions passing between us. I wanted to take his pain away. I wanted to comfort him just like he always comforted me—sweet, dependable Charlie who always saw my pain, even when everyone else only saw the rebellion and anger I chose to show them.

"Hey, you better pull it together without me there because you know Grace is going to have a break-up you're going to have to deal with pretty soon. You're going to need to be at a hundred percent to deal with that level of drama."

We both laughed, but his was restrained.

"Very true. She's already convinced she's in love with this guy and it's been like two weeks."

We both made a guttural noise at the exact same time and rolled our eyes, then burst into laughter.

"Why am I not surprised?"

I heard a knock at my door and my aunt peeked her head in.

"We need to leave soon, sweetheart."

"OK, I'll be right there, Aunt Cordelia."

She gently closed the door. I stared back into the phone to see Charlie's brown eyes narrowed, studying me.

"You're different."

"I'm the same old me, Charlie."

I glanced away. We both knew I wasn't fooling him.

"I think I'll have to come there in person and see for myself. I don't know how much longer I can go without seeing you."

I was in the middle of an emotional tug-of-war—elated at thought of seeing Charlie then simultaneously terrified for some reason, at the thought of him being in Tulsa. I pushed the unwanted emotions away, unable to decipher my confused thoughts.

"Maybe my dad and I can come back that way over Christmas break. I miss you and Grace so much."

"Miss you too, Ells."

He hung onto my name. Though I'd heard him call me Ells a million times before, somehow it sounded different suddenly.

"I gotta run. Chat soon?"

"Definitely." I pressed end on our FaceTime call. My stomach was nauseous and my mind heavy, remembering Charlie's mood, as I made my way to the kitchen to tell my aunt I was ready to go.

"Are you sure you feel up to going today?" Her worrying was sweet.

"Yes, I'm ready, Aunt Cordelia. I promise I'm fine."

She drove me to school and dropped me off five minutes before the bell rang for lunch. I walked to my locker and slowly began putting my books in, preparing for all the questioning glances and whispers that would no doubt be coming my way as soon as the bell rang. Fortunately, questioning glances and whispers were something I had become quite accustomed to over the years so I realized that wasn't what was making me feel so apprehensive. As I took inventory of my feelings, I realized what was bothering me—seeing Maverick. We hadn't discussed school and I was anxious to know how he would treat me. Insecurity seeped in as I relived the pain of him ignoring me on my first few days of school.

Great, now I really feel sick to my stomach. I might throw up. I couldn't bear the thought of being ignored by him again and I decided if he acted indifferently toward me, I would walk straight up to him and ask him who the hell he thought he was. There was no way I was going to be ignored anymore, especially not after the moments we'd shared.

The bell rang loudly, then the hallway flooded with open doors and the rush of footsteps. Slowly a familiar stirring awakened inside, telling me to turn around; and I obeyed. Immediately I saw him across the hallway, his blue eyes digging into my soul just like they had from the first moment I saw him. He started walking toward me purposefully, never taking his eyes off mine. With each step that drew him closer to me, I found it more difficult to breathe. The effect he had on me was tangible and I was positive that everyone else in the hallway, which was every student in the entire school, could feel the intensity that surged between us.

He was only steps away from me and I stood there, unable to move, waiting my fate which was undoubtedly in his hands. I couldn't tear my eyes away from his but I didn't need to look around to know that everyone in the hallway—the entire school—was staring at us and watching the emotionally charged moment between Maverick and me as we made our debut together at Heritage Hall Preparatory Academy.

I saw his little trademark wink as he walked up to my locker and it helped put me at ease. He reached down and put one of his strong arms on the locker behind me—pinning me—and my heart began beating almost out of my chest. He leaned in, and then the most adorable smile I'd ever seen spread across his face. I melted.

"Hey, Baby Girl." He flipped a toothpick back and forth in his mouth flippantly. I reached up and grabbed it playfully out of his mouth.

"You know I hate it when you call me that."

He leaned in until his lips were mere inches away from mine and his proximity took my breath away. "You love it," he said with smug self-assurance.

He kissed me on the forehead then wrapped his arm around my waist and led me through the halls, toward the front doors of the school. Every single eye was glued on us—a look of shock and awe covering their faces—as we walked by, the hallway splitting for us as if we were Moses walking through the Red Sea. Maverick never removed his hand from my waist and his posture was one of possessiveness, telling not only me but everyone who watched us that I belonged to him, and I undeniably did.

Maverick held my waist the entire time he walked me to his truck, then he opened the door for me and lifted me easily into his passenger side.

"Where are we going?" I asked.

"I'm taking you to lunch."

I glanced around nervously. "We can't just leave for lunch can we?"

"And all this time I thought you were a rule-breaker," Maverick teased as we drove away from the school. I rolled my eyes at him.

"Did you know the homecoming dance is next Friday?" Maverick asked as he reached across the truck and grabbed my hand.

"Nope, I sure didn't." I tried to sound disinterested.

"Well you need to get a dress," Maverick said. "I prefer red."

"I hope that's not your way of asking me to go to the dance with you," I said with disapproval, "because that's an absolutely terrible way to ask a girl to a dance."

"Oh really?" he challenged, "because I don't do chocolate and roses, baby, so that's as good as it's going to get." He glanced over and gave me another one of his winks.

"Well I don't know. I have someone else I might want to go with," I teased.

The tension escalated when I spoke those words. He looked over at me, anger in his eyes. "Don't even joke Elle. It's not funny. You're going with me and no one else and you know it."

I conceded but made sure to roll my eyes at him one last time. "Jealous much?"

"You have no idea," he said as he shot me a warning glance. It made me uncomfortable when he looked at me like that so I changed the subject.

"You would tell me what color of dress I have to wear. You're so bossy."

"You know you love it," he said.

I didn't even bother arguing with him but as we drove away—our fingers entwined and my head lying on his sturdy shoulder—I couldn't get his statement out of my mind. *You know you love it.* I stared out of the window, watching the large oak trees on Utica Avenue pass one by one as an unwanted thought in my mind took seed, and started to grow. *Why do I let*

Maverick tell me what to do? I was a girl who spent her entire life resisting anyone or anything that tried to tell me what to do or exert any type of authority over me, only to find myself inescapably in love with someone who was controlling and bossy in the most frustrating way imaginable. I found myself not only waiting for his direction, but craving it, wanting to do exactly as I was told if for no other reason than to please him. Suddenly I became angry—at him, but even more so at myself. A flood of emotions hit me, and I was swimming in a stormy sea, unable to keep my head above water and unsure of what direction was up and what was down.

"Maverick, pull over."

He looked at me, his brows creased together in concern, then slowly he turned onto a small street off Utica.

I pointed my finger at him. "You know what? You can't tell me what to do all the time."

He raised his eyebrows. Was he challenging me? But he said nothing.

"I mean it. You have some serious control issues and I'm telling you right now that I don't like being told what to do." *But you kind of do like it when he tells you what to do.* I silenced the voice inside my head. I was still confused about our newfound relationship and the onslaught of confusing emotions I experienced in Maverick Mason's presence.

"Elle," his voice was soothing, like a calming melody sung straight to my soul.

I looked away, unable to hold onto my will while his piercing eyes were fixed on mine.

"Elle, look at me." He quickly corrected himself, recognizing his normal controlling tendencies. "I'm sorry, let me try that again—Elle, will you please look at me?"

"No." *I'll show him he can't tell me what to do.* "This is just like the phone-tracking thing that I talked to you about earlier. It's *not* OK." I still refused to look at him, staring out of the window defiantly instead.

"Here's the deal—you're right."

I looked at him, shocked at his confession. Our eyes held each other's and for once I was speechless. He took a deep, labored breath and blew it out slowly. I watched as before my eyes, his mask began to falter. *Finally.* I waited in anticipation to hear what he would say.

"Listen, my parents make me go see a therapist. I know I have some issues with—" he cleared his throat, as though he didn't want to speak the next word—"control." He spat it out, finally, as though it made him sick when it rolled off his tongue.

I stared at him dumfounded. It's like I was seeing a crack in his seemingly impenetrable armor—realizing he was exposed—and perhaps he wasn't invincible after all.

"You go to a *therapist?*" My eyes were wide with disbelief.

"Well awesome. I'm feeling so great about sharing that little-known fact with you now. Thanks for your support."

"I'm sorry. That was rude. It just caught me off guard because you always seem so, um—" I searched for the right word but he beat me to it.

"Perfect?" He winked, and my body ignited in response. I rolled my eyes, annoyed at myself for how affected I was by him.

"No I was definitely *not* going to say perfect," I lied.

He reached over and grabbed my hand, kissing it gently.

"Will you accept my apology?" He looked up at me with those blue eyes—using all his power against me—knowing how impossibly handsome he was. I fought to hold on, delaying my response and looking at him with one eyebrow raised.

"I don't think I remember hearing one."

He chuckled. "So astute, Baby Girl."

"Seriously what is up with your vocabulary? I would bring that up in your therapy session next time if I were you because it's super weird for a seventeen-year-old to be using such obnoxious words."

He laughed—loudly—and I couldn't help but let a smile touch my lips in response. He was impossible to stay mad at, especially when he was laughing.

"Elle, I'm sorry. I know I have control issues and I'm working on them. Will you please forgive me?"

I paused again, trying to leave him hanging in suspense, at least for a bit.

"Yes, I forgive you," I finally answered.

He leaned across the truck—triumphantly—and moved toward me for a kiss. I held my hand up in front of his face, stopping him before his lips touched mine.

"But you better stop bossing me around all the time."

He held his hands up in surrender. "OK, OK, I said I'll work on it."

We stared each other down and I started to crack.

"So are we good now?"

I shrugged my shoulders continuing my ruse. He knew I was putty in his hands now.

"Can I have a kiss please, Elle?"

I ticked my points off on my fingers one by one as I made them. "Just to recap—no stalking, no phone tracking, no bossing, less control issues."

"Got it. Now can I kiss you *please*?" I could hardly wait for him to lean in, but I wanted to make him wait just a bit longer.

"I guess. Since you asked nicely," I teased.

He reached up and grabbed the back of my head forcefully—the look on his face rapidly cycling from playfulness to burning desire—fisting his fingers into the back of my hair. Then he pulled me toward him, crushing his lips on mine without pause. Our lips moved in perfect unison, passionately communicating so many emotions—anger, desire, forgiveness, promise, and a longing for so much more. When he finally pulled away, I was unable to breathe. He inhaled and exhaled several times, regaining his mask of indifference, then slowly started the truck and pulled away.

I couldn't tear my eyes from him as he reached into his console and pulled out a toothpick, popping it into his mouth. He tossed it around his beautiful lips aimlessly, as I watched, jealous—as usual—that it wasn't me touching his mouth. I was staring. He glanced over at me and I didn't even bother hiding the desire in my eyes.

"I'll fight with you any day, Baby Girl, if we can make up like *that* after." He gave me his signature wink. A smile of agreement spread across my face and I reached across to grab his hands, intertwining my long, thin fingers with his sturdy, masculine hands.

He turned into Utica Square and pulled up in front of a quaint little restaurant with a black-and-white awning and idyllic, red wrought-iron tables sitting outside. I kept trying to push away the nagging question in my mind. *Let it go. Don't ask him, Elle. You've already pushed so many issues today.* But per the norm, I silenced the voice of reason in my head. I needed to know.

"Maverick?" He halted—his whole body freezing—waiting for the question that he seemed to know was coming.

"Yes?"

"Why did your parents think you needed to see a therapist anyway?" I whispered the words, somehow knowing he dreaded hearing them.

A crushing sadness enveloped Maverick's eyes, turning them from a crystal-clear blue, to a dark, churning sea crashing with turbulent waves. It took my breath away. I was terrified by the unexpected storm I saw in his eyes.

"Elle, let's just go eat some lunch OK?" He looked away but our connection still spoke to me nonetheless. He was in pain—immeasurable pain. *Maverick has a secret.* The voice spoke and I listened. I knew she spoke truth. It was but a split second, but I saw another chink in his armor, a falter in the mask he always wore with confidence. And in that moment, I knew there was another side to Maverick Mason—something hidden beneath the perfectionism and control and self-confidence. The silence loomed as we drove away, but I pushed him no further.

We walked inside a little sandwich shop with the most delectable array of desserts I'd ever seen displayed openly in the glass counter in front of the register. We ordered a sandwich and some drinks, then took our number to a window seat and sat down. Maverick pulled his iPad out of his backpack.

"I have a lot to tell you." The mood in the room suddenly shifted. He was all business, opening his iPad and selecting a folder he had saved on his home screen. An old newspaper clipping with a picture of James Weston as a young man immediately pulled up as I heard Maverick explain. "I'm a teacher's aide for Mr. Jenkins during third hour and I convinced him I had a research paper I had to work on." I watched him scroll through the articles he found. "There's so much information here and I won't be able to read through it all until after my baseball game tonight." His fingers moved quickly across the screen and I found myself in awe of his skills with electronics. "There. I sent them to you. Get your iPad out and make sure they are there." I pulled my iPad out and he quickly moved straight to the utilities section of my iPad where he had clearly downloaded a slew of apps I had no idea how to use. "That one," he said as he pointed to a dropbox app. "You do it so I know you can do it on your own."

I crossed my arms in defiance and raised an eyebrow at him, refusing to do as he asked. He got my point.

"Sorry. I forgot."

"Of course you did." My arms were still crossed and I wasn't budging.

"Elle, can you give it a try *please?*"

I leaned forward. He was right to think I was completely computer illiterate and we both knew it, but I wasn't about to give up without a fight. I slapped his hand away from my iPad, asserting my independence. I tapped on the app then fumbled my way through until I figured out how to download the files. As I watched them appear on my screen I looked at him with satisfaction and crossed my arms with indignation, waiting for his apology.

"Wow, Baby Girl. You're a regular Steve Jobs." He smirked as he said it.

I narrowed my eyes. I had no idea who Steve Jobs was but I could tell he was mocking me. I made a mental note to look the name up when he wasn't around. I wouldn't give him the satisfaction of asking who Steve Jobs was.

Maverick stood up and took my plate for me. I followed him as he made his way to the door. "So you'll go through the articles and make notes about anything that stands out to you and then I'll see you at my baseball game tonight. We can talk after." I saw my opportunity to get him back for the Steve Jobs comment.

"Yes I'll look through all the articles. No, I won't come to your baseball game."

He glanced over at me and raised an eyebrow, assessing me and raking me over with his piercing-blue eyes. "Yes you will," he said confidently.

"We'll see," I challenged. He peeked over at me and I thought I saw a hint of appreciation in his eyes.

He likes that I challenge him. He likes that I'm strong. He likes that I don't fall all over him and do whatever he wants like all the other girls. I walked back to the truck with a newfound strut in my step.

We hopped back into his truck and he sped off, trying to beat the clock before our fifth-hour classes started. We hurried inside and kissed each other quickly then said goodbye as we ran to our classes. The second we said goodbye, I was incomplete and that familiar force was at work, always operating without cease to reunite us. I sat through my English class with only a few glances and whispers in my direction but when the bell rang and I opened the door, I saw three friendly yet inquisitive faces.

"There you are girlfriend!" Madison engulfed me in a huge hug. "We're so glad you're back."

"How are you?"

"Is your head OK?"

"Are you sure you feel ready for school?"

Madison, Macey, and Carly peppered me with questions but it was Carly who asked what everyone really wanted to know.

"I mean stop holding out on us girl. *What is going on with you and Maverick Mason?* It's all anyone is talking about!"

"We're hanging out," I answered coyly.

"Are you freaking kidding me?" Macey shouted. "You are hooking up with Maverick Mason and that is all the details we are getting? You are killing us right now."

I laughed as I walked away, indicating the subject was closed.

"Well are you at least going to his baseball game tonight?" Madison asked as she caught up to me.

"I don't know," I replied.

"Yes, you're going," Carly said definitively. "We'll pick you up at six so you better be ready."

"OK fine, I'll go." I said as I waved goodbye to them. I heard their catcalls all the way down the hall about me and Maverick and couldn't help but smile.

As I made my way down the hallway and rounded the corner that would take me to my next class, I ran straight into an unwelcome face. Glaring at me with a look that sent chills down my spine was Margot Weston. Although her face was positioned in that of a smile, somehow all I saw was a snake about to strike her prey.

"Well hey there new girl." That ever-present fake smile was plastered all over her face. The fire instantly began to burn. "Wow. I mean you really get around, don't you?"

The fire burned brighter and I had to take deep breaths. *She's not worth it.* I didn't give her a response so she continued her verbal assault.

"I mean first Caleb and now you're already hooking up with Maverick?" I still refused to speak so she spit more of her venom. "You know, two different guys *already*? Some people would call that a *slut.*"

Somehow—for the first time in my life—I miraculously contained my anger even as the fire burned rampantly inside. I pushed back, forcing the fire to simmer, and the look I saw in

241

her eyes told me it was the right choice. My control seemed to make her lose her own cool.

"I mean what could he possibly see in *you*? Look at how you dress." She eyed me up and down, making a noise in the back of her throat that communicated her disgust. She waited for my response but still I gave her none. I found it almost comical that she would think criticizing my clothes or my appearance would have any effect on me whatsoever. I let out a little laugh and her eyes filled with rage. Clearly the conversation wasn't going how she anticipated so she tried a different approach.

"You're obviously only with him because of his money. You are poor, white trash, and you found out about his company and thought he was your ticket out of your hellhole of a life didn't you?"

The words stung.

This girl is such a witch.

Wait. What is she talking about "his company"?

I heard my mother in my mind—*turn the other cheek, Elle*. I used the sweetest tone I could muster. "Are we done here?"

Margot's jaw dropped. I tried not to smile too big. I stepped around her, her glare tearing a hole in my back as I strolled calmly down the hallway. Before I rounded the corner, I gave her a kind smile over my shoulder.

"Have a great day, Margot," I said with a small wave. Then I walked away.

That day when school was over, I couldn't wait to get home to start my research about James Weston. I used the cover of still needing rest and feeling fatigued from my wreck to get some alone time in my bedroom. I closed the door, plopped across my tiny bed, and immediately opened the file folder that Maverick sent me. I used my right index finger to swipe the screen, flipping through article after article. They were in no particular order but they all had a central theme: James Weston.

I read through several pieces about his oil company, other start-up companies in which he had invested, his financial involvement in various charities, then more about his oil company. There were so many articles about his oil companies and investments but none of them held any information of importance to me. My eyelids drooped. I grew weary of article after article talking about WestCo Oil when I flipped the screen to the right and something caught my attention—a much older article from a publication I didn't recognize.

All the previous articles were from the *Tulsa World* or various Oil & Gas magazines, but this article was dated 1959 and it was from a paper called the *Osage County Herald*. Before I started reading, I stared at the black-and-white photograph on the front page of the article. It was of a man in a suit, his hands holding his lapels, chin slightly pointed up, and chest bowed out in an obvious stance of pride. I scanned below the picture and found the caption, "James Weston named Interim Chief for the Osage Nation." He didn't smile at the camera but instead stood stoically staring into the lens as if he were above the entire charade of having his photograph taken. The article told of the tragic death of the visionary Chief of the Osage Indians—Chief Joseph Blackwater—and the naming of the Chief's son-in-law—James Weston—as interim representative for the Osage Nation.

I took out a notepad and scribbled in large capital letters the name—*Chief Joseph Blackwater*—then underneath it I drew a line and a long, narrow box in which I wrote—*James Weston.* I tapped the eraser end of my pencil on my paper.

The article also spoke about important legislation the visionary Chief Blackwater was advocating for at the time of his death. The Chief's dying wish, which he expressed to his daughter and son-in-law on his deathbed, was for James Weston to finish the work that he wouldn't be able to complete himself—procuring legal rights to the gas and oil that was being produced on his people's lands.

The article concluded by chronicling the death of Chief Joseph Blackwater and told how his people mourned his loss because of the deep love and respect they had for their beloved chief. There was one final line at the very end of the article—"Chief Blackwater was predeceased by his loving wife who died giving birth to their only child, a daughter they named Rosemary."

I stopped and wrote down the name Rosemary in capital letters and for a moment I lost myself as my pencil took a life of its own. When I came back to reality I glanced down at the paper and saw a beautiful frame of roses I'd drawn around the name Rosemary; intermixed between the roses was the shape of a heart that looked like a necklace. It was the same necklace my mother wore around her neck when I was growing up—the same necklace that I had also worn around my neck in my most recent nightmare.

I slowly returned to my senses and before I began reading again, I jotted down some notes under Rosemary's name.

– Chief Joseph Blackwater's only daughter

– Married to James Weston

As I came to the end of the page, I moved to swipe the screen to the next page of the article, the name of Rosemary lingering in my mind. The next page popped up on the screen

244

and the first thing I noticed was a black-and-white picture in the lower right corner of the screen, the small black writing beneath the picture indicating that it was of a young James Weston and his new bride. As my eyes scanned the picture, I came to a halt as I saw a haunting picture of a young bride staring back at me with a pair of coal-black eyes I had seen before.

That's the woman from the reservation.

My heart pounded out of control. My breath became short and labored. I walked away from the computer screen and leaned against the wall, taking deep breaths; in and out. I pushed away from the wall and walked slowly across the room, toward my backpack, then reached in and pulled out the wooden box I was given on the reservation. Something guided my hands to two large, carved roses on either side of the box and without explanation, I knew to push. As I did, the top of the wooden box popped opened and inside I saw a beautiful rose-gold necklace. It was the same necklace my mother wore every day of her life; the necklace my father told me he buried her in.

The necklace sat delicately on a bed of plush purple velvet inside the box. Somehow, it called to me. I reached out for the delicate gold chain—slowly, reverently even—and placed it on my neck. It settled into that niche right below my collarbone and an unexplained peace washed over me. Then—carefully—I hid it under my T-shirt. My dad and aunt would never see the necklace. I found myself caressing it gently as I walked back toward the bed in a newfound state of calm contemplation.

I sat on the bed and continued my assessment of the picture from the article, the one with a young, beautiful Osage Indian woman looking slight but strong. She was wearing a stunning white, Native American wedding dress made of leather that was bound at the ends with beads. She stood next to her husband—James Weston—and looked up at him with obvious admiration. In her hands, I saw a small leather-bound object that looked like a book.

That looks like the same book I was holding in my nightmare last night.

I was interrupted by my phone chirping.

We're late, sorry. Be there in 5 so be ready. It was Madison. The clock read 6:30.

I looked down at my iPad one last time, zooming in on the grainy Polaroid on the screen. There in the picture of Rosemary and James Weston from their wedding day, I saw a tiny outline of a heart-shaped necklace around her neck.

Rosemary is the key to unlocking my mom's past.

CHAPTER 21

I was interrupted by a loud knock on my door but before I had a chance to answer, the girls rushed into my room excitedly.

"Let's go! We're already late," Carly said.

They dragged me out the door as I waved my goodbye to my aunt and my dad, then we all piled into Madison's shiny silver convertible. There was a chill in the air so we left the top up but rolled the windows down and rocked out to some old-school Justin Timberlake. In that moment with the wind blowing through my hair and all of us singing loudly to the radio, I almost forgot that I was different. I closed my eyes and let myself live the lie—even if momentarily—that I was a normal high-school student enjoying a car ride with her girlfriends on her way to her boyfriend's baseball game.

We pulled up to the baseball fields and I read the numbers on the screen from afar: five consecutive zeros on the top, followed by four zeroes on the bottom. The game was in the bottom of the fifth inning and it was scoreless. As we walked in, that familiar magnetic pull called to me, drawing me toward the commanding presence standing on the pitching mound. I froze, unable to move when I saw Maverick.

He had his baseball uniform on, fitted pants that showcased his muscular legs and a maroon jersey with a large HH symbol across his chest. I stood there—utterly spellbound—and stared in appreciation of how his uniform hugged his large, muscular frame to perfection. I would have stayed there in my trance the entire game but the girls finally grabbed my arm, laughing as if they knew exactly what I was thinking, and pulled me toward a seat in the bleachers.

As I walked away, I saw Maverick's leg raise methodically to his chest, then he plunged forward toward the mound and delivered a pitch into the catcher's glove. My jaw dropped as I heard the pop of the glove almost instantaneously. I turned toward home plate in disbelief and it was then that I noticed two rows of men, all with baseball hats sporting different logos: Texas Rangers, St. Louis Cardinals, New York Yankees, Houston Astros, and Chicago Cubs. There were others as well but I didn't recognize the logos. All of them held a small black object in their hands that they pointed toward Maverick when he threw a pitch. *Is he going to go play professional baseball?* Betrayal clawed at my heart but even more so unparalleled fear. *Why hasn't he told me? What will happen to us when he leaves to go play?* I immediately pushed the voice away, stupidity overwhelming me that I even dared to think of a future with Maverick Mason.

I felt Maverick watching me as I walked up the stairs. Right before I sat down, I heard a loud crack followed by the crowd's shocked gasps. When I turned to sit down, my suspicions were confirmed—Maverick had given up a solo home run. As he made his way back to the rubber on the pitcher's mound, I saw him glance in my direction. His eyes burned with anger; I knew that anger was directed at me.

The girls laughed and talked for the remainder of the game but all I could think about was the anger in Maverick's eyes. I listened to their endless chatter about school and about the scouts there watching Maverick play and how he would become a professional baseball player as soon as he graduated high school.

"Not that he needs the money or anything since he is seventeen and already started his own Fortune 500 company," Carly scoffed and all the girls nodded in agreement.

What does that mean?

"What company? Are you talking about his dad's oil company—WestCo?" I asked. They all stared at me in shock and my face flushed. I looked away, embarrassed at the way they were looking at me.

"He hasn't he told you about *his* company?"

I suddenly remembered Margot Weston mentioning a company as well and the realization that everyone else knew more about my own boyfriend than I did hit me full force.

How could I be so stupid?

I knew whatever she told me would be something that Maverick failed to tell me himself. My chest constricted. It moved to my throat, making it difficult to breathe. I wiped the look of hurt off my face, replacing it with indifference—a look I'd spent years perfecting. I hated for people to see that I was hurting; it reminded me of how the doctors and everyone in Brookville looked at me with constant pity after my mother died.

"This game is so boring. I'm going to get a drink from the concession stand."

I didn't invite them to join me. I stood up, held my head high, and stomped down the steps with wounded confidence as if the entire game was so beneath me. As I rounded the corner I felt Maverick's blue eyes on me but I didn't bother to look. I was too angry to care. I kept my mask of indifference on until I made my way into the bathroom and shut the stall door; then I leaned up against the wall and allowed myself to succumb to the onslaught of emotions attacking me.

Hurt. Anger. Fear. They smacked me full force in equal measures.

How you could be so stupid? He's going to do nothing but hurt you and leave you.

In a moment of complete honesty, I fully embraced my ignorance. I'd allowed myself to hope. I hoped that I could have a future; that I could have a semi-normal life; that I could love; that I could feel happiness instead of pain; and that I could do all those things with the mysterious Maverick Mason.

I laughed audibly as I thought of my stupidity; then, I took three deep breaths and walked out of the bathroom stall, my resolve set.

I'll shut him out. He'll never hurt me again.

The girls found me when the game was over and told me Maverick hit a three-run home run in the bottom of the 7th inning to win the game. I changed the subject quickly.

"Do you guys want to get out of here?"

"Are you freaking kidding me, Elle?" Carly asked. "You're dating Maverick Mason and you aren't going to stay and wait for him after his baseball game? All the girlfriends always wait after the games." She stared at me, shifting her weight to her left leg and placing a hand on her hip. It was a challenge. She knew I was being rash and was calling me out on it. Madison looked away awkwardly but Macey met my eyes and cocked an eyebrow, indicating her agreement with Carly. I shrugged and turned to walk away. They followed but I heard Carly voice her disapproval one last time.

"You are even crazier than I thought."

The words stung—because I knew they were true—but I refused to show anyone I was affected. I quickly rebuilt my wall as we walked past what I could only assume was the girlfriend's section—a throng of girls dressed to the nines—waiting for the baseball players to come out after their game. I saw Margot Weston waiting there and I knew who she was waiting for. I wanted to rip her blonde hair out of her head; but my pride wouldn't allow me to show her that I cared. I was too wounded anyway. All I wanted to do was run away and keep building my wall of self-protection to ensure that no one could hurt me.

We all followed Carly to the car and gradually the lighter mood returned as we drove to a burger joint on a street called Brookside. We walked in and ordered some fries to share as well as several milkshakes then we sat down in a corner booth. As we chatted, I covered my despondent mood with a fake smile and an occasional forced laugh here and there.

A few minutes later, I heard a loud thumping noise followed by a stirring inside my soul. A jet-black truck with black rims pulled into the parking lot. Seconds later the front door opened and Maverick's presence commanded the room. My skin began to tingle and I couldn't discern whether it was from fear or excitement—perhaps it was both. I couldn't tear my eyes from his as he glared at me with obvious animosity.

I crossed my arms in defiance and stared right back at him, matching his glare of disdain. He walked toward me and as he approached I found it difficult to breathe. The entire restaurant seemed to go quiet and I knew that all eyes were on us as he walked up to the table and addressed me with authority in his tone.

"Is it too much to ask for you to show up to my game on time?"

"Oh, I'm sorry." Sarcasm dripped from my words. "I didn't realize my father was here."

"Why don't we go outside and talk, Elle?" His words were soft, but I still heard the force behind his request. I pushed myself into the back of my seat and refused to move.

"I think I'm good here."

He stared me down, and the tension in the room escalated. My girlfriends were taking awkward sips of their milkshakes trying not to look at us.

"Oh, for God's sake you two just go outside and talk already." Carly could take the angry tension no longer apparently. "Maverick it was my fault she was late OK? I was late to pick her up and last time I checked she doesn't have a car?" I glanced at Carly with gratitude. She nudged me out of the booth. I almost fell out but Maverick caught my arm and helped me up.

"Will you please go outside with me, Elle?" I could see that he was trying so I let go of my anger, or at least some of it. I nodded my ascent and walked toward the door. He opened it for me and we walked to the side of the restaurant.

I whipped around, remembering all the pain and rejection I felt during the game, learning he had a company I didn't even know about and would probably be leaving to go play professional baseball. I lashed out in anger, my favorite defense mechanism.

"What's your freaking problem? Why does it even matter when I come to your baseball game or if I even come at all? Like any of *this* even matters!" I did a circling motion with my hands to indicate I was talking about the two of us. He grabbed my hands with force and pushed me up against the brick wall.

"*Never* say that we don't matter."

With those few simple words from Maverick, my wall began to crumble. *No! I need to keep it up.* He slowly let go of my arms, his body still holding me in place against the brick wall of the restaurant. He placed his strong arms on either side of my head against the brick wall, pinning me.

"*This*…is *all* that matters." He spoke with conviction as he used one of his arms to motion back and forth between the two of us.

I knew he was about to lean in and kiss me. His touch was all that I wanted but I was still hurt—remembering the pain I experienced when I found out he was leaving to go play baseball. The thought of him leaving made me unbelievably insecure; but I was also furious and suddenly knew why.

You allowed yourself to hope that you'd be a part of his life plans when he didn't even care about you enough to tell you about them. He's leaving you, just like she did.

I shot my hands up and pushed against his chest with every bit of strength I had but he wouldn't move. Enraged, I balled my hands into fists and beat against his chest.

"Get away from me!" I yelled at him. "Get away from me! *I hate you!*" I screamed the words as I pounded angrily on his solid chest that refused to yield. Externally I attempted to push him away with my words of hate and anger, while internally I begged for his comfort and protection.

Please don't leave me. I need you, Maverick. I'm incomplete without you.

I prayed he understood I was only pushing him away because I was terrified. I needed him to see past the anger and realize what I was truly afraid of: loving someone, only to be abandoned by them again.

"I said get the hell away from me!" I pushed against his strong body but he wouldn't move.

He dropped one of his arms from the wall behind me and grabbed my hand so I couldn't keep hitting him; then he grabbed my other hand and held it against the wall. He pushed his massive body up against mine, pinning me gently yet forcefully to the wall so I couldn't fight him. I held onto my anger, struggling against him with all my might.

I heard him speak to my soul without him even opening his lips. *I know you're afraid. Stop holding onto all this anger and fear. Let me help you.*

Then he looked at me with compassion and strength, and with his blue eyes, he guided me to calm; the waves in his eyes lapping at my fire gently, turning the boil to a simmer, then finally, stilling.

"Stop pushing me away." He used his index finger to raise my chin to his eyes. "Tell me what's wrong." He spoke with gentle authority.

I looked away, glancing around frantically, trying not to give into the confession that was forming on my lips—"I'm scared." The words fell from my mouth without my consent.

"Why?"

"Let's see," I said sarcastically as I held up my fingers and began to count off the reasons. "I'm scared because someone is trying to kill me and I don't know why. I'm scared because someone murdered my mom when I was ten years old and I watched her bleed to death and couldn't save her. Oh, yes and they never found the man who murdered her. I'm scared because I don't know what's happening. I'm scared that some old lady gave me a box with some mysterious necklace in it on the night I was almost murdered. I'm scared of the dreams and visions that I have and I'm scared of what they mean. And I'm scared that somehow none of this feels coincidental at all—me moving here, the reservation, even meeting *you*."

I finished my admission then looked up, hopeful he would buy the story I was selling even though I was leaving out the most crucial part.

"What else?" He pushed me further, our connection betraying me, alerting him to the fact that I was withholding something.

A war raged within me between what was and what could possibly be, that old part of me fighting to hold onto my coping mechanisms while the newfound piece of me struggled to let them go. It was confusing, exhausting, and most of all, frightening, but each time he ran his finger across my cheek I calmed as I let the old slowly slip away—for him and because of him. He used his strong hands to lift my chin again and when I saw his eyes I knew I would give him what he asked for, even though it scared me to death.

I closed my eyes and continued, fearful as I spoke. "And more than all of that, I'm scared of how I feel about you. I'm scared I'm going to lose you, just like I lost her." I found beautiful freedom in the honesty of my words.

"I'm scared too, Elle. Scared as hell." Maverick spoke softly as he leaned in toward me, touching his forehead softly to mine. "But I'm not going to let fear keep us apart. I *need* you."

I was speechless. My heart soared. *Maverick Mason* needs *me*? I couldn't even comprehend the words. They were too good to be true. How could I be living this dream? After all the brokenness and pain and fear, I could hardly comprehend being given such a beautiful gift.

"Elle?" He pulled back slightly, our foreheads no longer touching. His eyes locked on mine, his gaze leveling me. "Let's be scared as hell together, OK? Don't push me away."

It was a command, not a request. And in that moment, I loved his controlling tendencies. I shook my head yes. We both wanted the same thing. I didn't want to fight it anymore. I didn't want to struggle constantly to hold my wall in place and

255

push him away. It was too hard. I closed my eyes and let surrender wash over me as Maverick moved toward me. But just before our lips connected I pushed him back, somehow finding the will to stop. I needed one more answer first.

"Wait." I shoved back on his massive chest but he barely budged. "Why didn't you tell me about baseball?" I didn't give him a chance to answer before I continued with my next question. "And while I'm asking questions, why didn't you tell me about some company of yours that everyone keeps talking about?"

"Is that what was bothering you?" He sounded amused.

I nodded. "It made me realize how little I really know you and how stupid it was of me to allow myself to think that…"

"Elle—" he said my name like a prayer on his lips, one that I wanted to hear over and over, forever. "Look at me," he commanded. He understood my need for reassurance. "We still have a lot to learn about each other. We have to take it slow and let the facts catch up with our feelings. It will take time. You have to be patient."

I dropped my head. "I don't do patient very well."

"I know, Baby Girl."

"It just hurt, hearing those things from someone else instead of you."

"Why?" His eyes pried into my soul. He was challenging me, testing me, calling me to open up to him. I looked up into his eyes, determined to answer his question, even though it wouldn't be easy.

"Because it hurt to know that you might be leaving to go play baseball…" I paused, my heartbeat pounding erratically, trying to force the next words out. It was so difficult for me to open myself up to someone emotionally. But I knew I had to try, for him. "—without me." I looked away, uncomfortable with my confession and wanting to avoid his gaze. It was so soon—too soon—to be thinking these thoughts. I knew that. But I couldn't hold them at bay. The magnetism that surged between us, that connected us—it was an all-consuming force; as powerful as a hurricane, impossible to hold at bay, and unable to be controlled. I barely knew Maverick Mason, yet somehow I knew one thing without question—I couldn't live without him.

He used his finger to lift my chin toward him. "Elle, I don't know if I will go play professional baseball or not. I won't know until the draft this summer. But if I do, I want you with me. Wherever I go, I want you there. Always."

With those words of promise, I let go of my all my fight, my fear, and my questions. I allowed my wall of protection to crumble down at his feet. As we pressed our lips together passionately, I released my insecurity and allowed myself to feel what he was telling me with his touch—that he needed me as much as I needed him.

I was still dazed by our passionate exchange as he walked me back into the restaurant with his arm around my waist possessively. Everyone in the burger joint watched us. My face flushed. Maverick was calm, seemingly unaffected as usual.

We made our way back to our seats and I made a vain attempt to act interested in our friends' conversation. All I really wanted to do was leave, because I wanted to be alone with Maverick. After several minutes of forcing myself to make small talk, I finally saw Maverick stand, grabbing my hand to pull me up alongside him.

"I'll take Elle home so you don't have to go out of your way girls." My friends hung on every word he spoke and I rolled my eyes, annoyed that my boyfriend had such an effect on other girls.

"See you later." I waved to my friends then turned to follow Maverick out the door, elated.

We drove the whole way home in silence, Maverick's strong arm wrapped around me protectively, as we weaved our way through the narrow, midtown Tulsa streets. When we pulled up to the Mason estate and the gate swung open, I suddenly remembered another question he hadn't yet answered. I sat up and pushed myself away from his body so I could look at him while I addressed him.

"By the way, can you please fill me in on this company of yours since apparently I'm only dating you because of it?" I said with bitterness.

"It's not my company," he stated matter-of-factly as he pulled over in front of my aunt's cottage.

"Well several people have mentioned it to me and they definitely seemed to think it is *your* company and they accused me of being poor white trash who was only dating you for all your money."

He pulled over and put the truck in park aggressively.

"Who the hell called you *poor white trash?*" I loved how hot he looked when he was possessive and protective.

"Don't worry about it," I said, wanting to change the subject back to his company.

"Tell me who said it."

He wouldn't give up. "Margot Weston," I admitted.

"Of course she would say that. All she cares about is money," Maverick said with disgust.

"I couldn't care less about Margot. I want to know about this company everyone else seems to know about but me."

He took a deep breath and reluctantly started his explanation. "I've always had a thing for computers and electronics, from the time I was little. I developed a few apps last year that sold for quite a bit of money and my dad started a tech company with it that's doing pretty well. The company will be mine when I graduate from college." He looked at me as he said his next words. "*If* that's what I decide I want to do."

I tried to act unimpressed by his admission and fortunately, years of practice with my countenance of total indifference proved helpful in my endeavor. I faked swooning and placed my hand dramatically over my forehead.

"Oh my. Whatever will you do? Sign a professional base-ball contract for millions of dollars or run a multi-million-dollar company that's already waiting for you?" I let my hand drop and rolled my eyes dramatically. "I mean, your first-world problems are out of control, Maverick. I don't know how you do it, really, I don't. It must be so exhausting to be you."

In one swift movement, he was on top of me, tickling me endlessly and pinning me with his entire body weight onto the front seat of his truck. He lifted my arms above my head with one hand and continued his torture with the other while I laughed and screamed. When I could hardly breathe, he finally stopped tickling me. Suddenly the mood became serious.

His eyes seemed to smolder as he laid there on top of me, holding me down but no longer against my will. There was no place I would rather be. He lightened the mood between us as he whispered seductively in my ear.

"Say you're sorry."

"Never," I responded breathily.

He kissed my forehead and repeated his words. "Say you're sorry."

I shook my head no and then felt him kiss my right cheek before he said it again.

"Elle, say you're sorry," then he hovered over my lips and the longing for him was all consuming.

"I'm *not* sorry," I whispered between breaths, and before I even finished the words his lips were on top of mine, crushing me like a wave hitting the beach in a methodic, rhythmic flow both powerful yet perfectly peaceful. I never wanted him to stop but always the gentleman, he eventually pulled away—his rapid breaths betraying his need, telling me that he didn't want to be done either. Without thinking I grabbed his strong arms and pulled him back down then wrapped my legs around him. He kissed me again, passionately, and this time he had to rip himself from me. I pouted. He was shaken, struggling to regain the composure I had never seen him lose. I started to move toward him and he put his hand up, signaling for me not to move an inch further.

"Elle," he panted. "What are you trying to do to me? Your aunt and your dad are just inside the house for God's sake."

"So." I shrugged my shoulders and looked up at him from under my eyelashes. He shook his head and held his hand up, but I could tell he loved my brazen attitude.

"Why don't you go inside and ask if you can come over to my house for a while?"

I didn't have to be told twice. I hopped out of the truck and ran inside to ask my dad and much to my surprise, he gave his instant approval.

We made our way up the hill and as soon as the Mason mansion was in view, I remembered several weeks before when I walked up the steps of that mansion for the first time to go to Maverick's fall party. I was so determined to find Maverick and tell him how I felt about him, but then Caleb walked up behind me and sabotaged my plans for the night. I remembered playing truth or dare and I smiled at the memory, thinking about how furious I was with him that night, but even more so, at myself for wanting him so badly.

"What are you smiling about?" Maverick asked.

"Just thinking about that first night I came to your house for your fall party. I was so pissed at you when we played truth or dare."

"You were just pissed because you wanted me so badly and you couldn't have what you wanted that *very* instant."

I scoffed at his remark. "You wish," I said, but we both knew he had hit the nail on the head as usual.

We walked into his house hand in hand and I felt surprisingly at ease as he took me past the enormous double staircases in the foyer and into the kitchen. He grabbed a plate of snacks that were setting out for him and then took my hand to lead me down a long hallway. When we got to the end of the hallway I heard a melodic voice call out his name.

"Maverick? Is that you, honey?" I glanced through the doorway and saw a tall, elegant woman sitting in a reading chair next to the fire. She had dark hair cut into a long, asymmetrical bob that nearly touched her shoulders. She was breathtakingly beautiful.

"Yes, it's me, Mom," Maverick answered.

He led me into the room and Maverick made his introduction with a huge smile on his face. I walked straight up to her and held my hand out confidently, shaking hers firmly and telling her how nice it was to meet her. She stared at me with fascination as I tried to discern whether or not she approved of me.

"Oh Mav, she's even more beautiful than you said honey." She leaned in and gave him a loving kiss on the cheek then stepped away and winked at me. I noted that his mother was where he inherited that trademark wink from as well as the piercing-blue eyes. She shooed us away and told us to take our snacks and go study then she gave me one last hug and told me how nice it was to finally meet me. I was elated as we walked out of the room, knowing I had received his mother's consent.

We walked down a long hallway full of pictures. Maverick held my hand and led me, pulling me through the hallway. I sensed an urgency, though I wasn't sure why. The more he pulled, the more I slowed down, the pictures on the walls calling to me. I came to one large picture, a black-and-white one framed in a gorgeous gold frame. I recognized the cherub-faced angel instantly. *That's the same girl in the pictures in my aunt's hallway too.*

"Maverick who is that?" I pointed to the angelic girl with the perfect ringlets framing her face. I felt a connection to her, though I wasn't sure why.

"That's my sister." He was curt, refusing to look at me—and his tone indicated the subject was closed. *Eventually you have to talk to me about it.* I knew Maverick wasn't telling me something, and I knew I would ask him about it again. When the time was right.

I saw a staircase at the back of the room I hadn't noticed on the night of the party, probably because the space was crammed with dancing teenagers. Maverick led me over to the staircase and we climbed them, then landed in a vestibule with several doorways. I was trying not to act shocked or impressed by the enormity of the house but eventually I couldn't resist the urge.

"How do you even find your way around this place?" I commented dryly. "I bet you still get lost, don't you? Just admit it." I teased. He slapped me on the behind. I yelped in protest, then giggled.

Maverick opened two large double doors and then we were in his room—finally. I was momentarily taken back by what I saw which was more of a house itself than a high-school boy's bedroom. There was a large fireplace at one end of the room then a living area with a massive television and gaming chairs. On the other side of the room was a king-sized bed covered with lush bedding and pillows. I noticed a modern staircase in the corner of the room that seemed to lead to another loft area. As usual, I chose the sarcastic response because I didn't know what else to do upon seeing such opulence.

"This is exactly what my room back in the parsonage in Ohio looked like so don't expect me to be impressed by any of this."

He laughed and winked at me. "I bet. I hear parsonages in Ohio are all the rage."

"So your mom is cool with you having your girlfriends in your bedroom?" I asked, shocked.

Maverick was quiet, considering his words before he responded. "I've never had a girl in my bedroom before."

I'm the first girl Maverick Mason has ever had in his room? His confession made my heart soar with pride.

"And yes, my parents are cool with me having my girl-friend in my bedroom because they trust me."

"Well aren't you just the perfect child?" I rolled my eyes, annoyed at his self-righteousness.

He glared at me briefly, then chose to change the subject. "We've got a lot to do. Let's get to work." He pulled out his laptop and motioned to me to grab my backpack. As I fished through my bag, I smiled to myself thinking about my triumph.

I'm the first girl Maverick Mason has ever had in his bedroom.

I pulled out my notebook and showed him the infor-mation about Rosemary, James Weston, and Chief Joseph Blackwater. The whole time I absentmindedly fingered the heart-shaped necklace around my neck.

"What's that?" Maverick reached out and touched the locket.

I was terrified to tell him the truth, afraid he would think I was crazy. I took two deep breaths and summoned the courage to speak.

"Maverick, she was there that night, at the reservation."

"Who?" I could see the confusion written on his face.

"Rosemary." I pointed at the name scrawled on the note-pad in front of me. "She was the one who gave me this necklace. I figured out how to open the wooden box finally. There were two roses carved in the side and when I pushed them both, the box opened. This necklace was inside."

I held my breath as I awaited his response, fully expecting him to call me completely insane. Instead he reached out and grabbed me, pulling me onto his lap with one strong movement. As I sat on his lap, he reached up and examined the necklace with his sturdy hands. Seconds later I heard a click and, completely dumfounded, I watched him open the necklace, which I realized was, in actuality, a locket. Slowly he peeled the two sides of the locket apart to reveal a picture inside of two beautiful young women.

My eyes were drawn to the one on the left, the girl with coal-black eyes and long ebony hair. She was holding her large belly lovingly—obviously glowing with the joy of pregnancy—and her angelic face was lightened with a glowing smile of happiness. I was enamored by her.

As I looked at the picture, I knew the woman on the left—the one I was inexplicably being drawn to—was a total stranger; but for some reason, when I looked at her, all I could see was my mother.

CHAPTER 22

Maverick took me home not long after our discovery of the locket. I needed to talk to my aunt. My search for the truth superseded all else and my intuition told me she had the answers I needed.

"Aunt Cordelia, can I talk to you for a second?" I didn't waste any time getting to the point. I worried that my dad would find my request suspicious but he didn't even bother looking up from his book, much to my relief. I turned to walk down the hallway to my bedroom and my aunt followed.

Cordelia sat down on my bed, her eyes showing concern. I took off the necklace and opened it the way Maverick had shown me, then held it out to her. She took it from my hands and as she looked at the picture, the recognition on her face was instantaneous. I watched a single tear rolled down her face.

"That's my mother." She pointed at the girl on the right of the picture—the one with brown eyes and short dark hair cut into a bob.

"Do you know who this is?" I pointed to the girl on the left, the one with the long ebony waves and deep-set dimples.

She shook her head. "No, I've never seen her before but it looks like one of my mom's childhood friends. How did you get this, Elle?"

Don't tell her the truth. Protect her from this nightmare.

"I found it in one of my mom's old coats when we moved. Please don't tell my dad?"

My aunt nodded her head and I knew my secret was safe with her. She caressed the picture lovingly with her thumb before she closed the locket and handed it back to me. "I'm sure she would want you to have it. I don't know the woman on the left but the woman on the right is your grandmother, Margaret Smith." My aunt pushed my hair back from my face then stood up to leave, planting a kiss on the top of my head before she walked out of my room. I stared at the picture, confused.

So who is the woman on the left? She's the one who feels familiar?

Suddenly a different picture floated to the surface of my mind—a picture of a beautiful woman dressed in white, standing on the threshold of a yellow clapboard house, next to James Weston. I jumped off my bed and salvaged my iPad out of my backpack then clicked on the folder Maverick saved on my home screen with information about James Weston and the Osage Reservation. I scrolled through the pages frantically until I found what I was looking for—the picture of James Weston and Rosemary on their wedding day. I held the tiny picture in the locket next to the picture on my iPad screen, comparing the two, confirming my suspicions were correct. The picture in the locket was so tiny I didn't realize it at first, but finally I made the connection.

It's Rosemary. The teenage beauty pictured inside the necklace, the woman in the picture with James Weston on their wedding day, the woman on the reservation…they all are the same person: Rosemary.

I spent the evening doing more research but no longer focused on James Weston. Instead, I focused on Rosemary Blackwater-Weston. There was little information to be found but what I did uncover was in the *Osage County Herald*—an article from the early 1950s that was a feature piece about the school on the Osage reservation. I saw a black-and-white picture at the bottom of the article and I zoomed in on the students I saw standing in front of a one-room schoolhouse. There in the picture—standing on the back row with their arms wrapped around each other, joyous smiles spread across their faces—were two young teenage beauties. One had dark hair cut into a bob that landed just below her chin while the other had ebony waves falling down to her waist. I stared at the picture. The girls loved one another deeply.

Rosemary and my Grandmother—Margaret Smith—were best friends.

I continued my research for hours, but only found two more articles. One I'd already seen when I researched James Weston—the article about his marriage to Rosemary; the other was Rosemary's obituary. The obituary contained no picture, only a single column telling of Rosemary's untimely death just five months after her marriage to James Weston. The article lamented the death of the chief's only daughter, merely six weeks after the chief himself died, then it ended with one last sentence: "Rosemary was survived by her husband, James Weston. Authorities are still searching for their daughter who went missing on the night of Rosemary's death."

My head swam and although I knew pieces of the puzzle were shifting into place, the picture was still frustratingly unidentifiable. I looked at the clock and realized it was 11:30 p.m. The house was dark and still, and an eerie silence enveloped me, making me feel alone. I picked up my phone and texted the only person who filled the black hole that nagged at my soul.

I miss you.

His response was immediate. *I miss you too. Wish I could come and get you but I think we've been pushing the limits lately.*

I found the sad face-emoticon and sent it. I knew he was right, but I still would have risked sneaking out again to see him.

Always so responsible, Maverick Mason.

You know it, Baby Girl. Did you find out anything else?

Yes, too much to text. I'll tell you tomorrow.

My phone rang immediately and I picked up to see Maverick's face. An uncontrollable smile spread across my face.

"I couldn't wait until tomorrow. What's up?"

"So I asked my aunt and she told me she recognized one of the girls in the picture in my locket—it's my Grandmother Smith when she was a teenager. She didn't know who Rosemary was but I compared to the picture in the locket to the pictures in the newspaper articles and it's the same girl. I guess Rosemary and my grandmother were childhood best friends on the Reservation. And Rosemary was also Chief Blackwater's daughter *and* James Weston's first wife."

He was quiet, his brow furrowed together in concentration. It was me who interrupted the silence.

"So what about you? Did you find out anything about James Weston?"

"I looked into it but really the only information about him is all related to his companies and business dealings. It's almost like anything from his early years disappeared. I know there has to be missing pieces out there though." He smiled his most dashing smile, oozing with confidence. It leveled me even through the phone. "Don't worry. I'll find them."

"Oh trust me, I don't doubt you Maverick Mason. Not for a second." I smiled back at him, feeling our magnetic pull. A phone call wasn't close enough.

"Well I guess I better let you go before your dad comes in and gets mad at me for keeping you up too late."

"Are you scared of Johnny C Maverick? Say it ain't so," I teased.

"Johnny C," he chuckled. "I like that."

"It's what my best friends back home always called him."

Suddenly the mood turned more serious.

"I'd love to meet your friends some day." He gave me another one of his heart-stopping smiles.

He's talking about meeting my best friends. That means he's thinking about our future. I could hardly contain my excitement.

"I might be able to arrange that. Grace will *love* you by the way."

"I'm sure she will. Most girls do." He gave me a playful wink.

I shook my head and pressed my lips together in a firm line, showing how unimpressed I was by his overconfidence. I wanted to bring him down a notch—or two, or three.

"Grace might be an easy sell but trust me, Charlie won't be that impressed."

The mood shifted.

"Why do you say that?" He was defensive.

"Because he won't be." I wasn't backing down.

"Why would you think Charlie won't like me?"

I started shifting back and forth in my seat and was thankful we were just FaceTiming so he couldn't tell.

"I didn't say he won't like you. I said he won't be as easy as Grace."

"Why?"

I was starting to get irritated. "Oh I don't know, because he's not going to lose his mind the second you look at him and smile." I rolled my eyes.

"Is that all?"

My eyes were narrowed. "What do you mean is that all? If you have something to say just say it."

"Alright, I will."

"Please do."

"I guess I'm a little skeptical of you having a guy as a best friend. In my opinion, guys and girls can't be best friends."

"And why is that?"

"Because someone usually likes someone, they just aren't being honest about it."

I let out a disgusted sigh.

"You have no clue what you're talking about Maverick. I swear to God you think you know everything."

He refused to back down and so did I.

"I guess we will have to agree to disagree, Baby Girl, because that's the way I see it."

"Fine. We will agree to disagree then. Charlie and I have been best friends since we were two years old and I can assure you that neither of us feels anything but friendship toward each other."

"Whatever you say…"

His condescending tone annoyed me.

"Let's just change the subject, OK. I'm not in the mood to fight."

"Sounds good to me."

We sat there in silence for an uncomfortable period of time, until finally Maverick broke the silence with another taboo topic. He was being purposefully antagonistic, as usual.

"Have you gotten your dress for the homecoming dance on Friday? It's only three days away."

"No, I haven't," I said, perturbed.

"Well don't forget I like red." He winked at me playfully through the phone and my stomach did flip flops in response, even though I was irritated with him.

"We'll see. I like black." With that, I hung up the phone and threw myself back on my pillow, my heart beating rapidly after our exchange. *Will I ever stop feeling this way?*

I heard a knock on my door.

"Come in."

My aunt peeked her head through the door, her grey hair pulled back in a bun with her knitting needles—her signature up-do.

"Were you talking to Maverick?" she asked.

"Yes," I replied, that same giddy smile spreading across my face at the mention of his name. I coughed, covering my emotions, annoyed with myself for how weak I was.

"It's awfully late to be on the phone sweetheart." She sent a judgmental glance toward the clock, which read midnight.

I shook my head yes, looking up apologetically.

"I'm sorry Aunt Cordelia. I'm heading to bed right now, I promise."

She didn't move. She stared at me, something unspoken in her gaze, and it made my stomach churn. Finally, she walked over and sat on the bed, grabbed my hand, then patted it lovingly. My aunt could tell how Maverick and I felt about each other and it was if she knew that it could not be controlled, so she wouldn't even try; and for that I was thankful. At the same time, I could tell that something about our relationship worried her deeply—frightened her almost—and without her speaking it, that her fear was somehow related to what happened with my mother and Nathan Weston. I held my breath, hoping she wouldn't bring the subject up. I was unwilling to hear her thoughts on how mine and Maverick's relationship paralleled Nathan and my mom's, which ended in nothing but tragedy. Thankfully, she didn't.

"I have something I need to give you," she said. "Wait here." She walked down the hallway that led to her bedroom and was gone for several minutes before returning with a worn paper envelope in her hand. She sat down and held it in her lap, watching it intently, as if trying to decide whether to give it to me or not. Finally, she handed the envelope to me—ever so slowly—as though it was painful for her to part with. Then she stood up and walked out of the room, saying nothing.

I sat there with the envelope, unable to move after I recognized the writing on the front. I knew who the letter was from—my mother. My hands trembled at the thought of opening the letter and reading her words. Every single day I missed her and the pain of going through my life without her was unbearable. I still longed to hear her voice, to feel her touch, and to know the comfort of her presence. I knew seeing her words on the day she died would be excruciating. I didn't want to feel any more pain. I stuffed the letter in the inside pocket of my jacket lying on the floor beside my bed, and promised to find the courage to read it later.

I rolled over, escaping into my pillow—my thoughts swimming about my mom's letter and Rosemary. I fingered the heart-shaped locket around my neck absentmindedly as I lost myself in the past—a past that had more questions than answers, more pain than joy, and more darkness than light. Eventually, I found a restless sleep.

I awakened to a knock at my door. My first thought was of the necklace around my neck. I sat up and shoved the necklace underneath my T-shirt as my dad opened the door to remind me we had to leave for school in fifteen minutes. I jumped out of bed, threw on my school uniform and met him at the door.

I went through the school day as I did the day before, only slightly more accustomed to all eyes staring at me as Maverick and I walked down the hall together. We went to lunch together again but kept it light, not talking about any of the heavy subjects that we'd discussed on our previous lunch date.

Somehow Maverick always knew just what I needed, and what I needed was a distraction from the mysteries and nightmares of my past—and my present.

After lunch, we arrived back at school in time to sit outside for a while before the bell rang. Maverick put his truck bed down then turned his music up and before I knew it, a crowd had formed around us. Carly, Madison and Macey texted while we were at lunch so I pulled out my phone and sent them a message telling them to meet us in the parking lot. Seconds later they arrived and we sat on the truck bed, our legs swinging back and forth as we chattered endlessly about how hard the English test was in fourth hour and how Chesney Thompson threw up in the middle of chapel that morning.

"Elle, we're going shopping after school and you should come with us. I have *got* to get some accessories for my dress," Madison announced dramatically.

The other girls all chimed in their agreement as I sat there in silence. I knew I couldn't afford the price tags at any of the places they were accustomed to shopping.

"Elle, you're coming right?" Macey asked sweetly. "Don't you need to find some accessories for your dress?"

I laughed loudly. "What dress?"

I heard gasping from not only my three friends, but any other female who was in listening range of what I had just said. I rolled my eyes.

"Imagine the horror!" I grasped my chest for dramatic effect. "I don't have a dress for the dance on Friday night!" The girls all gawked at me as if I was certifiably crazy and I started laughing hysterically, which only made them more unsure of my mental state. "OK, OK, I will go shopping with you guys," I finally conceded. "But I get to choose where we're shopping," I added. The girls looked skeptical but agreed.

As we finalized our plans for after school, the crowd started to disperse slowly. The bell was about to ring. Maverick walked me to class—all eyes on us as usual—and deposited me right at the door. I knew I wouldn't see him again for several hours since he went straight to baseball practice after fifth hour, so when he grabbed me and pulled toward him with one swift movement and planted a swift kiss on my lips, I didn't protest.

"No PDA Mr. Mason," I heard Mr. Thompson, my fifth-hour teacher, admonish.

I pushed Maverick away at the sound of my teacher's voice and as I did, I saw him give me that wink of his. I turned to walk away, a smile plastered on my face.

"See ya later Baby Girl," I heard him say as I glanced over my shoulder to give him one last look before he walked away.

I met the girls in the parking lot after school as we had planned. I asked for the keys to my dad's new replacement for the Brookville Church of God van—a blue Ford Taurus with cloth interior that was at least a decade old—which was definitely not the type of transportation the girls were used to riding in to say the least.

I laughed as I told them to hop in and they all jumped into the Taurus with no hesitation. I Google Mapped my destination and with the windows cracked and the music turned up, we made our way down Riverside drive to the north side of town. I pulled up to a large storefront that had large, red capital letters painted on the front that said "GOODWILL". I saw the shock on their faces as I stopped the car and hopped out.

"C'mon girls," I said. "It's time for you to shop my way."

They piled out of the car, wide-eyed and perplexed. Madison—the fashion expert of the group—spoke up first as we walked through the front doors.

"OK, so first things first. We've got to get Elle a dress STAT."

We made our way to the back of the store where there was a section of old wedding dresses and second-hand gowns. Carly and Macey laughed loudly as they pulled out heinous dresses and held them up to one another but Madison and I were on a mission.

"What about this one?" I asked, holding up an emerald-blue sequined dress.

Madison turned up her nose at the dress. "That's so two-thousand and nine, Elle."

"Oh, my bad fashion goddess," I teased.

She held up a pale-pink short dress with a plunging neck-line. "How about this?"

"Heck no. There is absolutely no way my dad would let me out of the house in that."

She placed the dress in the cart anyway. "Well I want to see it on you," she argued.

I found two simple black dresses that I thought had potential and Madison found a purple silk gown that she insisted I try on even though I protested.

After we made our way through the entire row of dresses, we decided to try our luck at jewelry and accessories. Madison immediately found a gold cuff with a large embedded stone that looked like a ruby.

"OMG this is *perfect* for my dress!" she exclaimed with excitement. "And it's only fifty cents. Are you kidding me?"

I made my best "see I told you so" face and continued to usher the girls down the next aisle where Carly found a gorgeous old fur coat for $50.

"I've been wanting to borrow my mom's fur coat forever but she never lets me. This looks just like it and it's only fifty dollars!" She was beyond thrilled.

"And you guys thought Utica Square was the only place in Tulsa to shop…" I didn't bother to hid my know-it-all attitude.

We proceeded down the last aisle and as the girls were giggling and taking turns putting silly hats on each other, a flash of red caught the corner of my eye. At the end of the aisle, I saw a beat-up mannequin who was on her last leg, but she was wearing the most gorgeous red dress I'd ever seen.

That's the one. I laughed to myself as I thought of Maverick's request for a red dress.

"What are you laughing at?" Madison asked.

"Nothing," I lied.

"Yeah right. You better tell me."

"Just that Maverick told me he wanted me to buy a red dress." I glanced toward the dress and Madison's eyes followed.

Her jaw dropped. "Elle, that is absolutely gorgeous. You have to try it on."

I tried on all the other dresses first and saved the red one for last. When I walked out of the dressing room in the red lace sheath dress, the girls were speechless. I pulled my long dark waves up into a loose bun on top of my head and stuck a pencil through it to hold it up, then I looked at myself in the mirror. It was simple, but perfect.

"That's definitely the one," Carly said.

"Wow. You look amazing, Elle," Macey agreed.

"I can't even believe you just found *that* dress for twenty dollars at a thrift store," Madison stated with disbelief.

"Welcome to the world of thrift-store shopping, girls." We all laughed as I did a twirl in my $20 red dress.

I was in a dream world as I made my way back into the dressing room, thinking about my new red dress, Maverick in a suit, and an entire evening of dancing with his arms around me. As I picked up my jacket to put it back on, a white envelope fell out of the inside pocket, and my dream world instantly shattered.

I couldn't ignore my sobering reality any longer—there was no happy ending for me and Maverick, not unless I found out who murdered my mother and who tried to murder me.

I was completely preoccupied while the girls and I checked out, though I did my best to laugh and partake in their lighthearted banter. The letter burned a hole in my pocket. I needed to be alone to read my mother's words. I dropped the girls back off at their cars then headed home to the safety of my little bedroom in the back of the cottage. I opened the letter and took a sharp, painful breath upon seeing her handwriting,

Nov. 17, 2009

Sis,

I've missed you so much. Please don't be mad at me for not contacting you sooner. After the accident I didn't remember anything. By the time the memories started coming back, I had a beautiful daughter to protect so I stayed hidden. I wanted to forget my past and run from it so I could protect her, but now I fear my past will always haunt me and if I don't do something, it will haunt her too. Every day I remember more and as the memories return, I hope to find out the truth for myself, but more importantly—for my daughter Elyse. There is nothing I won't sacrifice to save her from the evil that haunts me. I've loved you always sweet sister and I will see you again, whether in this life or the next.

~Eleanor
John 8:32

I threw the letter down and reached for the Bible that sat in the nightstand next to my bed, flipping quickly to the gospel of John.

"Then you will know the truth, and the truth will set you free." John 8:32

As I read those words from the Bible, another piece of the puzzle shifted into place, making that unidentifiable picture somewhat clearer, yet still unrecognizable. Something began to take form. A heart-shaped necklace on Rosemary's neck, on my mother's neck, and on my neck. I knew that not only was the necklace connected to all three of us, but somehow all three of us were connected as well. But how?

I needed to go for a run. I threw on my shorts, a sports bra, a long-sleeved fitted shirt and my Nike tennis shoes and was gone in two minutes, calling to my aunt and my dad as I rushed out the door. My feet hit the ground hard and fast, pounding my frustrations, my fears, my questions, and most of all, my anger, into the pavement. I ran past the basketball courts and down the path that found its way into the woods, leading to the edge of the Mason property. I ran around the path that circled the pond until I came upon the boathouse. Momentarily, my thoughts shifted to the comfort of Maverick's arms around me and the flood of emotions I experienced that night, when we had our first kiss. But unfortunately, my thoughts could not stay there. The darkness called to me and as I continued to run hard, visions of Rosemary and my mother with a necklace around their necks clouded my thoughts. I ran into the woods as the last rays of sunshine began to fade into dusk and finally, the path ended at a massive oak tree.

Your mother and Nathan Weston fell deeply and madly in love. They would meet each other secretly at an old oak tree on the back of the property. My aunt's words echoed in my mind.

I walked up to the oak tree cautiously, placing my hand on the thick, dark bark that covered the massive trunk. I slowly rounded the tree. I thought about my mother—trying to reconcile the young, charismatic woman I never knew with the strong, graceful preacher's wife who raised me—struggling to make sense of her sordid past that was a secret not only to me, but to my father as well.

The texture of bark beneath my fingers changed. I stopped. Dusk was turning to darkness with each passing moment so I had to lean in closely to the trunk. Lines were scratched into the trunk of the majestic old tree. They were initials carved inside of a heart: "NW + ES."

This is it. This is the tree where my mom used to meet Nathan Weston.

Nathan Weston and Eleanor Smith, both tragically dead at far too young of an age, their secrets buried with them. I sat down underneath the tree, exhausted physically, mentally, and emotionally. I leaned up against the tree where my mother used to sit with her forbidden love in her past life and I let the tears fall. I let them fall for my mother, for her long-lost love, but most of all, I let them fall for myself, because of the betrayal I felt. There was no denying her past now: my mother had another life she hid from me entirely.

CHAPTER 23

I sat on my favorite stool in our tiny kitchen in Ohio.

My mother loved bright colors and she had the idea of painting each one of our old wooden barstools a different color. I chose purple. My mom chose a deep turquoise, and my dad chose black. I laughed as we went to the paint store and made the unanimous decision that our two votes vetoed Dad's vote for black. For the third barstool, we picked out the most brilliant shade of bright yellow.

I thought the purple barstool would be my favorite but once we were done, the yellow was by far the one I loved most. I always chose to sit on it and somehow it reminded me of her smile and hot Ohio summer days playing in the creek, the smell of her chocolate-chip cookies baking in the oven and mostly, the yellow floor-length sundress she wore so beautifully. Yellow reminded me of her.

My mother and I laughed as we blew out the candles on my cake simultaneously, then she handed me a gift to unwrap. She watched with anticipation as I opened the present to reveal a dark wooden box with beautiful carvings engraved deep within the mahogany wood. I looked up at her, an ominous feeling growing inside of me as I noticed the light dissipating within the room.

I opened the box and saw a heart-shaped necklace sitting on plush purple velvet. My mother's face was no longer happy. Instead, her features were etched with pain and sadness as she pulled the necklace out and slowly put it around my neck. The room darkened. My mother pushed the wooden box further into my hands, her eyes wide, begging me understand.

When I looked inside the wooden box again, I saw a leather-bound book. I pulled the book slowly out of the bottom of the box as the final streams of light evaporated from the room. I could no longer see my mother's face. I felt her presence though, as she leaned in and whispered in my ear.

"Elle…the truth will set you free."

I woke up disoriented. My name was being called, but by a different voice.

"Elle," Maverick's voice begged me to come back to him. "Elle wake up. You were having another nightmare. Your dad told me you went for a run. It took me forever to find you—"

I heard him, heard the concern in his voice, but didn't want to leave my darkness because she was there. I wanted to stay with my mom—forever—but that unnerving presence in the darkness was always with us. The man without a face.

Slowly I let go of my dream world and opened my eyes. I had fallen asleep against the massive oak tree on the back of the Mason property. It was nearly dark outside but I could see Maverick's crystal-clear blue eyes reaching for me, comforting me, protecting me always. He pulled me into an embrace until I calmed, then helped me up and ushered me back to his truck. As we drove off, I took one last look at the massive oak tree before it faded into darkness, and I swore I saw a figure standing in the distance. She was wearing white and had long silver braids. But when I looked again, she was gone.

As we drove back to the cottage, visions flashed before my eyes of Rosemary, then my mom, then me—all of us wearing a heart-shaped necklace around our necks and carrying a leather-bound book in our hands. My mother's words repeated in my head. *Then you will know the truth, and the truth will set you free.*

Suddenly I was back to being a little girl, sitting on the front pew of my father's church in Ohio listening to him preach, being expected to hold perfectly still. I would look up to see the intricate stained-glass cross behind the baptismal and stare at all its beautiful colors. I had every detail of those windows memorized, even the Bible verse that was interwoven into the stain-glass panels: *The truth will set you free.*

I looked up at Maverick, resolute. "Maverick, I'm going to Ohio. I think there's a book hidden there that might explain everything. I've seen it in my dreams."

The truck was silent. I bounced my foot up and down, nervously awaiting his response, wondering if he would try to control me and forbid me to go, and knowing that even if he did, I would go anyway. As always, his blue eyes pierced my soul, reading my every thought.

"Then I'm going with you," he said decisively.

Sadness gripped my heart and guilt overwhelmed me as I looked at Maverick and realized he had the whole world at his fingertips, and he was willing to risk losing it all, for me.

You can have any girl you want. Why me? I have nothing to offer you but pain and brokenness.

I was unable to hide what I was thinking. I opened my mouth to confess my insecurity, but before I could get the words out, Maverick reached up forcefully and grabbed my face with both hands.

"Elle. *Don't.* Don't do this."

I couldn't stop the self-doubt running rampant through my head. *You are so selfish for dragging him into your world of horrors. He deserves so much better than you. If you really loved him you would walk away.*

I dropped my head in shame. "Maverick, you don't deserve this. You should have a normal life. Date a cheerleader. Go to school dances. Go to college. Be a professional athlete. Run that company of yours one day. Marry someone and have two kids and a white picket fence. I don't know—I just care about you way too much to drag you into my darkness." Pain ripped through my body as I forced myself speak my next words. "You can't have a normal life with me. I'm too screwed up."

His blue eyes burned into my soul and without speaking, he told me he was angry, angry that I would dare to question our connection and more importantly, our undeniable need to be with one another only, no matter what the future held.

"I don't want normal, Elle. I want you."

A tear rolled down my cheek as I heard his confession, then unexpectedly, I burst into laughter as more tears streamed down my face. The irony of this blue-eyed boy who had the world at his feet admitting that I was anything but normal and he still wanted me made me laugh. I pushed myself into his lap, straddling him, and I kissed him while the tears flowed freely. We kissed passionately, desperate for one another, before he pushed away and held my face in his hands again.

"Elle, you're the only one for me. You're completely crazy and unpredictable and frustrating but that's all I want. *You* are all that I want. I knew the first time I saw you that you would be the only woman I will ever love."

I sat there speechless, reveling in his beautiful confession of love. Minutes before I had decided I loved him too much to be selfish, that I had to let him go so he could live a normal life. Now I was sitting in his lap listening to him confess his undying love for me and suddenly I was back under his control. If I was what he wanted, then that is what he would have. Without pause I gazed into his eyes and said the first words that came to me.

"I love you too, Maverick Mason. I'll always love you."

I stayed on his lap, his arms wrapped around me tightly, and while he held me that little black box in the depths of my soul—my coping mechanism that allowed me to survive during a time of great pain and sorrow—shattered to pieces. I let go of the pain of my past to grasp onto a future with Maverick; I was free, like a bird soaring on wings for the first time, coasting high above the earth with the wind beneath my wings.

From that moment on, there would be no more unspoken assumptions about our feelings for one another. Maverick and I both knew without doubt that we were in love with each other.

I pulled away, suddenly remembering Maverick's back-to-school party—three firm squeezes on my hand and his eyes burning into my soul, trying desperately to communicate something unspoken to me. I smirked as I grabbed his hand and squeezed it forcefully, three times. He winked at me, that quick little flicker of his eye that made me lose my mind every time I saw it.

"I knew even then. Three little words, Baby Girl."

I leaned in and kissed him, hardly able to control myself. I was still on his lap and we moved in perfect unison, our bodies clashing against each other yet still unable to find the closeness we desired. The fire of desire threatened to rage past the point of control and I knew he felt it too. Always in control, he stopped and pulled me backward as he let me down gently.

"Elle, you've been gone for hours now. Your aunt and dad are probably looking for you at this point." I pulled myself off him, not bothering to hide my frustration. He laughed as he started his truck and began the short trip back to the cottage. His mask of control returned quickly and when he opened his mouth I knew our passionate moment was over.

"We have to make a plan."

"Huh?" I asked.

He looked at me, slightly perturbed. "Ohio. We need to make a plan."

"Oh, yes," I said, unable to hide the sadness in my voice. I wanted live in my dream world awhile longer—the one where he and I were together, forever, and my past didn't haunt our future. But Maverick was always the realistic one. He was grounded and mature. He brought me back from my dream world because he knew reality is where we both needed to be if we had any hopes of having a future together.

"No, you're right. We definitely need a plan." I tapped my fingers on his dashboard, my mind formulating a plan as he pulled up to the hill that led down to my aunt's cottage.

"OK, tomorrow night is the homecoming dance, right?" He looked at me skeptically. "We're going to homecoming, Elle. You aren't getting out of it."

I smiled. "Of course we are. I already bought an absolutely beautiful *black* dress to wear." I put emphasis on the word black, knowing it would irritate him that I didn't get the color of dress he requested. He didn't show his frustration at my comment but I knew it was there.

"The girls are having a sleepover when the after party is over. They invited me. I'll ask my dad if I can go. You can come to pick me up and we will make an appearance at the dance, then we can leave for Ohio. If we drive through the night we should be there by the next morning. We can look for the book—I think I know right where it will be—then crash for a few hours at my friend's house then drive back. We should be able to make it back by late the next evening if we drive it straight through. I can come up with some reason that I won't be back that night or I can just go off the radar if it comes to that. It's not like it would be the first time…"

Maverick looked at me with disapproval. "What? Do you have a better idea?" I asked.

"Well I usually prefer the truth but in this case I don't think your dad will let you go if we try the honest approach so we're just going to have to go with your plan," he conceded but not without irritation.

"What are you going to tell your mom and dad?" I asked.

"The truth," he said flatly.

My eyes widened and I quickly voiced my displeasure. "You're going to just come right out and tell your parents you're going on a road trip to Ohio with your *girlfriend*?" I stood there staring at him in disbelief.

"Elle, my parents trust me because I've never given them a reason not to." He spoke to me as if I were a child and it pissed me off.

"Well your dad was never a preacher and you never had a million people judging your every single move, so that must have been really nice for you," I spat vehemently.

He laughed at me. I crossed my arms and glared at him in response.

"I've had people watching me and judging me my entire life actually. My dad owns one of the most lucrative oil companies in the world, Elle. I just realized at a very young age that breaking the trust of someone you love is an ignorant choice. I don't lie to people and I don't tolerate being lied to either."

I heard a warning in his words, and it irritated me.

"Wow. Have you thought about writing a book? I mean there has to be a huge market out there for your amazing words of wisdom." I rolled my eyes as I started to get out of the truck. He reached over and grabbed my arm.

"Elle, please don't leave while you're angry."

"What was that whole *I don't lie to people and I don't tolerate being lied to* speech because I feel like that was some passive-aggressive comment aimed at me somehow."

He took a deep breath.

"You're right."

"I know I'm right. And I don't like it when you act all superior and I hate it even more when you're passive aggressive. So if you have something you want to say to me, then say it and we will work it out. Quit playing games."

A smirk played at his lips.

"Alright, I will. Elle, don't ever lie to me. I know you've lied to your dad over the years and I'm guessing you lied to your boyfriends too?" He cocked an eyebrow expectantly. I didn't budge. He kept staring at me and it made me uncomfortable.

"Was that a question?"

"You know it was."

"Well I guess you're going to have to be more specific."

"Elle, did you lie to your other boyfriends?"

"Why does that matter?" I tried avoidance.

"It matters to me."

We stood there, staring one another down in a stand-off. He already knew the answer to the question, but there was something more he was getting at.

"This is getting old. If you want to know something just ask it and let's get this over with."

"Did you cheat on your boyfriends back in Ohio, Elle?"

You could cut the tension with a knife. For some reason, the fire began to rage inside while I simultaneously wanted to run away. He wasn't backing down and I found myself searching for an exit strategy. Finally, I conceded to get the conversation over with once and for all. It was stupid of me to not think he would have questions about my sordid past.

"Yes, I did cheat on my boyfriends back home." I dropped my head, not wanting to meet his gaze. "Why?"

"It matters because you said if I had something I wanted to say, I should just say it." He looked at me with an intensity that leveled me. I wanted to look away, but I couldn't.

"So I'm letting you know that's not going to work for me. If you cheat on me, if you lie to me, we're done." I was ashamed that he even felt the need to have this conversation with me, yet I knew my actions in the past warranted it. I looked away. I just wanted the conversation to be over with.

I looked up, meeting his gaze, pleading with him to see my feelings for him. I breathed—in and out, in and out, deeper each time, trying to find the words to communicate how I felt about him—that he was my very breath, my everything, and I couldn't imagine ever living without him.

"Maverick, I just want you to know—" I couldn't meet his gaze, what I had to say to him was too raw. I was stripped bare at the thought of even speaking the words. I looked out into the dark night, finding the will to continue—"that you're different than all of the others. Everything is different with you. I would never do that to you."

My words didn't seem enough, but I couldn't form any others. I was incapable of putting the depth of my emotions for him into words. The magnetic force between us surged, drawing me toward him. I knew he could feel it too. It called us to connection and it was painful not to answer the calling.

He reached over and pulled my chin in his direction, forcing me ever so gently to meet his steely gaze. "I know I'm different." His confidence was unbelievably attractive. "But just so we're both on the same page. If you cheat on me—even once—I will never give you another chance. We will be through."

I nodded my understanding and we sat in silence for several minutes, Maverick reaching across the darkness to hold my hand.

"There's one more thing I have to tell you." His tone suggested importance. "I asked my dad about James Weston since I couldn't find the information I needed."

I waited anxiously for his next words.

He continued cautiously. "He told me that Mr. Weston has pretty much been off the radar ever since his son Nathan died. He's mainly a silent partner in WestCo and his son, Philip, now runs his portion of the company." I could tell there was more he wanted to tell me but he didn't know how.

"Just tell me Maverick," I demanded.

"Well, this isn't known to the public yet, but James Weston has cancer. He's dying, Elle."

The fire raged. *How dare James Weston die before I have a chance to confront him about what happened to Nathan and my mother. I have to see him before he dies.*

Maverick watched me, his eyes prying into my mind.

"Well good. He deserves to die." I tried my best to act disinterested.

Maverick's scrutinizing glare made me uncomfortable so I scooted up next to him and lay my head on his shoulder to escape it. I knew he was trying to figure out what I was hiding from him. I had to get away from his prying eyes.

"I better get inside before my aunt and dad send out a search party for me."

He grabbed me and pulled me in for a kiss, still quiet and reflective. I kissed him back then hopped out of the truck and ran inside. His blue eyes seared into my soul even as I walked away.

CHAPTER 24

I sat through a late dinner with my family and made small talk, hoping they wouldn't recognize how preoccupied I was. After helping clean up, I disappeared to my room where I immediately reached into my backpack and pulled out my iPad. For a split second, I felt guilty for using the very device that Maverick had gifted me with to deceive him, but I quickly pushed those thoughts to the back of my mind. I had one focus: confronting James Weston before he died.

I started researching hospitals in the Tulsa area and after a frustrating hour, I still hadn't discovered the whereabouts of Mr. Weston. Obviously with a man as affluent and influential as James Weston, privacy was a luxury he could afford. I decided I would start with going to the nicest and biggest hospital in Tulsa: St. Francis. Something told me that Mr. Weston would be in a private room there.

I made my way out to the living room and put in some more face time with the family to avoid any suspicion, then at 10:00 p.m. on the dot, I yawned and professed my exhaustion before I walked back to my bedroom. I lay in bed waiting to hear the house go silent, then I jumped out of bed and made my way out of the window. I took off in a run up the hill and down the path that led to the pool house at the Mason estate. Ever since my wreck, my dad kept his keys with him for safekeeping, so I knew I would have to get inventive to find transportation to the hospital. The only idea I had was crazy, but I was desperate and had no other options. I knew Maverick's garage code—I watched him punch it in when he took me to his house a few days before—and I also knew he left his keys inside his truck.

I didn't even allow myself to stop and think through the insanity of my plan and the fact that I was committing grand theft auto. I was singularly focused on getting to the hospital and confronting James Weston before he died. Nothing else mattered. I punched in the code and opened the door to walk inside the Mavericks' huge garage. My heart dropped when I immediately heard a loud beeping noise.

Crap!

I fumbled around in the dark, trying to decide what to do when I heard four beeps; then the garage went silent. I crouched down by the truck and waited for my fate, my heart racing uncontrollably. I heard footsteps then I heard a voice from around the corner of the truck.

"Really, Elle?"

His condescending tone made the fire burn inside, yet simultaneously, relief flooded my body when I realized it was Maverick.

"Are you kidding me? Stealing my truck from our garage? *That* was your master plan?" He shook his head at me in disapproval but I also noticed a flicker of humor in his eyes. He ran his fingers across a red car with admiration as he walked toward me. "*This* is a vintage Ferrari two-fifty GTO." Then he walked over to a bright canary-yellow car that looked like some type of a spaceship. "And this…this is a Tesla Model S." With an exaggerated hand movement toward all the cars in the garage he looked at me and said with sarcasm, "You seriously think we wouldn't have an alarm on our garage?" He laughed at me and I flushed with anger as I stood up, arms crossed, fire raging, and ready to fight.

"Oh well I'm so sorry I'm not up on the latest rules for garages containing cars that cost enough to feed a freaking third-world country." I noticed he seemed hurt by my words.

"Elle, we give more than you could imagine to help others. Please don't ever insinuate otherwise." He responded with bitterness in his tone. I looked away, guilty for hurting his feelings but not ready to apologize.

"So please enlighten me on exactly where you planned on going once you pulled off grand theft auto," Maverick smirked.

"To the hospital," I answered matter-of-factly.

"Oh really. Which hospital?"

"St. Francis."

"And why are you going to St. Francis?"

Ugh. "Because I really love visiting hospitals late at night. It's a hobby of mine."

With an air of confidence, he pulled out some papers that he had hidden in his back pocket and handed them to me.

"Get in the truck, Elle."

I burned with anger as I opened the papers and read the admittance records for James P. Weston at St. John's Hospital. He wasn't at St. Francis at all. Shocked, I looked up at Maverick who gave me a smug look through the windshield of his truck. I wanted to walk out of the garage and flip him off, but I quickly realized he was my only hope for transportation. I dispelled that notion, at least temporarily. I hopped into his truck, crossed my arms, and stared out the window as we backed out, refusing to look at him. We drove for several miles before I spoke to him.

"How did you get these anyway?" I waved the admittance papers at him. I couldn't handle my curiosity any longer.

"I don't know if you've heard but I'm kind of a big deal when it comes to computers, Elle." There was playful arrogance in his tone.

"You hacked into a hospital's database?" He declined to comment on my accusation so I continued. "Maybe I'll turn you in and press charges."

"Maybe I'll turn you in and press charges for breaking and entering then," he quipped. I rolled my eyes at him and refused to talk to him the rest of the way to the hospital.

Maverick pulled over and parked half a mile down the street in a residential area and I looked at him with confusion.

"I don't want anyone recognizing my truck," he explained. He must have noticed the flash of admiration in my eyes as I appreciated his attention to detail. He laughed. "Why don't I make the plans from here on out, Baby Girl?"

"You know I *really* hate it when you call me that right?"

"You love it," he argued.

He hopped out of the truck and pulled me with him, then locked the truck and took off in a jog to the hospital. I refused to let his pace intimidate me so I kept up with long strides even though I had to take two steps to his every one step. By the time we got to the side entrance of the hospital, I was winded. I took several deep breaths while we stood at the door and discussed our plan.

I was more of the "jump first think later" type of person and thankfully, Maverick was more of the "think first then jump" type. He had calculated every part of the plan and as he stood there telling me where we were and how we would get in the side door and take the stairs ten flights up. He gave a trademark wink. I leaned in and gave him a kiss that was an apology and a thank you and so much more.

When I pulled away, I saw someone walking toward the door and Maverick immediately turned around so that his face could not be seen. I remembered him saying something about that in the plan, that we shouldn't show our faces, so before the person opened the door, I pulled my hoodie up over my head and looked away. After the person cleared the door, we followed them in quietly and started our trek up the stairway.

When we reached the top of the stairs on the tenth floor, we stopped at the landing and slowly opened the door, peeking through a tiny crack to see a nurse's station full of women in uniforms. I closed the door and sighed in exasperation, knowing we would never get into Mr. Weston's private room when it was being guarded by so many nurses. I looked over Maverick's shoulder and saw a flash of red and without thinking, I acted. I pulled the fire alarm and immediately a loud noise erupted throughout the hall.

Maverick covered his ears and looked at me like I was crazy. I cracked the door and saw nurses scatter, running about in a frenzied hurry then I signaled to Maverick to follow me as I ran into the hall unnoticed and slipped into Mr. Weston's room. The second I stepped into the room, I was enveloped in a feeling of dark, suffocating loneliness.

An old man, weathered by age and life, lay in a bed by himself. I expected to feel hate when I saw James Weston, but instead pity overcame me. Lying before me was a broken, sad man who spent his life amassing great fortune and even fame, yet on his deathbed, he was completely alone.

I walked to his side, searching his face. Who was James Weston, the mysterious man who was somehow an integral part of my mother's story? Eventually I heard the fire alarm turn off and I stood in unnerving silence, staring at the man who I thought killed my mother. His breathing was labored and

I heard a slow, rhythmic beeping sound in the background. He was but a skeleton with grey skin hanging off his bones. I knew I would get no answers from the despondent man who was knocking on death's doorstep. Unexpected peace flooded my body, and I turned to walk away from the corpse lying in front of me. As I reached to grab the door I heard a weak voice call out to me.

"Rosemary?" I turned to see a pair of grey eyes staring directly at me. He seemed to be in a world of his own—a world between ours and the world that we go to after we leave this life. He looked at me, but it was as though he saw someone else entirely. With whatever strength he had left he reached out to me and my heart softened. I walked toward him and leaned in as he seemed to want and need me to do. When I did, he reached out and touched my hair and smiled peacefully as he said the name again but this time as a statement, not a question.

"Rosemary." Pure contentment spread across his face as he touched my cheek.

I allowed the senile old man to have his moment without interruption. For some reason, the questions I had no longer mattered as I stared at the broken man before me who was trying so desperately to find peace in his dying moments. His features softened and he looked at me with love as he took a deep breath and found the strength to speak his final words.

"Rosemary, I'm so sorry. Please forgive me."

With those words, I heard the machines in his room sound off and I knew we only had seconds before a team of doctors flooded his room. We turned to run into the bathroom to hide but before we did I saw his hand fall open, and a flash of something silver caught my eye. In one swift movement, I grabbed the object from his hand and ran into the bathroom with Maverick, just in time to hear the doctors and nurses barge into James Weston's hospital room.

Maverick and I quietly made our way into the bathtub, where we were hidden by a white shower curtain, and we listened as we heard the team of doctors work to resuscitate a man we knew was already gone. In the dark, I let Maverick's arms encircle me, whispering comfort and safety. I held tightly to a cold, silver undefined object in my hand and in my mind, I heard these words: *James Weston didn't murder my mother.*

CHAPTER 25

I didn't tell Maverick about what I found in Mr. Weston's hand. We shared something transcendent that night, Mr. Weston and I, and something told me our connection was meant to be private. As we drove away from the hospital, I kept replaying in my mind the way a dying man looked at me with deep regret and complete sincerity as he apologized to me, thinking I was his long-lost wife Rosemary.

We drove home in silence, Maverick knowing what I needed as always. He held my hand, rubbing his thumb back and forth against my knuckles lovingly while the weight of the evening's events crushed us both and left us speechless. We pulled into his garage.

"Come inside with me?" The clock told me it was after midnight but I didn't want to go back to the solitude of my own room, so I nodded my head yes.

We didn't speak to each other as he led me into the house, up the back staircase, and into his room. I watched him set an alarm on his phone then we crawled into his bed and pressed our bodies as closely together as we could. The warmth of his body next to mine comforted me instantly and I drifted off into a deep and peaceful slumber as I heard him whisper in my ear.

"I love you, Elle."

It was still dark outside when I woke to his soft words in my ear again.

"Elle, it's time to get up." I ignored him, not ready to leave the security of his bed and wanting to return to my peaceful sleep. I felt his strong hands brush the hair off my neck and then his lips started traveling methodically up my neck. Suddenly I was wide awake and achingly aware of our magnetism. We were in the same bed, bodies pressed against one another and the electrifying force called us even closer still. I turned around and pressed my lips to his, resting my hands on his muscular chest as I did. His kiss was soft and gentle, and it left me wanting more. I leaned in and kissed him again, harder. This time our lips quickened, becoming more and more desperate as our breaths turned from soft and gentle to heavy and labored. He rolled over so his body was positioned above mine as we continued our passionate exchange, then—much to my disappointment—Maverick stopped unceremoniously and with one swift movement, he pushed himself off me, like he always did. My heart sank.

"Wait, Elle." He looked almost frightened as he got off his bed and sat down on a window seat on the opposite side of his bedroom.

I stood up and walked toward him, not allowing him to push me away this time. I grabbed his hair and pulled him into me and we sat there like that—his hands resting on my hips and his head buried in my chest reverently—me standing and him sitting. I could sense his vulnerability. Finally, he broke the silence as I heard his words reverberate through the darkness in the room.

"I need you to know something."

"What is it Maverick?" The wild look in his eyes concerned me. Usually I could read him, understand his thoughts, but the emotion on his face in that moment was uncharted territory.

"I don't want to scare you." I wasn't used to seeing him like this. He seemed—exposed.

"Trust me, that's not possible Maverick," I assured him. Clearly he didn't understand the depths of my emotions for him.

He took a deep breath then finally looked up at me with resolve. He was ready to share whatever secrets he was holding onto.

"I knew the second I saw you that you were it for me."

Is he really going to say it? My heart started pounding, my breath hitched, as I waited for him to finish his confession.

"My whole life, I felt like something was missing. I thought it was just because—" he trailed off, reluctant to finish his thought, then changed direction. "I just thought there was something wrong with me. That I was broken. That I couldn't love."

I know exactly what that feels like, Maverick. His words hit so close to home but I didn't speak. I held still, holding my breath in anticipation, euphoric that Maverick was finally opening up to me. I didn't want to do anything to shatter the beautiful moment that was happening between us.

"Then I saw you in the parking lot that day. I can't explain it, Elle, but I knew. I knew that very moment—you were what I had been waiting for. Something was calling me to you, connecting me to you. I tried so hard to stay away because I knew Caleb liked you, but it was painful. No, it was excruciating. I *can't* stay away from you. I can't breathe when I'm not with you. The thought of living without you, it terrifies me."

His words spilled out then he buried his head in my stomach. His breathing was deep and ragged. I watch his back heave as I ran my fingers through his hair, then down his neck, then along his back rubbing soothing circles. Finally, I spoke.

"Maverick, I know."

He looked up at me, desperation in his eyes. Our positions—him sitting and me standing—made me feel, for once, like I was in control, and the look of vulnerability in his eyes seemed to convey the same thing.

"I need you to know, Elle. This is forever for me. And that scares the hell out of me."

I lifted his head so that his crystal-clear blue eyes were looking up at me. He was waiting for a response, and I would give him one.

"I don't know how this will all turn out and yes, that scares the hell out of me too. We are so young. We just met. It feels like we have the world against us right now. But one thing I know without a doubt is this: I will never in my life love anyone the way that I love you, Maverick Mason. It's not possible to ever feel this way again. I knew that the moment I first saw you."

He looked at me with unparalleled passion and conviction—finally receiving the assurance he needed that I felt the same as him—then he stood up slowly. With determination, he lifted me in one swift movement and I wrapped my legs around him as he carried me with ease, back toward his bed. We kissed sweetly, softly, then he lay me down on the bed but this time he didn't hold himself away from me. Before he kissed me he pulled away one more time and looked into my eyes.

"You are mine, Elle Christiansen."

I didn't argue. We both knew his words were true. His lips crushed down on mine, the perfect mix of powerful but soft. This was different then all our other kisses; something had changed and I welcomed it. Maverick let go of his control and we stopped fighting the force that had called us to togetherness from the moment we'd first laid eyes on each other in the

Heritage Hall parking lot. We celebrated our confessions to one another, nothing left unspoken-finally. We were broken, scarred, perhaps even damaged—both of us—but somehow our imperfections made us perfect for each other. Where I was weak, he was strong. Where he had faults, I made up for them. We challenged one another. We fought. We pushed. We pulled. We were yin and yang; opposites attract; two people from two completely different worlds; yet somehow—it seemed—the universe gave us a gift, that we were perfectly created to fit together. Together—and together only—were we complete. In that moment with Maverick, I knew in my soul that we would no longer fight our connection, but instead we would fight to stay together.

When the first rays of sun began to show themselves out the window, we knew we had pushed our limits too far. Maverick reluctantly pulled himself out of the bed then pulled me up beside him as I pouted.

"Let's go. I can't even believe how bad my decision-making skills have become since I started hanging out with you. You're such a bad influence," Maverick teased as he pulled a T-shirt on then slapped me on the behind. "If Cordelia or your dad catches us—" He shook his head as if waving off some unwanted vision.

Maverick led me down the stairs and into his truck then drove me to the top of the hill that led to the cottage and dropped me off. I ran around to the back of the house, holding my breath as I crawled through the window to my bedroom, then pulled the curtain back and sighed in relief when I realized I was alone.

I scrambled into my bed and pulled the covers over me, still feeling a shiver of cold from being outside, then reached my hands into the pocket of my hoodie to help warm my body.

My fingers hit a small, cold object, and I remembered the hospital room and James Weston's dying moments.

I turned the lamp beside my bed on so I could inspect the object more closely and recognized it was a vintage watch—one of the large, round ones that were attached to a chain and worn by men in the early 1900s. As I opened it slowly, I saw a watch face on the right-hand side and on the left, a black-and-white picture. I recognized the woman in the picture immediately. It was Rosemary, standing on the porch of the yellow house on the reservation with her husband, James Weston. Her smile was exquisite and she radiated happiness. In her arms, she held a small baby with short, dark curls. The baby was smiling and I could see her two huge, beautiful dimples.

I sensed a strange familiarity toward the little baby although I'd never seen her before. I reached out and caressed the picture, rubbing my thumb over her smiling face. Slowly and with apprehension, I pulled the picture out of the watch and turned it over in my hand. There was tiny black handwriting in all capitals. It read: "James, Rosemary, and Eleanor, Jan. 1959."

Rosemary's baby was named Eleanor? But that's my mother's name.

I was reeling, struggling to process the information, but deep down I already knew the truth. I fumbled out of the bed and found the newspaper article about Rosemary's marriage to James Weston, frantically looking for the date they were married: March, 1959. Slowly, the pieces of the puzzle began to shift, coming together so I could see the shape of a picture beginning to form.

Rosemary is my grandmother. Rosemary had my mother before she married James Weston.

There were still so many questions and I knew the answers would only be found in the leather-bound book I'd seen in my dreams. It was the key to unlocking the mysteries of the past and understanding why my mother—Rosemary's beautiful, dimple-faced angel—was murdered in Ohio. I had to find that book, or my fate would be the same as theirs.

I jumped out of bed and dressed, anxious to get to school and get the day over. All that mattered to me was that evening and carrying out the plan Maverick and I made to leave the dance and make our way to Ohio. I made small talk with my aunt and dad over breakfast until I was interrupted by my phone beeping at me.

I'm picking you up for school.

Seconds later I heard a knock at the door. Cordelia ran to the door and gave my blue-eyed boyfriend a big hug and my dad followed suit with a silly grin on his face.

I watched the show, in awe of the power Maverick had over anyone and everyone in his presence. Once we got in the truck, I glanced over to see Maverick's typical smug look of confidence plastered on his face and of course, I felt the need to bring him down a notch or two.

"They won't like you quite so much when I tell them I stayed the night with you last night will they?"

"You wouldn't do that," he challenged.

"Maybe I will, maybe I won't."

He shook his head in exasperation but I knew he loved my crazy.

"Let's talk about tonight." Maverick changed the subject and as we drove to school, we finalized all the details of our plan to leave for Ohio. As always, Maverick thought through every single detail and I was in awe of him, though I refused to admit it. I kept James Weston's watch and what I learned about Rosemary to myself. I wasn't ready to share all my secrets with him, yet.

I went through the school day in a haze, tuning out my teachers in all my classes as my mind wandered, trying to assimilate all the information I had about Rosemary, James Weston, my mother, and Nathan Weston; but there were still too many missing puzzle pieces.

After school, we drove Madison's convertible to her house with the top down, enjoying the beautiful Oklahoma fall day. The leaves were just starting to change color but not drop from the trees yet, and something in the air reminded me of a different fall evening altogether—one that ended in tragedy. I pushed the unwelcome thought away and let the fresh air hit my face, determined not to let my demons ruin the homecoming dance.

We drove up to another gated fence with a keypad. Madison hit a button in her car and the gate swung open; I tried not to gape as we pulled up to a pristine white modern mansion with clean lines and floor-to-ceiling windows. We went up to Madison's bedroom and she directed me to a fancy seating area with a desk full of make-up in front of a mirror that was lined with Hollywood-style lighting. The girls pushed me into the seat and went to work.

I watched, in awe, as Madison transformed my eyes with smoky, sultry shades of browns and blacks. Next, Carly used a wand I'd never seen before to create long, dark waves in my hair. When she was done with the wand, she handed me over to Macey, who pulled my hair over one shoulder, used pins to hold it in place, then sprayed an obnoxious amount of hairspray all over my head to keep the soft curls looking like old Hollywood-style waves. Finally, they settled on a nude gloss for my lips then stood back to admire their work.

"That's what I'm talking about." Madison was beaming with pride at her work.

I picked up a handheld mirror and inspected my hair and make-up. "Madison, you are a miracle worker. I owe you, girlfriend."

"Maverick is going to die when he sees you." The girls all swooned and I rolled my eyes at their antics but secretly, my heart soared thinking about him seeing me in my red dress, with my hair and make-up done to perfection.

The doorbell rang, interrupting my thoughts, and I heard my dad's voice from downstairs.

"Alright girls I'm outta here. Thanks again for all of this. You girls are seriously the best." I blew them all air kisses as I ran out the door.

When we got back to my aunt's house, I rushed back to my room and slipped my red dress on then went to my jewelry box to find the small diamond earrings that belonged to my mother. They were minuscule—a gift from dad on their tenth wedding anniversary—but they were hers and therefore, they were perfect in my eyes. I put the earrings on then grabbed the heart-shaped necklace from my jewelry box and stuck it in my handbag. I heard a knock at the door.

"Elle, Maverick's here," my dad called.

I started my walk down the hallway and my feet moved over their own accord, drawn by that ever-present magnetic force toward the boy that I loved. Maverick didn't move when I walked into the room. He stared, his blue eyes wide and burning with desire.

His suit perfectly framed his athletic shoulders then made a tailored V down to highlight his trim waist. I couldn't control the passion burning in my eyes as I matched his gaze. I knew the feelings passing between us were recognizable to everyone in the room, but I didn't care. Maverick was all consuming, and nothing else mattered when I was in his presence.

"Elle, you're so beautiful. You look just like your mother." My dad finally broke the tense silence in the room as he walked up to me and hugged me awkwardly.

I blushed. "Thanks Dad." That was the ultimate compliment.

Maverick walked up beside me, offering me his arm, then he leaned down and kissed me sweetly on the forehead.

"You are without a doubt the most beautiful girl in the world, and I am the luckiest guy in the entire world." I beamed with pride at his words.

Maverick ushered me toward the door and I turned to call toward my dad before I walked out the front door, "Dad don't forget I'm staying the night with the girls at Carly's house."

Maverick opened the car door for me but before I climbed in, I turned to look at my aunt and dad one more time. *Tell them.*

There was an internal struggle as I tried to form the words, the new me wanting to speak them out loud so badly, and the old me trying desperately to hold onto the ways of my past. Determined, I locked eyes with my dad then my aunt, then back at my dad.

"I love you guys."

I turned and walked away, relief washing over me as I climbed into the fancy sports car waiting for me. I glanced at my dad one last time before we pulled away, and I saw a tear stream down his face. He hadn't heard me say those three little words to him in over six years.

Maverick drove me to the dance in one of his dad's fancy cars. I felt like a movie star as I stepped out of the car onto a beautiful red carpet that made its way into a gorgeous old hotel in historic downtown Tulsa. As we walked in, everyone's eyes were on us, watching us as we made our grand entrance. Maverick was calm and controlled as always, ushering me confidently through the crowd and directly onto the dance floor while my insides were a bundle of nerves. The live band started playing a song I recognized well—an Ed Sheeran classic—and Maverick directed me effortlessly across the dance floor, our bodies pressed as closely together as possible.

We were in our own world and in it, we were the only two people alive as he swayed me back and forth, singing the words to one of my favorite songs. I sighed. He had a beautiful singing voice.

"Is there anything you're not good at?"

He gave me one of his show-stopping smiles and pulled me tightly to his chest. I listened to the words he sang into my ear—letting the world fall away and allowing myself, if but for a moment, to live in a dream world with Maverick. His words seemed like a promise—*I'll be loving you, til we're seventy; when my hair is gone and my memory fades;* He was singing about forever, and he was singing it to me. As the song continued I reveled in where I found myself—in Maverick Mason's arms—and I reflected on the journey I had to take to get there; the pain I faced; the darkness I lived through; the loss I endured; somehow, it all led me to him.

People fall in love in mysterious ways.

Maverick's words resonated, parallel to my exact thoughts.

Maybe it's all part of a plan.

As Maverick continued to sing into my ear, my thoughts swirled uncontrollably. I couldn't quite comprehend everything that had happened since my dad and I packed up our van and moved to Tulsa, Oklahoma; but I knew one thing for sure—somehow I knew it *was* all part of a plan.

When the song was over, he kissed me tenderly and leaned his forehead down to touch mine. Our moment was over and he brought me back to reality with his words.

"Elle, we have to go."

"I know," I said, not bothering to hide my disappointment.

We stood there for a little while longer before I pulled away and told him I had to go find the girls.

"Ok I'll meet you back at the front in five minutes."

I searched for the girls on the dance floor but didn't find them, so I resorted to texting.

Where are you guys? Need to talk to you.

A response from Carly was almost immediate.

Bathroom. Get here.

I walked into the bathroom and heard the girls giggling and laughing to one another, discussing the atrocity that was Janie Jackson's Pepto-Bismol pink dress. I stood there and watched them for a minute—just taking it all in—wanting to stop for a moment and remember these friends and their simple laughter and teenage angst; these girls—my new friends—who had nothing else to talk about or consider in this moment other than homecoming dresses.

I smiled at them longingly, wanting to escape to their world and bring Maverick with me. I wanted to live in a place where my biggest problem was the accessories I needed for my dress and the only pressing matter I had to talk about was Janie Jackson's atrocious homecoming attire. My phone beeped. I knew it was Maverick and my five minutes was up.

"Hey girls. So here's the deal. I kinda told my dad I was staying the night with you but I'm not going to—" I trailed off, awaiting their response with nervous anticipation. There was nothing but silence for several seconds, then I heard a ripple of screams come from all of them simultaneously.

"Are you going somewhere with Maverick? You little slut! OMG you are the luckiest!" They were all speaking at once and

I couldn't even decipher all their words. I quickly shut them down.

"It's not what you think you guys. We're leaving tonight and he's driving me back to Ohio. I have some things I have to take care of back home and I can't tell my dad because he won't let me go if I do." The girls were still stuck on the fact that I was going somewhere overnight with Maverick Mason. No one cared about any of the details after they heard that juicy little detail.

I knew it was hopeless trying to convince them otherwise. I gave them all hugs and said goodbye. "Listen, if my dad comes looking for me, just tell him the truth. I don't want you guys getting in trouble or having to lie for me."

"Don't worry girl, we got your back." They hugged me and continued their assault of catcalls and whistles as I walked out of the bathroom, pausing to look over my shoulder and give them an exaggerated eye-roll before I left.

I made my way back out to the corridor and took one last glance at the dance that I was leaving behind. I saw Maverick's truck sitting outside and realized he had someone bring it to him to switch out so we didn't have to drive the sports car to Ohio; I was transfixed by how thorough and calculated he was. He never missed a single detail.

I sighed sadly as I allowed the acceptance of my reality to wash over me, then I turned away from the throng of high-school students dancing carelessly, realizing that I could never be one of them. With one last glance, I walked away from my dream world, the one where I got to be a carefree student at a dance with the man of her dreams, and walked toward my reality, the one full of nightmares and dreams and murder and darkness. Forlorn, I stepped toward the black truck.

When I saw Maverick sitting with his arm around the back of his seat, an inviting smile playing around his lips and a twinkle in his captivating blue eyes, I couldn't help but smile. I stepped away from my dream world and toward him, realizing that reality was perfectly fine with me because I was with the boy who captivated my soul. I would go back to Brookville, to the place my mother was murdered. I would go to that one-lane dirt road and confront my past, but this time I wouldn't go alone.

CHAPTER 26

I offered to drive numerous times but Maverick refused to allow me behind the wheel of his truck. He drank three Monster energy drinks and drove through the night. I tried to stay awake and keep him company but I was useless. I awakened when dawn was breaking above the horizon and looked over to see his tired, blue eyes greeting me.

"Good morning, Baby Girl. Did you have a good night's sleep?" I heard the hint of sarcasm in his voice.

"Hey, I offered to drive. Not my fault you're a total control freak and wouldn't let me."

"I value my life way too much to allow you behind the wheel at any point, much less in the middle of the night," he chided.

I looked out the window and saw a familiar old farmhouse on the side of the road.

"We're getting close."

I wondered if he heard the fear in my voice.

Maverick reached over to me, pulling me to his side and stroking my hair lovingly. He didn't say anything because he knew that there was nothing he could say. He was there, and his presence alone provided the comfort I needed.

"In about a mile, can you pull over please? I'll show you where." I pointed to a break in the road. "Right over there."

As requested, Maverick pulled over. He helped me out of the car and held my hand, waiting patiently as I found the courage to speak. I pointed at a road far off in the distance.

"That's the road where it happened."

Maverick didn't ask any questions.

"I always thought it was my fault she died, because I didn't get there soon enough to save her," I confessed. "Now I know I was wrong. There's nothing I could have done. Everything that happened—" I paused as I allowed myself to feel the truth in my words as I spoke them— "It was out of my control."

He grasped my hand firmly and we stood there together, staring off into the distance at the one-lane dirt road where my mother was murdered. I turned and walked away without saying another word, and Maverick followed. He didn't ask me a single question about that night or about my mother's death. I didn't think it was possible for me to love him anymore than I already did but in that moment, my love and respect grew even deeper for him.

"Where to?" he asked as we climbed back into the truck.

I pointed back toward the main road then directed him through the small town to a small two-lane road I knew like the back of my hand. A smile spread across my face when I saw a row of brick houses that held almost as many memories as my own childhood home—it was Grace and Charlie's neighborhood. Their houses sat in a cul de sac, separated by only one house in between them. It was early—far too early for visitors—but I didn't let that stop me. I hopped out of the truck, made my way over to Grace's window, and knocked. A few minutes went by before a curtain yanked back and Grace's tired green eyes stared at me with shock. I gave her a little wave. She yanked the curtains closed; I knew where to go. I made my way to her back deck and seconds later the door opened.

She looked straight past me and gawked at Maverick. She was speechless as he directed a charming smile toward her and extended his hand.

"Hello Grace, I'm Maverick." She was frozen.

"OMG Grace snap out of it." I literally snapped my fingers in front of her face, trying to awaken her from her Maverick Mason induced trance.

Maverick snickered. I cut my eyes toward him—warning in my look—but he just kept smiling.

"Uh—come on in," she finally stuttered.

We made our way to the game room off Grace's bedroom where we could talk. Grace was an only child and for her thirteenth birthday, her parents converted one of the other bedrooms in their modest home to a game room for all of us. It quickly became our favorite place to hang out, other than the tree house we built in Charlie's backyard when we were ten years old.

"Can you text Charlie and tell him to come over too?"

"Sure." Grace was slowly orienting herself to reality but she kept glancing at Maverick nervously. I gave him a sharp elbow to the side when he gave her another one of his dazzling smiles and shook my head at him. He was going to have to tone down the charm or Grace was going to be an incoherent, blubbering mess the entire time we were there.

Grace typed out a text and sat her phone down, taking three deep breaths while she stared at me, her mind obviously reeling.

"Okay, so what in the world are you doing here?"

An internal struggle was taking place—*Do I lie to her, and protect her, or tell her the truth?*

I decided on a version of the truth that would also still give her some protection. Grace was soft—always gentle—from the time we were little kids. If she knew everything, she would worry about me and I didn't want that.

"I'm here because my aunt gave me a letter from my mom. I think she left something here for me in Brookville and I had to come get it."

Grace was in shock. I never mentioned my mom. But before she could ask me any other questions, there was a knock at the door, interrupting us.

"Charlie!" I couldn't control myself when I saw him—dirty blonde hair peeking out from under his favorite Cincinnati Reds hat and his big brown eyes twinkling at me, making me feel like home. I pushed myself up from the beanbag I was sitting on and catapulted myself into his arms. He swung me around and didn't let me go. Charlie and I stood there hugging until I realized an uncomfortable tension was looming. My skin prickled and my heart began to race, our connection alerting me to Maverick's disapproval.

Well he's going to have to get over it.

I stuck my chin up in defiance, confident Maverick was reading my body language and knew I wasn't going to back down. Charlie was my best friend. Maverick was going to have to accept that.

Maverick walked over and offered Charlie his hand, his body language emanating control and possessiveness. I tensed as I watched Charlie take two steps toward him, not faltering in the least.

"I'm Maverick, Elle's *boyfriend.*" The way he said *boyfriend* made me cringe.

"Nice to meet you, Maverick. I'm Charlie, Elle's *best friend.*" I was mortified at how this entire exchange was going. Thankfully, another knock at the door broke the emotionally charged moment.

"Hi Momma T!" I jumped up and gave Grace's mom a hug. As I pulled away I saw a tear in her eye. She was like a second mother to me.

"Well I'll be, Elle Christiansen, what are you doing in my home? I had no idea you were in town!"

She glanced over at Maverick and her jaw dropped. She quickly collected herself though, in a more timely fashion than her daughter did, thank goodness.

"Momma T this is Maverick Mason, my boyfriend."

"Nice to meet you Maverick. Welcome to Brookville."

Maverick walked toward her and gave her a gentlemanly handshake.

"Thank you so much for having me ma'am. I'm honored to be here." Grace swooned, yet again, as she watched Maverick's niceties. I gave her a look of warning and she quickly covered up her wide-eyed-deer-caught-in-the-headlight look, with one of apology.

"Sorry," she mouthed. "I can't help it."

I rolled my eyes at her.

"I'm gonna run and get you guys some breakfast," Momma T announced.

She gave me another big hug, brushing away a strand of hair as she pulled away and looked into my eyes with a loving, motherly curiosity. She was perceptive—always had been—and I knew she sensed change in me. She smiled at me as she turned and walked away, calling over her shoulder as she did.

"Now you girls come on in the kitchen and help me here in a bit."

"Yes ma'am," Grace and I called out in unison, smiling at one another. It felt just like old times.

"So what are you doing here?" Charlie asked as soon as Grace's mom walked out of the room.

"My aunt gave me a letter from my mom and it made me realize she might have left something here for me in Brookville before she died. I think it's at the church."

A million questions flashed through Charlie's eyes. I held his gaze and we spoke to one another with no words. He knew I was protecting Grace somehow, so he wouldn't press me for the whole story in front of her.

Momma T called to us from the kitchen; Grace and I hopped into action, heading for the door. Before I walked out of the room, I turned to look at Maverick and Charlie, a strange sensation overcoming me as I saw them both standing there— in the same room, together. So many emotions consumed me, and the size of the room seemed incapable of holding all that I felt for both of them. Confused, I turned and walked out of the room. Running away was always something that came easy for me.

I helped pile a plate of pancakes onto a tray while Grace got the syrup, butter, and some orange juice. Momma T pushed me out of the kitchen and waved me on my way. I made my way back down the hallway, carrying my stack of pancakes. As I walked up to the door, Charlie's gentle voice stopped me in my tracks.

"You act like you own her. She's *not* your possession for God's sake."

I paused, unwilling to believe the exchange I was hearing between my best friend and my boyfriend.

"Look I'm just trying to protect her, Charlie. I love her, and I can't let anything happen to her." There was a desperation in his voice I had never before heard.

"Elle's the strongest girl I know. She can protect herself. She doesn't need you to do it for her."

"I know she's strong." There was an edge to Maverick's voice. He didn't like Charlie telling him things about me, as if he knew me better. *Because Charlie does know you better.* Again, I pushed the thought away as I listened to Maverick from the hallway outside the game room.

"Maybe she can protect herself and maybe she can't. I'm not willing to take that chance. Look, I lost someone I loved once before and it's never happening again. I can't lose her."

I almost dropped my tray of pancakes when I heard Maverick's confession.

He lost someone?

"Do you hear yourself? It's like you think you're God or something." There was disgust in Charlie's voice. I couldn't believe the way he was talking to Maverick.

I heard the laughter carrying down the hallway as Grace and Momma T walked up behind me. We all walked into the room together, Grace and Momma T oblivious to the tense exchange I just overheard between Maverick and Charlie.

We ate our pancakes and made small talk as I tried to put the conversation I had heard out of my head, unsuccessfully— *She's not yours to possess. I lost someone I loved before and it's never happening again.* Those two sentences were on a repeat reel in my mind, and no matter what I did, I couldn't turn it off.

By the time we cleaned up breakfast, it was close to 8:30 a.m., and I knew the church secretary would be arriving to unlock the church for Sunday morning services. Our time was running out, if we wanted to get into the church before the 10 a.m. service started. We said our goodbyes and I hugged Grace and Charlie, holding onto the embrace for longer than usual. I missed them already and I hadn't even said goodbye yet.

"Promise you'll come see me in Tulsa?"

"We will. How about a week this summer?"

I gave them both another hug.

"That sounds amazing."

Charlie kissed my forehead as he pulled away, which surprised me. But what surprised me even more was that I welcomed it—until I saw the murderous look on Maverick's face. I grabbed Maverick's hand and turned toward the truck, suddenly anxious to get the two of them away from each other.

I directed Maverick down our small Main Street and when I saw the steeple peeking over the hill in the distance, I pointed in its direction. He nodded his understanding and drove toward it, pulling in and parking his truck in the small gravel parking lot. We stopped, but Maverick didn't get out of the truck.

"He's in love with you, Elle." He spat the words out, rushed and clipped, very unlike Maverick Mason.

"Who? Charlie?" I laughed so loudly it caught even myself off guard.

"Yes, Charlie." Maverick spoke with certainty.

"Charlie is *not* in love with me, Maverick. We've been best friends since we were two. He doesn't feel that way *at all.*" I argued my point adamantly but as the words came out of my mouth they felt wrong, like I was trying to convince myself they were true. *You know he's right.* I pushed the thought away as quickly as it came to me, uncomfortable and not ready to accept the realization nagging at me.

Maverick stared at me, so much passion in his eyes it made my pulse begin to race and my blood boil.

"He's definitely in love with you. But it's not like I can blame him."

Suddenly, I knew it was time. I sensed a vulnerability in Maverick I had never before experienced.

"Maverick, I overheard you and Charlie talking." He looked at me, anxiety written on his face. We both knew what was about to happen.

"I heard you tell him you lost someone you loved."

The look in his eyes leveled me, immediately turning stormy and turbulent, pain etched into his every feature, turning his mask of control and confidence into one of agony and grief in a split second. Suddenly, a flood of memories overcame me—a comment Carly made once at school, Maverick telling me his parents made him see a therapist, my aunt's face when she saw me looking at the little girl's picture in her hallway, the massive frame of the beautiful little angel in Maverick's home—sadness hit me, enveloping me, as I realized what I had been missing.

"Maverick, what happened to your little sister? Why have I never met her?"

He catapulted his head forward onto the steering wheel—defeated—as though he could no longer stand the weight of holding himself upward for one more second. He left his head resting there, refusing to look up. For the first time ever, Maverick Mason was completely out of control. My heart ached for him. I scooted myself over to his side of the truck, placing my hand gently on his back. I said nothing, knowing there was nothing I could say to take away his pain. I, of all people, knew that better than anyone. The only thing I could do was show him—with my presence—that he wasn't alone.

He sat there, his back heaving up and down as he breathed in and out—sharp, painful breaths—until his voice cracked, finally breaking the silence.

"I didn't want you to know."

"Why Maverick?"

"Because I didn't want you to see me like this."

"Maverick, you don't have to be so strong all the time. You don't have to be perfect." His head still rested on his steering wheel in surrender, and I caressed the back of his neck gently, coaxing him, willing him to invite me in and let his walls down so that I could help him carry his burdens just as he helped me carry mine.

He nodded his head in agreement, glancing out the window. I knew exactly what he was doing—trying to find the courage to speak, to somehow put his pain into words.

"I was thirteen years old. Gracie was seven."

Gracie. The precious little girl with the ringlets. Maverick's sister. He didn't need to tell me who Gracie was. I already knew.

"Mom and Dad were out of town and Cordelia was watching us. It was February and there had been a huge ice storm. Gracie was obsessed with going down to the pond and checking it out."

Fear gripped my throat. I knew how this story ended—in tragedy.

"Cordelia told us not to leave the house without her, but Gracie was so convincing. She was impossible to say no to." I saw a smile touch his lips as he remembered the little girl he obviously loved hopelessly. "I let her talk me into going to the pond."

He paused, and I knew he was struggling to continue.

"What happened Maverick?" I knew he needed the release, so I pushed him to continue even though it ripped my heart open to see him reliving so much pain.

"I noticed one of the big oak trees had broken in the ice storm and I was walking around to see if there was any damage to the boathouse. I heard her call to me, '*Look at me Mav.*' " He mimicked Gracie's angelic voice as he stared off into the distance, recalling the horror.

"She walked out onto the tree that had fallen then made her way onto the ice. She was pretending to be a professional ice skater." He chuckled though his mask of pain remained. "She wanted to be an Olympic figure skater when she grew up."

I saw the tears forming in his eyes as he continued. He struggled to hold them at bay.

"I saw the ice crack and watched her go under."

I gasped out loud, covering my mouth in horror. The picture of the little dimple-faced angel with the dark brown ringlets—so full of life and energy—floated to the surface of my mind and I couldn't bear to think of what came next.

"I tried to save her Elle, but I couldn't. By the time I fished her out from under the ice, it was too late."

I held him in my arms as he let go. I comforted him with my presence and let him experience, through the transcendent connection we shared, that he wasn't alone. He didn't have to carry his burden by himself anymore. As I held him, I finally saw the complete picture: Maverick was just as broken as I was—my coping mechanism was anger; his was control. He was unable to save his little sister, so he lived his life trying to regain the control that he lost on that day.

I held him tightly, wrapping my arms around him and willing him to feel my love.

Individually we were broken—Maverick and I—but together, our love was so great that we somehow filled the holes in each other's hearts.

"Maverick?"

He turned his bloodshot eyes toward me and I knew what I had to say.

"It wasn't your fault. You couldn't save her, just like I couldn't save my mom. It just is what it is. We will never understand why we had to lose them." I watched a tear roll down his beautiful cheek, dripping off his chiseled jawline, as he accepted the truth of my words.

He shook his head as I watched him release the load he had carried for years. I lifted his chin to mine and planted a sweet, tender kiss on his lips.

It was unspoken, but as we held each other, our connection told us what was unspoken—our brokenness somehow made us perfect for each other. Together, we were complete.

We sat in the truck together as I watched Maverick slowly regain his composure. With each breath he took, the broken boy who told me of his sister's tragic death seemed further and further away, as his mask of confidence and control returned. Finally, Maverick reached over and opened his door, then he hopped out of his truck. He grabbed my hand and pulled me toward him, catching me before my feet hit the ground and setting me down gently, placing a soft and gentle kiss on my forehead.

"C'mon let's go check out your old stomping grounds. I've just been dying to see the *Brookville Church of God* ever since that day I saw you in the parking lot driving that gorgeous piece of machinery—the Brookville Church of God fifteen-passenger van."

I smiled, thankful to see he was back to his antagonistic self. As we walked away—hand in hand, arms swinging in unison—I couldn't contain a laugh as I glanced over my shoulder and saw my boyfriend's ostentatious pickup truck sitting in the gravel parking lot of the Brookville Church of God.

"What?" Maverick seemed confused.

"Brookville has definitely never seen the likes of you before Maverick Mason," I teased. "We're sticking out like a sore thumb here in that monstrosity." I pointed toward his black truck.

He feigned surprise. "What do you mean? I hear Brookville's a mecca for high-end vehicles…" he trailed off as he glanced around and pointed at a few of the other cars in the parking lot—a beat-up old farm truck that looked like it had seen its final day and a red Pontiac Bonneville belonging to the church secretary; it was missing a window and had paint stripped off the hood.

We laughed as we walked up the steps of the church but quieted as we entered the vestibule and made our way into the sanctuary. We were only there for a matter of seconds before a door opened and Marjorie, the church secretary, greeted us. Marjorie's jaw instantly dropped when she saw Maverick. She was clearly smitten and completely unaffected by the prodigal preacher's daughter returned home. She was too busy staring at my boyfriend to even notice me.

"Hello Marjorie." I didn't even attempt to hide my disdain. She glanced toward me just long enough to acknowledge my presence then returned to staring at Maverick. I stepped in between her and Maverick.

"Marjorie, I need some time alone in the church today before service starts. Would that be OK?"

She smiled a sickeningly sweet smile—I knew it was for Maverick—and conceded to whatever our wishes were. As she walked back into the office area, I locked the door behind her and turned to stare at him, crossing my arms and making my disapproval known. Maverick feigned innocence and threw his hands up in the air.

"What can I say? Forty-year-old church secretaries just really have a thing for me."

"Everyone has a thing for you," I retorted.

He grabbed me playfully and pulled me toward him. "Do you have a thing for me? That's all I care about."

I pushed him off and turned a cold shoulder as I walked away. "Maybe I do, maybe I don't." I refused to give him the satisfaction he wanted as I walked toward the front of the church slowly, memories flooding my mind with each step.

I took it all in—the wooden pews with the deep-red seat cushions, the stained-glass windows, the pulpit where my dad preached in his dress robes, the choir loft—and suddenly I remembered my life before Maverick. I saw myself in the middle of the ocean, a burdensome weight wrapped around my neck, weighing me down into the depths of an ocean of darkness and death. I was struggling with all my might to keep my head above water and somehow stay alive. It was a miserable existence. Then I saw a pair of blue eyes calling to me in the darkness and they bade me to come into the light. I held out my hand to him and he pulled me out of the depths of darkness and despair and into the light of his world. He broke down my walls. He blew the lid off my little black box in the depths of my soul, and he expelled the darkness. He replaced the fear and the pain and the anger with light, and with love, and with hope. I looked at the blue-eyed boy standing with me in the Brookville Church of God sanctuary with awe, and my heart filled with gratitude.

You saved me Maverick. I was drowning and you saved me.

He met my gaze and I knew he was reading my thoughts. He gave me a wink and I reached out and took his hand, leaning my head over on his shoulder and speaking to him in our own little language—thanking him for saving me, for protecting me, and for loving me in spite of my brokenness. Hand in hand, we walked to the stained-glass window and I pointed to the inscription.

"Then you will know the truth, and the truth will set you free.
That's what I heard my mom say to me in my dream Maverick.
I know the journal has to be here somewhere."

We looked everywhere, combing the entire sanctuary to no
avail. Finally, we sat down on a pew at the front of the church,
the air between us heavy with the disappointment of failure. I
closed my eyes, my thoughts racing, trying to determine how to
apologize to Maverick for dragging him all the way to Ohio for
absolutely no reason whatsoever.

Open your eyes, Elle.

I obeyed the faint whisper I heard, opening my eyes to see
the sun streaming in behind the stained glass, causing sunlight
to pour into the church, illuminating the cross. The word *free*
was written in a yellow pane of glass right below the cross as
the morning sun streamed into the sanctuary, I noticed a
shadow in the yellow pane. I walked toward it, this time
noticing a small notch in the steel that surrounded the yellow
cut glass. I pushed the notch and the corner of the yellow pane
popped up, allowing me to grab it and slide it out. When I
removed the pane, I saw a small book encased in shiny, dark
leather. On the front of the book was a small golden square,
exactly like I saw in my dream.

I took the book out and held it tightly to my chest with
one hand—just like Rosemary had done in the picture from her
wedding day—and with the other hand, I caressed the heart-
shaped locket I wore around my neck. Somehow my darkness,
my dreams, my pain, and all my nightmares had led me to this
very moment, and I knew exactly what I was supposed to do.

"Can you take me somewhere?" I asked Maverick. "I want
to read it in my old house, not here. Grace told me the church
hasn't hired a new preacher so no one's living in the parsonage.
We can go there."

He nodded and we walked out of the church hand in hand, then made the short drive to the tiny two-bedroom, two-bathroom house where I grew up. I grabbed the key from under the flowerpot by the door and unlocked the door. We walked in together and stood there in awkward silence, my vulnerability looming between us. Bringing Maverick into my old home was confusing and I was unsure of how to handle my past and my present colliding.

"So this is where you grew up?" He walked over and gave me a big, reassuring hug. I nodded my head yes. "I love those barstools over there." He pointed at the brightly colored barstools—the ones my mother and I painted together—that stayed with the parsonage when we moved, along with all the other furniture we weren't allowed to take with us.

"My mom and I painted those when I was nine." I smiled up at him and he kissed my forehead lovingly, coaxing me out of my shell. "She loved color. We weren't allowed to paint the walls so she always found a way to brighten up the house in other ways."

He glanced around the house with a look of longing on his face.

"I wish I could have known her, Elle. I know she was so amazing and so strong, just like you."

His words were so genuine and heartfelt, but I couldn't respond. I just walked over, into his arms, and told him how much his words meant to me in the only way I knew how—by speaking straight to his soul.

Eventually I pulled away from our hug and made my way to sit in front of the empty fireplace, holding the leather-encased book cautiously on my lap. Maverick followed me and sat beside me, then watched as I pushed the golden square on the front of the book. The square popped open and inside, I saw the shape of a heart. My hands moved of their own accord to the necklace hanging around my neck. I took it off then instinctively pushed the locket into the heart-shaped space inside the golden square. They clicked together immediately and I turned the heart to the right. The sides of the leather encasement popped free.

My hands were shaking too badly to lift the journal out of the leather encasement. Maverick was there in an instant. He pulled me toward his side and reached his strong arms around me; then, placing his hands over mine and steadying me by his touch, we opened to the first page together.

CHAPTER 27

(Rosemary's Journal, part I)

March 13, 1959

Yesterday was my wedding day and it was the happiest day of my life other than the day I had Eleanor.

James gave me this journal as a wedding present. He gave it to me inside of a pretty wooden box he carved himself with roses all over the outside. He also gave me a beautiful rose-gold locket with a picture of the two of us holding Eleanor. He showed me how the locket unlocked the journal. "They fit together perfectly. Just like us," he told me. He had a silver watch made for himself with the same picture of the three of us.

James told me to always remember how much he loves Eleanor and me when I feel the locket hanging above my heart. He told me he wants to adopt Eleanor now that we're married and we're going to be a family. He said this journal is to record a lifetime of our happy memories together. So that's what I'll do.

~Rosemary Weston

We continued to read numerous journal entries that spoke of the great love James and Rosemary shared, and of James' love for Eleanor—my mother—whom he adopted as his own daughter not long after they married. The journal painted a picture of love and happiness, and I realized why I experienced a connection to James Weston as I stood in his hospital room and watched him take his last breath. In a different lifetime, James Weston was married to my grandmother Rosemary and he loved my mother as his own, even though she wasn't biologically his child. James Weston and I were, in fact, connected by the love we shared for my mother, Eleanor.

Rosemary's journal continued to paint a beautiful picture of wedded bliss until December of 1959, nine months after she married James Weston.

December 17, 1959

Today my father left us to walk with the Great Spirit. I was holding his hand when he took his last breath and saw a look of total peace on his face. He must be so happy to finally be with my mother again.

My mother died giving birth to me so I never knew her. All my father would ever say to me about her was, "You have her gift." I never knew what that meant until my thirteenth birthday when I had my first vision. I was so scared when it happened and I didn't know who to talk to so I ran to Xo'ce, our village healer.

"Ehtah." That's what she said to me.

Too see. I knew what the word of my ancestors meant. Xo'ce told me I had a great gift. She told me I was chosen to protect our people, that I had the gift of sight just like my mother and my grandmother and my great grandmother before me.

Xo'ce told me stories of a great flood that could have destroyed our ancestors' village. She told me that my great-great-

great grandmother saw the flood in a vision and told the elders they had to move the village before the storms started. A few weeks later, the dam built by our people broke loose and flooded the entire valley in the middle of the night. If my great grandmother hadn't warned them, the entire village would have been destroyed and many of our people would have died in the flood.

I loved listening to Xo'ce's stories when I was a teenager. I went to her almost every day and begged her to tell me more about my gift. She told me about my mother having the vision of the "black gold". Xo'ce said my mother was the one who told my father where he would find the oil on our land. And she was right. Wherever my mother told them to dig, they struck black gold.

Xo'ce was always so proud of me. She thought I was a savior for our people; I didn't have the heart to tell her that I hated my visions and wanted them to go away. All I wanted was to be normal, like my best friend Maggie.

My visions keep getting stronger ever since my father died. I'm scared all the time. I see death and sadness and pain and I'm afraid I can't stop any of it from happening.

I pray every day that Eleanor doesn't get this so called "gift". I just want her to live a normal life. I can't stand the thought of my daughter having to go through what I'm going through right now.

I'm confused and I miss my father. I feel responsible for our people now that he's gone. He was working on an important law that was going to be good for our people when he passed away. He called it royalties and said our people would always have the rights to the oil produced on our land. He begged me and James before he died to finish his work and we promised him we would.

Now James acts like that conversation didn't even happen. I keep trying to remind him of our promise to my father but he acts angry and tells me not to concern myself with the oil business. There is a strange distance between me and James and I'm scared.

Last night I had a dream. I was drowning and Eleanor was crying. She was ripped out of my arms as I sunk to the bottom of a river of dark, cold water.

I'm so afraid.

~Rosemary

A chill ran down my spine as I read my grandmother's words and realized that her gift—or curse, as it should have been more aptly named—was my inheritance as well, whether I wanted it or not.

I picked the journal back up and continued to read Rosemary's haunting words out loud to Maverick as he sat quietly and listened to my grandmother's story unfold. Her journal entries became increasingly more troubled as she painted a picture of a husband who was changing right before her eyes, greed consuming him and transforming him into someone she no longer recognized.

February 3, 1960

Today is a council meeting and we vote on a new leader. James should win the vote since he had my father's blessing before he died but I don't want him to. I don't know what to do. I'm afraid he doesn't want what's best for our people. I'm thinking about going to the council and telling him they can't elect him. I have to protect our people.

A few months ago, James went to Tulsa to meet with a famous oil-and-gas attorney named Thomas Ballard. Ever since that meeting, there's been a wall between us. I can feel it. It's like he's changing right before my eyes.

James keeps telling me the law my father was trying to pass isn't what's best for the Osage. He says it's better to sell our land and our oil rights to someone who knows what they're doing instead of keeping it and receiving royalties like my father planned. I feel like I don't even know my own husband anymore.

My visions are getting worse and I keep seeing myself drowning. I watch myself sink to the bottom of dark water and I'm always reaching for Eleanor but can't get to her. When I wake up, I look over at James and he seems like a stranger. He's not the man I married. I lost Eleanor's father. I lost my father. Now I'm losing James. I'm so scared.

~Rosemary

February 5, 1960

Yesterday I told Maggie I was taking Eleanor and running away from everything. I know my baby girl isn't safe. I can't stop seeing the vision of me drowning while she is ripped out of my arms. Maggie acts brave and tells me everything will be alright but I can see in her eyes that she's scared too.

Last night Maggie gave me a picture of the two of us. It was a picture of us from happier times, when we were together at the end-of-the-school-year ice-cream social. She had just cut her hair into that cute little bob that fell right below her chin and I was pregnant with Eleanor. We had our arms wrapped around each other and we were laughing. Maggie gave me the picture and told me to always remember her and always remember the happier times we had together.

As soon as she gave me the picture, I got out my kitchen scissors and cut a small circle around our bodies then put the picture of me and Maggie in my locket. I took out the picture of me with James and Eleanor because I couldn't stand to look at it. We aren't that happy family anymore. Everything has changed.

Maggie and I held each other and cried. We know we have to say goodbye. There's no other way.

~Rosemary

I turned the page and noticed the handwriting changed. I flipped through the next few pages of the journal frantically, searching for my grandmother's handwriting; but it was gone. The journal entry on February 3, 1960 was her last and I knew exactly why. Rosemary was gone.

I felt Maverick's arm caressing my shoulder and bringing me back to the present. I looked over at him and saw deep, dark circles under his eyes. I reached over and kissed his chin, grateful for the comfort of his presence but also knowing he needed sleep. He could hardly hold his eyes open any longer.

"Maverick, there are several hours left of reading," I said. "You have to get some sleep. Let me read and I will fill you in when you wake up."

I leaned over and kissed him on his cheek then stood up and pulled him toward the couch. He didn't even argue with me. He and I both knew that he wouldn't be able to make the drive home if he didn't get some rest.

"OK. I'll just sleep for a couple of hours then you can wake me up and we'll head home. I'm sure your dad's already wondering where you are."

I glanced at my phone and realized I had missed two texts from my dad. I couldn't ignore him any longer so I picked up my phone and typed out a text.

Dad, I'm in Brookville with Maverick. I need you to trust me, please. I will be home tomorrow.

After I sent the text, I turned my phone off and picked up the journal to continue reading the entries with a new style of handwriting.

CHAPTER 28

(Rosemary's journal, Part II - Margaret)

March 15, 1960

Me and Eleanor are in Virginia now. A nice young man named Henry Smith picked us up at a truck stop in Oklahoma and offered to give us a ride to where he was going—a place called Fort Lee where he was stationed. I didn't even know where Fort Lee was but when he told me it was a two-day drive from Oklahoma, I said yes. I knew we had to get as far away from Oklahoma as possible.

Henry doesn't talk much but he's so kind. We don't ask each other any questions about our pasts in Oklahoma and I like it that way.

When we got to Virginia, Henry went straight to Fort Lee and they gave him a small one-bedroom apartment on the base. I told him to just drop us off at a hotel but he wouldn't do it. I didn't even try to argue with him because honestly, I have no idea where we'd go or what we'd do without him. Henry lets us sleep in the bedroom and he sleeps on the couch since there's only one bedroom. I feel bad about that but every time I offer to sleep on the couch, he says no way. He's so kind and I'm just so thankful for him. It scares me to think about what me and Eleanor would've done if he hadn't found us. Henry saved us.

Tomorrow I start my job as a cook on the army base and they have a daycare I can take Eleanor to. I hate leaving her while I have to work but I have no choice.

I feel afraid all the time. I'm afraid that James is going to find us or even worse, that Thomas Ballard will find us. I'm scared they will find us and we will have to go back to the nightmare we ran away from. I want to stay hidden forever and I want to keep my promise to Rosemary that I will keep Eleanor safe from all of it. It's all that matters to me now—keeping my best friend's daughter safe and hidden from our past.

~Maggie

May 7, 1960

Henry asked me to marry him and I said yes! I'm so in love with him! He is so kind to me and he loves Eleanor like his own daughter. He protects us and provides for us and I can't imagine my life without him. I go by Margaret now instead of Maggie, and now that my last name will be Smith, I hope me and Eleanor will stay hidden forever. I don't think anyone will ever find Margaret and Eleanor Smith who live in Virginia. I'm starting to feel like maybe we can finally be free of our past and have a happy future, with Henry.

I miss Rosemary every day. I hear her when Eleanor laughs and I see her dimples on her daughter's pretty face. Eleanor is just like Rosemary. She has that same fire in her spirit. People are drawn to her wherever she goes and she is loved by anyone and everyone who meets her. She is definitely Rosemary's daughter.

Every day I want to tell Eleanor about her mom. I want to tell her how Rosemary's smile could light up any room, how her laugh made you feel so happy, how she was fearless, how she was the most beautiful girl that walked into any room, and how she was the best friend I could've ever asked for. But I remember what Rosemary asked me right before she died, so I don't.

I pray every day I am enough and that I can raise Eleanor the way Rosemary would want me to.

~Margaret

August 8, 1960.

Eleanor is going to be a big sister! Henry and I are over the moon. Henry has been offered the head groundskeeper job at Fort Lee and he will start as soon as he's done with his training. I'm so proud of him and all his hard work.

Henry says I don't have to go back to work after I have the baby. I'm so glad because I want to homeschool Eleanor and the new baby when they get to school age and now I'll be able to. I'm afraid to send Eleanor to school because she has such a presence about her, just like her mother. Everyone notices her wherever we go, and I can't risk her being noticed.

I also want to homeschool the girls so I can teach them the ways of our people. If I don't teach them, they will never know their heritage. They are Osage Indian. It runs deep in their blood and they will know the ways of our people, because I will teach them myself.

~Margaret

I paused and looked over my shoulder at Maverick who was sleeping soundly on the couch then turned the next page slowly. The date at the top caught me by surprise.

October 1, 1973

I had pretty much forgotten this journal until today, when Eleanor turned thirteen.

She woke me up looking completely terrified. I took one look at her and knew exactly what had happened. All of a sudden a past I completely blocked out came back to me and I knew I couldn't run away from Eleanor's birthright. She had her first vision.

I held Eleanor and comforted her while she told me she'd seen a beautiful woman with long black hair. She said the woman gave her a birthday present—a beautiful rose-gold, heart-shaped locket. I knew she had seen her mother. I knew that Rosemary was trying to communicate to her, and I knew the exact locket Eleanor had seen in her vision. It was the same locket James gave Rosemary on their wedding day. It's the locket Rosemary gave to me on the night she died—the locket that opens this journal.

I've never even talked to Henry about my past. We both left Oklahoma so we could build a future together in Virginia. He doesn't know Eleanor isn't really my daughter. He doesn't know her mother died on the night he found us at the truck stop in Oklahoma. He doesn't know Eleanor is different—that she's special.

I'm afraid. The past found us even though I've tried so hard to run from it. I have this sick feeling all of this is out of my control, that Eleanor is on a path that's already decided and no matter where I take her or how hard I try to protect her, her visions will take her back to where it all began anyway. She has the same gift her mother had before her and there's nothing I can do about that. I'm afraid I won't be able to keep her safe. I'm afraid I won't be able to keep my promise to Rosemary.

I still have the necklace her mother gave me that night she died. Maybe Eleanor's vision means I'm supposed to give it to her? Maybe I should tell her about her mother? I'm so confused. I'm so scared.

~Margaret

October 8, 1973

Eleanor's visions are getting worse. She's seeing the past now too. She asks about a truck driving off a bridge and draws pictures of a beautiful woman with long black waves, a beautiful smile, and always a heart-shaped necklace around her neck. She's drawing her mother who she's never even seen before. Yesterday I walked into her room and saw pictures lining the wall of the Osage reservation. She hasn't been there since she was a tiny baby but she draws it like she's been there every day of her life.

I'm so afraid. I don't know what to do.

~Margaret

October 17, 1973

Yesterday Henry was called into his boss' office and told he no longer has a job. He told him about some other jobs he might be able to find then told us we had to be off the base in two weeks.

Nothing feels safe anymore.

I woke up to Eleanor screaming last night and found her in Henry's arm. He was rocking her while she sobbed.

"She's gonna die. We're gonna lose her," she cried.

"Who?" Henry asked.

I stood in the doorway where neither of them saw me and heard her choke out one word:

"Mom."

She was talking about me. I'm the only mother she's ever known. She had a vision that I'm going to die. Henry told her that wasn't going to happen but I know what he doesn't—Eleanor can see the future.

~Margaret

October 18, 1973

Henry called some of the people on the list he was given and has two job offers. One of them is in Oklahoma. I told him no way in hell would I move back there. He was upset with me because the job is a great offer and has free housing. We've never even fought before so when he told me about the job in Oklahoma last night and I slammed my hand on the table and yelled at him, he didn't understand. I've never told him about our past but now I feel like I'm going to have to.

I'm going to write Rosemary's story down in this journal tonight after everyone is in bed. Then I'm going to let Eleanor read it and Henry too so they will understand why we can't go back to Oklahoma. I don't know what else to do. The past found us, through Eleanor's visions, and I can't run from it anymore.

~Margaret

CHAPTER 29

(Rosemary's Journal, Part III - Margaret & Eleanor)

October 18, 1973

This is what I remember from February 4, 1960.

Rosemary had been telling me for months leading up to that day that she was losing James. She said ever since he went to go see Thomas Ballard for oil and gas advice, he came home a different person. He was obsessed. All he could think about was starting his oil business and becoming rich, so he would never end up like his father who was a broke, abusive alcoholic.

Rosemary could always see Thomas Ballard was evil and he was using James' biggest fears to manipulate him. But James wouldn't listen to her. When the Osage people refused to elect him because he wasn't from the tribe, he went off the deep end.

Rosemary and Eleanor came over to my house that afternoon after the tribal vote and she looked terrified. She told me she'd been having the same vision over and over for weeks and it just happened in real life.

James asked her to come to his office and when she and Eleanor got there he was sitting at a new fancy desk she'd never seen before. She said Thomas Ballard was standing behind James with his hand on his shoulder. She took one look at her husband and knew she'd lost James for good. His eyes were completely blank, overtaken by darkness and greed.

James gave Rosemary some papers and told her to sign them. When she asked what they were, James told her it was best for the Osage if he and Thomas Ballard controlled their lands and turned it into a successful business. Of course, Rosemary wouldn't sign the papers so James lost his temper. He grabbed her by the arm and jerked her across the table. When he did, he knocked over a candle that was sitting on the table and the hot wax spilled all over Eleanor. It burned her leg bad and Rosemary had to drive her to the hospital.

As I read Margaret Smith's words, I flash backed to a childhood memory. We were at the splash pad in Brookville and my mom was wearing a swimsuit. I noticed a scar on her right leg.

"What happened Mommy?" I asked.

"I don't know sweetheart. I've just always had a scar there."

Now I knew. I picked up the journal and continued reading.

Everything changed that night. Rosemary was scared Eleanor wasn't safe. She told me her husband was gone and that Thomas Ballard brainwashed him. She told me she was afraid of James and Thomas so she was taking Eleanor and running away. I'll never forget her looking at me with so much fear in her eyes and saying:

"Thomas Ballard is capable of anything Maggie, even murder. I have to leave to keep Eleanor safe."

We came up with a plan. We would leave that night while James was at a meeting with Thomas in Tulsa. We'd take the old farm truck my dad kept in his barn for hauling hay and drive it all the way to New Mexico where Rosemary's uncle lived. He would help Rosemary and Eleanor disappear, forever. After that, I would drive back to Oklahoma and tell everyone I had no idea where Rosemary and Eleanor were. Then in May when school was out, I would leave Oklahoma for good. Both of us would leave Oklahoma and never come back.

That night everything went as planned at first. I got the farm truck and waited for James to leave before I went to get Rosemary. When I got there she had two suitcases packed. They were hidden under Eleanor's crib. We both grabbed one and threw it in the back of the truck then she went back in the house. I watched as she stood there holding Eleanor, saying goodbye to the only home she'd ever known. Before she walked out the door Rosemary threw her arms around my neck then put something in my right hand—it was her heart-shaped necklace that she always wore around her neck.

"I want you to have this," she said. "I want you to remember me by it always. You aren't just my best friend. You're my sister Maggie. I'll never forget you."

Then she walked through the front door and got in my dad's farm truck without even looking back. She was ready to do whatever it took to protect Eleanor.

We turned left onto the road that would take us to the highway and we both saw a pair of headlights turn on from a dark road in front of us. When we passed the driver we saw who it was. It was Thomas Ballard.

Rosemary screamed when she saw Thomas and I slammed on the gas pedal. It was a one-way road so we were way ahead of Thomas by the time he turned around, but we saw his headlights behind us and we knew he was gaining on us. I drove as fast as I could and finally I saw Old Man McCoy's wooden bridge. It was all that stood between us and the highway.

Just before we made our way onto the bridge, I felt Thomas slam into us from behind. I stomped on the brake and the truck slid out of control then we slammed into the side of the bridge. The old wood railing couldn't stand the hit and the next thing I knew, the front right side of the truck was falling over the edge of the bridge.

My head slammed into the windshield and everything went black. It was the cries of a baby that finally brought me back. I forced myself to open my eyes and I saw Eleanor strapped in next to me, crying like crazy, but I didn't see Rosemary.

My eyes got used to the darkness and I finally found Rosemary. Her whole body was hanging over the bridge and she was holding onto the passenger side door, which was only attached by one small hinge. I pushed my way to the right side of the truck to try to reach for Rosemary but when I did, I felt the truck shift. Rosemary screamed at me not to move and I realized if I moved toward her, we were all in danger of falling off the side of the bridge into the water below.

I pushed myself back to the safety of the passenger side door then unstrapped Eleanor and pulled her toward me. I looked into Rosemary's eyes and I knew she had made her decision. She would sacrifice her own life for mine and for Eleanor's; but not before she said goodbye.

"Take care of her Maggie. Don't tell her about any of this," Rosemary said to me. Then I saw her fingers slip from the door and I watched my best friend let go of the truck door and fall into the darkness below.

The second Rosemary let go, truck shifted back to a safer place on the bridge. I grabbed Rosemary's backpack and I grabbed Eleanor then I pulled us out of the truck and I took off running with Eleanor. I had no idea what I was going to do but when I saw Thomas Ballard's sports car sitting on the side of the road with the door open and the engine still running, I jumped in without thinking. I locked the door and turned the car around then took off toward a backroad I knew would take me to the highway.

I'll never forget what I saw when I turned around and the headlights flashed down to the water. I saw Thomas Ballard standing down by the water. He watched Rosemary fall from the bridge and then he went down to the water to make sure she didn't come back up. Rosemary was right about Thomas all along. He was evil and he was a murderer.

I pulled over at a truck stop 40 miles west of the reservation and I went inside with Eleanor. I just sat there in shock. I had no clue what to do. Finally, I decided to open Rosemary's backpack since it was all that I had. I saw some snacks, a wallet that had $8 in it, a drink cup for Eleanor with some milk, and this leather book. I took off the necklace Rosemary had given me before we left that night and figured out it was a key to unlock the journal.

That's where Henry found us, sitting in a truck stop with $8 to our name, reading Rosemary's journal. He told me later that he loved me the instant he saw

351

me sitting there. I don't remember much for those first few months. I think I was in

shock from watching my best friend die and becoming a mother to her baby in the

same night. I was only eighteen years old and I left everything I ever knew, for

Rosemary, and for Eleanor.

It was Henry who finally brought me back. He gave me hope. He made me

laugh again. He helped me forget all the pain. He gave me a beautiful family and

I've lived a life with him that I wouldn't trade for anything. Being Henry's wife and

raising my two beautiful daughters, Eleanor Rose and Cordelia Ann, has been my

greatest joy. I have lived simply but have loved greatly. Even in spite of the pain, my

heart is full.

~Margaret

I stopped reading momentarily and took a deep breath as several large parts of the mystery fell into place, allowing me to see an almost complete section of the picture that had eluded me for so long. Margaret Smith was not my biological grandmother, but she raised my mother as her own daughter. She raised my mother because her best friend, Rosemary Weston, died tragically. Margaret took my mother and ran away to Virginia where she married Henry Smith and had my Aunt Cordelia. She lived her life in hiding, trying to protect my mother from the evil of a twisted past that included Thomas Ballard and James Weston. I felt a gratitude and love toward Margaret, the grandmother I had never met, and I needed to know what happened to her.

I had to talk to my Aunt Cordelia.

CHAPTER 30

I didn't dare turn on my phone for fear of my dad's angry texts and voicemails. I saw Maverick sleeping peacefully on the couch so I walked over quietly and grabbed his cell phone from the edge of the couch; then I walked outside to call my aunt.

"Aunt Cordelia?"

"Elyse Rose!"

I interrupted her before she could continue her angry onslaught. I needed my questions answered.

"Aunt Cordelia," I said in a forceful tone, "I need you to listen to me." She paused when she heard the urgency in my voice. "I need you to tell me about your mom. I need to know about Margaret Smith."

When she spoke, her tone was almost scolding. "Well, she wasn't just my mom, Elle. She was your grandmother too." I had offended her by referring to Margaret as only her mother so I quickly rephrased my question.

"I'm sorry, Aunt Cordelia. I need to know about my grandmother Margaret, please."

"Well what do you need to know?" she asked.

I paused, knowing my questions would cause her pain.

"How did she die?"

I heard a long sigh and several seconds passed before she finally answered.

"She died when we still lived in Virginia, Elle. I don't really remember much about it. I was only thirteen years old. Your mother was fourteen if I remember right."

As she spoke, she confirmed the same story Margaret had written in Rosemary's journal.

"My mom died suddenly. It was very unexpected. My dad found her sitting in her rocking chair and they think she had a stroke and died immediately. I don't really remember much. It was an extremely difficult time. She was there one day then gone the next. We barely had time to finish the funeral before our dad moved us to Oklahoma for a new job he was offered."

"The job for James Weston?"

"Yes. The job for James Weston. He owned the estate before the Masons bought it."

"Then when you moved, my mom met and fell in love with James Weston's youngest son correct? Nathan Weston?"

"Yes, Elle, that's right." I could tell she was getting irritated with my questioning but I continued.

"Do you know what made your dad move to Oklahoma after so many years in Virginia? Don't you think that's kind of strange? Did he ever mention what made him move back?"

She sighed in exasperation before she answered. "I don't know, Elle. That whole period is a blur to be honest."

"Please Aunt Cordelia," I begged. "I need to know."

She finally conceded. "It seems like I remember my dad saying that someone called his boss in Virginia and told him about the job in Oklahoma. He said it was an offer he couldn't refuse. That's all I know."

"I really need to know who called and offered Grandpa Henry the job Aunt Cordelia," I pushed. "Is there any way you can find out for me?"

"I don't understand any of this," she argued.

"I know. I don't understand it yet either," I admitted. "All I know is that my mom always told me that the truth would set me free. I need to know the truth, once and for all Aunt Cordelia, and I need your help."

There was a long silence on the phone before she answered.

"I'll look through my dad's old chest and see if I can find anything."

"Thank you. Call me on Maverick's phone if you find anything. Mine is turned off." I added one more thing before I hung up. "And Aunt Cordelia...can you please try to make my dad understand?"

With that, I turned off the phone and returned to my reading. As I turned the next page of the journal, I took a deep breath and fought back tears as I saw my mom's beautiful handwriting scrolling across the page. I gasped as I read the date, written in my mother's own handwriting, as I realized she had written in Rosemary's journal on the day she was murdered.

November 17, 2009

Yesterday I told John and Elyse I was going to a weekend women's conference with my ladies Bible study group, then I got in my car and drove to Oklahoma. I got a hotel once I got here and I will drive back tomorrow after I find what I'm looking for. I hate lying to them, but I have no other choice.

I've been seeing visions off and on again for nearly three years, and finally, they've brought me back home. They brought me back to Oklahoma. No matter how hard I've tried to run away from my past, it found me again.

The first vision I had after my accident was on Elyse's seventh birthday. She was blowing out her candles and I was singing "Happy Birthday" to her. Suddenly the room went black and it was if I was transported to a different place. I saw a woman rocking in a rocking chair and she was holding a leather-bound book in her hands. It seemed to be a journal. Behind her stood another beautiful woman with long dark waves hanging down her back. She took a heart-shaped necklace from around her neck and handed it to the woman in the rocking chair, who used it to unlock the journal. Together they looked at me, smiled at me with love, and offered me the journal and the necklace.

After that vision, I remembered my mother. I recognized her as the woman in the rocking chair and I had this memory of her looking very troubled, writing in this very leather-bound journal that I had seen in my visions in the days before she died. I remembered moving from Virginia to Oklahoma. I remembered a boy. I remembered that I loved him and he loved me. I remembered him reading to me from the pages of that very journal my mother had held in her hands, underneath the shade of a massive oak tree that had our initials carved on it.

Each time I had a vision, a memory from my past would also return to me. At first I was frightened by my visions and memories returning. I wanted to run away and forget the darkness of my past, and I tried. Then I had a vision that changed everything.

A few days before Elle's eleventh birthday, the room went dark again. I found myself on a dirt road. I was running from a man. He had no face but I knew he was evil, and I knew he wanted to kill me. Then I saw my sweet Elle. She was on the road with me and she was terrified. I grabbed her hand and we started to run together from the man with no face but no matter how hard we ran, we couldn't escape him. He was gaining on us with each step and I knew he would eventually catch us. When I returned to reality, I knew what I had to do. I knew what the vision meant. I couldn't run from the man with no face forever. I had to stand

and face him. I had to confront all the darkness and pain and misery of my past, in order to save my daughter.

So, I made my plan. I told John and Elyse I was going to a women's conference and instead, I drove to Oklahoma. I woke up early this morning and went to find the journal. It was just where I left it, tucked deep in a crevice of an oak tree with initials carved on it: ES + NW.

Nathan Weston. I remembered his name the second I went to that oak tree. My past came flooding back to me as I recalled how much I loved him and how much he loved me. I remembered we were forbidden to be together by his father, James Weston, and I remembered why. Nathan and I found Rosemary's journal together—in Margaret's old hope chest—and we learned how to unlock it using the heart-shaped locket. I remembered Nathan reading to me from the pages of the journal as we uncovered our family's shameful secrets and learned of our parents' tragic love story.

After reading Rosemary's journal, we realized why Nathan's father would never allow us to be together. I was a constant reminder of the woman he had loved, and failed to protect. I was Rosemary's daughter, come back to haunt him for his sins.

So, Nathan and I decided we would run away together. I was supposed to wait for him underneath the oak tree that night, but he never came. It was someone else who met me there—the man with no face from my visions. I remember seeing his dark shape walk through the woods toward us and I hid the journal deep in the trunk of the oak tree where Nathan would always leave me poems and I would leave him letters. I remember the evil man. I can hear his voice but I can never see his face. I remember him demanding I give him the journal and when I wouldn't, he took me.

I don't remember all the details. I've blocked the memories of pain out for so long that it's hard to remember now. I know I was in the back of Nathan's truck. I was tied up and gagged and Nathan was beside me. I remember a struggle, then Nathan reaching over and opening my door. I remember our eyes meeting right before he pushed me out of the truck and knowing he was saying goodbye. He sacrificed himself for me. The last memory I have is of the car swerving wildly then flying off a bridge.

Obviously they found me in Ohio but I don't remember how I got there. I had no memories for years after that. I look back now and wonder if it was truly amnesia as the doctors called it, or if it was the power of the mind protecting me by blocking out all the pain and loss and fear that I had to experience.

I have blocked out the past for too long. I know I can't continue to run from it. For my daughter's sake, I have to face my past. I have to face the darkness. I am going back to Ohio with this journal and I will continue to remember. I will hide it at the church, where no one can find it, then as I have visions and my memories return to me, I will go get it and write them down. I won't fight my visions any longer. I will embrace them, and I will write everything down until the pieces of the puzzle are complete. I will write for my biological mother—Rosemary—and I will write for Nathan. I will write until I understand my past. I will write until I uncover the truth, to protect my Elle.

I hate leaving Oklahoma without talking to Cordelia. She thinks I'm dead and has for years, and that breaks my heart. She is all alone. She lost Mom, then me, and then Dad. I saw her through the kitchen window of our cottage before I started walking to the oak tree and I had to fight the urge to run to her and tell her that I'm alive. I pray we see each other again but I know that can't be today. I have to get home to Elle. I have to protect her and I can't do that unless I solve the mysteries of my past. For now, all I can do is leave a note for Cordelia and tell her that I'm alive and she has a beautiful niece, and that I pray we'll see each other again one day.

~Eleanor

I turned the page frantically, searching for more of my mother's writing and wanting to hear more of her words, but I knew that her journal entry on November 17th would be her last because she died that night. I found her at the end of a one-lane dirt road and held her as she took her last breath.

Suddenly exhaustion consumed me. I pushed myself toward Maverick and lay my head down on the couch, desperate for relief from the visions that flooded my mind with pain.

CHAPTER 31

I was on a one-lane dirt road, the same one-lane dirt road that haunted me in both my dreams and my reality, for years. It was already dusk and I could feel the darkness closing in on me with each passing second, but I was surprisingly at peace. I knew that in the darkness I would find truth and freedom—even if that liberty was only found in death. Although my soul felt like it would rip apart as I turned away from the light, and the boy with the blue eyes who lived there, I stepped into the darkness—alone once again.

I awakened startled and disoriented to find myself in the living room of the parsonage I grew up in, Maverick sleeping peacefully on the couch beside me. I looked outside to realize it was dusk and in a moment of complete clarity, I knew exactly what I had to do. As always, the answers were there, in my visions.

I didn't even allow myself time to feel fear. I silently set Maverick's phone back down on the couch beside him and grabbed his keys; then I made my way quietly out the front door, careful not to wake him. I knew he would be angry when he awakened and found me gone, but I couldn't drag him any further into my world of nightmares. I had to say goodbye, because I loved him.

When I got in the truck, I turned my phone on, ignoring the seventeen voicemails I had that were no doubt from my very angry father. I sent a quick text to my aunt.

"If you find out an answer to my question, you can text me on my phone. It's turned back on."

I sat my phone down and drove to the one-lane dirt road, my heart beating rapidly as I approached the place that held so many memories of pain and darkness. As I neared the turn off the highway that would take me to that forsaken road, I heard my phone beep and I looked down to see a response from my aunt.

"The man who called and offered my dad the job in Oklahoma was named Thomas Ballard."

Another piece of the puzzle shifted into place and as I turned off the highway and parked Maverick's truck, I knew who would be waiting for me when I made my way to the end of that one-lane dirt road.

I walked slowly down the road—fighting the memories that plagued me from when I walked down that very road as a ten-year-old girl—and when I reached the end of the path, a black SUV with dark tinted windows sat; it was barely hidden by the tall grass that grew on either side of the path. I stopped and waited until finally, someone opened a door and stepped out of the vehicle. He walked toward me and I stood tall, undaunted in a moment that warranted fear. I was ready to face the darkness. I was ready to face the man with no face.

The man stopped several feet in front of me and we stood there, each of us evaluating the other, but neither of us speaking. He was middle-aged and wore an immaculate, black fitted suit. He exuded wealth and privilege, but I could see past his polished veneer and straight into his soul. There I saw a monster.

"Thomas Ballard?" I asked, my voice strong and steady as I searched for the answers I needed. An evil laugh ripped through the air, sending a cold chill down my spine.

"Thomas Ballard is an old, old man, my dear." He strolled around me as though he were a lion stalking his prey. "No, I'm not Thomas Ballard. But he is my mentor, and my grandfather," he said with pride.

I struggled to process his words.

"Grandfather was right. You do look so much like your mother," he said as he appraised me knowingly.

"How did you know my mother?" I asked.

"How did I know your mother?" he repeated with a hint of humor in his words. "Well, I was in love with your mother once upon a time." He stared at me with an intensity that made my skin crawl.

I remembered my aunt's words about the Weston brothers—Philip and Nathan—both falling madly in love with my mother when they met her.

"You're Philip Weston." I said it as a statement, not a question. He didn't acknowledge my words but just continued to rake me with his evil eyes.

"You look like Rosemary too." I heard the disdain in his voice when he said my grandmother's name.

"How do you know about Rosemary?" I asked. "She was dead before you were born because your grandfather killed her," I accused. The fire within was beginning to burn.

"That stupid Indian woman ruined my life. Of course I know who she is," he answered. "And my grandfather showed me a picture once."

I could hear the prejudice in Philip Weston's voice and though before me stood a seemingly polished and professional business man, I saw but a broken young boy who was abandoned by his father and brainwashed to hate by a greedy grandfather.

"Rosemary, Rosemary, Rosemary. She was all I heard about growing up. A stupid, uneducated Indian woman who grew up on a reservation for God's sake. My father was never the same after he lost that stupid Indian woman. My Grandfather Ballard told me she brainwashed my father— bewitched him somehow with her Indian magic." He turned to me and pointed his spindly index finger at me as he screamed violently—"Just like your mother did to me!"

It was obvious that Philip Weston hated Rosemary and he hated my mother for not loving him back; but what was even more evident was that he hated his father for loving an Indian woman instead of his beautiful, blonde socialite mother; I looked at the man standing before me and realized his hatred and resentment, along with the influence of his evil grandfather, had twisted him into a monster.

"My father never even loved my mother." He shook his head as if trying to rid himself of a painful memory. "He flat out told me once he only married her because Grandfather Ballard would have exposed him if he didn't. I grew up with a father who hated my mother because of who she was— Thomas Ballard's daughter—but mostly he hated her because of who she wasn't. She wasn't that stupid Indian woman, the love of his life—Rosemary. My father blamed my Grandfather Ballard for losing Rosemary and for forcing him to marry a woman he didn't love. He hated my Grandfather with every fiber of his being, and he hated my mother and me, too. From the time I was a little boy he would tell me I looked and acted just like a Ballard. I could see his disgust every time he looked at me. The only people he cared about were his beloved

Nathan, who looked just like him, and Rosemary, his stupid, dead Indian bride."

My stomach lurched and I thought I was going to be sick as I watched him relive a painful past that shaped him into the terrible person I saw in front of me. My mind was reeling.

James Weston married Thomas Ballard's only daughter after Rosemary died. He was blackmailed into marrying her by Thomas Ballard who wanted control of the oil on the Osage lands. He never loved his second wife. He had two sons with her—Philip and Nathan. Both of his sons loved my mother. Nathan was good. Philip was evil, like his grandfather. Philip and his grandfather, Thomas Ballard, blamed my mother and Rosemary for everything. They hated them. They murdered them. The hatred coursed through my veins as all the puzzle pieces finally came together.

Philip paced around me, staring at me appraisingly. My blood went cold. I knew he was looking at me and seeing my mother, and feeling the pain of scorned love all over again.

"Did you know that my little brother and I both loved your mother the second we saw her?" he asked. "She chose him of course." I heard the animosity for his brother in his voice. "One night Nathan brought your mother to dinner to meet our parents and that was when everything changed. James Weston, my powerful, wealthy father—" he laughed mockingly. "He took one look at your mother in her beautiful yellow sundress then he turned completely white and walked out of the room. He was never the same again. He went completely insane. For years he thought Rosemary and Eleanor were both dead, so he lost his mind when he saw Eleanor. He was convinced she was Rosemary—his long-lost love—come back from the grave to haunt him and punish him for his sins. No one could convince him otherwise. He forbade my brother from ever seeing your mother again then locked himself in our house and became a recluse. Grandfather Ballard knew my dad was going crazy. He saw a past he worked hard to bury threatening to surface." He looked up at me, the evil in his eyes burning as he spoke his next words. "So we did what we had to do."

"So you *murdered* them?" I accused. "Say it. I want to hear you say out loud that you're a murderer."

An evil grimace touched his lips then he laughed again as a chill ran down my spine. He answered my question with a question of his own. "What would you know about protecting an empire? You're just a little girl. We run a multibillion-dollar corporation! You have no idea what has to be done to run a company like WestCo."

I knew the "we" he kept referencing was himself and his grandfather, Thomas Ballard.

"My dad has been incapable of running WestCo for years, ever since that night he saw your mother. He slipped into a dream world, living in the past and blabbering on like a crazed fool about 'Rosemary, Rosemary, oh my Rosie, I'm so sorry Rosemary'. He is an embarrassment. My grandfather and I are WestCo—past, present, and future. We had to take on a partner when we first started the company for financial backing but we will take care of the Masons soon enough then we will change the company to its rightful name—Ballard Oil & Gas."

I glared at him, repulsed, as he stood there confessing his evil plans to overtake WestCo oil from Maverick's family.

"You and your grandfather are murderers," I accused again.

"It was their fault," he responded defensively. "If they would have given us that damn journal like we asked, none of this would have happened. Grandfather was right. He said your mother was exactly like Rosemary—stubborn and stupid."

The second he spoke those words about my mother, the fire raged out of control. Without thinking, I lunged at him, attacking him with all the strength I could muster. As I attacked, he moved to the side, causing me to fall to the ground, and I felt the weight of his body on top of me instantly. He pinned me down and I found myself staring into his dark eyes, allowing me to see into the depths of his hollow soul. I struggled but my small body was no match for his strength. I was at Philip Weston's mercy as he spat his venomous words at me.

"Where is the journal, Elle? Tell me where it is," he demanded angrily.

"What journal?"

"I know you came back here to find Rosemary's journal."

"I don't know what you're talking about." I tried to feign innocence which only angered him more. He flew into a fit of rage.

"I know about the journal! Don't you dare lie to me!" he screamed at me. "My brother came to me that night and told me he was running away with your mom. He told me Eleanor found a journal that proved our Grandfather Ballard was an evil man and a murderer and they were going to turn him in to the authorities."

He continued to pin me down as he reached into his back pocket and pulled out a gun.

"Don't move." He pointed the gun at my head with warning. I obeyed.

"I know about all about the journal. My grandfather and I have been looking for it for years," he confessed. "When Nathan told me about it, I went straight to Grandfather and he told me I had to find the journal at all costs. That it could ruin us." He slipped back into a dream world as he relived his past.

His eyes glossed over and he recalled the events of the night his brother died as if he was a robot, and he was completely unaffected by the horror of it all.

"That night, I took one of my dad's guns from his safe, then I went to his study and stole his big hunting knife. I found your mom and Nathan at the oak tree where they always met each other, and when they refused to tell me where the journal was, I tied them up and put them in the back of Nathan's truck. I was just going to take them to an old warehouse on the outside of town to buy more time until my grandfather could come up with a plan, but Nathan got loose and threw your mother out of the car to protect her. Then he grabbed the wheel and the truck spun out of control. We went over the bridge." His next words and the way he spoke them as if he had no emotion whatsoever, sent a cold chill running up my spine. "I woke to water filling up the truck and we were sinking to the bottom of the river. My brother was unconscious, and I could've saved him. But I left him there to die."

I wanted to tell him he was a monster but I held my tongue. There was still another piece of information missing and I needed him to give it to me desperately.

"What happened to my mother?" I asked him.

"I don't know. We looked for her for years but she just disappeared. One day ten years later, she showed up out of the blue. My grandfather always had people watching your aunt's cottage in case she came back. She was seen leaving a note in your aunt's mailbox and my grandfather called me and told me what to do. I got the note out of Cordelia's mailbox then followed your mom back to Ohio." He paused to evaluate me. "In the note, she spoke of a beautiful daughter she had to protect—you, I presume."

I wanted to attack him but I knew I had to wait. He still hadn't told me how my mother died, and I needed to know everything.

"If you took the note from my aunt's mailbox, then how did it get there years later?" I asked. "My aunt said she got the letter a few months ago."

"What are you talking about?" He looked at me as if I were crazy. "I still have that letter in my safe at home. Your aunt never got that letter," Philip argued.

I started to open my mouth to protest but something stopped me. Somehow, in that moment, I remembered a woman in a white dress on the reservation. I remembered how she handed me a carved wooden box and a necklace and I realized there were events leading me to that very moment, that were beyond my understanding.

"How did you kill my mother, Philip?" It was time to press him for the truth. "Tell me about how you plunged a knife into her body and left her dying on the side of the road. *Look at me*, you coward, and tell me how you murdered the woman that you supposedly loved."

I raised my voice to a scream and noticed he started to cower at my words—obviously distraught. The gun remained pointed at my head.

"It was an accident!" he screamed in desperation. "All she had to do was tell me where the journal was." He kept running his fingers through his slicked-back hair, giving a disheveled look to his previously refined appearance. He was starting to fall apart. I saw my opportunity.

"What did you do Philip? Tell me about the knife. I found her. Did you know that? I saw what you did to her. I saw her covered in blood. I was with her when she took her last breath."

He looked traumatized by my words. "It was an accident! I told you! I was just holding the knife to her throat to scare her into telling me where she hid the journal." He was almost whimpering. "I didn't plan on actually using it. But when I threatened you, she completely lost it. She attacked me!"

"What do you mean 'when you threatened me?'"

"I followed her all the way to Brookville like my Grandfather said to do and she drove straight to the church and went inside. I hid in the back of her station wagon while she was inside."

He followed my mom from Oklahoma then hid in the back of her van when she went inside the church to hide the journal, the journal I just found.

It was almost too much to process all the information I was finding out at once.

"Then what happened, Philip?" I pressed him to continue his confession. I need to know everything, once and for all.

"When she got back in the car I held the knife to her throat and told her to turn onto a dirt road off the highway so we could talk."

I was sick to my stomach as I listened to him recount the night he murdered my mother but at the same time, I hung onto every word that came out of his mouth. Finally, I would have the answers to the questions that had plagued me since I was a girl. He continued as I stared into his eyes and past them even, into the blackness of his soul.

"I asked her to tell me where the journal was and she refused to tell me. So I threatened you. I told her if she wouldn't tell me where it was then we would come after you. She went insane when I said that. She grabbed the knife with her hands and pushed the knife away from her throat. Then she attacked me. We struggled on the ground and when I stood up, she didn't move. There was blood everywhere and when she rolled over I saw the knife plunged into her chest." He looked terrified as he relived that moment. "It was an accident! I never meant to stab her!" He buried his head in his hands momentarily and I saw my chance.

I grabbed a rock that I felt pushing into my rib cage underneath me and with all my strength, I slammed it into the side of his head. He cried out in pain as I pushed my body off the ground and took off in a sprint. He was standing in between me and the path that led to the truck so I had to turn and run in the opposite direction—toward a small path that led to the river.

He pursued. His footsteps pounded behind me. His evil presence closed in. Just as the sun was setting over the river, I came to the edge of the small path and my heart sank when I saw a large, forty-foot drop into the river with jagged rocks below. I took a deep breath and peace overcame me over me as I stood staring at the river rushing below me.

I knew I was going to die.

Then you will know the truth and the truth will set you free.

I heard my mom's words echo in my mind and I turned around, determined to face my attacker and make my final stand with strength and dignity. I found peace in knowing that I would die, finally understanding the truth of what happened to my mother.

Philip pointed the gun to my head then used his other hand to whip me around. I didn't move as he reached into my backpack and found what he wanted—Rosemary's journal— then he tucked it safely inside the pocket of his suit coat. I formulated a plan to attack.

I'm not going down without a fight.

As Philip placed the journal inside his coat pocket, I pulled my right leg up and stomped as hard as I could on his right foot. He loosened his grip. I thrashed my arm out in desperation toward the direction of the gun he held at my head. I was fortunate to hit my target and the gun tumbled to the ground a few feet away.

We both dove toward the ground, fighting for possession of the gun and as we wrestled, we rolled dangerously close to the edge of the chasm. We both grasped for the gun frantically but I gained possession first. I felt Philip grasp my leg and use it to drag my body toward him. I pulled my other leg back then kicked at him with all my strength, landing a hard blow right to his chest; then, I watched in horror as I saw the man who killed my mother began to tumble over the side of the cliff and into the ravine.

No! He has the journal.

Without thinking, I dove toward Philip Weston, desperate to regain control of Rosemary's journal—the only piece of evidence that could prove the Ballards' murderous affairs as well as their illegal involvement in acquiring the Osage lands. He grasped his hand out in desperation as he flew over the edge and I reached my hand out to his.

As we connected, the weight of Philip Weston's body began to pull me over the ledge and threatened to take me with him. I looked around, panicked, frantically trying to find something to stabilize us both and keep us from going over the edge of the cliff. Just as I started to slip over, I spotted a large root of a tree protruding from the ground and I fished my left leg underneath it, bending it to use the tree limb to anchor my body. He tumbled over the edge and the top half of my body followed with him but we stopped as I connected with the root and halted our fall. We sat there, me holding onto the tree limb with my leg, the lower half of my body safely on the top of the ravine and my upper half over the edge, holding onto the murderous man who killed my mother. We made eye contact, a knowing glance passed between us.

"Give me the journal and I'll pull you up."

"Do you really think I believe you?" he answered. "No way. Pull me up then I'll give you the journal."

We stood there sizing each other up, each calculating our enemy and trying to gage our next move. I felt my foot beginning to give way and decided to call his bluff. I loosened my grip.

"I swear to God I'll drop you right now if you don't hand me that journal."

He still didn't budge so I started to drop my hold on him. My tactic worked. He started to fish in his coat with his free hand. He found the journal and started to hand it to me but before I could reach it with my free hand, I felt my foot slip free from the tree branch. I was falling.

My life flashed before my eyes as my body made its way over the edge of the cliff. I accepted my impending death and peace enveloped me.

I will die knowing the truth and I will die knowing love.

The last thing I saw was Maverick's beautiful blue eyes as my body made its way over the ravine and started to fall to the jagged rocks below.

I jerked to a stop, something stopping my fall. Then, I watched the body of the man who murdered my mother plummet into the ravine, bouncing off a large rock like a rag doll before falling into the rushing river. He was gone. The man with no face, who plagued my nightmares and visions for years, was gone.

The journal hung precariously on a rock beside me and I became singularly focused on retrieving it. I reached out for the journal and when I did, I felt myself slip; but it didn't matter. All I cared about was getting that journal. I reached further, then felt myself slip another inch. My fingertips were mere inches away from touching the journal. I had to reach it.

"Ells."

I recognized the voice, soft and gentle, but it was like I was dreaming.

"Ells, give me your other hand."

Only two people ever called me Ells. I awakened from my dream world, to see a pair of welcoming brown eyes, and a red Cincinnati ball cap. It was Charlie.

Something shifted, and I listened to him. I had always listened to Charlie, ever since I was a little girl. I paused, torn at the thought of leaving the journal behind and struggling to accept what that meant—that I might not ever be able to prove what Thomas Ballard and Philip Weston did to my family; that I might not ever be able to expose them and show the world what monsters the two seemingly perfect and polished businessmen men truly were. *One little fingertip and I can reach it.* I started to slip.

"Ells, you gotta give me your other hand *now.*" He was calm, as always.

Suddenly another pair of eyes appeared above the cliff, piercing-blue and magnetic. I could see Maverick's lips moving in desperation, but couldn't process what he said. Everything shifted, our connection drawing me toward him, more powerful even than the darkness that called me toward the journal. Slowly, I turned away from the journal, letting go of justice for my mother, for my grandmother, and for Nathan

Weston. I let go of darkness and murder and generations of confusion and pain; and I turned toward him.

I gave Maverick my other hand and with one sudden movement, he and Charlie pulled me away from the darkness and into the light.

CHAPTER 32

I hugged Charlie and refused to let go of the embrace, wishing he and Grace could just pack up and come to Tulsa with me. Maverick watched from the steps of his dad's private plane, giving us the moment we needed even though I could sense his tension.

"Thank you, Charlie." I let out an exasperated sigh. "It sounds ridiculous even saying those words. I mean, you saved my life…"

He dropped his head, humble as always, stuffing his hands into his pockets bashfully.

"Maverick deserves some of the credit too, Elle. When he woke up and realized you had taken his car, he ran over a mile to my house to get help, for God's sake. I think he made it in under five minutes."

I peeked over my shoulder at him. He was commanding, even from a distance and I was being drawn to him by the undeniable force that surged between us. But for once, I pushed it away.

"But you were the one who made it to me and saved me before I fell over the cliff and *died…*" I nudged him playfully. "Seventh-grade track champ still has it goin' on, huh?"

He tried to stifle a laugh unsuccessfully.

"Yeah I guess I can still turn it on when I need to." There was a twinkle of pride in his eyes.

"Well thank God for me, or I'd be dead at the bottom of the river right now."

The silence loomed, and the unspoken tension between us made my heart beat at an uncomfortable rate. I was thinking of another witty comment to break the silence when I heard his gentle words.

"Hey, Ells. I'm always here for you. You know that right?" I looked up to see his usual concern touching his tender brown eyes, but I noticed something new behind them.

Has that always been there but I was just too selfish to see how you felt, Charlie?

I averted my eyes, uncomfortable with the emotions that seemed to be passing between us.

"I know Charlie, and I'm always here for you." I squeezed his hand gently. "Take care of Grace for me, OK?"

I gave him one last hug, then turned to walk away. With each step I took, a sadness gripped me as I realized I couldn't bring him with me. Charlie was staying in Brookville, and I was going back to Tulsa, with Maverick.

When we stepped off Mr. Mason's private plane, Aunt Cordelia and my dad were waiting there for us, as well as Maverick's parents. That night when I lay my head on my pillow, I had another dream. This time I was walking with a beautiful, aged woman in a white leather dress with turquoise beads tied along the bottom. We walked along a peaceful mountain road, a gurgling brook twisting its way alongside the path.

I knew the woman I walked beside was Rosemary, my grandmother. There were so many questions I wanted to ask her: did she really die that night in the river? If so, how did she meet me in the yellow clapboard house that night on the Osage Reservation? How did she give me her wooden carved box with the heart-shaped necklace in it when that necklace was buried with my mother? Did she put the letter from my mother that Philip Weston stole in Cordelia's mailbox after all those years?

Most of all, I wanted to know if she was a ghost, forced to walk among earth until her murder was solved, or if she had truly been alive all these years and never really died in the river that night so many years ago.

I turned toward her to ask my questions but for some reason, as I looked into the depths of her coal-black eyes, I couldn't speak. She grabbed my hand and when she touched me, suddenly none of my questions mattered. We took a few more steps down the path together and then my mother joined us. She was radiant in a bright yellow sundress. My mother smiled at me, that smile that touched her eyes and showed those gigantic dimples etched into the sides of her face. She grabbed my other hand and we walked purposefully down the path together, all three of us—Rosemary, my mother, and me—until we came to a crossroads.

We stopped at the crossroads and I was confused. On the left, I saw a road ahead with nothing but sunshine and beautiful blue skies reaching out for miles into the distance, but on the right I saw a different path. I saw a road with hills and valleys. There were times where I couldn't even see the road and others where I thought I saw storm clouds on the horizon; but there were also other stretches of the road where I undoubtedly saw beautiful skies and glorious sunshine. It was unmistakable that the road on the right was an unknown and uncertain path full of both sunshine and storms, while the road on the left seemed to offer nothing but perfect serenity.

I looked at the road on the left and I knew it was the road my mother and Rosemary had to walk. They walked as far as they could with me on my journey and it was time for them to take the road with nothing but sunshine, blue skies, and peace. I looked to the right. A force called to me, telling me I was meant to walk down the path that was uncharted and unknown—the path that obviously still had some storm clouds yet to weather.

My mother and Rosemary let go of my hand and they both smiled at me lovingly, and with approval. They didn't need to speak. I knew they had to go left, and I knew I had to go right. I looked to the right and at the end of that road I saw a pair blue eyes far off in the distance. My mind was set. I would part ways with Rosemary and my mother and I would take the road to the right.

We hugged and said our goodbyes and with complete peace and calm—knowing that they would always be with me on my journey because they were both a part of who I was—I walked onto the road on the right; the road that was completely unknown.

EPILOGUE

I woke up on the morning of my eighteenth birthday to a chorus of people in my room singing Happy Birthday. It was an instant reminder of how my world had completely changed in the last two months since I moved to Tulsa, Oklahoma.

I sat up and rubbed my eyes then a small smile spread across my face as I looked at the blue-eyed boy sitting next to me on the bed. He stood by my side through all my darkness. He turned my world upside down, helped tear my walls down and unravel the secrets of my past, and loved all of me—even the broken and ugly parts. With him sitting by my side, holding my hand, I let my friends—Macey, Madison, Carly, and Caleb—and my aunt and my dad, sing Happy Birthday to me at the top of their lungs. I smiled from ear to ear, when I noticed Carly and Caleb holding hands. Then I blew out the candles and made a wish, the first wish I had made since I was ten years old.

Maverick handed me a beautiful little red box with a perfect white silver ribbon tied around it.

"Open it," he said with his calm and commanding tone.

I slowly pulled apart the ribbon and opened the box inside to see two tickets. "*One Republic? Are you kidding me?*" I screamed with joy.

I jumped on top of him, unable to control my excitement and completely indifferent to the fact that my father, my aunt, and my four friends were in the room with us. They were all used to our magnetic connection by now. When we were together, nothing else mattered.

"Seriously? We are going to see One Republic?"

He shook his head yes and gave me that signature wink.

"Thank you. I can't wait," I whispered in his ear.

I spent the day with Madison, Macey, and Carly. Maverick, of course, had arranged everything. We started with brunch at my favorite restaurant in Utica Square. He ordered a table full of my favorites. After brunch, Maverick scheduled a blow out for all of us.

"What in the world is a blow out?" I asked the girls as we walked into a salon.

They all looked at each other then let out a loud laugh. "It's a salon where all they do is wash and blow-dry your hair for you," Madison explained.

"Oh. Well that sounds absolutely ridiculous. I can wash my own hair thank you very much."

"OK, do you want us just to call Maverick then and cancel the appointments?" Madison challenged.

I rolled my eyes in defeat. "No, I'll go."

"That's what I thought," Carly said as she pushed me down into a seat at the salon.

After our blow outs, Maverick instructed my girlfriends to take me shopping and pick out a new outfit for the concert. Apparently he called ahead and gave his mother's saleswoman at Saks Fifth Avenue his credit-card number and made Madison promise she would get me to pick out an entire outfit.

I almost threw up when I walked into the store and picked up the first pair of jeans.

"Three-hundred dollars for a pair of jeans? That's just insane. I'm leaving."

Madison managed to turn me back around and, with the help of Carly and Macey, they got me back in the store.

"Oh no you don't. Maverick made us promise and you aren't leaving here without a new outfit or we're all going to be in trouble."

I agreed not to look at the price tags and we finally settled on a pair of leather pants that were so tight, they seemed to be painted on. Madison assured me they were *so hot*. I was unsure but I knew she was a fashion goddess, so I trusted her. Plus, I wanted to see Maverick's face when he saw me in them. Next, she picked out an off-the-shoulder black shirt that hung perfectly on my body and a pair of camel-colored peep-toe booties. She finished with accessories— a bright-red shade of lipstick and a leopard-print clutch that was the most beautiful thing I'd ever seen. I held my breath when the lady behind the cash register gave us our total, but Madison assured me she had already OK'd all our purchases with the man in charge—my boyfriend. The girls came over to my house and helped me get ready. They fixed my hair and even put on my new bright-red lipstick and when I looked in the mirror, I could hardly believe what I saw.

When Maverick came to pick me up he clearly appreciated the new clothes and especially, the red lipstick. He couldn't take his eyes off me. When we got in the car he grabbed me and pulled me over toward him until I was nearly on top of his lap. He pushed my hair aside and whispered into my ear. "Damn, you look hot."

We were barely able to keep our hands off one another as he drove me downtown to celebrate my birthday at the One Republic concert. Before we pulled into a parking garage, I saw the exact same shiny silver building that my dad and I had passed almost two months ago as we pulled into Tulsa. I couldn't help it. I laughed out loud.

"What?" Maverick asked as he stroked the back of my neck with his hand and ran his fingers through my hair.

"I was just remembering the morning my dad and I pulled into Tulsa. We passed this very building and I saw the billboard flashing that One Republic was going to be playing here."

"And why is that funny?"

"I was just remembering that my dad drove all through the night because I got pissed at him and threw a Diet Coke at his head when he told me we were moving to Tulsa and I had to go to Heritage Hall Preparatory Academy."

"That sounds about right." Maverick scoffed as he pulled into a VIP parking spot at the BOK center.

"You know you love my little bit of crazy," I teased as we got out of the truck.

"More like *a lot* crazy." Maverick grabbed me and pulled me toward him. He was leaning against the back of his truck and he positioned me in between his legs. "Mmm," he murmured into my ear with approval as he reached around to grab my backside in my leather pants.

I pushed him away and reminded him of his words as I shook my index finger back and forth playfully in front of his face.

"*A lot* crazy? Isn't that what you just said?"

"Oh c'mon Baby Girl, you know I was just teasing."

"Nope. I don't know that you're just teasing so you aren't allowed to touch," I said playfully as I slapped his hands away from me. I walked away and smiled at myself, feeling triumphant as I felt his blue eyes watching my every step. He was at my side in a second, holding my waist possessively, as he ushered me inside the building.

"Mr. Mason, please right this way." I heard a tall man in a dark security suit talking to Maverick then the guard directed us through a back door and escorted us down a long hallway. We stopped when we saw a pair of dark-red velvet curtains in front of us.

"Wait right here," I heard the guard say while he disappeared momentarily.

I looked up at Maverick and crossed my arms in defiance. I knew he was up to something spectacular, as usual.

The guard reappeared. "Right this way. We're ready for you, Mr. Mason."

He led us through the opulent curtains and into a lush lounge with several dark-leather couches and dim lighting. Maverick sat down in one of the leather lounge chairs and pulled me onto his lap. The next thing I knew I saw Ryan Tedder—the lead singer of One Republic—walk into the room, followed by several of the other band members. I was certain I was dreaming as the lead singer of One Republic walked up and introduced himself to me.

"Happy birthday, Elle. Maverick requested this one for you." He picked up his guitar and started strumming slowly. Then I heard his signature voice rip through the silence of the small backstage room. It was a song I'd never heard, apparently something new. Yet somehow it seemed the lead singer had written a song—the perfect song—for us.

So I'll take all the pain because it led me to you.

Maverick pulled me to my feet, wrapping me in his arms protectively as we swayed back and forth to our own impromptu unplugged concert. I rested my head on Maverick's solid chest and let peace envelop me as the singer's melodic voice hit the refrain.

I can't stay away. You are magnetic.

385

Everything about that moment with Maverick was perfect. I remembered where I was and even more importantly, who I was only two months before—an angry, sullen, bitter, and emotionally damaged girl. That girl now seemed like a stranger to me. The boy who held me in his arms helped me change. He broke down my impenetrable walls. He pushed past the anger and the secrets and the brokenness and the hurt and found a girl hidden there that only he could see; and he loved me with an all-consuming love that changed me.

As I looked up into his eyes, I realized I was at complete peace with the pain of my past, because it led me to him. I let the freedom of acceptance wash over me as he held me in his arms and I heard him whisper the words of the song into my ear.

"I can't stay away. You are magnetic."

THE END

Author Bio

Carissa Miller writes a lifestyle and design blog called CC and Mike, where she and her husband blog about their experiences designing, building, and flipping houses in the Midwest. She was inspired to write her debut novel-Magnetic—because of her firsthand experience living with the trauma of an unsolved violent crime, her mother's attempted murder. When she's not writing, blogging, or designing, Carissa loves Oklahoma summers on the lake with her husband and three children, going to Oklahoma State sporting events and cheering on the Cowboys, and traveling cross country with her family in the RV she and her husband renovated. Carissa laughs loudly, loves with her whole heart, tells it how it is to a fault, and enjoys living life to the fullest, every moment of every day.

You can follow along with Carissa and her family on Instagram - ccandmikecreative, Facebook - CC and Mike, Pinterest - CC and Mike, Twitter, or by subscribing to their blog - www.ccandmike.com/.

A Word from the Author

"The weak can never forgive. It is an attribute of the strong."

- Mahatma Ghandi

On September 16, 1990, my mother went to the grocery store, and never came home. I was ten years old, days before my eleventh birthday, when I found out a man had hidden in the back of my mom's minivan at the grocery store with a hunting knife. When she turned onto a road less than a mile from our home, her attacker came out from his hiding spot in the back of her van. He plunged his knife into her right lung, lacerating it, then attacked her repeatedly. He left her, bleeding to death, in a ditch on the side of a road in McAlester, Oklahoma. My mother's attacker was never found. He was never held accountable for his crimes or brought to justice for attempted rape and murder.

I know firsthand the pain of living with an unsolved violent crime. I know the journey it takes to find forgiveness and healing. For twenty-five years, I walked that journey—never truly facing the fears and pain of my past—until I wrote this book. That is when I finally forgave the man who tried to murder my mother. I see now that until I forgave, I was the one who was a prisoner. So, to anyone who has suffered something unimaginable—a crime, violence, rape, murder, injustice—my message to you is this: You too can be free. Your freedom will be found in forgiveness.

I hope you will find the strength and courage to rewrite your story, as I have rewritten mine.

Here are some resources for victims of violent crimes: Victim Connect Resource Center (find local help for Victims of Violent Crimes), National Center for Victims of Crime, or contact LifeChurch and ask to speak to a minister to guide you toward healing and forgiveness.

Acknowledgements

First and foremost, thank you to my three beautiful children—Easton, Emmy, and Cohen. Thank you for being my biggest fans and constant encouragers. Thank you for believing in me far before I had the courage to believe in myself, and for being relentless in pushing me to become an author, even when I doubted myself and wanted to give up—*especially* when I doubted myself and wanted to give up. Without you, Magnetic would have stayed a secret, nothing but a Word document on my computer that I never told anyone about. Thank you for not letting me take the easy way out. This book is and always will be, because of you, and for you. I hope you will also have the courage in your life, to not take the easy road, and to remember what Vincent Van Gogh said: " Normality is a paved road. It's comfortable to walk, but no flowers grow there." Just like you pushed me to walk off the paved road, I encourage you to do the same, my three sweet babies. Have the courage to walk off the paved road in life.

To my girlfriends—Kassidy, Molly, Amy, Brady, Sarah, Bethany, and Christy—who read this book in its unedited, raw form, and still believed in me, and believed in Maverick and Elle. I'm forever grateful because you planted a seed of hope that took root and grew, and eventually led to me getting this book published. Kassidy—you, most of all, were my constant encourager: asking me for chapters and pages and revisions; knowing when I was on the verge of quitting and having just the words I needed to hear to continue pushing forward; being there to listen when I wanted to pull my hair out and scream and give up. You were by my side, every step of the way. Thank you for walking this journey with me.

To Keri Mitchell, for dreaming with me and for lending me your editing skills.

To my editors and designers—The Artful Editor, Katie McCoach, Anna Hogarty, and Dane at ebook launch, thank you for your endless patience in helping me through the painstaking process of becoming a first-time author.

To Michael, for putting up with a creative, scatterbrained hot mess who lives her life in a dream world. You are my entire world, and you always have been from the moment I first saw you in the Union High School parking lot. Thank you for doing life with me, and for loving me so completely and unconditionally.

To my mother, for modeling not only the courage to fight, but also the greater courage it takes to forgive.

And finally, to you, my readers—anyone and everyone who reads this book. I will never find the words to express how much each of you mean to me. Every person who picks up this book, is participating in rewriting a story of pain, and turning it into something beautiful. *You* are a part of my story. Thank you.

Made in the USA
Middletown, DE
30 October 2017